Author: Ernestine Nicolussi Smyth.
Swiss, born in Austria. Emigrated aged 17 to Switzerland.
Married to an Englishman. Two daughters, 5 grandchildren in Vancouver Canada.

Occupation: Hotel/Restaurant management
Last long term employment in management team Grand Hotel Palace Bellevue Bern.
Also worked as fotomodel, stylist through model agency Special, Zürich.

This novel encompasses romantic, loving and lifelong relationships, but also those which fell apart. The 1st World War. Between the wars: Abolition of aristocratic titles, escape, adventure, concentration camps. The 2nd World War. Then the peaceful times after the war with the need to rebuild and recover a sense of belonging. Christine's eventful youth, as a Red Cross child in Switzerland, in the nunnery, as an acrobat in the circus, back home in her father's company, the rock and roll years in the 50s and the day she, still a teenager, emigrated to Switzerland.

The events in this book are factual and historically correct.
The lives of the characters in this novel reflect the *Zeitgeist.*
I spent a long time pondering all these experiences before I finally decided how to tell the story.

By that, I mean that anyone who tries to write a fictional story about 5 generations of one family has to draw from a *Fundus* and this Fundus came from the lives of many people; in particular from notes, voice recordings, reports and photos which I discovered during my research.

Every character, every generation looks for its own way to come to terms with society. One tries with conformity, another with resistance. In writing this, let's say, cultural history, I discovered the characters and their stories by research which I then developed little by little, because, in all cases the line of action was not clear at the beginning.

The life of Franz von Dorn, who was born in 1900, was the starting point and his story led me to write this novel. Since he, himself, wanted to write a book, he left behind much of the material which I have used.

It has taken me 5 years of lengthy, historical and biographical research to complete this book.

A one hundred and fifty year family history!

Starting with the aristocratic great great grandfather, over the great grandfather who unacceptably married a serving girl, the grandfather a brush maker with eight children, to the father who took an Hungarian artiste as his second wife and, with her, had one child after another; his first daughter Christine who would have loved to have had a higher education but instead because of her gymnastic talent was forced to work as a circus acrobat with three of her siblings and still as a teenager managed to escape and emigrate to Switzerland.

Two families of completely different backgrounds come together here; the aristocratic land owners and the travelling performers and artists; the blue blooded communist who believed in freedom, equality and justice, who fought in the underground against fascism and through betrayal landed in a concentration camp.

The people and their destinies pass in front of the reader as if in a film so vivid is the description in this book. The author presents a completely personal story of her family over five generations. It took her years to put together the whole story from what her father and mother told her and what she found in letters, documents, tape recordings, photographs etc. Some names of people and places where changed to protect the author and the people still living but the historical facts have been accurately reflected.

Quote from the original German lector:
Heide Reyer: "A huge undertaking and an enthralling read".

Aristocrash

A history through 5 generations

Ernestine Nicolussi Smyth

Order this book online at www.trafford.com
or email orders@trafford.com

Most Trafford titles are also available at major online book retailers.

Printed in the United States of America.

ISBN: 978-1-4269-7003-0 (sc)
ISBN: 978-1-4269-7004-7 (hc)
ISBN: 978-1-4269-7005-4 (e)

Library of Congress Control Number: 2011907884

Trafford rev. 05/21/2011

www.trafford.com

North America & International
toll-free: 1 888 232 4444 (USA & Canada)
phone: 250 383 6864 • fax: 812 355 4082

I

Albert Karl von Dorn, took after his sensitive mother, much to his father's dismay. The strict upbringing, to make out of him a steadfast and competent man who would impart new energy into the family estate, so that they could at last live "according to their station", bore no fruit. So the attention turned to the stronger daughter. His son was set aside. He was left to fumble about and work on the estate as best he could. Albert looked after the animals, went out riding and loved to fish in the nearby river. The farm labourers and house girls liked him, because he was always ready to help out wherever his limited strength could be put to use.

One day he helped a young laundry maid who was trying to lift a washing basket full of wet clothes onto a handcart. She was really shocked as his helping hands touched hers and lowered her eyes. He asked her name. Her heart was beating fast when she said her name was Anna. Her voice trembled as she added that she had only started to work there a few days before. Afraid, she took up the handcart with the washing and ran, barefoot down the stony path to the river without a backwards glance. From that day on she avoided meeting him. But she could still feel his hands on hers.

Anna had a hard childhood, but it was full of love. When she was 12 years old, she left her home to make her own living. In those times that was normal. If there was not enough to eat on the table then the children had to seek work elsewhere. Most of the children went to work in factories, a house or went to the farmers. Some of the boys went into the coal mines.

So, one day, Anna left her family, without thinking about where she was going. Her father thought she should walk northwards and that she should watch out, because there were many 'ne'er do goods' about. Her family wished her luck. She left her parent's small house, surrounded by its paltry fields which could not bring in enough to feed the whole family.

Days passed. Chilly nights and fear, as she slept under the open skies, sapped her strength. On the 6th day, after having knocked on many doors, she met a peddler, who said, "I've been watching you. You're not begging, are you?" Anna wanted to run away. He stood in her path. "Let me pass, I'm looking for work," she murmured. "Ah! then let me think." He wrinkled his brow and thought. He knew many people in the region. Finally he suggested that she go to the estate owned by the Count von Dorn. He had heard that the laundry woman there was old and no longer able to do the work. But then, he also said that she would have to give him some of her wage if they ever met again. He said that that was the normal reward for this kind of information and she should not forget it. Anna promised not to forget him, if she was hired. She smoothed her dress, straightened her hair and ran up the hill as quickly as she could to the estate. Out of breath, she reached the estate, stood in front of the giant gate and rang the bell. She had to wait until the servant, with a huge dog on the leash came and opened the gate. The dog barked furiously and Anna, shaking with fear told him about her meeting with the peddler. He thought she might find work there as a laundry maid. The servant gave her a critical look, from top to bottom and asked her where her possessions were and, without waiting for an answer said, "Come."

Anna had only the clothes which she was wearing. When it was hot, she rolled up the sleeves and when it was cold she rolled them down. The same went for the high neckline; open when it was hot, closed when it was cold. She had never had her own pair of shoes. At home, behind the door, there was a pair of large shoes. She was only allowed to wear these shoes when it was cold and she had to go out. They were made of hard leather and the soles were made of wood. If your feet were small, you stuffed the shoes with straw until they fitted.

Anna had been on the estate for some time and she was happy there. Very early, one morning she had to go to the river to wash the soap out of the laundry. This was normal. She should have done it the day before, but the weather was stormy and it was impossible to do anything out of doors. Anna needed all her strength to pull the heavy sheets out of the fast flowing water which was spitting and swirling. When she turned round, she saw the young Count Albert, who was fishing next to her. He was also surprised, since he had not seen her behind the bushes. They both stood there, neither knowing what they should say. The first rays of sun shone on Anna's young face, reflected by the water; her wet clothes clung to her body, revealing her youthful, but already feminine shape; the mist over the meadow surrounded her so that she appeared like a delicate painting. It reminded Albert of the picture which his grandmother had given him for his first communion, showing the Mother of Jesus surrounded by gentle clouds.

Seeing that he was embarrassed, Anna simply said, "Good day" to break the spell and went on with her work. "Wait! I'll help you" he said as she bent to lift the washing basket onto the cart. She remembered, that, a long time ago, he had helped her once before and she was disappointed when he said, "I don't remember meeting you before. How long have you been working for us?" Anna thought, "Is it so long since our first meeting that he cannot remember?" For Anna, it was as though time had stopped. "Once a year I can go home," she thought, "and I have been home twice, the second time only a short while ago" In reply, she stammered, "More than three years, Sir". She was a little angry that he could not remember that they had already met, because she could remember the meeting very well and also the first time they touched. No. She would never forget it. "I have never seen anyone at the river so early. I'm almost always here at this time." He gave her a searching look.

"I couldn't finish the washing yesterday because of the storm," she explained and looked away. Albert saw that her hands and arms, up to the elbows were very red. He asked himself why she had such red hands and asked her if that was from the strong bleach, which was used in the laundry, or was it from the cold water in the river.

In the laundry there was always so much steam that he could not really see who was working there.

In the meantime, Anna had fastened the wash basket on the cart and was ready to leave. Putting his hand on her shoulder, he stopped her and advised her to spread butter fat over her arms and hands overnight. Her short answer was, "I don't have that," and she wanted to leave, but, his hand still on her shoulder, he did not let her go. "Tomorrow I'll bring you some," he said, "when will you be here?" "After the second bell rings at the house, but not before." He took his hand from her shoulder, let her go and watched for a while. Anna pulled the cart behind her. She had the feeling it was not so heavy as usual and she felt happy about the next day, but she still did not want to show him her reddened hands and simply arouse his pity.

In spite of the hard work, Anna was happy with herself and the world. Of course, she had her dreams. Soon I'll be 15; I have two dresses and the third will be a Sunday dress. She looked forward to finishing it.

She had bought the material for a good price from the peddler and next time he had promised to bring her the buttons. The second hand shoes which the old laundry woman – God bless you! - had left her, along with other things, were no longer too big; they fitted better now and her feet had grown to fit them. She should have everything ready before the harvest festival.

She could also put aside a few farthings. If she were to marry one day, she did not want to stand there like a beggar. If no one wanted to marry her, then, as God wills, they would be for her old age. Anna sighed, when she stood in front of the washing line. She would rather have children who would look after her when she was old. In secret she prayed every day that God would listen to her.

Anna gave most of what she earned to her family. Her mother was very thankful for it. Last time she had even been able to take a bunch of corn cobs, carrots and apples. As much as she could carry.

A few days after the old washer woman died, Anna was allowed to move into the tiny room. It had no windows and it was behind the horse stable. In one place the planks were not close together so that a little daylight broke through. On the wall there hung a misshapen cross made of two simple pieces of wood, held together, in the middle, with a rusty nail. In the middle there was a handful of flowers, which had long since died. Below this there was a jute sack filled with straw, which she could use to sleep on. The straw smelt really fresh. In the middle of the sack there was an opening, so that every morning Anna could move the straw about and air it. In the evening, when she was exhausted, she just let herself fall onto the sack.

Up till then she had had to sleep in the humid laundry, in the farthest corner, in a long, wooden trough.

The time was fast approaching when she should meet Count Albert at the river. The whole night she tossed and turned in her bed. She thought she was very foolish. Her thoughts were elsewhere when, in the early hours of the morning she carelessly put her dress on backwards. She laughed at herself. When she left the room, she had to pull herself together. She was afraid that the others on the estate would want to know what she had to laugh about. But no one took any notice of the others. It was still too early for anyone to be fully awake. They walked around like sleep walkers. No wonder, in this season there was much to do, maybe in winter you could sleep a little longer.

Anna lit the fire under the wash boiler. She sorted the laundry and finally started to beat the linen, which she had put into the lye yesterday evening, with a large flat wooden beater on a wooden board. She had to fold it many times and beat it and then boil it in the wash boiler.

Just as she had finished the washing, she heard the second bell sounding from the estate tower. Swiftly she took the cart, piled the laundry on to it, and started to pull it. She tried not to walk too quickly. She had to avoid the pointed stones, so that she did not damage her feet, which were, really, already quite hardened.

Still a long way off, Anna looked to see if Count Albert was already there, but saw nothing. Maybe he is behind the bushes, she thought, when she reached the river bank. She did not look around, but started to work. It doesn't matter, she thought if he doesn't come. Up to now I've got by without using butter fat. Well, sometimes it burns horribly, but maybe he will still come?

But the young Count was already there. He was sitting on the top of the river bank and he was watching her. The roar of the river swallowed every other sound. He had a warm feeling in his heart, and started to pluck the flowers around him to make a small bunch. When he saw Anna wringing out the last piece of laundry, he came nearer. The first thing she saw was the flowers in his hand, and then she looked at him and was happy that he had really come. She straightened up, smoothed her dress and said, "Good day, my Lord!" When he saw her looking at the flowers, he said, "Do you like the flowers?" "Yes," she said, "they are very beautiful." She did not trust herself to say more. "Good, then you can have them." He dived into his jacket pocket and brought out a small, wooden box. "And here is your butter fat. It is good. Many times it has healed my skin. You have to spread it on your hands and arms every evening before you go to sleep. I'm going to come here often and look at your hands." Albert put the flowers and the wooden box on a piece of wood which was lying on the ground. Shyly, she murmured, "Thank you." She asked herself, did he not want to touch her?

Then he wanted to go up-river. He said that he wanted to catch a few fish. They loaded the washing in no time and Anna went on her way. Her thoughts were totally confused. Now he wants to know how her hands are!

Her thoughts were all over the place and she almost forgot the flowers and the box. She went back to pick them up. Then she went into her room and fastened the fresh flowers on the cross, which she had straightened. She put the box with the butter fat on a jutting plank on the wall and stroked it gently with her fingers. "These are the first things a man has ever given me," she said aloud, "and they were from Count Albert! If the others knew that he had given me flowers! What would they say about it? Should I tell Marie? She has already told me some of her secrets. I think, sooner or later everyone finds out everything about everyone. I don't think anyone has any secrets here."

Anna realised that she had been speaking her thoughts aloud and looked around. Had any one heard her?

Later, at dusk, when she was taking the dry clothes off the washing line, she saw Marie, a house servant coming back from the fields with the labourers. She wanted to say something to her, so she called her. All of them looked, with curiosity at Anna. She knew that she was blushing and she added that it was something which she had to tell Marie, and that it had nothing to do with any one else. A young labourer said to the others that he would also like to say something to Anna and that was also not anybody else's concern. All of them laughed and, as they went on their way, added a few inane remarks. Marie showed that she would come to Anna's room, as soon as she had finished her work. Anna nodded her head, but she was no longer sure that she should tell Marie what had happened. She had already heard similar stories from the cook. She had warned Anna that she should keep her thoughts to herself, and stay away from the labourers. Any relationship with the labourers would only end in misery.

The door to Anna's room stood open. Marie came in and sat down next to her on the straw mattress. Anna was smoothing butter fat on her arms and hands. She was holding the box between her knees. She sat there, without saying a word. Marie wanted to know what she wanted to say and if it had anything to do with that. She pointed her finger at the box which Anna has holding, demonstratively, between her knees. "Yes, I wanted to show you that. And do you know who gave me this? You'll never guess!" Marie had never heard Anna speak so arrogantly and simply said, "Well, the young Count always gave us that when he saw that we needed something for our wounds, because if one of us could no longer work much of the work remains undone and if two of us were suffering, then we couldn't catch up with the work. They really need more workers, but every mouth has to be fed and there are too few of us who really need the work. Even you must have noticed that." Anna sighed and thought, "Oh, so that's how it is; and I was stupid enough to think that..." Suddenly she remembered the flowers, "But how many of the others has the young Count given flowers to?" She looked at the cross. The flowers did not look so fresh, but never the less, she thought.

"Oh yes? And what about the flowers?" she asked Marie and surprised herself with her haughtiness. Marie looked at the cross and crossed herself. Anna was amazed. "Jesus Christ, child" exclaimed Marie, "I hope you haven't done something really stupid. I would never have thought the young Count could do something like that. Whatever, there is always a first time, but with you? Hopefully you won't be pregnant! The old Count would never accept the child as his grandchild and it would break the old Countess's heart. I've heard that she suffers greatly because the father completely ignores the young Count." Marie was in a fluster and the words spilled out from her. Anna jumped to her feet, "What are you saying? I have done nothing wrong. I never expected to hear something like that from you. I will marry before I bring a child into the world so God help me. You must believe that." "Yes, yes, many have already said that," shouted Marie, "just look around the estate. There are several children who don't come from married parents and the maid servants, the mothers, get almost no money, because the Count has to feed the little ones. They can't go anywhere else with the children and they can certainly never go back to their parents. That would bring shame on the whole village if the people there learnt about it. They are called bastards, the priest is not allowed to baptise them; they are not allowed to take the sacrament and..." Anna sat there, her mouth wide open. The she interrupted Marie, "But now you have to believe me. Nothing happened! I got the ointment and the flowers. Just like that. That's what I wanted to tell you and nothing else." Jesus, Maria, thought Anna, how quickly you can get yourself into such a mess, even if there is nothing in it. And then when people start to talk...No, there is nothing to talk about.

But her thoughts kept going back to the young Count. He was coming to take a look. Hopefully no one sees him. Or had he already been to others? She no longer trusted herself to ask Marie.

They were both lying on the straw mattress. Marie knew a lot and talked about women servants who had to take their children with them into the fields. They always took some fermented fruit juice with them. When the little ones started to cry they soaked a rag in the juice, so that they could suck on it. Then they were quiet and most of the time they slept. But, sometimes they lay too long in the sun and were sun burned. Most of the fathers were farm labourers, but sometimes they were farmers or even the noble Count himself. If a farm labourer fathered a child, then part of his wage was deducted. Most of the farmers were not bothered by this, because they could deduct the cost of the food for the children from the taxes and there were a few who profited and saw this as a small income on the side.

Marie had also quite a lot to tell about the neighbouring farmer's wife who had been made pregnant by a farm labourer. The farmer knew that he was not the blood father and withheld a third of the labourer's wage. And the farmer was legally allowed to do this.

Marie went on, "Some of the children are brain damaged by the alcohol in the fermented juice. Then they stay on the farm for the rest of their lives and, for good or ill, are totally dependent on the farmer. They are forced to do heavy work and some of them are mistreated in the worst way possible by the farmer or the labourers. I've seen that where I used to work. I chased a ferocious, horrible labourer away with a manure fork. I saw him doing impossible things with the animals in the meadows and in the stalls. You have no idea what sort of creatures there are in the world." Marie shivered when she remembered all the horrors. A cold shower ran down her spine. And then she saw, that Anna had fallen asleep and was not listening.

Marie was too tired to walk across the courtyard. It was pitch black outside. During the day the sun had shone on her without pity. Her feet were sore from walking through the stubble. So, in the dark, Marie searched for the butter fat to also ease her wounds.

The next morning the sun was shining through the cracks when someone knocked loudly on the door. It was the voice of the young Count calling them to work. Anna and Marie were shaken out of their sleep, jumped up as if they had been stung by a wasp and rushed out of the door into the courtyard. Marie shouted, "We didn't hear the bell." Both of them took the piece of black, roughly baked bread and the wooden bowl with the milk, which they were allowed, every morning, but which was often thinned with water. They sat down on a bench and saw, that they were not the only ones who had arrived too late. The foreman came, swearing, "When I find out who took the bell from the roof, then I'll give him something to think about." Everybody started to giggle. Anna looked down and grinned, privately. Then she saw the straw which was stuck to her calves with butter fat. It looked so funny, that she laughed, quietly. Marie couldn't believe her ears and gave her an indignant look. Then she looked down, saw that her feet were also full of straw and laughed, just as Anna had laughed. The two sat side by side, made a sign to each other and folded up in laughter. Still laughing, they swept the straw from their legs. They were still laughing when the angry foreman, with the whip in his hand, drove them out into the open. The day had started so merrily. Anna was full of joy and happiness. She sang the whole day long. In high spirits she put a daisy in her hair. She tucked her dress high on one side, and fastened it with her cloth belt, before she went to the river. She knelt down on the jetty to swing the washing many times in the water. She had not a care in the world and did not notice that she was not alone.

Count Albert thought that Anna was so enchanting that he did not show himself. He could not take his eyes off her; she looked so lovely. The songs she sang made him happy and he hoped that today, the river would flow more quietly so that he could understand the words better. After a while he crept into the bushes and lay down in the high grass until Anna left. Anna's good mood had infected him. For a long time he had not felt so good as on this day. He looked up to the sky and murmured, "Thank you Anna. Just the magical sight of you touched my heart. My greatest wish is that you were lying next to me in the grass and that the clouds would carry us both into a world of which I have often dreamed." From that day on, the young Count often came to this place. He often enjoyed watching her work. But she always ran up the slope and always looked to see if anyone was following her or was hiding. She never knew that he was there.

One day the watchdog broke free from his leash which he was always chewing, when the foreman had to fasten him up for some reason or other. At first the animal chased a large bird which flew over the courtyard towards the river. Anna was standing right on the river bank and was drying her face which was wet from the river spray. She did not see the dog, which was rushing on, collided with her and pitched her into the river. Anna's cry reached the Count, who was still dreaming in the long grass. He jumped up and ran through the bushes, saw Anna's dress floating on the surface and called the dog, "Fetch! Fetch!" The dog prepared itself for a long jump and disappeared into the water. Count Albert saw Anna thrashing about with her arms. Then he saw the dog Fetch her dress and swim to the bank. The Count jumped into the river, Right there, the water was flowing more quietly; where the river bed widened. Here he knew every bend. He saw the dog swimming towards him, with Anna. They were very close to the bank. She was still thrashing wildly with her arms. The Count grabbed her dress and her shoulder and held her above the water. Then he tried to get a better hold on her. She threw her arms around his neck and clung to him. He could scarcely breathe. He could hardly keep his feet; his boots slid about on the river bed. Luckily, just then, the foreman came running down, wondering why the dog was barking so loud. He saw the Count with Anna, who was soaked through and through, with her arms round his neck. He ran into the water and helped them out. On the bank the Count wanted to stand Anna on her feet, but she sank out of his arms and fell unconscious to the ground. Her dress was in disarray and the foreman pulled it together and covered her as best he could. He lifted Anna onto his broad shoulders, carried her to her room and laid her on the straw mattress. He said to the Count, who had followed them with the dog, "She'll come to, it just takes a while." Then he took the dog and went on his way.

The count looked around the tiny room. At first he had to adjust his eyes to the darkness. A reel of thread with a needle on a half finished dress. Next to this a pair of shoes neatly fastened together. On the wall there was a simple wooden cross with a faded bunch of flowers. On a jutting plank stood the empty box, which had contained the butter fat. He remembered that he had given it to her and looked at her hands and arms. He saw that they were still very red. He sat down. She was lying very close to him; her wet dress clung to her young body and revealed her pleasing figure. Suddenly her chest rose and fell and rose again. She's coming to, he thought. Then Anna opened her eyes. "Where am I? Am I dead? It's so dark here," she called. The Count leapt to his feet and opened the door wide, so that there was more light. "It's all right," she heard someone say, "you're lying on your mattress. You should take off your wet clothes. I'm leaving you now and I'll send you a woman who can help you, so that you can get on with your work." Having said this, the Count went out of the door.

Anna was too exhausted to take off her wet clothes and she was certainly not in any condition to work. She fell asleep. Marie, who had heard what had happened, left all her work in the field, which was close by and ran to Anna. She saw the young Count leaving Anna's room in his dripping wet clothes. He called to her that it was good that she had come; otherwise he would have had to send someone to help Anna to her feet. After all, no work could be left undone, time was short enough. "If you need anything, I'll be in the stables," he added. What he really wanted to say was: Please, help Anna so that she can get over the shock.

Marie removed Anna's wet clothes, which was not easy. She then looked around for something to cover her with. All she could find was the half finished dress next to the bed. The straw mattress was also wet; it should be taken out to dry in the sun. Marie ran to the stables and asked the Count if she could get something dry. She did not mean that he should go to the house and bring something, but that is what he understood and left. Marie looked around the stable and spotted a bundle of sweet smelling hay between the horses. She took it and carried it into the room. That's even better than straw, she thought, because everyone knows that fresh hay works wonders. She put it next to the straw mattress, rolled the exhausted young woman on to it and covered her with the unfinished dress. When the Count came back, he had a bed sheet and a heavy, brown blanket under his arm. He stood in front of the door, and when he saw that Marie was trying to drag the wet straw mattress out, he put them down and helped her. One strong pull and the jute sack was outside; both of them nearly fell over and they both laughed at their clumsiness. Marie opened the slit in the straw sack so that the sun could shine on it. The heat of the sun caused the damp to rise.

While Marie was doing this, the Count thought nobody was watching and went to look at the sleeping Anna. He saw her slim, well shaped legs and then he looked at her face. He wanted to stroke her wet hair away from her forehead, but he did not trust himself to get so close to her. Shudders went down his spine and he went back to the house to change out of his wet clothes, but he still meant to go back later and see how she was.

Marie was amazed at what the Count had left in the room. Of one thing she was certain; his father should not hear about it. It was not the best of bed sheets, but for the labourers it was much too valuable. She suddenly had a suspicion that the Count could have fallen in … No. That cannot be true. Thoughts went through her head, if it were so, that would be a disaster for both Anna and the Count. The old Count would explode and Anna would be thrown out. Then there would nothing more to laugh about. Especially for her, Marie, who had always gone about her hard work happily and without any problems; yes, and who would listen to her? Up to now they had been able to tease each other and exchange their little secrets. It was good for them both to kneel before God Almighty and ask Him to fulfil their dreams or to thank Him for a pleasant day. Up to now it had been peaceful. No, her thoughts went on, for the love of God, I had to explain everything to her, before it happened. What more could I have done? Marie looked at the cross on the wall and snatched the dry flowers, because she knew that these flowers came from the young Count. I'll bring her a fresh bunch. There are enough flowers in the meadows. She ran out of the door and picked some flowers, not forgetting some daisies, which she knew Anna loved. She bound the flowers together and hung them, with the heads down, on the cross. She also spread the wet dress over a large boulder and then went to look for the cart with the laundry, because the laundry should be hung on the line. She let Anna sleep, but she had to hurry, because soon the bell on the roof would call the workers to their mid-day meal. Marie would bring the stew, which they always had at mid-day, to Anna. Maybe then Anna would tell her exactly what had happened.

The bell rang, calling them to their mid-day meal. Since it was a nice day, most of them were out in the fields, so only a few came into the room where the food was given out. Marie held her own bowl and Anna's under the ladle. "And since when do you have two bowls?" the cook wanted to know "Well, haven't you heard? Anna fell into the water. So I'm taking her food to her." "She should come herself if she wants to eat," said the cook and turned her back on her. But the servant girl who was doling out the food gave Marie an extra large portion in Anna's bowl and winked at her. Marie ran to Anna and saw her sitting up on the hay. "Oh, it's you Marie," said Anna and smiled weakly, "I heard the bell." Then her face became serious and said, "Something terrible happened to me today. I can't even remember that I took my clothes off." "You didn't undress yourself," Marie said, "you were in no condition. I undressed you. Look, I've brought you something to eat, but don't stuff your mouth so full that you can't tell me how it all happened. I only heard that you fell into the water and then you were lying here in your room, soaked through." Anna started to eat, but she had no appetite, because her stomach was still full of water. She pushed the bowl to Marie and told her what had happened. Marie shovelled the food into her mouth, because she was very hungry and only stopped when she wanted to hear something which she thought was really exciting. The bowl was empty in a flash. When Anna had told her everything, Marie started to talk like a waterfall. She told her where the blanket had come from and everything else which had happened. She warned her to take care. Anna dragged herself to her feet, which were still a bit shaky and she was only listening with half an ear. Then she asked Marie to bring her dress and to take the sheet and blanket back to the count. Marie did as she was asked and fetched the dress, which was still not completely dry, and went to look for the young Count, to return the things. As best she could, she stuffed everything under her ample blouse, so that nobody could immediately see what she had hidden there. Marie was absolutely certain that the young Count had asked no one and had simply taken the things from somewhere. She ran to the stables and handed him the blanket and the sheet. But, she was amazed when he refused to take them and simply said that Anna should keep them. Marie should return them to her. And, stroking his horse all the time, he asked, as if it were of little importance, how Anna was. Marie thought that he should already know.

When Marie arrived back, Anna was no longer in the room. She saw that she was already by the washing line. So they both went on with their work. The thought went through Marie's head, let's hope we don't have another day like this, I don't think I could stand it. However, one good thing came out of this. You think about life, whether it be short or long, good or bad, you start to wonder about it. How can you make sense of it? She trotted along the path and saw a horse-drawn cart coming. Look! Hans, the junior forester from the Schlossberg forest was driving the cart. She had not seen him for a long time. He had been at the last festival and had danced with her. "Hello, Marie," he called, "have you seen young Dorn? I've got to tell him something and I've something to give him as well." "Yes, hello," said Marie, "the young lord is up there in the stables with his horses." Then Hans added, "Marie, can we meet sometime? I'd like to talk to you. If you're interested, you know where I am." Then he drove on. Marie lifted her head and said to herself: "Ah! I think my life does have some meaning." Then, smiling to herself, she skipped over the track.

What a day, thought Anna as she dragged herself across the courtyard to her room; "I just want to sleep, sleep, sleep". When she came to the stable door, she saw Count Albert coming out. She greeted him and wanted to pass by. Then she heard him ask how she was. "I'm fine now," she answered, "and thank you for everything." She opened the door to her room and saw that the blanket and sheet were there again. She wanted to pick them up and give them back to the Count, but he was standing in the doorway and said, "You can keep them." He looked so deeply into her eyes he almost took her breath away. He came closer and shut the door behind him. Now he was standing very close to her. He took her in his arms and kissed her gently on the lips. Anna did not resist and neither knew how it happened. Suddenly they were lying on the ground, in the hay, and hugged and kissed each other till the morning dawned. He stood up and whispered, "I'll see you this evening," and disappeared. She pulled the blanket over her and dozed happily for a few minutes.

Albert von Dorn came almost every evening. They talked about all sorts of things and were very happy, but made sure that nothing disturbed their joyful time together. They had found the love of their dreams. She did think about the next day. She just counted those wonderful moments when they could be together. Love and tenderness made her forget everything else. But then came the day when Anna felt queasy. Her food rose in her throat and she did not feel well. This began to happen more and more frequently.

In the meantime there were more people on the estate and that meant for Anna more laundry. She had been given help for the heaviest work. A plump girl who was the child of a house servant. She had strong arms and had no problem in lifting heavy weights.

I'm not going to tell Albert that I feel unwell, thought Anna, he'll only worry unnecessarily about me. And I've hardly seen

Marie since she met Hans. She hasn't got much time for me and up to now that was all right for me too. Anna would have been reluctant to tell her what was happening. But then there came the day when she really felt she should speak to Marie.

Anna made sure that she did not miss the land labourers when they were returning from the fields. Today, they had had a long day. At midday they stayed in the fields and their food had been brought to them in baskets. There was Marie. Anna waved at her and ran up to her, "I've got something to tell you." The labourers who heard her, shouted, among other things, "And I'd like to talk to you as well," and they grinned at both of them. "Yes, that is just about your level," Marie shouted back. Then the two young women hid themselves behind a large lime tree. Anna told her how sick she sometimes felt and that she tired quickly. Had she picked up some illness, what could it be? Marie thought for a moment. "There was a woman in the fields. She was the same, but she was pregnant." "Pregnant!?" shouted Anna, and turned pale. She held her stomach. "I don't believe that! I mean, that can't be t-r-u-e-!" For Marie it was clear. "Is it possible that something has happened that I warned you about?" "I'm certainly not pregnant." Anna broke into tears and ran into her room. Marie did not want to leave her alone and ran after her. Anna sat on the straw mattress and cried as if her heart would break. Marie stroked her head, "Is there something between you and Albert?" Anna nodded. "Does he already know?" "What? What should he know? It's nothing. I've just got stomach ache. I just wanted to know why I feel so sick. That's why I waited for you." Marie gently asked, "Can I feel your stomach?" Anna lay down, arms against her sides. Marie saw the swelling. The skin was stretched. "Your periods? Anna, when did you have your last period?" "I don't know. I've forgotten. It's a while ago."

Marie said, "Come, Anna, I know a woman who knows about these things and she can also hold her tongue if she has to." She took Anna by the hand and pulled her outside. They walked for half an hour through the growing dusk till they came to a hut, an almost derelict small house.

Marie knocked on the door and opened it. Anna was shivering. "Don't be afraid, I know the people who live here."

The glow from a lantern came closer and shone on Marie's face. Anna heard a woman's voice say, "Ah! It's you, Marie, so where's the fire?" In the feeble light she could just make out an old woman's face. Hcr eyes took in Anna's tear stained face and looked at Marie. She only said that she was not sure if…. . The woman dismissed her with her hand. Marie hat not mentioned Anna's name, on purpose. The woman sat down on a bench in front of the hut. The two young women sat before her on a stone. "Now, tell me". She tapped Anna on the shoulder, "do you feel something?" Anna told her what had happened to her recently. The woman asked her a few more questions, took hold of Anna's hand, touched her stomach and all she said was, "Yes, you are going to have a child. Make sure that you marry the father of this child before it is born and hurry. People will soon notice your condition." Then she stood up, went back into the house and closed the door behind her.

Marie dragged Anna with her. She felt a lump in her throat. Anna cried all the way home. It was now pitch black. The stones under their feet seemed to be sharper than before. At last they came to Anna's room. In silence they sat down and thought about what they could do. Marie pondered about the various ways in which Anna could tell the young Count. Worse, the old count. How would he react? That was Marie's greatest worry. Then they started to talk about the problem. Suddenly there was a knock on the door. "What are you talking about so late in the night?" It was Albert's voice. 'Now you have to tell him.", whispered Marie in Anna's ear and left the room with a "Hello" as she passed Albert. "What is it, Anna?" he asked as he entered the room. "I'm pregnant." The words just came out. He quickly lit a candle which was standing on a block of wood. He looked at her and his whole face lit up. He took her in his arms and pressed her to him. "Now you have to marry me. Do you want to be my wife?" Anna stood there, speechless. She felt dizzy. She sat down and stared at him. "Don't think about it too long. Say something. Do you want me to be your husband?" Anna stood and said, at first with a weak, but ever stronger voice, "Yes! Yes, my Love, my sweetheart. I want to be your wife. But is it possible?" Albert answered, "We'll make it possible." They kissed each other gently and they were in seventh heaven. Suddenly Albert took her head in his hands, "I'm dizzy. I've so many thinks in my head. It's better that I go now. Sleep well. Until tomorrow." And then he was gone.

Close to the house Albert saw there was still light in his sister Marie-Louise's window. That's good, he thought, she can certainly help me to get my thoughts in order. But how can I tell her? How can I tell my parents? What does one need to marry? He stood in front of the door, knocked and asked if he could come in. He heard his sister's voice, "I was getting ready for bed, but just come in." He went in and sat down. "Well, what's the matter?" "My dear sister, I need your advice and probably even your help." He told her what had happened and what he wanted to do about it. "Oh, my God," she shouted, "this is really a nice mess. We're going to have to think very carefully about what we tell Father. It won't be easy for him to accept a marriage with a serving wench. What are we going to do when he says 'no'? He has always hoped for a good marriage. One that would contribute something to the estate so that one day the property would be what it once was and of which he could be proud. Anna is a pleasant, pretty girl. I can understand that you gave her more than a passing glance, but you shouldn't have … Oh, what am I saying, it is as it is. First of all, we have to tell Father. We can't avoid that. Early tomorrow morning, when we're all together around the breakfast table, we'll choose the right moment and tell him the news. Hopefully everything will come out for the best." Albert remained silent and seemed disturbed. "Come, my brother, all we can do now is pray."

Marie-Louise took the Bible in her hand. She knelt down and put her hands together in prayer.

That was the moment when it became clear to him what a burden he would have to shoulder if his father did not agrec. Up until now he had taken everything as it came, without doing much about it. But now the world looked different. Dark thoughts came to him. The ease of his life up to now was coming to an end. Up to now everything had been in order. His father had never given him much attention, but this had not bothered Albert.

The next day, at breakfast, when all the family members were sitting silently round the table, Albert laid down his spoon, cleared his throat loudly and looked at his father and mother. Marie-Louise leaned back and gave Albert a nod. He searched for the right words in his head and finally began to speak. "Father, Mother, I have to speak to you. I ask for permission to marry Anna." He swallowed hard and went on. Quickly, "She is expecting my child. She is only a laundry maid but she is honest and good and I love her with all my heart." The old Count sprang from his seat. The chair fell over. His face was deep red. Aghast he looked at his only son. "Say that again." And Albert repeated what he had said, "I want to marry Anna." "Shame!" shouted the old Count, so loud that everyone at the table winced. "Tell me that it is not true. You don't make jokes about things like that!" he uttered between closed lips. "Yes Father, it is true. As true as I stand here, it is not a joke," then he stood up, slowly. "Get out of my sight!" thundered through the room. "Get out". The Count was beside himself with anger. Then he let his hands fall onto the table, like one defeated and collapsed. The Countess hid her face behind a cloth, close to fainting. Albert looked at his sister and left the room.

Days went by. The family members avoided each other. Not a word was spoken about the incident. Albert work from early to late as he had never worked before, he shouted orders at the labourers and only visited Anna for a moment. Of course she knew that something was wrong, but did not dare to ask what.. She was happy just to get a look from him, when, sometimes, he sat next to her and could stroke her hair. It was good for him and he was pleased that she did not push him.

A couple of times he rode out with a fully loaded horse. No one knew where he rode. One evening he said, "Anna, tomorrow is a very important day for us. Put on the best dress you have. I'm going to take the horse cart and drive with you into town. Please, don't tell anyone about it. We'll be leaving very early, before anyone can see us. It will be our day." And even though he did not say it, she knew it was going to be their wedding day. She ran to the laundry. The water in the boiler was still warm and she washed herself from head to toe. Back in her room she laid everything out for the next day. Her head, still wet from washing, was full of questions. Why should no one know about it? Does anyone know about it? It was all so strange. He had not introduced her as his bride to anyone, not even the registrars. And she knew that that was normal before you could marry. What was happening? She began to have doubts. Is it really going to be the day?

She hardly slept. Very early – it was still dark outside – she arranged her hair, put on her dress, which she had never worn before and lay down again. Then she heard Albert calling quietly, "Anna, get ready, we're leaving soon. There's a fresh wind, take a blanket to put over your shoulders." She hurried and ran outside. Albert helped her onto the cart and they drove off.

When they reached the small town, it was already light. The sun had begun to shine and spread its rays onto a large building, where they had stopped. "Come," he said to her, "we have to go to the registry office and then to the priest. I've arranged everything." In the registry office there was a heavy, ornamented oak table. Standing on it were flowers and two candles. In front of the table there were two chairs covered with yellow velvet and behind the table there was a magnificently carved chair. The registrar came in, greeted Albert and Anna and asked them to sit down. He lit the candles, laid a thick book beside some printed sheets and placed next to them an inkwell and a beautiful long feathered quill. Then a side door opened and a man wearing the official clothes of a government officer, accompanied by two other men came in. The three of them shook hands with Anna and Albert. The man dressed as a registrar said some words about marriage, their rights and duties and asked if they had understood everything. Albert and Anna looked at each other and with one voice answered, "Yes, we have understood everything." Then, at the end of the ceremony they gave each other the 'Yes' word. The registrar asked all those present to sign the thick book and all the other papers. Albert signed first. She stood there and did not know what she should write. Albert noticed this and asked for a piece of paper so that he could write it down for her. "Now you only need to copy it," she heard him whisper. So she wrote, Anna von Dorn and the rest went almost automatically. She looked very uncertain and wanted to say something, but Albert took her face in his hands and kissed her gently on the mouth. Everyone congratulated them. Then they all went to the church.

Anna knew no one there, only the priest and his house keeper. She was holding a bunch of pretty flowers ready, which she pressed into Anna's hands. And she put something green in her hair. Anna blushed, because she had heard, that anyone who was no longer a virgin wore something green in her hair or in her veil. Most people no longer clung to this tell-tale tradition. At the church door stood the village teacher and asked if he should play the organ and held out his hand. Albert gave him some money and he disappeared immediately. Then they heard the music coming from the church. The pair followed the priest to the altar and knelt down on two red hassocks which had been placed on the altar steps. The marriage ceremony could now begin. Anna had to pull herself together. She still had not eaten anything and she was beginning to feel dizzy because of the incense. She did not understand the Latin and everything else the priest said was the same as she'd heard in the registry office, except that here they spoke of God and sins and it all lasted longer.

Finally the rings, secretly pressed into Albert's hand by his mother, could be placed on their fingers. Now they were man and wife, also for God and all the saints. Anna looked at Albert through misty eyes. He kissed her, took both her hands and lead her from the altar steps to the few people who were gathered there for the ceremony and who now congratulated them both. Then they left the church. The fresh air did Anna good. They went into the inn which stood next to church, accompanied by the priest and his housekeeper. It was good that everything was already laid out on the large table, since most stomachs were rumbling. There was lamb with bread and grapes, and a large jug of wine. And, of course, the wedding cake. The inn keeper told a few funny stories and everyone was very happy. The priest did not seem to be averse to good wine. His nose was covered with dark read veins. For Anna, it was hot and her cheeks were blazing. She had only taken a few sips, but she was not used to drinking wine. She pressed Albert's hand hard under the table and gave him a beseeching look. She needed some fresh air. So Albert stood and said, "It's time to go." But the priest wanted to give a few more words of advice for them to take on their way, "Now you both must be strong and stick together. There will be hard times as well as happy times. May God be with you on your journey." As they left, he blessed them once more. Anna looked at the ring. She could still not trust what had happened, she turned round and asked the priest, "Father, are we now really married before God and the world?" Everyone laughed out loud. "But of course," said the innkeeper. Then they took their leave.

As Albert and Anna drove into the courtyard, the head servant rushed up to them, "The Count has had us all looking for you. You have to come to him immediately." Then his eyes widened and he stared at Anna, sitting there in her beautiful dress and with the bouquet in her hand. Albert had already carefully removed the green sprig from her hair. He looked at her tenderly and kissed her lovingly. "It almost looks as though you've been to a wedding," said the head servant in confusion. "Yes, and that seems to amaze you," answered the young Count, "We've been to our own wedding." Then he added, loud enough for all those standing around to hear, "You may congratulate us." The head servant stammered a few words and the rest shouted their best wishes. Albert and Anna descended from the horse drawn cart. The young Count took Anna by the hand and led her to his father's house. He knocked on the massive oak door. His mother opened the door and took both of them in her arms. They heard the father roar, "Stop that! What did you have to sneak away from? Answer me!" With sure steps Albert went to his father and showed him the marriage certificate, "Yes, although it hurt us to do such a thing, we have married against your will. My conscience would not let me do otherwise. My child should have a father and one who is no coward, and, not least, we love each other." The father snatched the certificate from his hand. "She's signed with the name von Dorn. What were you thinking of? I will not permit it. She is not from our class. Never shall she call herself by this name. I forbid it, now and forever. She is not a von Dorn and she is certainly no Countess. Get out! And you, just get on with your work," then he pointed at Anna, "and she won't be here much longer! I don't want to see her in this courtyard. This little piece of filth has bewitched you. She should be burned at the stake." "That's enough," shouted the mother, who up to now had just been crying softly, "you don't know what you are saying. Don't forget that she is carrying your grandchild under her heart. That's something you can't change, my dear. It is as it it is and it's in God's hands." "Get out," roared the old Count, even though both of them had already gone out through the door, without turning round. Anna was shivering all over.

When they were standing in front of the house, Albert held her shoulders and said, "Everything will be all right. I'll look after everything. Please believe me, I'll never let you go. We belong together." He looked deep into her eyes. She smiled and nodded, "I believe you. Your noble father probably didn't mean what he said. We angered him because we did everything behind his back. Nobody likes that." "Everything is all right," he repeated and pressed her to him.

On the estate nobody wanted anything more to do with Anna. Everyone turned away. She shrank away from every little sound and she was almost at the end of her nerves. It was almost unbearable. Albert worked every day until he was dead tired and tried his best not to leave her alone. He knew very well, that she was not feeling good. "And I'm really homesick," she said, "no one at home knows that I'm married and expecting a child." She almost cried out her soul. This cannot go on, thought Albert and smoothed her hair. "As soon as the weather is better we'll go to your home. I promise you. And now, calm yourself. It won't be long."

For days on end there was torrential rain. The fields were flooded. There was nothing to do except try to divert the water. One morning, when it finally stopped raining, Albert said to Anna, "Come, now we'll go to your parents. We'll take the long road through the woods. That way we won't get stuck in the mire."

Anna's face lit up. She threw herself round her husband's neck, kissed him and said, "I knew it. You are the best husband one could wish for. I love you with all my heart. My dear husband, many, many thanks." He was happy to see her joyful again.

When they got to Anna's home, the whole family were happy for the visit. Anna introduced the man who had accompanied her, "This is Count Albert von Dorn, my husband." That silenced them all. Then Anna and Albert laughed heartily and infected them all. They also laughed. They were congratulated. Hugged and everyone was happy and when they heard that a child was on the way, the surprise was even better.

Later Anna and Albert listened to all the interesting stories about what had happened in the meantime. The parents told them the biggest news. Their eldest daughter, Elfriede had eventually married. She was living close by with her husband, Hermann on a small, leased farm. "You should go there now," said Anna's father, "we can't leave the farm and with the horse drawn cart, you'll be there in no time." He gave Albert an almost beseeching look, "It would make us very happy if you would visit them." Albert was tired after the journey, but he agreed. Anna almost exploded with joy. She did not seem in the least bit tired. They took their leave from everyone. Anna waved back until she could no longer see her family.

Hermann and Elfriede's farm was very small. As they reached the hill top, they could hardly see it. When they arrived, Anna's sister and her husband were waiting. They had seen the cart in the distance. They greeted each other warmly. Soon they were all sitting at a rustic wooden table, drinking apple juice, eating bacon and bread and talking about all sorts of things, which families normally talk about. However, they did not hide their worries. Both sides spoke openly. So they found out that Elfriede was also pregnant and in the seventh month. It was difficult to see, because she had put on so much weight. Afterwards, Elfriede heard what had happened in Albert's family and made an offer. Anna should stay with them. They could help each other in this situation. Albert and Anna thought this was a good idea. So, the next day, Albert drove back alone. It was the first time they had been separated, since they had got to know each other intimately. Albert promised to return quickly and bring Anna's other possessions with him.

Time passed. Anna's sister gave birth to a baby boy, without any complications. Straight after the birth Elfriede left her bed and was soon fit again, as though giving birth was the easiest thing in the world. Anna's time was approaching. She did not feel strong. She was always happy when Albert appeared and now he was there again and gave her the strength to hold out. Albert and Anna also had a son. Although he weighed little, she had a lot of pain during the birth. He was a sweet child and they named him Hans. Right after the birth Anna had to get out of bed and, supported by Elfriede take a few steps. Anna's recovery was slow and Albert was worried, but his mother calmed him. It had been the same for her, she told him. Then came the day when Anna felt good and happy again. She did all the housework and looked after the two boys. It was amazing how well she worked. And the whole time she hummed a melody.

A few months later, Anna had the feeling that she was pregnant again. The first person she told was her sister. She looked worried. It was too early. Albert hid his feelings behind a smile, told Anna and his son to go outside in the sun, winked and said, "Everything will be all right. The second time is always better. You know how it is." He wanted to calm Anna and himself with these words.

Months passed. It was colder and winter came. It started to snow without a break. Much snow fell. It was almost impossible to keep the few steps from the house to the stables clear. And in this weather, it was impossible for Albert to make the journey. After a while the little farm was completely snowed-in. For a time it had been possible to push the snow off the hill and let it roll down, but suddenly there was nothing more to be done. There was simply too much snow. Christmas, with the three adults and the two boys was a very quiet, thoughtful and also a happy time. They fooled around, played with the children; it was just a pity that Albert was not there.

They dug out a path to the stables. There was not much work to do. You just had to make sure that the smoke found its way out of the chimney. Anyway, it was not the first time that the area had been cut off by the snow. That's what the neighbours told them. A few years before, the snow had been so heavy that for a long time, some of the farmers had no contact with each other.

Anna's sister could not rid herself of her worries about the birth of Anna's second child. The last time that Albert had been there, he had said that if it was another boy, then it should be called Karl. Anna was happy with the name, but, if truth be told, she wanted a girl, a Magdalena. Her time was due in a few weeks. But she did not think that Albert would be able to be present at the birth. The snow was much too deep and it was bitterly cold. These thoughts made her a little sad. That is God's will. Everything is in His hands, she thought. She turned the ring on her finger. Sometimes she had the feeling that the Lord was very close to her. She dreamed that angels took her on a long, pleasant journey. And then, one morning, Anna could not get up from her bed. The pains were coming ever more frequently. She felt terribly hot. Pearls of sweat ran down her face, yet the sweat felt cold. Anna's sister and her husband were very worried. If only that turns out for the best, they thought. The child seemed to be lying in the right position, but it still went on, right through the night until, finally, in the early morning a healthy, strong boy took his first look at the world. They were all surprised. They had expected a more delicate child. Anna was exhausted and, at the same time happy that it was over. And her sister and brother-in-law were also relieved. Both of them danced for joy round the bed, kissed each other, smiled and, in their hearts, they did not forget to thank God. Anna and her sister were moved by the beautiful words which they found and sent up to heaven. After such a wonderful event they were all overcome by tiredness and slept for a while, even in the light of day.

After this birth Anna was very weak. Her breath was laboured, she was feverish and none of the healing plants which they brought her seemed to help. They all looked at her, helpless. Hermann tried to find a way thought the snow to get help.

The snow seemed to have settled a bit, but the horse sank deep and could no longer move. He had great difficulty bringing it back to the stable. The snow shoes, which he had made himself, were a little more useful. Maybe, the next day he could get to a neighbour, for today, it was too late. Anna's sister tried to bring her confinement fever down by applying cloths soaked in vinegar. Hermann stayed in the stable with the children or in the living room and looked after them as best he could.

So another night passed without sleep. Finally, in the early morning, Anna fell asleep and her sister slept, half upright, next to her bed. When the light came up over the snow, Anna's sister woke and went to see where the others were. All around everything was quiet. She found the children and her husband in the stable. He was taking care of the animals and the small boys were watching him. "I didn't want to wake you," he said, "I saw that you had fallen asleep. How's Anna today?" His wife looked at him and did not know what to say. Yes, how was she? She only remembered that Anna was lying there, peacefully. Even her breath was still. Still? She was shocked by the thought. She turned round and, tripping over the stable threshold, rushed into the room where Anna lay. She leant over her sister, looked at her peaceful face. Her eyes were not quite closed and her mouth was a little open. There was a small smile on her lips, but she could neither hear nor feel any breath. She touched Anna's shoulders and shouted "Anna! Anna!" But Anna did not react. Screaming, Elfriede shook her. Hermann had followed her and he understood what had happened. He prised his wife away from Anna, took her in his arms and they both started to cry bitterly. The children clung hard to the hem of her dress and started to cry. The baby cried. It seemed as though their whole world had collapsed around them.

It was the first time that they had both felt awkward, alone and deserted. The children calmed down. Elfreide gave them something to eat and put them on their mattress in the corner. The parents did not think long about what they had to do.

Hermann brought a candle and a fir tree twig. Elfriede washed her sister, combed her hair and dressed her in the best dress she had. Then she made a bier and laid Anna on it. She placed her hands together. Then Hermann took the wooden cross, which Anna had brought with her, from the wall, placed it under her hands and decorated it with the fir twig. He lit the candle and placed it on the side table. Then they stood at her feet. They looked at Anna, who looked like a Madonna. They knelt down and prayed.

Anna lay there for two days. Then she had to be buried. Hermann shovelled the snow to one side and tried to dig a grave. The earth was frozen. He hacked at it with his pick. It took him hours until he finally had a grave which was deep enough for the corpse. As he was putting the shovel to one side, he heard a call in the distance. He listened and then shouted, "Is someone there?" "Yes. It's me. Hello." It was Albert's voice. Then he saw his brother in law looking down from the mountain of snow. He could see his breath in the cold air and his clothes were steaming from his exertion. Smiling, Albert came closer and took off his snow shoes. "A horse drawn cart with a snowplough from our estate brought me close and the rest I had to do with snow shoes. Tomorrow they'll come to collect me." With a serious face Hermann took him in his arms and brought him into the stable. Before Albert had the chance to greet Elfriede, Hermann told him that Anna had given birth to a healthy son and, after a brief pause, added that she had died a few days after.

Albert fell to his knees. Hermann dragged a bundle of hay to him, so that he could sit on it. He laid his hand on Albert's shoulder and tried to take in his grief as best he could. After a while they went into the living room. Albert greeted his sister in law, who broke down in tears. He hugged the children and looked around the room for his new born son. He took him in his arms, pressed the child to him and broke down in tears, sobbing. His sister in law took the child from his arms and led him into the room where Anna lay. She left him alone with his beloved wife and quietly pushed the door to, but she did not close it completely.

Elfriede made something to eat, while her husband busied himself in the stable. After a long while, Albert came out of the room. Without saying a word, he sat down at the table. After some time, he asked what had happened, exactly. His sister-in-law described everything. Hermann joined them, carrying all the things which Albert had brought with him, including the wonderful winter shawl for Anna. It was now given to Elfriede. Naturally, no one expressed any happiness as would normally be the case during a visit. They were all in deep mourning. They sat at the table for a long time and talked about what should now happen. Anna should be buried on the next day, in the early morning hours. They wanted to keep Hans, the first born, but Albert had to take Karl with him and find a wet nurse for him. Albert remembered a farm servant. Marie. She had just had a child. She would surely have enough breast milk to feed Karl as well.

And that's how it was. Marie had always been a good friend to Anna and there was no problem. So the tiny Karl von Dorn arrived back on the estate of his grandparent's, Count Franz Johann von Dorn and his wife, Charlotte. The Countess took the child warmly in her arms. But the old Count simply asked, what was happening and took no further interest in his grandson. He showed not interest in the events. But the old Countess was very pleased whenever Albert brought little Karl, who was always happy, to her. Right from the beginning she had taken him to her heart, but did not want to show it, as though she was afraid that someone would be against it. As time went by, Albert suffered and his mother knew it. He could not get over his grief for Anna. He ate little and he found it difficult to talk to people.

One day, Albert was found, completely deranged, crouching in a corner of the stable next to his favourite horse. He was murmuring unconnected sentences and his eyes seemed to be searching for something. He gave no answer to any questions.

The head servant called his father, the Count. He looked at him and called for another servant. Together they carried Albert into the house. The head servant was ordered to bridle the horses to the cart. They wanted to take the young Count into town to the doctor. His mother would have preferred that the doctor be brought to the house, but she was unable to achieve her aim. She could only ensure that Albert was washed and dressed in fresh clothes. Recently Albert had not shaved or had his hair cut. He had a wild look about him and his eyes were deep sunken. They filled a wash bath with warm, soapy water and laid him in it. The old Count called for scissors, took hold of Albert's beard and cut it off with one straight cut. Then his long hair was held back on the nape of his neck and a servant girl had to cut and clean his finger and toe nails.

Albert let all this happen. The warm water seemed to relax him, because his eyes were closed the whole time. After they had bathed and dressed him, the head servant took his undernourished body with the blanket and carried him to the cart. Albert seemed to be in a deep sleep. His mother had infused him with herbal tea and valerian while he was lying in the bath water. "Maybe that is why he is drowsy," his father said, threw another blanket over him and drove off.

The track into town was bumpy and full of potholes. When they arrived in front of the doctor's house, it was covered in dust. Without looking at his son the old Count went straight into the house to fetch the doctor. The waiting room was full. An unpleasant smell offended his nose. Ignoring the people who were waiting he called for the doctor, went to the door at the end of the room and opened it. A young woman with a bandaged arm was sitting in front of the doctor. The old Count, after a brief greeting, said what was happening. The doctor looked at him, looked through the window and saw a man lying on the cart. "Go ahead, I'm coming." he said and turned back to his patient. Soon after he came and looked at the man. Shook him, tried to find a pulse and said, "I can do nothing. The man is already dead." Then he pulled the blanket over Albert's face and said to the Count, who was in shock, "Come with me. I'll write the death certificate." They went into the house. The doctor sat down at his desk and asked, "Who is this man?" In a strangled voice, the old Count said, "he is my … my only son, Count Albert von Dorn." The doctor stood, gave the Count his hand, his face showing his sympathy. He wanted to know how it had happened. Listened to everything, went once more to the cart, to check the facts and wrote on the death certificate, "Died of a broken heart." As he gave the document to the grieving father, he saw his colourless face and that he staggered. He offered him a glass of spirits and drank one himself. Before he let in the next patient, he gave him a few words of advice about what he should do next. Count von Dorn took his leave. With shaking hands he carefully covered his son, drove the horse to the town fountain and then straight back to the estate, where Albert was to be buried. On the third day, early in the morning he was laid to rest.

The old Countess made sure that her two grandsons were cared for. But the old Count wanted nothing to do with them. Little Karl was not allowed in the main house, and certainly not allowed to sit at the table with the other von Dorns. That didn't seem to bother Karl. Since he was still at the breast, Marie gave him enough warmth that nothing could disturb him. His grandmother loved him very much. However, she suffered from gout and could not do a lot with him, but she did make sure that he learned to read and write and do arithmetic. Hans, on the other hand had no interest for such things. He wanted to be like the people with whom he was growing up. He was not brought to the estate after his parents' death. Aunt Elfriede, Uncle Hermann and their children were his family and, in spite of having to work hard he felt comfortable there. When the old Countess called for him, once in a while, he had an uneasy feeling and when she died all contact to the estate stopped. The brothers rarely saw each other.

When Hans and Karl were older, they were both able to work self-employed. Hans was a farmer, with little wealth, but he was content with his lot.

Karl fell in love with Sofie, the daughter from a small farm. He became a broom binder, specialised in brushwood brooms and moved close to town. The brooms sold well and as soon as he put some money to one side, he married Sofie. When he signed the marriage certificate, it was the first time that he used the name which was his right, "Karl von Dorn." He left the title 'Count' out, because this was not mentioned on his birth certificate.

He should have also left the "von" out, because that was also not on the document, but Mr. Korn, the oldest official to have checked the papers, knew Karl's family and officially corrected the birth certificate. Then Sofie had to sign with her new name and she was proud to sign, "Sofie von Dorn."

Later, when they met over a glass of wine, Karl discovered that Mr. Korn had known Karl's great grandfather, Count Franz Johann von Dorn very well. Old Mr. Korn told him that his grandfather and the Count had been in the same hunting club. "The count was always very proud of his ancestors." Up to then, Karl had no idea that he had relations in Sweden and Finland and that these people were very well respected. "In the club, your great grandfather told many stories and he was always a jovial fellow. We had a lot of fun together. I was still very young, but his stories always interested me."

Mr. Korn noticed that Karl knew very little about his own family and carried on.

"Unfortunately your grandfather, Count Albert Karl von Dorn had to take over the estate and all responsibilities, very early. Then, he was forced to marry your grandmother, Charlotte. He respected her, but he didn't love her. He only married her to bring some money into the estate. With the marriage the estate was able to pay off the debts. That was more important than anything else." And he went on to say that he and Charlotte, after a time, got on well together and were content with their lot.

It was only later that Karl and Sofie found out, that his grandfather had had a secret love called Katharina and that this Katharina was the mother of the official, Mr. Korn, who had examined and corrected the certificate.

Karl worked hard and he soon had two employees and showed them how they could swing from branch to branch to collect the thin branches for the brooms. Sofie was happy in her small rented house. It stood not far from a brick factory. There were always people passing by who greeted her and sometimes time for a gossip.

She had long dreamed of such a life, and her dream was fulfilled. She thanked God and the world for her happiness. She was always in a good mood, often went to church and had warm words for the poor people who knocked at her door. She gave them some bread and warm soup to help them on their way. On Sundays Karl went to church with her and although he was not too comfortable, he never let it show. After the Mass, people met on the square in front of the church, or they went to drink a glass of apple juice or wine in the "Mönchskeller" 'Monks Cellar' or the "Gasthaus zum Engel" - 'Angel's Inn'. That was where he found out where he could do some business, or where he could be of help and, of course, be paid for it. He also made money writing letters. He had beautiful handwriting and was discreet. The people were happy to let him write their letters. Sofie also learned to read and write. At first she thought it was a waste of time. It was enough that one person in the family could write.

But, with time she started to enjoy it and she did her best to make her handwriting look good. Reading became very important to her. She could now read the Bible. She did not understand much of what was written in it. She thought that there must be a good reason why you did not understand everything immediately. You must be patient. Yes, patience, that is a virtue. How often the priest in his pulpit had said that you needed patience to read the Bible and understand it. Sometimes Karl had enough, when the only thing in her head seemed to be the church. At those times he could speak quite strongly about the priests.

"These know alls! These Pharisees! I can tell you, that they promise much, but they can't tell you what happens to the alms which they take from the people. There are people who give up their last farthing to pay for their sins and mostly they are the poor people." Usually Sofie closed her ears and simply said, "You heard these words in the inn, where people drink more than needed to quench their thirst and can't even find their way home." She had noticed that he often went to the inn and that he enjoyed it there. Since she became pregnant, he went there more often in the late evening. However, after the birth of their first son, called Karl junior, they were once again as contented as they had been at the beginning of their marriage. She was happy at her work. Karl was happy with his new work shop, which he built in a wooden shed. He was clever with his hands and could make and repair all manner of things for the local people. He was friendly and mixed easily with everyone. They enjoyed going to his work shop. Sometimes it was really loud and merry. He also heard wildest stories from the region and spread them further. Now and again a little was added to the story, or maybe even left out, depending on whom they were talking about and sometimes, when they had thoughts in the backs of their minds which they could possibly really carry out. For example, during a festival, they cut a man's beard when he was drunker than a lord. They hid stolen women's underwear in the clothing of a man who was known to be unfaithful and so on and so forth. That was great fun and they laughed about it for days.

As time went by Karl acquired more tools, which he did not need for making brooms, but which he could use for repairing all sorts of things for his customers. For the farmers it was more a case of bartering, because they had very little money and they wanted to get rid of their agricultural products. So Sofie always had enough bacon, flour, bread, fat, butter, milk, cheese, fruit and vegetables in her store.

Sofie had one child after another and soon there were eight. But a boy and a girl died shortly after birth. So they had four sons; Karl, Alois, Alfred and Franz and two daughters; Senta and Berta. The children, the house and the garden gave her a lot of work. But they were a contented and happy family.

Until the First World War broke out. Very soon hunger and need were their daily companions. Many were unemployed. Everyone saved where ever they could. There was almost nothing to buy and no one was ready to exchange anything with Karl; not even a broom to sweep with. Only the essentials were brought to him to repair. His sons, Alfred and Karl found work in the coal mines, even though they were only 12 and 13 years old. Even Senta had to go to work as soon as she was 13. She went to the glass factory. She had no other choice. Berta stayed at home, took care of the garden and the land around it. She tried to help her mother and to comfort her. The mother suffered a great deal, because everything had changed.

Franz was the last to be born in 1900. He was the smallest in the family, but he was agile and got on with everyone, just like his father. Franz and Alfred still went to school, when that was possible. Father was now alone in his work shop and over the years his customers changed. Now they were mainly women, who asked for advice and help. At the beginning he could help, but as time went by, more often, Karl had to send them away.

The First World War came to an end. The von Dorn family were lucky. All of them survived the war. But many were still unemployed. There was misery and poverty all over Europe. Many trusted to luck and emigrated, in the hope of finding a better life in another, foreign, country.

It was truly a terrible time. Once, mother Sofie queued for four hours for bread and at the end she got nothing. She managed to get the last loaf in exchange for cigarettes which she had hidden away from father, but then it was over. She also saw the mayor's servant going to the baker's back door getting a cake. She ran to the house and knocked on the door, which was closed. She knocked until her knuckles bled. Then she gave up. She did not know what else she could do. She was overwhelmed with despair and crying, she thought she had never been so low in her life. The son, Hans, could not bear it any longer. He packed a few things, went into the hills and knocked on every farm door. He wanted to exchange the few things which he had in his bag for flour, eggs, potatoes or anything which he could get. If he was lucky and did not come home with empty hands, then his mother's eyes shone again and that was the most wonderful present he could have. Franz also went around asking if anyone had anything to repair, or if he could bring them something from town. He was a smart boy and was happy with the smallest success. In this way he was always able to organise something and even get work for his father.

One evening, father Karl came home very drunk. He staggered about, threw up and, since he could no longer reach the bucket, it went everywhere. He also soiled himself and there was a terrible smell. Disgusted, Sofie shoved her husband out of the house and into the work shop, locked the door, took off his stinking clothes and scrubbed him clean. The next day she washed his clothes in the well. In the house Berta busied herself with cleaning up. It tool a long time before the sour smell went away. Late into the night the windows stood wide open, although it was very cold.

Every morning their father went to the inn. He always hoped that he could make some business, but instead only increased his debts and rather than eating something he drank whatever the people offered him. He tried gambling, just to get a little money, but that was useless. He lost more and more and at the same time money was continually losing its value.

There was no point going 'hoarding' to the farmers in the valley. That is what they called bartering. The farmers gave nothing more, because everything was rationed. Every family got their rations, and they were minimal. You could neither live nor die from them. Some suffered from pains in their sternum. Many died of hunger and illnesses caused by hunger. Work in the coal mines was hard and dirty and they got little to eat. From the canteen in the glass factory, Senta could, apart from the money, occasionally bring something to eat. Now they counted on her. One day, she was ill. The company doctor sent her home, because she had 'head flu', as they used to say and she should stay in bed. As soon as she felt a little better she went back to work. She was afraid of losing her job. Senta was deeply disturbed about her family's suffering. It was not long before she fell ill again and this time it was very serious. As if that was not enough, awful news arrived; her friend, to whom she was secretly engaged, had been killed in the war. For days she grasped his photograph in her hands. She was slow to recover and kept repeating the same words, "Everyone must come home healthy. Everything is going to be all right." And she kept on repeating these words until she was very old. She started to laugh constantly and became mindless. So they put her into a mental institution for a while. Physically she was healthy, but her mind remained very disturbed.

Father Karl Dorn – he dropped the "von", because he felt it did not fit in with their impoverished state – after a long search, found a place in town, since he could no longer pay the rent for their small house. It was a single room in a very old house. The gravity lavatory was at the far end of the corridor. If you needed to go, someone else had to go with you, because there were also strangers about.

One fine day Berta ran straight into the arms of a thief. She started to scream and the thief pushed her down the stone steps. Her spine was damaged and she was given a corset to wear. It was a long time before she was better and could walk without the corset. Later the doctor diagnosed a curved spine. In the hospital Berta was forced into a corset again, which was extremely painful. She could hardly sleep. Only when she was exhausted did she fall asleep. After a while the corset was removed and she was fitted with a support which held her spine straight. Then the pain was not so bad. The pain stopped and she could walk upright again. But the distortion of her spine continued and she developed a hump back which was clearly visible. She stopped growing taller. She remained small and in later years she shrank even more. In town they called her the "hunch back". No one could help her. For the rest of her life she was marked out and mocked. Years went by before people left her in peace and she found once more her sense of humour. She was very attached to Senta, because she was also handicapped. So the sisters stayed together for ever.

Berta was not the only one in the town with a crooked spine. For example, there was the worthy tailor Mrs. Wattenweil. She also had a hump, but was happily married. One day she heard about a young man who had the same problem and who had been rejected by his family because he was a "cripple" and labelled as a "bad child". She told people that she was looking for him. A man brought the miserable, stinking being, clothed in tatters and delivered him, saying, "This is what you are looking for. He wanted to hide himself on my property." Mrs. Wattenweil said, "He can stay with us, if he wants to." The man looked at her, amazed and went, muttering on his way. The youth gave Mrs. Wattenweil an inquisitive look. She took hold of his chin and looked at him. "You're a good looking youth. What's your name? Are you hungry?" He didn't answer and she led him into the house. She gave him some milk to drink and a slice of bread and honey. "Would you like to stay with us? You don't know us, but let's try it for a while. Maybe we'll get on together and become friends. So, what do you think?" The youth shrugged his shoulders and stayed.

He was a good looking, confident youth. His name was Willhelm. His back was less crooked than Frau Wattenweil. With her tailoring skills it was easy for her to hide his small hump. He allowed her to do everything. But, in the beginning, with Mr. Wattenweil, he did not like being stroked on the head and ducked, because at home and when out and about, he had often been beaten. The Wattenweils did not have children and had given up all hope of having any. The youth was very happy with the couple. One day, out of the blue, he said that he would have loved to have had them as his parents. So they went to see Willhelm's parents, without him and asked them to give him free for adoption. The whole process took very little time. In the parish they were amazed that an adoption could happen so quickly. The Wattwenweils gained a great deal of respect from the people in that small town. A few years later they got to know Senta and Berta and quite often spent time with them.

Sofie Dorn, who had taken to her bed and seemed to have lost all will to live, worried them all, particularly Franz, who was very fond of his mother. Sometimes with tears running down his cheeks, he sang funny songs to her.

He had been able to get a few potatoes from somewhere. The pan with hot water was standing on the fire so that they could quickly make something to eat, if they got anything which had to be cooked. When Franz came in with the potatoes, Berta washed them and put them in the water. They could hardly wait until they were ready. So that they could eat them straight away, she cooled them in cold water. Everyone got two potatoes. Berta his two potatoes for her brothers, Karl and Alois, who always came home late in the night from their shift in the coal mines and brought their work rations home with them so that everyone got a small portion. Mother Sofie could eat almost nothing. She had become weaker because of the lasting distress and sadness. One day she did not recover from a cold and died. They were all there, except Father. Karl ran to find him. He ran from one inn to another. Finally he found him sitting at a table with the mayor. He was tipsy and his face was jovial, because he had finally secured a contract to supply brooms for the parish.

"Now things will be better," he said, just as he saw his son, who was out of breath, standing in front of him. "Come, Mother has died," he spluttered and took his father by the arm. Karl Dorn went pale and, shivering, got to his feet. Unbelieving he looked his son in the face and they both ran home as quickly as they could. The father tore open the door and with a smothered cry, threw himself, crying over his wife. "Why now? Now, when things are looking up," he sobbed, "could you not have waited just a little longer? I've got a large order for brooms! Wake up! Can you hear me? A broom contract! You can't go now, not now, please… ." He got an advance from the parish to pay for the funeral. Berta managed to scrape together something for a meal. People who they had previously helped remembered her and also brought some food with them. It was well known that everyone had very little to offer.

In those days many farmers' wives and their children had to take care of the fields alone. The women worked until they dropped. In town they collected and bartered what they could. There was little food to be had in the shops, but after a few years it got better for the Dorn family. Miraculously they did not succumb to typhoid, dysentery, smallpox etc.

Karl junior and Alfred got used to working in the coal mine and they were promoted. Alois, who worked in a glass factory, was promoted to shift leader. It was a good job and soon he married his girlfriend, Ingried. They had two children.

Alfred made it to head of department. He married Gerda, a local beauty queen. However, the marriage did not last long. Gerda wanted more from life. She did not want to be a housewife. They had one son, Peter, and she felt tethered to him. One morning, she left the family. Peter, abandoned by his mother, became a chronic bed wetter. Then, many years later, Gerda came back. She was lonely and clearly dependant on alcohol. At least she tried to show her son some affection and succeeded, because Peter did not get on well with Grete, his father's second wife. She was somewhat younger than Gerda, had a loving nature, was pretty and always happy, but there were always tense moments. She could not and did not want to replace his mother. So, when he was 14, he went to live with his beloved mother and stayed with her until she died from a liver tumour. When he was 23, Peter married Anna, who was the youngest sister of his step-mother Grete and they were very happy together.

Berta and Senta stayed with father Karl Dorn in the old flat. The two spinsters received a small pension because of their handicaps. They also got a little money from their brothers. With this they got by.

The youngest Franz was now working in the coal mines, but after the first kick in the backside that his boss gave him, he often reported in sick. Later he became a miner.

It meant for him, that whatever the weather he had to work mostly outside. In addition, the pressure to meet deadlines was too much. So he was soon, once more, unemployed. Up to then he had been content with life, because he had been able to do odd jobs. With his wife, Luise, he had five children, but two died shortly after birth. He was only 20 when his first son, Franz junior was born. They called him Franzi. Soon after came Erwin, Aloisia, Irmgard and Maria. Money was in short supply. Franz started gambling and was sometimes lucky. But it was barely enough. One day a returning wanderer told him that in the harbour in Hamburg, it was a lot easier to earn money. So he hitch hiked to Hamburg, mainly in trucks. Now and again he sent money home, but it did not go far. Luise worried about the children. Irmgard was always at the doctor's. She died when Franz was in Hamburg.

A widowed neighbour asked Luise to be his housekeeper. The pay was not bad. Later she helped him in his confectionery shop. So that her three children were not left alone in the house, she asked her sister in law Berta to keep an eye on them. One of Franz's friends wrote home regularly. That is how Luise found out that he was working hard and about a year later, that Franz was having problems, that he got to know every bar in Hamburg but having been hit during a fight in the red light district, he stayed more at home.

One morning Franz was shocked when he discovered that a room mate had stolen his clothes and run away with them. Franz jumped up and, half naked behind the door, shouted down that the man should bring his clothes back.

A woman in the entrance heard him shouting and asked what the matter was. He told her briefly what had happened.

The the old woman took a deep breath and went back into her flat. After a while she knocked on his door, offered him a few clothes and a hat and said, "There a few things from my dead husband. God bless him." Before Franz could say anything, she blew her nose into a prettily embroidered handkerchief, went back to her flat and closed the door behind her.

Franz put on the clothes which were a little too big, but he still felt good wearing them. Then he packed together all his remaining things and crept out of the building. Suddenly he was afraid. He was not sure if his colleague had paid the rent and asked himself why he had let someone take his worn clothes? The thought went through his head that something must be wrong.

He then went to his favourite bar and told them that he had had enough and was going to try his luck in Switzerland.

Soon he was in Lindau in southern Germany, but he and a colleague he had joined up with on the journey, were turned back at the border. When they both asked why, the border officer answered in Swiss German, "You just want to collect cigarette butts and roll cigarettes from them, wander around like tramps and make it with our girls. We don't need people like you."

So Franz staggered on towards his Austrian homeland. But he did not get far, because his money was almost gone. So he plucked up courage, jumped on to a goods train and, with a good portion of luck, he finally came home, with no money, no food and totally exhausted. He greeted his wife as though he had never been away. He stood in front of her in his grey, pinstriped suit, white shirt, tie, waistcoat with a grey hat on his head. In his hand he had a suitcase with his dirty washing and a large shell with a ship painted on it. Apart from that, he had nothing. They greeted each other warmly, but neither of them knew what they should say. Luise said, "Do you want some tea? … and , well, how was it?" Franz avoided the question and asked about the children. He knew from his colleague that Irmgard had died. When he started to tell his story, she was not really listening. She had already heard some things from people who had written letters or had come home to visit their families. But her dear Franz could not know that. Whenever she heard that someone had come back from Hamburg, she had asked about Franz and what he was doing. She had never heard a bad word about him, only that he could not go on doing heavy work for long and that other work was difficult to find, but that he was clever enough to earn a few pennies here and there. To save paying rent he had slept with workmates and colleagues. Nobody knew, until now, that a widow had given him her dead husband›s clothes and shoes. Actually, Franz did not want to tell any one, but his brother, Karl, to whom Luise sometimes brought something to eat, wanted to know why he had come home wearing such fine clothes, but had sent almost no money home. Karl kept on asking until Franz finally told him the truth,

"It was like this…," and he told him what had happened.

His brother Karl asked him in no uncertain terms, what he intended to do now. Franz calmed him down. He had already started looking for work. He could help cooper Florenz until his helper came back from hospital. The frame-saw had split and had badly injured his shoulder. He had managed to hold the gaping wound closed and stagger the half kilometre to the hospital.

Franz liked working for the cooper. Florenz was a very jovial person and was still unmarried. He said, "I like women and can find a woman to my taste since there are more than enough around. But first I want to improve my situation, so that I can start a good situated family." However, there was something which annoyed Franz. Florenz always whistled the same melody the whole day long. It was a blessing that the saw machine was fairly loud and the workshop was anyway noisy, for instance, when the metal bands were beaten onto the wooden barrels. Were it not for that, the continuous whistling would have not been bearable. After work Franz and Florenz were happy to go for a drink and Franz often drank more than was needed to quench his thirst. Across the street from the cooper's workshop, Ferdinand, a good school friend ran a restaurant together with his living partner. It was always merry there, especially when the strong women came to drag away their men or demanded money out of their wage packets. Franz could not stand that. He could not imagine that his wife, Luise would ever enter this male domain and then, in front of everyone, demand money. No, he thought, she would not do that. But she stood outside, hidden in a corner and whenever someone she knew went by, begged them to tell Franz he should come out and then she added that they should not say that it was she who was waiting. Since he did not like that either, there were often arguments back home, although she was discreet. Of course, Franz showed little interest in the children.

Berta had more and more washing to iron. She was very good at ironing and people got to know about it, so more and more people brought her their washing. She had a good circle of customers and earned good money. Senta was constantly washing. She was happy to do it, she did it well and was praised for her work. Every Saturday, Berta and Senta took the liberty of going to the pub on the ground floor where they lived. Often there was someone there playing music and singing. They sang along and some of the guests offered the singers a glass of wine, which they were happy to accept. Sometimes there was a good soup or a cutlet. They looked forward to this day all week. Along with the washing they often got presents of presentable clothes so they were always well dressed and infected other people with their good mood. They thought that now Franz was home, they would not have to take care of the children so often. However, unfortunately, that was not so. At first Luise gave up her job at the neighbour, but she soon went back. She could not take the accusations that she needed too much money and although she could account for every penny she spent, Franz did not listen and just shouted that she was doing something wrong, otherwise it would not be so. And on and on and...

One day, Franz suddenly realised that actually his wife was very pretty. At the same time he asked himself why she cared so much about her looks when cleaning for the neighbour. He also saw the fine clothes from the neighbour lying about the house. Before, it had not interested him, because he was always somewhere else. Now it disturbed him. He started to stay away from work on Mondays. Then he complained about the alcohol at Ferdinand's. He reckoned that he served his guests a mixture of cheap wines. "Then they poison you," he yelled when he had to run outside to vomit. From then on Ferdinand gave him only a quarter of wine mixed with fizzy mineral water and made sure that he got no drinks from anyone else and from that time on, Franz was a little better, since, thank God, he had no interest in going to another inn.

Franz went on working at the cooper's, but soon had the idea of making toys from the left over wood and for that he needed to use Florenz's machines. He took the toys with him wherever he went, to sell them to anyone who was interested. Franz always had better ideas. He made funny and noisy toys and painted them in bright colours. The children loved his things. With time he started working to order, but he noticed that Florenz was not too pleased.

Franz spoke to him about it. Florenz answered that he had barrels to make and also that he was using his machines and anyway, the left over wood was needed for the fire which they used in coopering. Franz tried to continue making the toys at home, but that did not go well. The flat was too small and he always had to clear up. He could not leave things lying around because of the children. He told his wife he was losing precious time. Later he got the idea of buying the wood from Florenz and that is what he did. He let him store the wood in the workshop. In the evening, he went home, cut out the templates, drew them on the planks and thought about how he could cut them. He knew that Florenz always hid the key to the workshop and never took it home, because his way home was dark and he was afraid of being robbed or losing the key. There was only one key for this old, complicated lock and it was too heavy to carry it around in his trouser pocket. One evening, Franz plucked up his courage and searched for the key. He looked for a long time, but he did not find it. It was too dark. He should have brought a light with him. Where was it? In which cranny and under what plank was it hidden? He had to go home without finding it. The following evening he left work as usual, went into the attic and from there, although it was dark, he could see where the key was hidden. He waited until there was no one about, took the key and went into the workshop. Franz did not want to turn on the lights. At first he lit a match and then he found the remains of a candle, but the light was not good enough for him to cut out the shape which he had drawn on the piece of wood. And it was eerily quiet. What will people think when they hear the machines running? Although, at this time of night there was no one in the courtyard. With these thoughts in his head he trotted home. "I give up," he said to himself. And, his conscience was disturbed, when he thought of cheating on his friend and employer. He calmed down, after all, he had not stolen anything, but his conscience still worried him, but he did not want to give up. He fell into bed like a beaten man. What will happen when the other employee comes back to work? Then I'm going to get even more problems, he thought. With these thoughts in his head, he fell asleep.

Days passed. Every evening Franz and Luise were surrounded by the children and all their questions. Berta had started sending the children back home at mid-day, so Luise always had some work to do in the evenings. Franz started to become interested in what Luise really did. Instead of asking her, he spied on her. There was the neighbour, who had a confectionery and who started to work very early in the morning when most people were still sleeping. Apart from him and the miners who were changing shifts, no one else woke up so early. And there was something else, the baker was a widower.

One evening, when the children were already in bed and Luise was wrapping sweets in coloured paper. Franz stood behind her. Her freshly washed hair smelled so sweet. He stroked it, took her by the shoulders. Then he touched her breasts. He wanted to kiss her, but he sensed her resistance. Defensively she said, "The sweets have to be delivered early tomorrow morning." "Have you forgotten about married duty?" he hissed, poisonously in her ear. She started to quake and pleaded him to speak more quietly so as not to wake the children. "You're getting your pleasure elsewhere, with the baker, or am I wrong? Show me what you do with him. You make yourself very fine for him. I'm a complete idiot that I haven't realised until now how my dear wife spends her time when I'm working my socks off for you creatures." He threw her and the chair to the floor, kneeled over her, tore her dress from her breasts and pulled her skirt high. Then he opened his trousers and took her by force. In shock and pain, she cried and whimpered. She had never known him like that. When it was over, he laid heavily on top of her. She thought he was going to crush her with his weight. With a great effort she pushed him on one side and stood up. She was on fire with pain and went quietly into the children's room. A few minutes later she heard the front door crashing to and was glad that he'd gone. Shaking with anger she took off her torn dress which was covered in sperm, pushed it into the stove and set alight to it. It disgusted her. She had a sickening feeling deep in her stomach. Then she started to wash and scrub her violated body. She was in such an awful condition that she did not even notice the wounds which he had inflicted on her. The stove was smoking badly. The dress did not want to burn. Luise took it out, shoved it in the wash bucket, opened the window, through it out and watched it as it landed in the bushes.

Luise lay down on her bed, but she could not sleep. She got up, went to the children and cuddled up to her little daughter,

Aloisia. For a while she snoozed. When she heard Franz return, she pulled the blanket over her head. Coughing loudly he fell into bed. Later his snoring woke her. She listened for some time and then she decided to get up and go on wrapping the sweets. Outside it was getting light. Luise ran into the garden, picked the bucket out of the bushes and threw its contents into the rubbish pit. Back in the house she took the box of sweets under her arm, ran to the confectioner, sneaked in and put the carton on the table. Bending down she ran back to the house. She did not want anyone to see her swollen lips. The children were already awake and waiting for their slice of bread and the warm milk which they all loved. Then Franz came from his bed. He washed and shaved without looking at anybody. The children were quiet. He took a slice of bread, drank the milk without sitting down and disappeared without saying a word. Franzi was the first to speak, "Mummy, why have you got such a thick lip?" "Oh, I was careless and ran into the door." In the evenings Franz came home later and later. That made daily life a little less unbearable. They had little to say to each other. Luise went on doing the housework and working for the confectioner as well as she could. Franz heard that the baker went to the cemetery almost every day to visit the grave of his much loved wife. He showed no interest in anyone else, not even Luise. That calmed him down for a while.

One day, as he was on his way home, Franz saw a horse drawn caravan entering the town. Brightly painted on the caravan he read that they were artists, performers and magicians. The wagon stopped. A young woman came down and asked a group of people for directions to the castle park. Somewhere near here there must be a junction. Franz came closer so that he could hear what was being said. He offered to walk in front of them and to lead them there. He also asked if they were sure they wanted to go there, because the owner never opened his door to common people. Even he had never been in the castle park, although "blue blood" flowed through his veins. He added that he had a very modest life and up to now, he had never had any idea of visiting these noble people. The young woman laughed and said that he should leave all that to her. She was amused about the "blue blood". Franz led the entertainers to the castle park and when the young woman saw the iron gate, she thanked him. A man from the group in the caravan blew loudly on a silver horn. After a while someone came and opened the gate. The caravan drove through the gates and disappeared into the park. Franz was amazed, went home and told his wife about it. Luise thought, "Maybe they are the same people who perform in the town hall. I saw a large poster in the town." And that is exactly as it was.

Franz planned to see the show. When it came to the point, he was excited. He had seen many bawdy shows in Hamburg. They cannot show anything like that here, without risking being thrown out of the town. At the entrance to the town hall, which was also used for dramatic productions, stood the young woman, he'd already met, in a glittering dress and heavily made up. On the other side of the entrance stood a stout man with a well trimmed moustache, slicked back hair wearing a shiny red uniform. Franz went up to the young woman. She recognised him immediately and welcomed him so loudly that everyone around heard, "Good evening, Mr. Franz von Dorn. I'm glad that you could come." He was totally perplexed that she knew his name and he was embarrassed. He felt that he was becoming red, bowed a little and spluttered, "My pleasure. Good evening, gracious lady." The gracious lady did not let Franz pass. She called her sister, Anna and asked her to take Herr von Dorn to a place in the front rows. Franz would have preferred a place in the back rows, since he did not want to be noticed. "Are you accompanied?" asked Anna politely. Without waiting for an answer she led him to a single seat in the middle of the second row. She laughed, whispered, "Enjoy the show" and left. Franz squeezed passed the people who had already taken their seats and he was not unaware of some envious looks, amongst them a few from the town's better society members. He excused himself many times as he pushed passed them. A rather large woman turned her face, when he came in contact with her fat knees. And, naturally, he had to sit next to this corpulent woman! She breathed heavily and managed to fill half of his seat as well. On the other side was a man who was also not exactly thin. Franz began to sweat even before he had taken his seat. Soon he started sweating more profusely when he sat down next to the fat woman, whose heavy perfume was mixed with her perspiration. It was almost unbearable. He sneezed and coughed. He could hardly bring himself to breath in the air which was full of sweat and dust and struggled against his claustrophobia. So there he was, sitting in a good seat in the second row squashed like a crushed dwarf!

Finally there was a fanfare and the stage was bathed in light. Two men drew back the heavy velvet curtains. The audience clapped franticly, although there was not yet anything to see. The programme was announced in various languages, alternately by the young woman whom Franz had already met and a young man whom he had never seen before. Franz was impressed although he did not believe there could be so many foreigners in the audience. Then there was an old violinist who played Hungarian music while three couples, wearing traditional Hungarian costumes, danced. The women's dresses rose up, so that their lacy underwear could be seen. An eye opener for the men! Loud applause, followed by a short pause. The gracious lady, Anna, who had shown him to his seat and an other girl came onto the stage and performed the splits and other acrobatics. At the side was the violinist, now playing a concertina. He accompanied their movements with a romantic melody. The three women wore loose, sleeveless, collarless vests and full, white, knee length bloomers. Their dark, long wavy hair hung to their hips. A tall, slim, somewhat older regal looking woman, dressed in black and with a lace scarf covering her head, assisted in that for every exercise she handed them a different article. A silk scarf, a staff decorated with coloured ribbons, a ball and so forth. After the performance, the applause in the hall was tremendous. Franz clapped so hard that his hands hurt. Then there were magic tricks and between the acts a clown appeared. When the performance was over, Franz went home, his head full of all these impressions. He wanted to tell Luise all about it, but she put her finger to her lips, lay down and went to sleep.

The next day a man who Franz had seen the previous evening on the stage came to the cooper's workshop. Florenz was not there, so Franz asked if he could help him. He said he was from the artistic group and needed to replace the leading pole for the horse drawn caravan, because the one he was now using had only been roughly repaired in an emergency. All he needed was a long, round pole. The rest he could do himself if he could borrow some tools. He had brought the old pole with him, so that it could be measured. Franz offered to help him and as the man left the workshop, he saw one of the three young acrobats, the girl he had not yet met. He greeted her and said that yesterday evening he had been in the second row and that he had enjoyed their act. Jokingly he added, "My hands are still hurting because I clapped so much." She was pleased and introduced herself as Miss Rosa. She put her hand in front of her mouth and giggled. Franz went to look at the pole and examined it closely. Well, he did not have a round pole, but he was sure he could find a square pole. They went through the wood store and found something which would serve. The man introduced himself as Igor Pfeiffer and he was Miss Rosa's brother. He spoke German with a strong accent, even stronger than his sister's. It turned out that their mother was from Hungary their father from Burganland on the Neusiedlersee. They travelled a lot so that the children had been born in many different countries.

Igor worked expertly on the wood in the courtyard. He had nothing against his sister, Rosa being with Franz in the workshop the whole time, talking about her travels. Sometimes she forgot to hold her hand in front of her mouth. She just went on chatting. So Franz could see that she had lost one tooth from the top row and two from the bottom row. He remembered the wide smile of her sister Anna, who he had met the evening before. Anna had sparkling white teeth like pearls. Even Josefine, the young woman he had met first still had all her teeth. But Anna attracted him most. She had an open, honest look and a genteel, reserved manner, just like his mother. When Igor had finished his work, Franz was pleased, because he had had his fill of Rosa's chattering. And then she had begun to flirt with him. He thought she was a bit too forward. She had even suggested that they could drink a glass of wine together when he finished work. She would make time for him, before the show began. Luckily, at that moment Igor came into the workshop and they did not make any arrangement. They agreed a price for the pole, but Igor wanted to take it to the castle park and make sure it fitted before he paid. Franz did not like that one bit and he reminded Igor that he had brought him the sample. Then Igor wanted to take the sample with him and also wanted the price reduced, because he had provided the sample. That was too much. In a stern voice, he said he could only take the sample and demanded his money. So Rosa took a few notes out of her blouse and gave them to her brother. Igor stopped trying to make a deal, paid, took the poles and left with his sister. Franz wished them a good evening, rushed into the workshop to check the tools and everything else which Igor had used, because he had become suspicious.

He was a little ashamed of his suspicion about these travellers. In the past he had always defended them. He had always said to those who mistrusted them, "There are good and bad travellers just like us." The Pfeifers were performers and artists. They are a pure folk and an exception. They were forced to live in caravans. Any other shelter for their family and their animals would have been too complicated and too expensive.

Franz asked himself why he had qualms. In the end they had paid. They had only tried to get a better price and that was all. But there were still a few questions when he thought about it. Then Florenz came into the workshop. Franz put his thoughts to one side, told Florenz what has happened and gave the money to his boss. Florenz said that he had visited his assistant at home and that he would be starting work again on the following Monday. Franz knew that this day would happen. He found that the assistant had taken a lot of time, but that now the day had come. "So, that means this week," Florenz said. Franz enjoyed working with wood. It kept him away from drinking and smoking and calmed him down. Smoking was only allowed in the courtyard and, truth be told, he no longer wanted to smoke a cigarette so often. He had put on a bit of weight, but people who knew him said, "You look fine," so he was not worried about it.

One evening, when he came home from work, he heard his son Erwin crying. "What's happened?" he asked. Erwin had a bleeding head wound; his knees and elbows were grazed. "I was playing on the stairs and suddenly I was dizzy and I fell down," he sobbed. "Where is your mother?" "She said she was going to the baker with a delivery." "What the hell?" he shouted, took the child on his lap, looked at the cut on his head and saw that he did not need a doctor. He bandaged his son's head with a clean piece of cloth, asked him everything was all right and disappeared to the baker's. On the way, he thought of his sister Berta. He could not get it out of his head that she was a cripple, because someone had pushed her down the stairs.

When he arrived at the baker's he was so angry that he burst though the door. Then he heard his wife and the baker laughing. He strode up to her and hit her hard across the face. Luise fell over a box and lay there. The baker ran to the door and shouted for the police. The people on the street stood still. They wanted to know what had happened. "Dorn Franz wants to kill his wife. He's gone crazy." A strong farm labourer heard that and marched into the shop. He saw Franz kicking his wife in the ribs, grabbed Franz by the collar and almost strangled him, took his legs from under him, dragged him to the door and let him fall on the path. Franz coughed, struggled for air and thought he was going to suffocate. In the meantime a policeman had arrived. Franz had recovered a little. He shouted as loud as he could, "This bitch leaves the children alone in the house while I'm working and she's having it off with the baker." The policeman asked him to stop shouting and told the bystanders to go on their way. "Our son fell down the stairs at home and he's probably bleeding to death right now," he shouted.

Luise was still lying there, not moving. An older woman dressed in black with a colourful silk scarf over her head, bent over her and saw the wounds which Franz had caused. Then she took her under the arms and helped her to stand. Luise grimaced with pain, but she wanted to go home and see her young son. She realised that her helper knew something about injuries and gave her a pleading look. The woman nodded and took her back to the house. Then she looked at Erwin's cut. He was happy that his mother was there and explained what had happened.

It came out that the woman had once been the Red Cross leader in the area and was the widow of Dr. Zernic. Mrs. Zernic looked around at the order and cleanliness and thought that the children could not have been left alone for very long and confirmed this by talking to Lusie. She took Luise and the children to the doctor's surgery, which her son, Walter, had taken over. Although it was late, he examined the child, who was clinging, fearfully to his mother. When Erwin drew away from her, he saw blood on his arm. He started to cry loudly. It was his mother's blood. The doctor treated them and said to Luise, "In three weeks the bruises will disappear, but Erwin would probably have a small scar from his head wound." Then he took his leave, "Please excuse me, I still have a visit to make," took his doctor's bag and went out of the door. Mrs. Zernic gave them diluted wild berries to drink and also gave the children a few sweets. Sweets, which Luise had often wrapped. Mrs. Zernic then led them to the door and promised to visit them the next day.

When they came home, their worst concern was father's violent temper. Luckily he was not yet there, so they hurried up and went to bed. They felt protected by the blankets and

Luise prayed quietly. The powder which the doctor had given her started to take effect. The pains in her head were not so strong and she did not hear Franz coming in. The next morning his trousers lay beside the bed and she could only see his hair peeking out of the covers.

Luise tried to get up, but it was not so easy. She clung to the edge of the bed and with difficulty, she stood up. Her legs were shaking as she went into the kitchen. The little Franz followed her. Luise realised that she left the bag with bread and a little butter at the baker's. So she sent Franzi to the confectioner's. It was the first time she had done this, so she said, "Go straight to the baker's, get the bag and come straight back. Have you heard?" Franzi nodded and ran off. There was enough milk. Since she could buy milk from the baker, which was actually not allowed, she could be sure that the milk had not been diluted with water. In the milk shop you often heard customers complaining that when they boiled the milk it did not have a layer of cream because it had been diluted with water.

Berta could always see the funny side of things and said, "Everything has its advantages and disadvantages. The milk doesn't boil over and you remain slim as a film star." When she said that, Luise could only laugh. She had no problem with her figure. "Only eat half," was her daily motto so that the others would have something on their plate. There were people who had a so-called water stomach, but that was caused by under nourishment and not from full cream milk or too much food.

Out of breath, Franzi came back with the bag. Luise praised him and kissed him gently on his forehead. Franzi also had a letter in his hand. He gave it to his mother and said, "That's for you and no one else." Luise looked at it briefly and hid it in the folds of her dress.

She unpacked the bread and carefully the soft butter. Quickly she took care of the children and then tidied herself. Because of her head wound, she combed her hair, more than usually, over her forehead, rolled down her sleeves and pulled on her stockings. She put milk, bread and a small glass dish of butter on the table for Franz, went to see if he was still asleep and went out to the lavatory. A little light came though a hole in the door. With trembling hands she held the letter to the light and started to read it. The first line said that she could no longer work for the baker after what had happened last evening, and he begged her not to come to his house. He could not simply sweep the thing under the carpet. Luise's eyes filled with tears. The letters were no longer clear. She read on. "We have both been accused of things which are not true. My good name and the honour of my best beloved, deceased wife have been ruined." He would send someone to her, he wrote on, who would bring her the remaining money which she had earned and she should be so kind as to give this person the goods which she still had in her house. There was a knock on the lavatory door. Luise was shocked. She wiped her tears away on her skirt, disposed of the letter and opened the door. It was only a neighbour who wanted to use the lavatory.

When Luise returned to the flat, Franz was standing in the middle of the room. She stopped in the doorway. He lifted his hand, pointed to the children and said, harshly, "From this evening on, I don't want to see any of you in this flat and I mean that. You have only brought me bad luck. Now, because of you useless creatures, I'm registered with the police. You're a real useless baggage" He went to the door and shoved Luise, who was trying to protect her head with her hands, to one side. In the doorway he turned back and said, "For a long time I've suspected you foisted these children on me. They are not my flesh and blood. Just look at them. None of them look like me." Luise started to boil inside and shouted, "That's enough, enough!" She grabbed a pan with boiling water and threw it at him. Franz reacted quickly and shut the door behind him. She threw open the door and saw that he was wrapping his left hand in a handkerchief. She picked up the pan which was lying on the floor and threw it after him down the stairs. Because of the noise, neighbours came out onto the stairway, saw the scene and were witnesses to a totally broken marriage. The scene was later told during the divorce proceedings and of course, everything they had to tell went against Luise. She went back into the flat, took several deep breaths and tried to seem calm in front of the children. But they had gone to hide. In Luise's eyes were no tears. She called the children, "Everything's all right now," and she hugged them.

How many years has this been going on, went through her head. She gathered her thoughts. What was going to happen now? She tidied the bed covers and the pillows in the usual routine, but she was in pain in body and soul. Actually she should lie down, she thought. But everything happened so automatically as if she should then go to work as normal. She took the children to Berta. She heard Berta singing, so she obviously had no idea what had happened yesterday. Luise knocked on the door and called, "I'm in a hurry. See you later," and went on her way. She did not want Berta to see the mark of Franz's hand on her face. Meanwhile Erwin was telling his grandfather, in every detail, about his accident. His grandfather was still lying in bed, because, as he said, "I just don't feel too good." Senta got on well with the children and created simple things with them. She also told them stories, sentence for sentence when she was washing the clothes. Her mental condition had improved only a little. She often repeated, out of the blue, the well worn phrase that everyone should come home safely, Berta, Senta and grandfather liked having the children around them, but only in the mornings. Because of all the work they had to do no other time was available. Luise was happy that Berta's house was peaceful and that she enjoyed having the children.

Luise went back home to see how much money was still there. She calculated how much money she would need to get by. After all the drama, she could no longer count on Franz. She was sitting at the table with her head down when there was a knock on the door. The door opened and there stood Mrs. Zernic, a smile on her face and an overflowing bag in her hand.

"Good day. How are you?" she asked in a friendly voice. "Oh, Thank you. I am not too bad except that I can't touch my head and I've got big bruises on my right hip and thigh. If I had some raw meat I could put it on them. I don't even have anything to offer you, or, maybe there are still a couple of apples." "Forget about that, Mrs.von Dorn. I've got a few things in my bag, which I'd like to give you, if you would like them. Where are the children?" "Please, Mrs. Zernic, let the "von" drop. Dorn is enough." As Mrs. Zernic was unpacking the bag, Luise told her about everything which had happened. She showed her the letter from the baker and told her what her husband had accused her of. "This evening he'll come home and find us still here. Then he'll really let all his anger loose on us. I don't know where we can go. What on earth can I do? I'm so desperate I can't even cry." Mrs. Zernic looked at her with eyes wide open, "Yes, but your husband can't simply throw you out of the flat. Surely he said that because he was angry. He must know that he has a duty towards his family." "No," Luise replied, "this time he's deadly earnest. You should have seen him, then you would believe me. Mrs. Zernic, I have to get out of here and I don't know where to go. I have no relations here and Berta doesn't have the room. There's no room in town where I could live with the children."

Mrs. Zernic looked thoughtful, "There is one solution, but I don't know if it would be suitable. But I mean it wouldn't be for ever." Suddenly Luise fell to her knees. "Please! I'll take the last rat hole if I can protect myself and the children from this madman then I don't care where." "Come, stand up. I'll show you this small place. It belonged to our caretaker, who died. It's a lot smaller than this flat. No, I shouldn't have mentioned it. Oh God, how stupid of me to think that it would be suitable for you to live there." Luise begged her to show her the room. Mrs. Zernic thought that was the least she could do. So the two women went there.

The room was at the back of the town hall. You had to cross a courtyard and through a stone archway. From there the stairs went up and down. Luise stopped, then she heard Mrs. Zernic say, "Come, the one room flat is almost in the cellar. The only window looks onto the alleyway. It was completely dark at the bottom of the stairs. Mrs. Zernic felt the wall, trying to find the switch. It took her a while, until a dim light glowed. Then she searched for the key which should have been left somewhere. When she could not find it, Luise started to help her and searched every nook and cranny with her finger tips. Finally they heard something fall on the ground. Luise picked up the key and gave it to Mrs. Zernic, who put it into the lock and turned it until it fell into place and they could open the creaking door. The lock and the hinges will have to be oiled, thought Luise. The lighting in the room was better. There were two light bulbs on the ceiling under a pretty lampshade. There was a light coloured curtain on the window and under it there was a wide bed. It looked as though it had been lived in recently. All the caretaker's things were still there. His clothes still hung in the heavy wardrobe, which had a mirror on the middle door. Mrs Zernic looked around and said, "My son wanted to use this as a store room, but you can move in with your children. For a while it will suffice. But what are we going to do with all these things that the caretaker has left here? We've looked for relatives, but nobody has come forward. There was no address in his papers which could help us find any family. He was a very private person. He fell of the roof when he had finished repairing the gutters and died instantly. That's quite a while ago, so it's high time the flat was cleared out." Luise said, that if she and her son agreed, she could get rid of the things. She also saw a few things which she could use.

Mrs. Zernic said that everything was hers and she could do what she wanted with the things. She did not want any of it and neither did her son. A solution had been found and she thought that everyone had profited. She handed Luise the key. In that moment Luise realised that they had not talked about the rent. Mrs Zernic replied that right now she wanted no money, but if the arrangement lasted some time then there must be some recompense. Luise felt a stone fall from her heart. At least for the moment, the rent would not be a problem. Mrs. Zernic then told her that she should ask Mrs. Kidritsch on the first floor about the use of the washing room and the lavatory in order to avoid any problems in the house. Then she said she had to go. Luise thanked her for the things which she had brought her. "Yes. I just hope that some of them fit you," and with a laugh, added, "but you haven't even looked at them." Mrs. Zernic felt good, that she had once again been able to help someone in need.

Hesitantly Luise began to look into the cupboards and drawers. She took her time. She eyed up the earthenware crockery. Everything was there, but it was covered in dust. She only needed some warm blankets and her children could bring their own pillows with them. On the bed there were two good mattresses lying side by side. I'll put one of them on the floor, she thought and the two boys can sleep there. Aloisia can sleep with me in the bed. She smiled. Hopefully they won't argue about who sleeps with me. She found pencil and paper and made a list of all the things she must take with her. Then she went home, spread a large sheet on the floor and laid everything which she needed on it. She worked swiftly, because by midday everything must be ready and the children would be back. Berta would certainly bring them home, because of Erwin's head and knee wounds.

She laid the things which Mrs. Zernic had brought on the table. I don't have time to look at them. But then she took a dress and held it up, looked at herself in the window, as if it were a mirror and she was happy. Her whole face smiled. You might think that everything which had happened yesterday was only a nightmare. Luise made three bundles of her possessions and looked around to see if she had forgotten anything. She would certainly not have any opportunity and also no desire to come back to this flat. Then she saw the photos which were on display and there were more in the cupboard in a pink box together with souvenirs, documents and other things. She sorted through them and left those which belonged to Franz. The bell on the tower struck midday. I have to intercept Berta and the children before Berta reaches the flat. Right now I am not in the mood to review what happened today and yesterday. No, for to-day that's really enough.

Luise met her small family group in front of the house door. She greeted Berta and the children with a kiss on the cheek. Berta was surprised. She had not embraced her like that for a long time. She stroked her cheek while Luise held one hand over her bruises and listened to the children's chatter. "Is something wrong?" Berta asked. "Why?" Luise replied. Berta laughed and said, "I was surprised by your kiss on the cheek. I can't remember the last time an adult kissed me." The children looked at both of them and wanted to know why Berta was laughing. Franzi pulled at Berta's skirt, "Now that I'm going to school, no one is allowed to kiss me." Erwin nodded since he agreed. Aloisia said in contrast that she always wanted to be kissed especially on her lips. "Oh, yuck!" shouted the boys and ran into the house. Luise hugged her sister in law, who had no idea what was going on and took her leave. I hope I haven't made a mistake, she thought, Berta can be very sensitive sometimes.

The children saw the bundles on the floor, asked what was in them and wanted to have a look. Erwin spotted one of his wooden soldiers peeping out. "That's mine. No one else can have that. It's mine and no one else's," he said angrily and put it in his trouser pocket. Aloisia could not find her doll and started to cry. Franzi was the only one who did not know what to look for, because he was so upset. Luise took each child, sat them on the table and explained that Daddy wanted to live alone in the flat and they had to move out. Crying, Franzi protested, he did not want to go away. He wanted to go to Aunty Berta, Aunty Senta and grandfather. The other two nodded. Luise explained that they would only be going three houses further down the street and stroked Franzi's back, because she knew how much he liked his mother doing that. Then, somewhat calmer, he said he wanted to see the new flat. "Agreed", said Luise, taking the largest bundle on her shoulder and giving the other children something to carry. They each took an apple and set out.

Luise noticed that at midday there were very few people about. After the second house there was a path to the courtyard. They passed the windows where they were going to live and Luise saw that they were all heavily barred. She did not know if she should feel protected or imprisoned. She had a strange feeling. She felt uncomfortable. When they came to the stairs, the children ran up. Luise had to call them back. Then they went down stairs. Aloisia was afraid in the dark, but when Luise switched on the dim light, she felt better. When the children heard the creaking door they dropped everything and all ran out into the courtyard. Luise had not reckoned with this. Quickly she switched on the other lights. There was also a lamp over the stove and a standard lamp beside the bed. She called the children back, took Erwin and Aloisia by the hand and took them inside.

Franzi was fascinated by the large mirror on the wardrobe. He looked at himself and smoothed down his hair. Erwin started jumping on the bed, until his wounded head began to ache. Aloisia touched everything and left her fingerprints every where in the dust. "How did you get so dirty?" Luise asked. "There are black stones lying about outside in the courtyard." Later Luise saw that it was a mound of coal. "And now I have to go to the lavatory" yelled Aloisia. "Me too," "Me too," shouted the boys. "Oh! I don't know where the toilet is," said Luise and, somewhat confused, looked at her children. "I just want to go to the lavatory, not to the toilet. I have to pee," Aloisia explained. Erwin wanted to known what a toilet was. "We'll go back to the house to use the toilet," Luise decided, "can you wait that iong?" Aloisia said, "Yes, but we must be quick, otherwise I'll wet my knickers." Both boys ran ahead, making it a race. Luise switched off the lights and hid the key in a crack in the wall.

She hurried after the children who were running to the lavatory. Luise locked the door and busied herself at the stove.

She could make bread soup very quickly. None of them had eaten anything apart from an apple. While the children were waiting for the food, they gathered together the last of their treasures. After they had eaten, Luise tidied up, pushed two bundles to the door and noticed the cardboard box which was for the baker. She heard footsteps and without waiting for someone to knock, she opened the door. She had never seen the man who stood there. He greeted her in a friendly manner and gave her an envelope, saying that she should open it immediately and count if the amount was correct. Then she should sign the receipt. She wanted to close the door, but the man put his foot in the opening and asked about the goods which he was supposed to take with him. Luise blushed and excused herself. "That's all right," she heard him say, as she picked up the box. When the man had gone, she called the children and told them that now they had to leave the flat for good. She put the key in the place where Franz would find it and gave Franzi and Erwin the lighter bundles to carry. "Show the people how strong you are," she said, to encourage them. In the new flat she arranged things as comfortably as possible and after a while went to look for the "toilet". The letters "WC" were written on the door. Later Mrs. Kidritsch told her what it meant. "That's English and it means Water Closet" she said, teaching her something, "the German is Wasserklo. Klo is a short form of closet. But actually a closet is a small room. Toilet comes from the French and means a lot of things but doesn't mean that here you can pee and empty your bowel. Whatever," she laughed, "pee in the middle and not on the side. That's my best advice." The children were amazed they had never seen a toilet-loo-WC before. You had to pull a chain and then the water came down, making an awful noise and then there was a rush of air which was frightening and it sucked everything into a hole.

When Franz came home the door was locked. He found the key and when he went into the flat at first he did not notice that the family had left. It looked as though everything was still there. But when he looked in the wardrobe and there were no clothes hanging up, and then it dawned on him what had happened. His wife had really left with the children. He sat down on a kitchen chair and suddenly could not hold back his tears. His stomach went into spasms. That's what he wanted, or not? She should leave and take the urchins with her. Had he not said that? He blamed himself. How could one so young be so stupid to have brought children into the world! He felt empty and alone, but only for a moment. Then he saw another chance. I can start afresh, he said softly to himself and I know how. He felt himself freed from all his burdens. Finally alone, finally free, free, free. He stood up and skipped to the door. I have to go to Berta. But, he thought, I hope they are not there. Then everything is for nothing. Although he knew Berta well enough to realise that she would not set such a burden on her shoulders. He went across to his sister, listened at the door and only heard Senta singing quietly. After a while he left. He did not have enough courage to ask about Luise and the children. He ran through the streets looking for some sign or hearing some word from somewhere, but it was just like any other evening.

Back home he took a block of paper on which he had already made notes and drawings for some new toys. He found the rest of the bread soup, which he ate cold, and buried himself in his notes and drawings far into the night.

The next morning, he got up earlier than normal. The most important thing was to come to some agreement with Florenz. He wanted to be allowed to use his machines from time to time. For example the plane and the band saw. Maybe he could also buy some waste wood. There was certainly enough of it. With an empty stomach he hurried to Florenz and asked to talk with him. "Good," said Florenz, "but make it short, I don't have a lot of time right now." Franz told him everything and Florenz said, "That all sounds fine, but I have to think about how we're going to work out the bills and if we have to make a written contract. As far as I'm concerned, you can start right away, as long as I don't need the machines myself." Florenz showed Franz the wood which he could have and went on with his work. Franz took as much wood as he could carry, went home with it and laid it on the table. Then he went shopping. In the largest pot he could find he cooked enough polenta for the next few days. He also boiled up the milk. It had been thinned down with water. He would complain to the milk woman. He would not stand for that. He had not asked for skimmed milk. After he had had eaten something he started to draw animals from the templates onto the wood. He made sure that he made the best use of the wood. He saw that Florenz's band saw was too wide to cut sharp angles and he needed lacquer with which to paint the figures. So he bought a few basic colours, sandpaper and a smaller band saw. He also bought a couple of brushes from the blind brush maker. Then Franz really got going. Very soon the flat looked like a small workshop and in no time he was able to display a few samples of his work in a shop. When children in the shop showed interest, the shopkeeper was ready to take his first order.

IV

Franz had already been alone for almost two weeks and only, the artist, Josefine Pfeiffer had visited him. Just by chance, of course, because, as she said, "I was in the neighbourhood and had a little time on my hands. I hope I'm not disturbing you." Josefine did not say that her mother had sent her there to find out if Mr. von Dorn was interested in her. The two women had heard, in the food shop that Luise von Dorn had moved out. Obviously the whole town knew about it. Mother Pfeiffer thought it would be a good opportunity to marry off one of her daughters. She wanted to see her daughters married while soon she would not be able to travel with them any more. Innocently and just by the way, she asked if the family flat was free. The answers was, "No," because Mr. von Dorn was still living there and they told her the street and the number. Mother Pfeiffer pushed her daughter in front of his door and gave her a hard look. Words were not necessary. Josefine knew what was expected of her, so she knocked on the door.

Franz was just taking a breather, as he said, and showed Josefine in. He saw that she was not alone. She was holding a small child by the hand. "Hello, he said to the boy, "and who are you?" Josefine nudged the boy, "Tell him who you are." "I'm Emer, and today is my birthday. Now I'm four years old." He held out his hand to Franz and counted on his fingers. He gave him a small flat wooden horse and said, "I haven't had any time to paint it, but here are some paints. You can colour it yourself." Then he poured a little colour onto a piece of wood and gave it to the boy. Then Franz turned to Josefine and said he could make some tea. She offered to help him and while they were talking at the table she skilfully painted a few wooden animals. Franz was pleased that in the two hours she was there, all the planed animals were nicely painted on one side and had been laid out to dry, much to his satisfaction. She suggested that she could come back the next day and paint the other side. Because it should look the same on both sides. She was happy to do that and that was actually the truth. Franz agreed. He did not yet know that she intended to bring little Emer with her and move in for ever.

Mother Pfeiffer was very happy. She wanted to know everything. Josefine told her and added that Franz had nothing to eat, but that he already had a buyer for his toys and could make some money with his business. Mother suggested that, on the next day, she should not go to Franz with empty hands. She would buy some food, which she could take with her. That is how Franz and Josefine started a new life, together with little Emer.

The toys sold very well. Two sales representatives were employed and very quickly, they needed more workers. There were enough relatives who wanted to earn a little extra money. Franz and also the others came up with new ideas. They made trains, cars, whole villages and doll's houses. They glued, hammered and nailed, often late into the night. Sometimes it disturbed the neighbours and because they were envious, they complained. One fine day, two policemen came to the door and wanted to know what was going on. They were very surprised to see so many people in the flat. After their visit, many unpleasant things happened. Complaints about disturbance of the peace; the flat was not registered as a place of work and there was no trading licence. Work had to stop immediately, otherwise all tools and material would be confiscated.

Cooper Florenz was not very surprised. He had already thought about the situation, since he was also profiting from it. However, he did know how to get a trading licence without many problems and he also knew where to find suitable premises. In the courtyard, next to his workshop, there was a large and a medium sized room. Both rooms had large, grilled windows and they had previously been used as living accommodation. The tiled stove was still in place. The wooden floor had been covered with dark oil to protect it from insects. There was a double entrance door which was wider than normal. Next to this was a vault and through this, on the way to the cellar was a large hall. But it was musty, because it was very damp. There was only one window in the room and that was hidden behind cardboard boxes, old furniture and other rubbish. Then there was a staircase leading down to the cellars. The house owners were a Jewish family called Weisser and they were very respectable people. They lived above the vault. Their linen shop stretched to the main road. Few people knew them personally. They kept themselves to themselves and normally spoke Yiddish. In fine weather, they had many visitors in their large garden, a so-called garden house. The garden could only be seen from the cooper's attic.

Josefine was very good at languages, because she had travelled so much. She even knew some Yiddish. So she wanted to speak to the owners about the rooms. Mrs. Weisser, an elderly lady, scrutinized the unknown young woman who stood in front of her door one day. When she heard that it was about renting the rooms, she invited the young woman into the office at the back of the shop. There they would not be disturbed, but Mrs. Weisser could still keep an eye on the shop. She asked Josefine to take a seat, offered her tea and started the conversation, "Now, tell me who you are and how you heard so quickly that the flat was free." The old woman thought that Josefine had come about the flat on the first floor. Josefine was pleasantly surprised that there was also a flat for rent. She did not show that she knew nothing about it. "Yes, yes, the flat, but my future husband is interested in something else." She spoke a mixture of Yiddish and German and in her enthusiasm the words fell like a waterfall. Mrs. Weisser interrupted her, politely, "I have known Mr. Dorn Franz for a long time. He's a very polite man. I know that he works for the cooper Florenz, but I think it would be better for me to talk to the two men." She stood up, took her leave from Josefine who went into the courtyard and fetched both of them. She led them to the shop door and told them that Mrs. Weisser also had a flat to rent.

Josefine was very proud to have made the first step. She took Emer in her arms and kissed him. When the two men came back, she was almost bursting with curiosity. But Florenz went straight into the workshop and Franz screamed loudly, "What have you done!". She should pack her things and go back to her band. She had only chased after him like a bitch on heat. He had never promised her anything and there had never been any talk of marriage. He was not even divorced. Josefine was deeply shocked and covered Emer's ears. But he started to cry, "I want to go home, back to the caravan." It was difficult to calm him down. Franz turned his back on them and said, "You can leave the key under the doormat. Have you understood?" He left her standing there and went to Florenz. Josefine took her boy in her arms and ran with him along the back way beside the stream to the flat, where she burst into tears. She promised Emer that they would go back to the caravan and he was overjoyed to hear that. With eyes red from crying, he helped her stuff their belongings into the rucksack. Thank God the little boy did not know what a long journey they would have, because her family had already moved on. Josefine packed some food and a few toys which she could sell or exchange on the way. She had a little money hidden in the folds of her dress. From outside, no one could see the hidden pockets. She then rolled up a large mattress and a woollen blanket and fastened them onto the rucksack. Before she left the flat she tried to gather her thoughts. Her head was heavy. She would have preferred to lie down on the bed with Emer and sleep for a while, but she pulled herself together, placed a pocket knife in one of her hidden pockets and left, holding her boy by the hand.

She had some idea where she could find her family. On the way she asked everyone if they had met actors or artists and she found someone who told her, "Yes, but it was a while ago. By now they have probably gone over the pass to the next village." Then she asked a lorry driver and it turned out that he was going in that direction. But she had to sit on the load area, because he did not have a passenger seat. Josefine sat on her blanket and took Emer on her lap. It was a stony road and she was thrown around. Her back started to hurt and at every bend she was afraid of being thrown out. She clung to the sides with all her strength. When they came to the pass summit she slid backwards. As the lorry started on the descent she slid with full force forwards. She held Emer tightly to her. After a while the driver signalled to her that they would soon be there and pointed in front. About five minutes later he stopped so abruptly that she hit the back of her head. "Terminus," shouted the driver, but she barely heard, as if he was shouting through a wall. She could hardly move. Her whole body hurt and she had red marks everywhere. Thank God Emer had been well protected on her lap. Later she saw that he had only a few bruises.

The driver went into a barn close by and came back with a farmer who was limping. "So, do you not want to get off? He said with a dominant tone. "I'm not going any further." Josefine could not say anything and Emer clung to her as though the next corner was coming. The farmer asked the driver to help them down, because both of them had been badly shaken. The driver climbed up and threw the rucksack and the other things far out. He took hold of the child and let him slide down. Then he took Josefine under her arms and helped her until her feet touched the ground. When he let go of her, she fell to one side. The farmer helped him to lay her on the grass. The farmer gathered her things together and piled them up close by. He noticed that her arms were grazed. He called his wife, who was busy sorting the vegetables which the lorry driver had come to collect. She took one look at the mishap and shouted, "What's happened here?" "So that's what I get", the driver said, defensively, "I only wanted to help her on her way. She jumped onto the loading area so easily that I thought she had often ridden on a lorry. How was I to know that she could be injured?" The farmers' wife gave him something to think about. Did he not know that they had nothing to hang on to on the loading area? "Look at the little boy. He can't speak. He's in shock. You, you're a monster! How could you let this happen? Come. Help us to carry the woman into the house. But carefully! We may even have to call the doctor. She's in a terrible state and she's so pale."

And while the men went on with their work she talked softly to Josefine and Emer. She examined Josefine gently who felt really sick. However, it seemed that Josefine had come out of it with, as they say, just a black eye. The farmer's wife could find nothing apart from a few grazes and red marks. "Nothing broken," she declared, "you might have a slight concussion, young lady. Just lie quietly on this bench for a while. I'll give the child some milk and bread." Then she turned to Emer, "You can have an apple if you tell me your name." But Emer just looked at her with big eyes and clung to his mother. "All right," said the farmer's wife softly, "you can tell me later and now drink your milk. It will do you good." She fetched boiled water and also gave the mother a few sips of milk. She helped her to wash and spread a cooling ointment on her wounds. She covered her and Josefine, exhausted, fell asleep. She gave the blanket, which they had brought with them, to the child. Emer sat down on it, held close to his mother and soon fell asleep with the hem of her dress in his hand. The house cat had been wandering round him for sometime, now it lay down at his feet and began to purr. The farmer's wife was deeply moved. She put the slice of bread and the apple by the boy and went about her work. The farmer came to have a look and saw that his wife was wiping a few tears from her eyes with the end of her apron. She did not see him, so he went quietly back into the barn.

Finally, after three days, Josefine began to feel better. The farmer family, their name was Katz, liked having them both there. The evenings were entertaining, because Josefine had a lot to tell them. Even Emer became more trusting. He said that his father heard and saw everything that he and his mother did. He was always there, only you could not see him. He was a great magician. The farmer family was amazed, but Josefine told them how it really was. Five years ago Emer's real father, Emil Selznik, to whom she was engaged, disappeared. Now he was officially registered as dead. He never knew that they had a child. "It was like this," she recalled, "one evening he came to me and said that he had to go away for a long time." He put his finger to her mouth and kissed her goodbye. His last words were, "Don't ask any questions," and then he gave her a handkerchief with some money and a letter wrapped in it. In the few lines which he had written, he swore he loved her and confirmed his intention to marry her. As soon as he, Emil Selznik returned home, he would take Josefine Pfeifer as his wife, as long as she was still willing. But in the next few years she heard nothing from him. He seemed to have disappeared without trace; even the Red Cross could not find him. Even today she still asked after him at every opportunity. Josefine was sad, but did not want to admit that in the meantime she had been together with another man who had humiliated and exploited her. She just talked about the toy production where she had worked and that, for various reasons had to close. Now she was making her way to her family, but she did not want to show them all her bruises. The farmer's wife said, "It's harvest time. There's a lot to do here, at least for the next few weeks." "Then can I stay here?" asked Josefine, full of hope, "and my son too?" "As far as we're concerned, yes." So she worked and helped where she could. Emer loved the house animals and was busy with them the whole day long.

Three weeks later Josefine and Emer left the farmers. They had become very close. The farmer's wife had no children under which she suffered greatly. It made her sad when Emer hugged her and gave her a toy to remember him by. The farmer's wife gave Josefine some money for the work she had done. Josefine thanked her, kept a small amount for the journey and hid the rest in the folds of her dress. In the meantime she had collected quite a tidy sum which gave her immense joy. Laden with fruit, bread and other good things, she went to the nearest village and took a bus to the next large town, Klagenfurt. When she arrived in the town, Josefine asked at the local authority office if entertainers and artists had been there. The answer was "Yes, there were some here. They're probably in Marbach now." She was lucky and managed to catch the last train to Marbach.

Josefine was really longing to see her family again. In spite of the hard work she had done for the farmer, she was fully recovered. Emer looked well. He had rosy cheeks and soon he would be able to sleep in the caravan again. He was greatly looking forward to it. It was already dark when Josefine spotted a few caravans in a field. She peeked through a window and saw her mother. She knocked. When the door opened her mother was amazed, "What are you doing here?" Josefine said, "Hello mother. I'll tell you about it. Nothing bad has happened, but first can I take care of the boy? We've been on the road all day and he must be very tired." Emer had already crept onto the bed, without saying a word and had fallen asleep.

Thankfully no one else was there, thought Josefine. They were all in the theatre where they were performing. So she had time to tell her mother, who she always greeted formally, to reveal what had happened. But she did not tell her everything. She left out the shameful way Franz had treated her and she did not mention the terrible journey on the back of the lorry. She simply said that they had been able to rest for a few days with a very nice farming couple, before setting out on the rest of their journey. In return her mother told her that Anna, and particularly Rosa, were none too pleased that she had moved in with Franz von Dorn. They had accused her of going behind their backs. She had had to put them sharply in their place and make it clear to them that it was not easy for a woman with a child to find a man. When she had said that, Rosa was very angry. Her anger boiled over and she cried hysterically.

"They will not welcome you with open arms," said mother to Josefine, "and anyway, what have you arranged with Franz? When are you going back to him?" Josefine was prepared for the question. So that there would be no quarrels in the next few days, she said that Franz wanted to start up his business and that in the meantime she should visit her family. When everything was arranged he would send her news. "Of course, it could take a while until all the licences are in order to start up the new company," she added. "Well then we'll have to be patient. After all, it's your future, my dear which looks at the moment very rosy. We don't want to do anything hasty."

Mother was already seeing Josefine as a company partner and her dark eyes glinted. "Give me your hand. I want to read your future." Josefine held out her hand and her mother moved it back and forth under the light from the oil lamp. She pressed it, looked at the crease next to her little finger and jumped to her feet. "You're pregnant", she shouted, "I can see it quite clearly." Josefine did not answer immediately. She had not reckoned with that. "Have you let yourself be seduced again? Or did you want it? You stupid thing! Franz is still married. What if everything goes wrong? Then you'll have two bastards in tow." Josefine looked closely at her hand. Her face was now blood red and shouted, "No! That's not possible. How can you frighten me like this? I don't believe in palm reading. What you say can't be right. I know that for a fact. Let's leave it for now. I'm tired. Please, where can I sleep?" Angrily, mother hissed, "Under the caravan and no where else!" She threw Josefine's things out of the caravan. Then, some motherly instinct made her throw a couple of horse blankets after her. Josefine went outside. She knew that the best thing she could do for the moment was to get out of her mother's sight.

She looked under the caravan, pushed her things under and took some apple juice and bread out of her rucksack. Am I pregnant? Or maybe not? She had no idea and it was too soon to know. Just wait, she said to herself and wondered how she could make herself comfortable underneath the caravan, so that no one would discover her. She went to the horses and took a bundle of hay which she spread out so that no one could see her or her rucksack. She took the bed cover which she had brought with her, crept into it and covered herself with her woollen blanket. It smelt sweetly of fresh hay. Although she had been very nervous, she quickly fell into a deep sleep.

Franz tried to get together everything which the authorities wanted to grant him a licence for toy production. He had already been promised premises, but the flat on the first floor had been rented to Mrs. Schorch. Previously, the old woman had worked for Mrs. Weisser in the house. She got the flat because she could take care of Mrs. Weisser's two German shepherds, because Jews were not permitted to keep pets. So, if anyone asked, the two dogs belonged to the new tenant.

When Josefine had been away for a week, Franz found the courage to visit his wife Luise and his children, but it was already dark when he knocked on the door. He heard the key turn in the lock and Luise stood in front of him. But what did she look like? Her face and arms were thin, but the three children looked healthy and beamed all over their faces on seeing their father. Luise put her hands over her stomach, but Franz knew at once that she was pregnant again. He was embarrassed and put all the money he had with him on the table. He sat down on a stool and asked for a glass of water. Luise said, "It's good you have come. I wanted to send Franzi to you. Berta said I shouldn't show up at your place. I don't know why she is so cross with me. She won't speak to me and when she sees me she avoids me. Just recently I knocked on her door, but she didn't answer. We always got on well together. I simply don't understand." "Leave it to me," said Franz, "I'll have a word with her." Then he chatted with his three children and told them a few jokes. To Luise he said, "It'll soon be all right again. You'll hear from me. If you really need something, send Franzi to me. I can't promise you anything right now. Everything is with the authorities. I'm going to talk to them tomorrow. I hope they won't make me wait too long for the trading licence. So, I'll see you again." He went to the door, but the children clung to him. They didn't want to let him go. Luise called them back and sent them to bed.

Then she counted the money which Franz had left and pressed it to her heart. We can get by with this for a while, she thought. A little relieved she crept under the blanket. The next day Berta came to her. She was sorry, but she hadn't known how she should react after Luise had left Franz. "Father is ill," she said, "he's got flu again. I hope he doesn't infect us all. And now I have to go to the chemist to get some medicine for his fever. How are you? You do not look very rosy." Luise said, "It's just the pregnancy that is giving me problems, but now I'm eating more. I'm not going to collapse as quickly as that."

Shortly after, Franz came again, but he was complaining. "Who knows when I'll get the licence? Every time I have to fill out another form, sign it and today I had to pay again for some official stamp. They told me that for any further time spent on the case, I would get a bill. Getting a trading licence is not cheap. Now I really have to try to find work. I'm going to ask if I can work as a miner again." He looked at Luise and advised her to go to the social office, because he had no idea when he would next earn any money. Go to the social office! That was the last thing Luise wanted to do! That was shameful. Up to know it had turned out all right in the end. She had enough clothes. But she had to think about the children. She started to care for a bed-ridden woman. Dr. Zernic had given her the address, but she did not want to tell Franz about it and she had good reason.

Franz always made sure that he was well dressed. He had three suits, matching ties and white shirts. One never saw him without a hat and suit. His trousers always had a knife-sharp crease, but he did not iron them. Every evening he laid them carefully between two boards under the mattress and lay on top of them. He was very vain. As time went by, he even started to colour his eyebrows with a crayon and almost no one noticed it. That's how he went to the labour office and there was a job to be had in the mines. He could start straight away and the wage was not bad. He remembered the dirty work and outside whatever the weather. That did not suit him one bit. But he had no choice, he had to take it, he thought. Let's hope it's not for long. After a week he asked for an advance which was refused. They could only do that next week since the first week's wage always remained there, just in case.

Since Franz was working again, Berta was ready to lend him some money. She had taken charge of father's income and her sister Senta's pension. She had the household firmly under control.

Since there was a lack of accommodation in the area she rented two beds, with full board, to two young men. So, thanks to her, there was always money in the house.

Finally, after almost three months, Franz had his trading licence in his hands. The official asked him for one last signature and asked him, "How do you want to sign? I've noticed that the word 'von' in front of your family name is not used by all of your relations. Most of the time you simply sign, Franz Dorn. As you can see, the trading licence is made out in the name of Franz Dorn. I wonder why your father did not refuse the title 'Count' officially, when you do not use it. He also stopped using the 'von'. Franz scratched his head. He was embarrassed. "Yes, my father was a very self-willed individual. At some stage he started to call himself simply Dorn. As far as I know that was after the burial of Franz Josef Count von Dorn. That would have been my great grandfather and they didn't get on together. Since then there are no Counts or 'vons' in the family", he claimed. In fact, since the monarchy was disbanded in 1919, officially, Austrian titles were no longer acceptable, except if the title had been acquired abroad and brought into Austria, which was the case for the von Dorn family. But that he didn't want to discuss further, although it was both a family and political matter. "I am aware that some titles are now allowed by the new government and some have been abolished. So let's wait and see," said the clerk. Franz set no value on the title, at that time, since his political leanings were more in the direction of communism.

Franz rushed to Mrs. Weisser, to negotiate the rent contract. She was very pleased and said, "I won't want any rent for the first month, since the rooms have been used as a warehouse. The walls will have to be painted and in some places the floor needs attention. All the junk will have to be taken away. My brother has a lorry. I'll ask him if he can take the stuff which has to be thrown away to the rubbish dump. But first, you should have a look to see if there is anything there you can use. I seem to remember an old writing table and some shop furniture. Here are two keys. Now you can go since you've got a lot to do." Franz thanked her and went into the courtyard. Now he was going to take a look at "his" workshop. He went to the two entrance doors and opened the first. It creaked, loudly. The second would not budge until he gave it a powerful shove. It smelt of old things and antiseptic. The first thing to do was to open the windows and let in some fresh air, but he could only open the first one a little, because it was so obstructed. To get to the other window he had to scramble over furniture and cardboard boxes. Even with some daylight and a solitary lamp hanging from the ceiling he could see almost nothing. He looked around as best he could. There were certainly things there which he could use; the shop counter would serve as his workbench. He could also make use of the shelves and he could also find a use for the large plywood chests. Yes, yes, he thought, I can make something out of this and he promised himself that he would come back the next morning.

The next day he tried to find a few people to help him, but at such short notice he only got his brother, Alfred. He was not exactly excited about it, but he was curious and his foreman was ill. Franz thought about Josefine. She would have been very welcome. She could get down to work and she knew what was what. But, he thought, how can I find her so quickly? A policeman named Precinschek lived in the building where he now had his workshop. When he saw Franz and Albert carrying things into the courtyard, he asked what was going on. Franz explained everything in a few words and complained that he had too few people. "If I only knew where Josefine was. I could use her right now. She's gone to visit her family, but I don't know the name of the place. I know which way she went, but God only knows where she is now." Mr. Precinschek said, "That isn't too difficult, because travellers have to register and de-register in every town. We can find them immediately if you want. That will only take a few telephone calls." "Well yes, if it isn't too much trouble, I'd be very glad." "All right. I'll let you know as soon as I have any news."

The very next day Franz knew where Josefine could be found. He made an excuse for leaving work, went to his brother Alfred and asked him if he could take him on his motorcycle to Josefine. Alfred was none too pleased to have to get out his splendid motorcycle, which he only used on Sundays, but Franz convinced him that it was very important. He could leave him there and drive back immediately. Anyway, there would be no place for all of them on the motorcycle. Josefine and he would take the post bus or the train. So, they set out. It took them about two and a half hours. Once they arrived at the place, it was not difficult to find the travellers. They only had to ask once. When they saw the caravans, Alfred stopped and let Franz get off. Franz thanked his brother and gave him some money for the petrol. Then Alfred started for home.

It was midday when Franz knocked on the door of the caravan. Josefine's mother poked out her head and shouted over her shoulder, "About time! Peppi, Franz has come for you." Josefine almost chocked as she was eating. She was sitting at the table with Emer. She hated it when her mother called her Peppi. "Please come in. My daughter has been longing for you." Josefine wanted the ground to swallow her up. In Hungarian her mother said she should hurry up and pack her bundles. He should not know that she had been sleeping under the caravan.

Franz greeted Josefine with a kiss on the cheek and stroked Emer's hair. Then he sat down at the table. Mother gave him something to eat and drink. Franz thanked her. He was hungry. Then he told them what had happened in the meantime and how much work there was to do. "Now we have to work quickly so we can finally earn some real money," He nceded all the workers he could get. "We can't waste any time," he said to Josefine, with such an impertinent self evidence as if nothing had happened. "We have to go back today. There must be a bus or a train. I'll go and find out. In the meantime pack your things." Mother said, "Say something, child. He has surprised you, hasn't he?" Then quietly in Hungarian, "You don't have to tell him right away that you're pregnant. Thank God, you can't see it yet, So wait a while."

To Franz she said, "I'll show you where the train station is. The buses go from there as well." When they were some distance from the caravan, she said, "Mr. von Dorn, I'm going to tell you a big secret which has to remain between us. Only I and my man know about it. There are some things in my life which I don't like to talk about, but since you have noble blood, you should know. Anna's and Josefine's father is an Esterhàzy. As you surely know that is an old, noble Austrian-Hungarian family. My present husband is a kind and generous man. He was aware of my situation and was a trusted employee of the father of my two daughters. I was very lucky that he married me and gave them his name and I am eternally grateful to him. But hush! I have already said too much. Please, swear on all that's holy to you that you will tell no one, but really no one, what I have told you." Franz stood there, flabbergasted. She took hold of his right hand and laid it over his heart, "Now swear." He made his oath and she let him go. Later he found out that the Esterhàzys were a very lively family and did not take fidelity very seriously. He kept his oath until shortly before he died.

Franz, Josefine and Emer took the post bus. They had to change twice and the journey was long and strenuous. Franz dozed off now and again and they did not speak much to each other. It was dark when they reached home and they soon went to bed. Early in the morning, it was only four o'clock, Franz woke Josefine, saying, "We have to get up. I'll take you to the new workshop which we have to re-arrange before we can start producing the toys. There is really a great deal to do. I'm sorry, but up to the end of the month I have to go on working at my job and finish a project. Only then, can I start here. At the moment, I can only be in the workshop early in the morning and late in the evening." Josefine drank her tea, put food and something to drink in her rucksack, took Emer, who was still sleeping, in her arms and went to the workshop. Franz opened both entrance doors and told her what she had to do first. He helped her move a few pieces of furniture and then he disappeared. Elmer was put onto a few cardboard boxes and went on sleeping.

Josefine started folding cardboard boxes and carrying other things which were not so heavy down to the cellar. About midday, more and more neighbours and the cooper's customers came by. They were curious to see what was going on. Josefine answered all their questions, without stopping work. She even made use of their curiosity and asked them to help her to carry things out or move furniture into their proper place. She borrowed a bucket and rags from the cooper to clean the windows. With a broom she got rid of the spiders' webs on the walls. She swept and cleaned and soon one could see where the walls needed to be painted and where the floor would have to be repaired. A green tiled stove in the corner was taking up a lot of room. If Mrs. Weisser agreed, she would remove it. There was a cast iron stove in the cellar which would heat the room. Mrs. Weisser agreed. Alfred brought tools from the mine, Mrs. Weisser had a wheelbarrow and they started on the dusty, soot filled work right away. Noisy work was permitted from 7 o'clock in the morning to 10 o'clock in the evening. Very soon they had removed the tiled oven. With the help of several different people the workshop was ready for use in about two weeks.

Mrs. Schorch, the new tenant on the first floor, was almost everyday in the courtyard or the garden with the two German shepherds. At first Josefine and Emer were afraid of the two dogs, but with time the dogs stopped barking at them at every encounter. They got used to the animals, without having to touch them. For safety's sake they were always kept on the lead. Josefine soon managed to build up a good relationship with Mrs. Schorch and she was also the first to learn that Josefine was expecting a child. Mrs. Schorch worried about her. "With all the hard work you've been doing you could easily have lost the child." "Yes," replied Josefine, "but I'm a strong woman, if not, I would have certainly miscarried. I'm not very proud to be pregnant, because Franz is still married to another woman. I'm ashamed, but nothing can change it." Then she added, "I must beg him to put things in order. Divorce and marriage won't be easy." Mrs. Schorch said, "Jesus, Mary. Then you really have to put pressure on him," and gave Josefine a sympathetic look. Josifine said, "He doesn't even know that I'm expecting." "What?"Mrs Schorch exploded, "he doesn't know, oh dear! You have to tell him and quickly. That's the only advice I can give you" Josefine said, "Yes, I'll tell him this evening. Yes, certainly this evening." She knew, now, that Franz was relying on her.

It was getting late and Franz would soon be home. Josefine took care to put good food on the table, but she was not a great cook. So she went to the rear window of the inn, down the alley way and asked them to put some goulash in the pot she had brought with her. The cook said, "You'll have to go into the inn." Josefine said, "I'm not properly dressed. Please, give me the goulash through the window. I'll be really grateful." Muttering, the cook took the pot, disappeared into the kitchen and came back with it full of goulash. Josefine paid, thanked her and hurried home. When Franz came home there was bread, goulash and salad on the table and it smelt very appetising. He saw the table was only laid for one. "Have you already eaten?" he asked. Josefine answered, "Yes. Emer was very hungry and couldn't wait." Emer and Josefine had eaten what she had cooked. It had been edible, but that was all.

Franz sat down at the table and said that the workshop looked good. "Luckily the hardest work is finished," said Josefine and sat down opposite him. She had taken care of her appearance and started to talk and chatter. By and by she asked him whether he had noticed that her stomach had become round and that she was expecting. It was now time to put some order in their private life. "We have to make sure that we can marry as quickly as possible. If a child is on the way, the local authority does things quickly so that the child is legitimate at its birth." So, she had said it. She took a deep breath and thought that it not been so difficult after all. Franz sat there, chewed on his food and said nothing. You could feel the tension in the room. Then, he stood up abruptly, wiped his face, combed his hair and left the flat without saying a word. He came back late in the night and lay down on the bed without undressing. He stank of alcohol. After a while he threw up. Josefine ran for a bucket and put it down next to the bed. Then she got a wash bowl and cleaned the floor. She was almost finished when he vomited again and it went everywhere. She stepped to one side, but still got some on her house shoes. She cleaned up again, but then she also began to feel sick. She started to cry, sobbed for a while and then took her blanket and bedclothes into the corner next to Emer and tried to make herself as comfortable as possible. She must have fallen into a deep sleep for the rest of the night, because she did not hear Franz get up, clear up everything and go to work. The window was wide open to air the room.

Josefine and Emer went down the street to the workshop. On the way they bought milk and bread. In the bakery they met a friendly young woman. It turned out that she was a kindergarten teacher. She was known as Aunt Hellen. She asked if Emer lived in town. If he did, then he could come to the kindergarten. "If you want, you can come and have a look round," she said to Josefine. "How about right now?" Josefine asked, "right now I've got time." Hellen said, "Of course. Come with me." The kindergarten was very pleasantly furnished. Emer immediately took possession of the toys and the rocking horse. He smiled broadly and did not want to get down from the rocking horse. "You can leave the little one here until after the midday meal. His midday nap he can take at home, if you agree." "Oh yes," said Josefine happily, "if there are any problems, I'm close by. We have a workshop at the back of the courtyard. That's where we will be working in future." She asked Emer if he wanted to stay there and said that she would collect him after the midday meal. He agreed. Hellen gave Josefine a form. "You have to fill this out and have it stamped by the council." Josefine went back home, rang by Mrs. Schorch and told her what had happened on the previous evening. "It's good that you have told Franz everything and hopefully you have also asked for marriage. I think it's a good idea, with the kindergarten and it's good that they still have a place for Emer. If you want, you can show me the form and I can help you fill it out, then you can go to the council and get the stamp."

The questions seemed to be simpler than they really were, for example: *Where have you lived in the last five years? Place of residence...... District/es......* Mrs. Schorch spoke with Josefine and suggested, "So, we write Traveller with postal address in Klosterberg." Josefine did not like that one bit. "I know what people think about travellers," she said vehemently. But we are entertainers, artists with a good reputation. No one can say anything bad about us." Mrs. Schorch said, "All right, we'll write: For artistic and professional reasons, up to now no permanent residence. Postal address was in Klosterberg" "All right, that's better." Then came: *Parents family names:... Father's first name:.........* They wrote: Disappeared; Declared dead. Then they answered other questions. *Mother's maiden name:....... Religion:...... Child's birth certificate registered in/on........... Registered in our district since;...... Address.........*

When they had almost completed the form, Josefine went to the council office. The building was close to the town square. There was a small park close by where people sat and watched who went in and came out. Josefine took a deep breath and went into the building. There was a highly polished copper plate fixed to the wall which showed where each office was.

Josefine took a quick look and knocked on the first door. "Excuse me. Am I in the right place for the kindergarten stamp?" "On the second floor, Room 3." O.K, up the stairs, knock and enter. "Hello. Please, I need a stamp for the kindergarten."

She heard a woman's voice, "You have to wait outside until I call you." There was a large clock on the wall. Every floor had the same clock. After half an hour she was called into room number three. She presented the form which she had filled out. The young woman looked at it and handed it to one of her colleagues who was standing at a desk and wearing black protectors for his shirt sleeves. The two of them spoke quietly to each other. Then the young woman turned back to Josefine, "Have you got your residence confirmation with you?" "No. Where can I get it?" "In room one on the ground floor." O.K, down the stairs, knock and enter. "Excuse me..." A man with a bushy moustache stopped her short. "We are closed between twelve and three. Josefine said, "But the clock shows it is only twenty to twelve." "Come back at three. We have our lunch break." Then he turned his back on Josefine. "Lunch break," Josefine repeated in an annoyed voice and left the council office. She went back to Mrs. Schorch and told here what had happened. Mrs. Schorch asked, "Have you identity papers and a birth certificate for your son with you?" "Oh, God, My mother has the birth certificate. All I've got is my own identity card, but Emer is also registered on it."

Mrs. Schorch said, "They're going to ask you for other papers. I'm sure of that. But first of all, I would go there and ask what they really want. For example, if you want to marry you have to have an identity card and proof that you are free to marry and so forth. It might also be a good idea to ask at the same time what papers you need for a divorce."

"Thank you Mrs. Schorch. Now I've got to collect Emer. He'll be waiting for me."

At the kindergarten Emer was waiting behind the glass door. An older kindergarten teacher opened the door. "You're a bit late. Next time you must be punctual. Have you filled out the registration form and had it stamped?" "No, not yet. The office must check my details and that takes some time." "Oh yes, we know that these officials take their time when they want to. Well, we'll just have to wait." "But can I still bring Emer tomorrow" Josefine asked. "Yes, yes, tomorrow." shouted Emer. Both women laughed. "All right, and when you're here by 8 o'clock, you'll also get breakfast."

When they left the kindergarten Josefine had two papers in her hand. One had the kindergarten times, the rules about clothing and the other told her what was forbidden and what was allowed. Josefine read both of them very carefully. She did not want to make any mistakes.

At a quarter to three Josefine and Emer were standing in front of the council office. The council employee waited until the clock had struck three times before he opened the door. The people who had arrived later pushed passed Josefine and ran in. On the stone stairs every step sounded very loud. At room number One there was a bench. It was already fully occupied. Politely Josefine asked if everyone wanted to go in and pointed to the one. "Yes," said a woman wearing a colourful headscarf, "you'll have to wait at the end, like they do in Paris." The others sniggered quietly and made jokes about Paris. Little Emer sat on the floor, took a couple of buttons and a thin yarn out of his trouser pocket and tried to thread it into the buttons.

The wall clock did not move. Finally it was Josefines turn. For a moment she forgot why she was there. She held out the kindergarten registration paper to the officer. "You're in the wrong place. You have to go to the second floor, room three." "I've already been there but I don't have a confirmation of residence." "Why didn't you say that right away? You're wasting my time. That's why officers are always blamed when things take so long. Ah! So you want to be resident in this district. Where are you living and how long have you been there?" He wrote everything down on a note pad. "Show me your papers." Josefine gave him her identity card. "Is that your child? Where are his papers? Have you nothing with you?" Josefine felt as though she were standing in front of a judge when she had to explain why and how and that she wanted to get married. "Very nice, but that needs two people," the officer laughed. She asked him to write down what documents she needed, particularly for the marriage. The officer laughed again. "Fantastic, fantastic. Don't you think so Mr. Kogler? Please take care of this case and don't forget that we need confirmation from Dorn. No he should come here personally in the next few days. With all his papers. And by the way, I haven't heard that he is divorced." Josefine tried to turn the conversation around, "My mother has the boy's birth certificate and probably all the other documents which I might need." "One thing at a time," said the officer, who had now taken over the "case", "to get a confirmation of residence you have to make an application to the council for yourself and your son." Josefine felt that she was being treated like a gypsy. "But," he went on, "that is not necessary if a marriage is planned. However, then you need a legally acceptable confirmation of a divorce between Luise and Franz von Dorn, which has not yet taken place, otherwise we would have registered it here. Josefine asked him to write down everything necessary for a divorce.

The officer looked at her for a long time. Then she blurted out, "I'm pregnant and from him. This child should be born into a regular family. I've heard that if there is a pregnancy then all this red tape is dealt with more quickly." She did not want to say red tape, but in the heat of the moment she could not think of a better word. The officer permitted himself a quick smirk. "My dear woman, it won't be so easy to get out of this mess. As far as I know, his wife, the woman to whom he is still married, is also pregnant with her fifth child." Josefine turned as white as a sheet. She had to contain herself. Finally she muttered, "I didn't know that. For the love of God, No! No!" Then her legs collapsed and she fell to the floor. She felt someone press some water to her lips and felt the water running down her blouse. Someone else brought her a chair and they sat her on it. Emer started crying and wanted to go back to the caravan. As soon as she could stand, the officer gave her the list of documents which she needed and said, "If you have any other questions come straight to me. I've written down my name. Because of your condition, you don't have to wait in the corridor. Are you feeling a little better?" "Yes. Thank you. I'll just sit down on the park bench for a while and then I'll go home."

Once she got home she felt better. She looked out a recipe which Mrs. Schorch had given her and made a potato soup with bay leaves. The soup smelt wonderful. Elmer was already sitting at the table. He was hungry. She did not wait for Franz, but spooned out the hot soup which both of them found very tasty.

V

Franz came home late. Emer had been in bed for a some time. He had to be up early the next morning. He was looking forward to kindergarten. Josefine was very tired. Franz said, "I've been in the workshop till now. From next week we will be there all the time and then we will really have to start working hard to make something out of it. So then the money will flow in." Josefine shared his enthusiasm and was sure that they would succeed. While Franz was eating his soup, she told him that Emer had been in the kindergarten, that he had been really happy there, that he was going again the next day and had also been given a good meal. To keep attending, Franz must fill out a form and take it the council. "They asked for confirmation from you that we are living here," she said. "Yes," Franz answered, "I'll write it for you tomorrow, but now I'm going to bed." Franz took her hand and pulled her close to him, "It's good that the little one can go to kindergarten. Then we'll have more time for the workshop. I hadn't thought of the kindergarten." He started to stroke her gently. Josefine said, "The officer in room two said that you should go there personally in the next two to three days. He said I should tell you that. "Everything has to be regulated," he muttered and drew her closer. Then he stood up, and pressed her upper body against the back of the chair. "Ow!" she cried, "the back of the chair is cutting into me." He grabbed her thighs and pulled up her skirt, dropped his trousers, pressed himself between her legs and satisfied himself loudly and violently. Then he let her free and went into the other room. After a few minutes he came back and took a slurp of milk. "How can you be so rough? My whole stomach hurts," Josefine complained. "Ah, yes," he said without showing any remorse, "you should be happy that it didn't take me very long. Many women are happy when they are treated that way. It heightens their desire. And so, good night! I'm going to bed."

Emer was happy to go to kindergarten. The workshop filled up with material from the flat and new material which had been bought. Brother Alfred came to work almost every day and recorded his hours in a small book, which he always carried with him. "Maybe one day there will be a lot of money," he said, only half joking. Everyone seemed to be waiting for the big money.

Franz had finished his last day of employment. His wage was paid into his hand. It was not much, since almost every week he had asked for an advance, but he was pleased with what he received. He was in a good mood when he walked up into town. Today I can really afford something, he thought. I'll visit Anderl›s Pub and invite Florenz for a good glass of wine. Now, for once, it›s my turn. In front of the town hall, he was met by Mr. Kogler, the officer from room one. "Well, hello Mr. Dorn," he said "you still haven't come to me. Did your new partner not inform you? You should come to the council offices for a talk and for a few new documents which we have to draw up. Do you know what? I've got time, right now. Just come in. We can get it behind us. Is that all right for you? Walk in, Mr. Dorn, we are situated in room one." He gave Franz no time to consider and politely opened the door. "Yes, she did say something, said Franz, slowly, "but what it was all about does not come to mind." "Well, now you're going to find out. We've prepared everything apart from a few things which are not quite clear and we can certainly work those out together, if that's all right with you." Franz said, "Well, if it's really necessary." "Right, let's begin with Miss Josefine Pfeifer. She and her son are living with you. We have the confirmation right here. Read it through and then please sign it. So, that's that. Is Emer your son?" "No, no. I've got enough children of my own and a fourth is on the way." In truth, the fifth was on the way.

The fourth child was Irmgard, but since she had died, she did not count. "Do you mean from your wife or your present partner? As far as I can count one and one make two. Is that not so?"

Franz was totally perplexed. How did he know all that? "Well, it's not clear that my wife's child is mine. She's been unfaithful to me for years. When she told me about it, I threw her out." Kogler asked, "In that case are the children with you or not? Because in divorce proceedings if the wife is guilty, then the children are put into the care of the father. You must know that. However, Mr. Dorn, as long as you are not divorced and your wife has other children, then according to the law, they are your children. Have you started divorce proceedings?" Then it was Franz's turn to speak, "She took the children with her because I had to take employment elsewhere to earn some money." After a short pause he added, "As far as the divorce is concerned, there is no hurry." Mr. Kogler looked at him, "Am I to understand that your wife gets regular upkeep for herself and the children from you or from another institution?" "How should I know? She got money from me until I was unemployed. She goes to work. She always wanted to do that. As far as I was concerned she could have stayed at home. Then all this would not have happened with our marriage." He became angry and stumbled over his words. "What has all this to do with you? That's my private life. I'll apply for divorce when I'm ready, or maybe not. That is my business. Right now it is not important." Kogler answered, "It may not be important for you, but it is important, very important for your two pregnant women. They want to know where they stand and what your position is towards them. I don't want to be too personal, Mr. Dorn, but be reasonable and bring some order into your life. This cannot go on; or are you thinking of going back to your wife? It doesn't look like it."

"You say it can't go on like this? I'll show you," Franz shouted and his voice almost cracked, "Who do you think you are? You can't lay down the law to me. Peppi, I mean Josefine came to me of her own free will. No one forced her and there was never any talk of marriage. She can work for me and live in my flat and that's all I have to say about the matter." Then, quietly he added, "Bloody women, you only have to touch them and they're pregnant. All you get from them is problems. Life is hard enough. Is there anything else?" His face was as red as a turkey. The officer said, "I think that for today we've heard enough hot air," and looked at him with a mixture of contempt and sympathy, "if you want to talk about something, then come back. Your situation is now a little clearer. As far as the documents are concerned, I'll speak to Miss Pfeifer. I'll ask her to come here. Goodbye, Mr. Dorn." With the sentence, "Good day, my pleasure", which all Dorns used to say, he took his leave and left the council building.

Suddenly he had a very bad conscience about Luise. He went to the courtyard entrance in front of Luise's flat, took some money from his wages and held it in his hand. He knocked and heard a timid, "Come in." He called, "Hello," in a friendly voice and entered. It smelled of urine, the remains of food were lying around and it had not been tidied. Luise was lying on the bed, in the dim light. "I'm not well," she said in a weak voice, "Hours ago I sent the children to Berta to get help. I have a high fever and I'm shivering. The good Lord has sent you. I need a doctor. I think the child is coming. I can›t get any air. Please fetch Dr. Zernic. This little flat belongs to him. He knows me well. He'll come straight away when he knows what condition I'm in. Hurry. Wait, give me first some water to drink. Please, hurry." "Yes, it's all right. I'm on my way." And now this, thought Franz on his way to the doctor. His heart was beating fast. Awful thoughts went through his mind. Let's hope that nothing terrible happens. His eyes filled with tears. My God, what have I done? His head hurt.

Dr. Zernic packed a few things and sent Franz with a thermometer back to his wife. He should measure her temperature before he arrived. Franz hurried back, gave Luise the thermometer and quickly tidied up. There was a night pot next to the bed, full of urine and stools. Franz took it into the courtyard and emptied it into the drain, rinsed it out and went back to the flat. He left the door wide open to get rid of the smell and let in some fresh air. The doctor was already there and asked him for hot water. “There isn't any. I'll have to light a fire first,” Franz said. The doctor turned back the bed covers. There was a smell of rotten eggs. He read the thermometer. “She has to go to the hospital immediately.” He ordered Franz, “Go to the police station across the road. They must send for an ambulance. Do it quickly. There's no time to lose.” The hospital was only about a kilometre away. The ambulance came quickly, with a lot of noise and blue lights. “You can come to the hospital tomorrow,” then Dr. Zernic called out to Franz, “now you're only in the way. If need be I'll let you know.” “Franz. The children,” whispered Luise as they lifted her into the ambulance. Franz gathered up the blood stained bed clothes and went to Berta. He heard the children laughing. “Ah yes, and have you forgotten your mother?” he shouted, angrily. “No,” Franzi answered, “Aunt Berta had a lot of warm water and we all washed ourselves from top to bottom.” The children giggled. “But your mother sent you to get help.” “Yes,” said Berta, “we were just going.” Then she saw the bed clothes. “What stinking things have you got there?” She unfolded the sheets, saw the blood stains and was shocked. “Is that from Luise?” “Yes. She's in the hospital. We can visit her tomorrow. She's very ill. Hopefully she'll pull through.” Aloisia started to cry, “I want to go to Mummy.” Berta took the bed clothes and plunged them into the warm bathwater which was still in the tub. The water went red. That night the children stayed with Berta.

Luise gave birth to a tiny girl, but she arrived much too early. Would she survive? Luise was in a very bad state. She still had a high fever. There was talk about who would take the children. Berta said she could not take all three. Grandfather Karl, on the other hand would have liked to have all his grandchildren with him, since he seldom went away. But Berta only wanted two. So Franz agreed to take his daughter Aloisia with him for the time being.

Josefine was amazed, when he arrived with the girl. "That's Aloisia," said Franz, "she'll be staying with us for a few days. Give her something to eat and make a bed for her. It's only for a short time, until we know what is going to happen." Then he said to Aloisia, "That is Peppi." "Oh, no," said Josefine, "you can call me Mrs. Josefine. But what has happened? I take it that she is your daughter." Franz answered, "Yes. Who else?" in a surly manner. "How am I supposed to know?" asked Josefine, "it's the first time I've seen her." The only things she knew about his family she had heard from the council officers. Franz started to speak loudly, "Stop asking questions, you're confusing the child." All this time Aloisia was standing, shyly by the door. "All right, tell me about it later," Josefine said, trying to calm him down, then she went to Aloisia and said, "Come here little Luise, sit down. Are you hungry or thirsty?" "I don't want anything," Aloisia said defiantly. Josefine said, "I'll put milk, some bread and a peach on the table. Then, when you feel like it, you can take what you want. Don't be afraid, I won't harm you." Aloisia ate nothing and drank nothing. She did not even want to go to bed. Franz held the milk to her lips, pinched her nose and tried to force her to drink. But Aloisia screamed like a stuck pig and went blue in the face. Then Josefine intervened. He should leave her in peace. That did not please Franz one little bit. "If you do that once more then you'll get something that you'll never forget for the rest of your life," he threatened. He was frothing with anger. "She gave as good as she got and in an aggressive tone she said, "We'll see about that. Watch out what you say and, not least, what you are going to do. I'm warning you, there are people who will stand fully behind me. You don›t have that. And there's something else I'm telling you. Up to now I haven't tried to protect myself when you've offended me, but in future I'm not going to take it. Now I know enough people in the town and in the district. Either you treat us all decently or I'll tell everyone, in the minutest detail how you behave and how you treat me. No more loud words. Have you understood?" She stood proud and upright in front of him. She threw the words at him and forced him to look into her eyes. A few times he wanted to interrupt her, but she gave no chance. He looked at her in wonder and then, in gentle tones, "Yes yes. Just calm down, otherwise Emer will start to blubber."

But Emer was not impressed by his mother's angry words. He went to Aloisia and offered her the bread and the peach, but she fended him off. She would not let anyone touch her. She sat on the floor, leaning against the wall and after a while she fell asleep. When Franz picked her up he noticed that she had wet herself. Very carefully, Josefine undressed her, put her into the bed and covered her with warm blankets.

In the night she woke a few times and called for her mother. She was afraid of her father. The next day she avoided him whenever she could. She did not let him take her hand and she did not speak to him, and she still would not eat or drink. As evening came, he decided to take her to Berta. She was none too pleased. But Grandfather took her in his arms and she ate from his plate and drank from his cup.

In the hospital Luise began to recover. The children visited her every day. Lusie always kept something from her hospital food in the bedside table for her children. She said she could not eat so much. The baby was not doing well. The priest said that the child should be baptised. "I agree, Father. She should be named Maria."

A catholic nurse stood as godmother. The tiny girl was baptised on her seventh day. Dr. Zernic visited his patient every morning. He said that Lusie should have eaten more during the pregnancy, then she would not have had such problems. She said that it had been too difficult to get food. The shops had little on the shelves and only the so-called better people got things that were sold "under the table". Apart from that, she had many debts, in Mrs. Gasser's general store and in the milk shop. The only shop where she did not want to run up debts was the bakery. When Franz gave her some money now and again, she sent Erwin to the bakery. He gave him whatever he had. Some flour, maize or semolina; now and again there would be an egg. But Luise had always thought she had eaten enough.

Then she added that every day, early in the morning she walked along the fence where the fruit trees hung over and collected the fallen fruit. After heavy rain there was more fruit to be found on the ground.

Franz entrenched himself in the workshop for a day and a night, whilst Josefine tried her best to put something edible on the table. Because of this she was often on the streets and she was not ashamed to ask people who had a full bag, if they could give her something to eat. She had a good trick. She made the most of her swelling stomach so that everyone could see that she was pregnant. Sometimes she even pretended to be sick. She said that she had had nothing to eat for days and now she felt unwell and she made a suffering face. She had more luck with the farmers than with the town people. When she did this, she also took a few toys with her, which she could exchange for food. In the shops she left the toys there on commission or exchanged them for food. She would come back from time to time and ask if anything had been sold. That worked well, because the people were often ready to give their last farthing for a small toy so as to give their children, in these miserable times, a little pleasure.

Soon it was time for Josefine to call the mid-wife. The birth was easy, quick and without complications. She gave birth to a boy and she called him Reinhard. Oh! Shame. She now had two sons from two different fathers and worse was to come. After four months Josefine was pregnant again and Franz was still not divorced.

Fate hit Luise hard. Her little Maria died, at home, a month after her birth. When Josefine heard, by chance, that Luise was a little better and that she had even started to work half days for Dr, Zernic and had got a somewhat larger flat on the first floor, she started to push Franz to start divorce proceedings.

Franz went to talk to Luise and was amazed at her reaction. She agreed immediately. He had expected that she would be against it. At any event, as Franz was leaving, she said that he should not forget the children and that she would by pleased if he would go on providing them with food. Josefine knew nothing about this.

To get a bit more money, Luise had taken a lodger without informing Franz.

Luise and Franz were now divorced. The guilty party was Luise, "because of her "relationship" with the baker, although both swore by God and all the saints that this was not true. In addition Luise and Franz were forbidden to marry for one year.

That meant that Josefine's third child would also be illegitimate when he was born. Once again, it was a boy. He was named Alfred, but they always called him Fredi.

Josefine always said, "He's a good boy." She had chosen Fredi as her favourite son. If anyone said that to her, she simply said, "He's a very well behaved, happy boy. You have to like him."

The toy production progressed well. They sold, exchanged and dealt. But they lost sight of the big picture, how much came in and went in materials, goods and money. Mr. Gosch, an insurance agent and businessman, who had a flat in the same building often came to them, hoping that one day Franz Dorn would take out insurance through him. One day, when he was there, Franz asked him if he knew someone who could do the book keeping for him. Mr. Gosch said that he could do that himself. He knew about bookkeeping and if necessary he could also write business letters. He was a very sincere person, but he did not let any one come too close to his family. That did not worry Franz.

Mr. Gosch told Franz that such a business would soon need, at the very least, basic insurance. Franz asked cooper Florenz, what he thought about that. "You know what," Florenz said, "today we'll go and visit Anderl at the pub. I'll bring my policy with me and we'll have a look at what you need." "All right. Let's say in an hour, if that's alright for you." "Of course," said Florenz, "we'll meet there."

In the pub Franz paid for the first round of wine. He told Anderl, that a Mr. Gosch was now taking care of his book keeping and that he, himself, was looking for a woman who could keep house for him so that Josefine could spend more time in the workshop. "Oh," said Anderl, "now he's better off than us. Who would have thought it?". Florenz said, "Yes. I hadn't looked at it that way. I see him making his toys everyday, but I never thought of that." Franz calmed them down, "No, it's not like that. I haven't got as far as you both. You shouldn't exaggerate."

Then he said, "It's like this. Josefine has no idea about cooking. What she can do, she has learnt from me, so you can imagine what it looks like." Franz described her cooking skills colourfully, and all three laughed heartily. "And with the washing I tell you, it's all mixed up. But now it's getting a bit better. The dirt is out, but the stains are still in." Another guest joked, "In, out. In, out." The others grinned, but Franz went on, unperturbed. "I take all my white shirts to Berta. I don't think Josefine has noticed. No wonder, when she has so much to wash. So it would be good if I could find someone who could help in the house. But she shouldn't be too expensive." "Go on Anderl. Bring us another round." Florenz ordered. It's a long time since we had so much fun together. Anderl brought them a round and then he gave them another round "on the house" as he said. "Well," he said to Franz, "as it happens, I do know someone. Gerdi lives close by. She would certainly be happy if she could get work again as a house help. I'll send her over to you tomorrow. You can take a look at her. But apart from that, nothing more," he added mischievously and laughed, so that the other guests also laughed and each one wanted to share a joke.

It was a jovial evening and the insurance, for which Franz had come to the inn in the first place, they did not get round to discussing. Then Anderl looked at the clock. A guest asked, "Do you want to close? Is someone waiting for you?" "That's private. That's none of your business," answered Anderl, "It's late. It's closing time, my friends. I don't want to hear any moaning from your wives tomorrow. Go home!" Everyone started to laugh and wanted to say something, but Anderl started a song, which they went on singing in the street. From a window came a bucket of water. "Quiet!" someone shouted, "or I'll call the police." It was only then that Franz realised he had drunk far too much. He couldn't walk straight. He staggered home and, balancing on tip-toe, went into the flat. Josefine smelled the alcohol and turned her back. She didn't want Fredi, who was sleeping next to her, to wake up.

The next morning Josefine brewed tea for breakfast and spread jam on a few slices of bread. She waited for Franz to come and sit down at the table. He did not show that his skull was buzzing. "Look, Franz," Josefine said, "yesterday Mrs. Schorch came to me. You know her. She's the tenant on the first floor. She told me she was leaving to live with her aunt. She thinks that we could rent the flat with a small separate room from Mrs. Weisser. We could join that room to the flat. We would simply need to break through the wall which was only built in the last couple of years because Mrs. Weisser wanted to have a separate guest room. That would be a good idea. We would have more room. What do you think?" Franz replied, "We'll talk about it later. I'm going back to bed for a while. I've got a terrible headache." "No, no," said Josefine, "you can't go back to bed now. Drink your tea and eat a slice of bread. Then you'll feel better. At this time you're normally in the workshop. Think about it. If we get the flat then we won't have to walk through half the town everyday. Everything would be easier. Mrs. Schorch is even ready to leave us the furniture, for the time being. When she needs it, she'll give us enough time. She thinks she will be away for a few years. She said that she really trusts us. Then she said that we should not talk about it. I had to really promise that. People will notice soon enough that she has left and that others are living there. She'll put in a good word with Mrs. Weisser. So hurry up, Franz. You know that Mrs. Weisser always gets up early. She's always saying, "The early bird catches the worm."

Franz was persuaded and went straight out. Mrs. Weisser saw him coming and waved to him. "Come in, quickly." "Good morning, Mrs. Weisser." She pulled him by his sleeve into the shop, "I need to talk to you about the flat. Yes. You already know. You wanted the flat some time ago, didn't you? With or without the guest room?" But Franz was thirsty and asked her for a glass of water. Because he had drunk so much alcohol last evening, his throat was dry. She gave him a glass of water out of a crystal water jug. He drank it down in one go. Then he said, "What does the flat look like? I've never been in it. I'd like to see it first." "Yes, just go up. Your future wife, and I hope she soon will be, already knows the flat well. She likes it. Mrs. Schorh is already up. Just knock. Don't ring the bell, because you'll wake the other people in the house." Mrs. Weisser opened the back door and pushed Franz into the corridor.

He had never been in the house before, only a couple of times in the shop. It was a bit dark. He looked for the light switch, found it, but there was no light. He went up the stairs, lit a match, saw the doorbell and pushed it. Then he remembered that he should not have used the bell. But the bell was very quiet. Mrs. Schorch had put some paper behind it. She opened the door, "Good morning," she whispered, "did anyone see you? Sorry. I mean is anyone else awake in the house?" Franz said, "Good morning. I didn't hear anything and I didn't notice anything. Does everyone here show so much consideration for the others? I hope my children won't upset the neighbours if we really move in here, because you can't keep them quiet all the time." Mrs. Schorch said, "No, they're used to noise, even if it's just from the dogs. If the bell rings too loud, then they start to bark. Apart from that they're quiet and obedient." The dogs were under the table. "Please, sit down. Would you like a coffee?" She poured him a coffee. "Oh," he said after taking a first sip and almost burning his tongue, "but that's hot." Franz hated anything hot and thought it was not healthy. "Could I have a glass of cold water?"

She had to go into the corridor to get water, came back with a jug and poured him a glass full. In the meantime Franz had taken a look around. Luck is on my side, he thought and touched wood, although he was not superstitious. It's going well with Josefine, the workshop is successful and now the flat with the nice furniture. "I'll take the flat and you can leave the furniture here. Of course, because of the children, I can't be sure that there won't be a few scratches. We'll take care, but I can't guarantee anything." "What can I do?" Mrs. Schorch asked, "I can't put them into storage and I can't take them under my arm. It's an emergency. My aunt is chronically ill. I have to go and look after her." She turned her back and swallowed a few tears. Franz comforted her, "It will all be for the best. You'll see. Everything takes time." "I'll miss Josefine," she said sadly, "we understood each other. She promised me that she would take the dogs to Farmer Katz. She thought that would be a good place for them. I can't take them with me and Josefine said that they couldn't stay with you. Mrs. Weisser will be very sad, when the dogs are gone, but I understand you. You have children who are not used to dogs in the flat and the dogs are not used to children. That would certainly be a problem. They will certainly have a good life on a farm. Now I'm going to tell Mrs. Weisser, that you agree to renting the flat. She'll bring you the tenancy contract." Franz thanked her for the coffee and said that if there was anything else, she should come to him. Apart from that he wished her all the best and that she had good times with her aunt.

Mrs. Schorch only took with her what she could carry. Josefine thought that was strange. She had a feeling that something was wrong. She helped Mrs. Schorch to carry her things to the bus and asked her if there was some other reason for her leaving, apart from her aunt, because she was leaving so many things in the flat. "Well, yes, Mrs. Schorch said, "I trust you, dear Josefine, but how can I explain it? My aunt is half Jewish and I have just found out that I am an eighth Jewish. I didn't know that. The Aryan investigation office found it out. You must have noticed that Jews are no longer welcome here. More and more people disappear and I ask myself, where are they? It is really frightening. There are observation stations everywhere and everything is reported. I couldn't take all my money from the bank. Otherwise I would have been suspected. As long as there is no security for us here, we all want to leave. I have to go to the border. My aunt is waiting there with a few other people, but I don't know where we are going. Everything I have done up to now and everything which I am going to do has been discussed in the family." Josefine looked at her, thoughtfully and full of sympathy. "Now when you mention that, a lot of things are going through my head but I can't put them quite in order. I feel quite agitated." Mrs. Schorch said, "When I'm in safety, I'll try to send you my news, but I hope that one day I can return. Come, Josefine, let's sit on the bench. The bus stop is just there. I don't want to give any acquaintances the opportunity of asking where I'm going."

Josefine thought for a while and then suddenly said, "Mrs. Schorch, can I look at your hand?" "Yes, but why?" But she slowly held out her hand. Josefine looked closely at her palm, stroked a few lines with her fingers, closed her eyes for a moment and said, "You'll come back to your flat. It'll take a few years. Everything will be all right. The journey you are now taking will be difficult, but you'll come through." Without saying another word she pressed Mrs. Schorch's hands together, stood up and left. Mrs. Schorch was not too sure what had happened. She watched Josefine leaving and as if in a trance, she got on to the bus. Josefine was sure that she was right. She had already read the hands of Florenz, Anderl and the farmer's wife Katze. By the two men it was easy to prove whether she had correctly interpreted the signs. It was indeed so. But they only laughed about it and forgot the whole thing almost immediately. Josefine often thought about her mother, who had only ever read the hands of her family and closest friends. She did not want to be seen as a gypsy. Most people thought that only gypsies could read the future.

VI

As time went on, Josefine, because of her knowledge of languages, was often called to the council offices to interpret. The first time was when a covered lorry came into the town square. There were people from the east in the lorry, Romanians and Bulgarians who had been on the road for several days and the lorry had been in the square since 3am. After about an hour, when Josefine had been called out of her bed, everyone had to get out of the lorry. They were surrounded by security officers. The people had not been able to wash for days. They were allowed to go to the fountain, wash themselves, drink some water and satisfy the call of nature over the drain. Some of them had to clean the floor of the lorry. Then they were given cabbage soup and old, dry bread. The people pushed forward to get something to eat, but they kept themselves quiet. Then, they were called one by one and split into three groups. Each group was assigned a specific work location. The lorry driver was Hungarian. He only had to drive from one place to the other. Then he should have been replaced. He had no idea where he had to deliver his "goods." He had collected them in east Hungary. And someone should have taken over the lorry at the border. Both of his companions had stayed there. Someone had simply explained and written down the directions to the next station. A small man in a brown uniform came to Josefine and said that now she had to interpret. She had to tell the driver that he had driven over the wrong border and that the transport had already been registered as "missing". She also had to ask him where he had got the fuel for the long journey.

For Josefine this was anything but clear. In the meantime the lorry's petrol tank and even the reserve tank were filled. That must be still a long journey, she thought. The people were lying around in the courtyard, most of them were exhausted. Josefine wanted to find out what it all meant and spoke quietly and secretly to a few people. She had left the house in such a hurry, that she had covered her head with a scarf and in the dark, she did not stand out and did not look very different to the women from the lorry. She could not understand why people, who were supposed to get work were brought from so far away when there were so many unemployed people right here. A Bulgarian woman said that she had simply been collected. She had not even had time to say goodbye to her husband even though he was just next door with the neighbours. She had been chosen to join the workforce. But where? Why so far away? Tears ran down her face. She asked Josefine to send a message to her village. Josefine went to find something to write with. When she came back, they were all on the lorry again and were accompanied by armed personnel.

Josefine saw that a civilian from Vorderberg had a pistol protruding from his jacket. A new driver was drawing nervously on his cigarette butt then he drove off. The Hungarian driver was taken away. She never saw him again. All those present were taken into a side room where a man in a brown uniform told them in no uncertain terms that they had seen nothing and they were sworn to total secrecy. They raised their right hand and swore. Much later Josefine found out that the people from the east had to work in ammunition factories, in appalling conditions and for a minimum wage. When she was interpreting, she sometimes saw transport lists on the office desk, which were marked "special detachments". She did not trust herself to ask any questions. Repeatedly she heard that people disappeared without trace. There were a few informers amongst them.

At home everything was going well. There was a lot of housework. The paid help, Gerdi, was always busy with washing and cooking. Most of the time Josefine was in the workshop and she took the youngest, Fredi with her. Were ever she went he was with her.

Franz had become a little more friendly, but he was often deep in thought. He was always writing notes, which no one else understood. In the night he crept away, secretly. Josefine asked him what was going on, but his answer was always, "Nothing, nothing. I just can't sleep so I take a walk. Don't think anything about it." Once she watched him and saw him moving a plank under the cupboard and sweeping the floor with a cloth. She waited until he and the boys were out of the house, checked that Fredi was sleeping and then tried to pull out the plank. But it was somehow blocked. With all her force she pulled on the blank and fell over backwards as it came free. At first she only saw an empty space. She fumbled in the dark until she dragged out a book and a few loose sheets and a small newspaper. She gave them a quick glance and realised that it was all against the present Nazi regime. That it was underground material. She stood up and hurriedly locked the flat door. Then she opened the book. Inside was a pistol. The pages had been cut out so to make room for it. Josefine was shocked and thought about what could happen if someone discovered it. Her first thought was to throw everything into the stove, but then she put the things back in their place, put the plank back and unlocked the door. She was frantic.

Franz cannot even shoot, she thought. Once at a church festival he wanted to shoot for her a rose but each time he had been way off the mark. She had taken the gun from him and shot the rose herself. Her first shot had met its mark. Her head was spinning. I've got to calm down. Somehow I'll find out what it's all about. I won't ask any questions, but I'll watch everything that happens very closely. There's that Lanegger, who's always raving about Communism. To quieten down she held herself onto a chair and took a few deep breaths.

Yes, Mr. Lanegger, who was a neighbour had a lot of good to say about Russia and Communism. He took every opportunity to talk to Franz and explain Communism to him. "There are no poor and rich there," he said, "everyone is equal; everything is shared; no one goes hungry. Everyone can afford to go to school.

Anyone who wants to go on with their studies can do it without paying. There are no poor houses like here. The old people live in a nice old people's home. There is work for everyone, but they have to work hard, of course. Everyone has the same rights. That's what counts. And that is why we are fighting. It's possible, if only everyone has the will and believes in it." Josefine had once broken into such a discussion and told them that she had seen with her own eyes what was really happening in the eastern countries and that it would take generations for them to achieve their aims. "I'll just say one thing," she said vehemently, "watch out for yourselves. If anyone hears, how you are praising Communism, then it will be your turn. The SS will strike immediately. You can already here about how they treat activists like you. In the cities they would have already caught you. Here it's still relatively quiet." Franz said, "Rubbish," and that she should stay out of it. To Mr. Lanegger he said that he did not want to discuss the matter in the workshop. Mr. Lanegger whispered to him that there would soon be another meeting which he would be organising personally. Josefine was still able to hear what he said.

That must be it was he thought that went through her head, Franz had let himself be convinced to join the group. I don't know what I should say about it. Mr. Lanegger had often visited southern Russia. He speaks a strange Russian dialect. I've also been to Russia with my family when we performed there. Often we had to perform for noble guests, while they sat on comfortable chairs, ate opulent food and where the vodka flowed in streams. But the poverty outside was horrific. You saw people chewing on sunflower seeds. They spat out all the time, where ever they were. They tried to still their hunger with alcohol. A terrible drink, which they had distilled themselves.

Josefine interrupted again. She asked Mr. Lanegger where he had been looking when he visited Russia. She had never seen or heard all this splendour which he described. "Yes, yes," he said defensively, "this is already true in some communes. I was in Russia's granary. That is where you can see the idea of the collective at its best. We have to keep on trying to convince the people. Communism exists and works, not only in Russia. The people in Moscow have a lot to learn and must change and believe in the good which will come in the future. We'll bring them on the right road as soon as we are strong enough." Josefine replied, looking him straight in the eye, "What you are suggesting, Mr. Lanegger, is a time bomb. I don't want Franz to get mixed up in this. Apart from your wife you have only one son who will survive you. And he, in contrast, won't just leave his child without a father, but he will endanger our very existence, which we have built with our own sweat. And not just that, innocent people who earn their daily bread honestly will be dragged under with you." Franz wanted to calm her down, "It isn't what you think. We are always careful. Mr. Lanegger is often travelling getting us work" "But that just makes it worse." "No, no," Mr. Langegger said, trying to reassure her, "look," he turned his collar round and showed her the Swastika, "when things get dangerous, I pin that on my chest." Josefine was appalled, "Jesus, Mary," she shouted, "what sort of people have we got in this house? Friends of Hitler, Friends of the Communists, an eighth Jew, full Jews, strict Catholics and protestants. That's going to lead to problems in the future, because one thing is certain. It certainly won't be as easy as you imagine."

"I'm telling you, Franz, only if we remain neutral can we protect ourselves from the worst." Suddenly a thought flashed through her mind. "Can I see your hands, Mr. Lanegger? Just out of curiosity." He held out his large, strong hands. She asked him to sit in the light. "Stop that," shouted Franz, "forget that nonsense." But Mr. Lanegger just laughed and sat down. Josefine felt his hands, moved them about, pressed on his palms and then looked closely at the lines. Her face became serious. "What can you see?" asked Mr. Lanegger. "Shush," she answered. After a while, she said, slowly and in a hushed voice, "For a while everything will be alright for you, Mr. Lanegger, but round about autumn there will be dramatic changes in your life. Pain. You will be separated from your family for a long time." Little beads of sweat gathered on her forehead then she continued, "Betrayal. I can smell leather. Black leather. There are black shadows coming to get you." She looked up, "Mr. Lanegger, please take care." She was shaking. She stood up, went into the next room, washed her hands and wiped the sweat from her face. Mr. Lanegger sat there, flabbergasted and speechless. "Don't take it so seriously." Franz said to him. "It's clear that she smelt leather. We have some here." Mr. Lanegger laughed uncertainly and said, "I think it's time I left. Comrade, you know how it's going to continue. So, I'll see you soon." Josefine came back into the workshop. "You certainly put the wind up him," Franz remarked, "but maybe that's not a bad thing and, in future he might think about what he says. Did you hear? He called me Comrade. Anyway, what was that all about? I thought only gypsies could read hands." "Don't you remember? I read Florenz's and Anderl's hands and I was right." "That was just coincidence," Franz replied, but he thought about it. Josefine let it be.

They went up to the flat on the first floor. It was comfortable there. In the evenings when the children were already in bed and Gerdi had gone home they listened to the radio, which Mrs. Schorch had also left in the flat. There were a lot of reports and speeches. They said that things were going to get better. That now almost no one was unemployed. That criminals like the Jews and other low life, as the Nazis called them, would finally be cleared out. The speeches over the microphone were shouted rather than spoken. Now and again they listened to an illegal transmission which reported about terrible camps which were being set up everywhere. They reported about persecution of Jews and gypsies, which the SS were collecting from everywhere and transporting them in cattle wagons full of people of all ages. Josefine had told Franz about the transport which she had seen when she was interpreting. After all she had not been sworn to secrecy. Then she said, "It's a long time since I saw Mrs. Weisser's children. They have probably left." "The youngest daughter is still there," Franz knew, "just a while ago I saw her in the garden with old Mrs. Weisser. Sometimes strange things happen. Recently I saw Frühwirt and Gosch coming out of Mrs. Weisser's flat. It was about one o'clock in the morning. She hadn't switched on the light and none of them spoke." Josefine remembered that she had seen Mrs. Weisser's brother in the council office. "You know. The one with the furniture lorry. He took away the rubbish from the workshop."

Josefine wanted to know more. She thought up some excuse and knocked on Mr. Gosch's door. She had heard people moving about in the night. Had he not noticed anything? She no longer felt safe in the house. "Don't be worried, Mrs. Dorn. I think that now I can call you by that name," said Mr. Gosch, "but it's good that you are here. I have something important to tell Franz. Can you ask him to come to me in about half an hour and – please, don't say a word to anyone else. We have to be very careful about everything which is going on here. You know, the enemy hears everything. That's why I advise you to put the radio somewhere else, because even walls have ears. I don't want to breed any informers in this house." Josefine went to the workshop. There were still two employees there who were fastening the last postal packets. When they had left she told Franz that he should go to Mr. Gosch. He had something important to tell him. "Where did you meet him?" he wanted to know. "I went to him because I thought he might know more than us about what is going on in this house." "So. Once again you couldn't wait. Your curiosity got the better of you and now we have problems. All of us want to know what is in store for us. In future keep your curiosity under control." As soon as Franz had closed the door to Mr. Gosch's flat behind him, Josefine emptied a bucket of water onto the corridor and started to clean it up. Maybe I can see who goes in and out, she thought, but unfortunately nothing happened. And Franz said nothing about what was so urgent between him and Mr. Gosch.

The next day Josefine had to go to the council offices to interpret. A uniformed office brought two Croatians up from the cellar, who claimed to know no German. He pushed the pair in front of him and Josefine saw that they had been beaten. One had a bloody nose and the other was holding his hand under his stomach. The younger was crying and swearing. Josefine understood every word. The uniformed officer asked her what the Croatian had said. "He is in pain," she lied, "there's something wrong with his stomach." "Ask them why they are here, where they came from and if there are any others with them?" Josefine made as if she was interpreting correctly, but what she really said was completely different. "You were obviously looking for someone here, in the area and now say something, otherwise we'll have problems." The older one quickly got it and said that he understood what had been said. Josefine said, "They're looking for a Family Varnislav who apparently live in the region." Luckily she remembered the name of a Yugoslav who had left the area, "they wanted to visit them, but no one has ever treated them like this." The older one said something but made sure that his speech was unclear. said, "They don't live far from the border", translated Josefine and gave him the name of a village. She wanted to help both of them.

An ostentatious council officer nodded, disappeared for a while and came back with a file. Yes, a family with that name had actually lived in the region. He smiled and asked if he could offer them some tea, but he also had some home-made schnapps. The Croatians would have liked something to drink, but only the uniformed officers were served. The Croatians whispered to Josefine that they had escaped from a work transport. The official asked what they had said. Josefine replied, "They asked if they could now go. They both need to go to the lavatory, urgently". One of the officers was told to accompany them to the lavatory and then he should give them back the dirty, ancient papers which were lying on the desk. He turned to Josefine, "Tell them that the next time they should bring their passports with them, then they won't have problems like this." The passports, if they had any, had almost certainly been taken by the boss of the work transport. Back home you always had to carry these papers which were now on the desk, the older man, who had now cleaned the blood from his nose, said. Josefine glanced at the papers, saw Cyrillic letters and instead of interpreting described an old garden house across the stream, right behind the railway. You can hide there. "Help will come after dark." The younger said a few polite words. "They say that with these papers they will certainly not get home." The council official was clearly irritated, but not for long. He stamped the papers and wrote, "For the return journey to the home town."

As the Croatians took their papers, Josefine saw that their hands were very fine. "So, and now, Mrs. Dorn, please take tea with us," the official said after the two had left. Josefine said she would be happy to drink a cup and the officer disappeared to fetch the tea.

For a moment she was alone in the office and noticed on the desk a cleanly ordered written list of names. A few names had been crossed out and remarks had been written in the margin. She noted a few names which had not yet been crossed out and one of them was Weisser. When she heard footsteps she took a piece of paper pencil and then looked out of the window. "I have to go to the girls' room," she said and hurried along the corridor. In the lavatory she quickly wrote down the names she still had in her head, shoved the paper into the folds of her dress. She flushed the WC and went back to the office, where the tea was waiting. She buttered up the official and made him compliments. She said that she was surprised how quickly he had dealt with such an awkward case and she noticed that he was pleased by her remarks. She drank her tea, which was only lukewarm and saw that he was looking at his watch. The she left the office and sang. "I wish you a pleasant day. Good bye. Au revoir."

Josefine ran along the path next to the stream to the workshop. Franz was not there. She went up the stairs into the flat. He was sitting there at the table, reading the newspaper. She sent Gerdi into the workshop under a pretext and as soon as she was out of the room, told Franz what she had seen and heard and showed him the paper with the names. "Mrs. Weisser?" he stuttered, "but she has an exit permit and a visa for Palestine."

Just yesterday she said that in case she went away for a while, Mr. Gosch would take over the house administration and Mr. Frühwirt would run the business. Contracts had been signed.

So everything would remain the same. For the quarry and her brother's lorry she had provisionally found someone. But, she thought, did he know what he had taken on? "Yes. He's a strong man and a good lorry driver who knows the region well." Franz thought about it, "Don't tell anyone, because if someone gets to hear that we are in the know it could be dangerous for all of us. I'm going to Mrs. Weisser and you must watch the entrance and give me a signal that the air is clear. Now we are in great danger."

Josefine looked around, took the rubbish bucket and emptied almost half of it in the entrance. Then she took a broom and pushed the stuff from one side to the other. She gave Franz a signal by moving the broom from side to side without touching the floor. He knocked briefly on Mrs. Weisser's door and disappeared inside. Mrs.Weisser heard the knock, but had not noticed that Franz was already in the flat. In the first moment she was shocked, because the door was normally closed. Franz put his finger to his lips. With the other hand he showed her the piece of paper with the names on it. "You're on the transport list. You know what that means? I'm working for the resistance. No one here knows that, not even Josefine. Unfortunately, I don't know when the transport will set off. You must go over the border as quick as possible."

He found out that Mrs. Weisser's brother had often driven people in his lorry close to the border. "My brother has already escaped and is now in safety," she said hastily, "just recently he realised that he was being watched in the hiding place where he let the people off the lorry. They were also at the quarry. He wanted to change the colour of the lorry. I don't know if he was able to do that. He also managed to get other number plates. The lorry is in Greisensteg Castle. It is parked legally in the castle tunnel." She put her hand to her heart and sat down on a chair. "I wanted my Edda, our youngest daughter, to leave the country, but she didn't want to leave me, her old mother alone. I think we could ask Mr. Dvorak. That's the person who will take over the sand quarry. I think he is a very brave man. He knows the lorry and he can drive it. My brother always said he could get away from anyone who tried to catch him. At the moment Dvorak is driving the taxi for Grossmeier, who's ill. The taxi rank is next to the bus stop in the main square. I'll write him a note telling him where he should be, tonight, with the lorry. Please take it to him." She looked at him, almost begging. "Yes," said Franz, "of course I'll bring it to him." "If anything goes wrong, then you, Mr. Dorn have the tenancy of the sand quarry. I'll put that down in writing." "No, Mrs. Weisser, we don't want to tempt the devil." But Mrs. Weisser could not be dissuaded. She wrote the note for Mr. Dvorak and the attest for Franz, complete with the company stamp and gave him both, "Here. Now you must go." She pulled back a brown curtain which hung in front of the rear door, opened the door just a crack and looked out. The air was clear. Josefine signalled Franz to go. He ran quickly through and outside he slowed his pace.

Franz wandered towards the main square. Now and again he stopped in front of a shop window and saw, in the reflection what was going on behind him. That is how he found Grossmeier's taxi. Dvorak was sitting in the driving seat and his arm was hanging lazily out of the window. A bus drove up. Franz took the opportunity to go to the taxi. "Dvorak?" He nodded. Franz pressed the note into his hand, went to the bus and asked the driver something. When he turned round he saw that Dvorak was lighting a cigarette with the note and was giving him the thumbs up. Franz went round the bus and took the path behind the church back to the workshop. Josefine was at work. "I have a headache," he lied, "I'm going to lie down for a while." "All right" she said, "I'm here." He went up to the attic where the women hung the washing out to dry when the weather was bad. If you went into the eaves you could see the whole main street. Franz lay there for almost three quarters of an hour before he saw the taxi drive by. It soon came back, stopped and something was taken off the windscreen. That was the sign that he and the lorry were ready to move. Franz crept into the flat saw that he was dusty from top to bottom and quickly changed his clothes. Gerdi had not noticed anything. She was busy with the wash board. He hid his clothes in the cupboard so that he could shake them out and brush them later.

Josefine's thoughts were with the Croatians, Who knew when they had last eaten. The day seemed to be very long. Evening would not come. Josefine did not want to tell Franz that she had suggested the garden house as a hiding place. She was afraid that he would think she was unreasonable, because now that they had the stamped papers, they could move about freely. There was not even a date when they should go back over the border. Maybe it was really stupid of me she thought. In spite of that, as soon as it was dark she wanted to go to the small garden house and bring them something to eat, if they were there. She had already hidden bread and a bottle of milk in the pram. But she was still sitting at the table with Franz. Gerdi still had some things to tidy away, then she would be finished. Fredi was in the pram and fidgeted a bit. Josefine stood up, looked around to see if everything was in order. That was her opportunity. She nicked Fredi on the bottom and he started to cry. "Gerdi, help me to carry the pram outside. We'll go out in the fresh air. That will do us both good." She pushed the pram up along the side of the stream and went alongside the fence to a narrow bridge which she crossed. Then she reached the garden house which was very overgrown. She looked around and then called softly in Croat, "It's me," through the leaning door. Her heart was beating strongly. After all she did not know the two men. Nothing stirred. The door opened outwards. Josefine looked around her again and then she opened the door, but there was no one inside. She held still and then put the bread and milk on a ledge by the door and walked back home.

Franz was often away in the night. Josefine could only really sleep when she heard him return. He did not need much sleep. Four to five hours were enough for him. But then, after the midday meal he had a snooze, as he called it.

VII

One day Luise knocked on the workshop window. Her face was tearful. Franz went outside and she told him that Franzi had volunteered to join the army. "He's still a child," she sobbed. Then she told him that he had worked in the glass factory for a while and had been living with Berta. When she took a subtenant, he did not want to stay there, even though things were better after that. "In the beginning he had had problems with Berta. For a while he had to sleep in the town park. The reason was that he had not given her any money from his first wage, since he had had to buy shoes. He could not work in the glass factory with his worn out shoes. You know Berta. If you don't pay punctually, you get nothing, whatever the situation. Erwin told me that Franzi would never forgive Berta for that. Now he's in the army. He had counted every single day until he would be old enough to join the army. But really he's a timid boy." She wiped the tears from her cheeks. Franz said, "What can we do? We can only hope that he doesn't have to go to war. There's no easy way to get him out of the Nazi claws. I'll have a few words with Berta. She should have told me about Franzi. When he has leave I will talk to him. Right now, there's nothing more we can do." He gave her a few bank notes, which she accepted, gratefully. Then she left. Josefine had never had any contact with Luise, but had slipped the children money, now and again.

A few weeks later Luise knocked again. The subtenant had made Aloisia pregnant. "She's not even fifteen," Franz heard. "She admitted that she hasn't had a period for three to four months." Said Luise ashamed. "Where is this dirty swine?" Franz ranted, "I'll show him something." He threw off his work apron and went with Luise to her flat. She bawled, "He's basically a pleasant person, a good person" "So now you want to defend him," spluttered Franz, "I'll bring him before the magistrate, the child molester. He belongs under lock and key." In the flat Willi and Aloisia were sitting hand in hand on the sofa. "Get away from each other," shouted Franz, "what a disgrace!" He went for Willi, who had sprung to his feet, and wanted to plant one on his face. But Willi caught his fist in a strong grip. "I don't want to fight with you. Your daughter and I have decided to marry. Of course we need your consent." "You're much too old for her, you idiot, you swine." Aloisia shouted: "Stop that. Father, you're just making everything worse than it really is. I don't think Willi is too old for me and I love him dearly. It's all my fault. I let him do it. And anyway, the age difference is the same as between you and Josefine. You can't accuse us of anything." "But you are still a child." Franz was in no mood to calm down, "and that's the difference." He sat down and thought for a moment. Luise brought him a cup of tea, "I knew nothing about all this," she cried. Willi said, "I'm really sorry about what has happened. I know that many people will gossip about it. But I have a good job here with chances of promotion. I'm not going to run away from it."

Franz sat there and hung his head low, "You can forget any ideas of promotion. When they hear what has happened, then they'll throw you out." Willi tried to bring things onto a lower level, "Aloisia looks older than her years. Who knows how old she really is." "Oh stop," sobbed Luise, "as far as I'm concerned, you can marry. It's your problem how you're going to arrange it." Then she became angry, "Damn it. That is really a load of filth. You're destroying everything, but everything." She turned away and crossed herself. "Yes!" interjected Franz. "Now that everything is going well in our private life and in the workshop. And then there's the political situation, but that we can manage. Things are happening, but you will hear about it in good time, before the putsch comes." He picked up his hat and left.

After a time Willi and Aloisia were able to quietly get married. Luckily they found shelter, close to the next large town, at Willi's grandmother›s. That was better for everyone. Willi had to take the train to work. Often the train was halted and men in black leather entered to control all the passengers' papers. Armed soldiers made sure that no one could run off. Without the correct papers, you were in big trouble. Willi was proud to show his Aryan pass, which he always carried. They often heard shots fired, but no one dared to look out of the windows.

In the workshop they sang and laughed, in spite of all the problems. They tried to remain contented and happy and avoided talking about any subjects which could betray them.

VIII

Then, one day, Franz found himself in really hot water. He was on his way, with a jute sack full of bread and tea, to the refugees' meeting point, when he heard a man's voice roaring, "March, left, right, left, right." He dropped everything and, overcome by fear ran zigzag through the woods. He heard shots behind him. Exhausted he came to a small, isolated house and managed to get through the door. A woman was sitting in front of the stove. She wasn't the least bit shocked when he fell into the house. "Can I hide here?" he said panting. He thought, either she helps me or I am lost.

Without saying a word she pushed the basket of wood next to the stove to one side and pointed to a hole. "Jump down there. It's not deep and there is straw on the floor." Franz jumped into the hole. He could see nothing, but he heard her closing the hole and moving the basket of wood over it. Not long after there was a knock on the door, which, in the meantime she had closed. "Open up!" someone shouted. The woman opened the door, "Jesus, you gave me a fright," she said, and put her hand on her heart. A soldier pushed her roughly to one side, marched in and looked around. "Have you seen or heard anything? We're looking for an escapee." "Well, I've seen a few strange people further down the hill, but no one has come up here to me. Since my son died in the army, it's as though everything has died up here." She looked at the photograph of her son in uniform with a black ribbon on it "Go on," shouted the soldier and left, "we mustn't lose him. We should have brought the dogs with use." The woman waited until she could not hear the soldiers, moved the basket to one side and opened the hole. Franz's knees were so weak that he had problems climbing out of the hole. He took a wary look out of the little window. "They won't be back," the woman said, "they've gone down the hill and it's difficult to come back up. I've got some polenta. You can eat it, if you want, and I've got some acorn coffee."

While Franz was eating, Mrs Kramer, that was her name, told him what had happened to her son. She took a letter from behind the crucifix. "They wrote me a letter and I don't believe a word of it. I know my son. What they wrote was that he was in a field close to the border and that he died there, with others and that he was buried there. I went there, but no one knew where his grave was, not even the police." She started to cry, "Why could he not be buried here in his native soil? There wasn't even a burial service." Tears ran down her cheeks. Franz tried to console her and it made him think. After a while he suggested that she should put a few of her son's personal things in a box and bury them next to the cross which was only a few meters from the house. She could also write a letter and plant some flowers. "If your son is in heaven, and he must be there, then he will know that you have made a memorial for him. That will bring you peace and he will be happy when you go there to pray and you're with him in your thoughts. Come on. You can write the letter and put together a few of his things and I'll go and dig out a place for them." Mrs. Kramer thought that was a good idea, "By the way," she said, "my name is Irma, and your name?" "My name is Ferdi," he lied, because he did not want to give his real name. He asked her for a shovel and he had no fear of being discovered. When Mrs. Kramer brought a large porcelain urn with a cover and they had buried it and surrounded it with a few flowers from the garden they both knelt in front of the cross. After a few minutes Franz stood up, put his hand on her shoulder, turned away and went down the hill through the wood.

All his life Franz kept on saying, "I can't explain why I say I believe in God. Praying and all the other things which people do, that I don't understand. And why does God, if he is all powerful, bring so much suffering to the world? Now that, I'll never understand."

About a week after the chase – Franz was in the workshop and Josefine was somewhere on the way – a couple of men came into the house, showed identity cards bearing the swastika and started to ask questions. They had Mr. Lanegger and another man in tow. Only Gerdi and the children were in the flat. The men searched the cupboards, the beds and everything where something could be hidden. Without any consideration they tore everything out. Gerdi was frightened and took the children to one side. Then they saw that Emer was staring at one particular floor board. They did not know that there was a secret place there, but one of the men saw where the child was looking. He took out his pocket knife, lifted the board and found the book in which the pistol was hidden. They also found a few notes which they could not read, otherwise nothing.

They collected Franz from the workshop and took him with them. A few inquisitive people were standing around in the street. Josefine was on her way home when she saw Franz get into the black car. "Where are they going with my husband?" she wanted to know. "To the police station," whispered someone standing next to her. She knew what that meant and ran into the flat. It was in chaos. Quickly she went to the hiding place under the floor, knelt down and felt the whole space with her hand. She got a mirror and a torch just to make sure, but there was nothing there. Gerdi was still sitting there, shivering and crying. "What were they looking for?" Josefine asked. "I think Emer knew about the hiding place. He kept looking at it," sobbed Gerdi. Emer defended himself, "I didn't betray anything, "men already came in the school and asked us questions, but I said nothing, because they didn't ask about the hiding place."

It almost took Josefine's and Gerdi's breath away and they thought, now it's even happening in the schools. Josefine looked Emer in the eyes and said to him, in a friendly voice, "Come, Emer, tell us exactly what happened in school. Take your time and think about it." Emer thought he was very important and walked up and down thc flat, just like Franz when he was thinking. Finally, Josefine said, "Now sit down and tell us what happened." "One of them kept smacking his cane on the teacher's desk," he began, "all of us noticed it. Then he said that anyone who knew something and did not open his mouth would feel the cane. Then the men asked some of the boys. ‹Do you know anything about this?›. The man with the cane picked out a few of the boys and asked each of them. ‹What›s your name?›. Another man went through the school list and wrote down some of the addresses. A few names he called out and the pupils had to answer. ‹Here!› The man with the cane then looked at them closely. He came to me and forced up my chin with the cane. After the men had left, the teacher told us that we should tell our parents what had happened, but I forgot". "Is that all?" Josefine asked. "No," Emer said, and he was embarrassed, "something else happened, but I don't want to talk about it, because I'm ashamed and the others were also ashamed." "Now tell us. You don't need to be ashamed, not in front of Gerdi and me." Josefine was trying to calm him down.

"The man with the black hat asked us if in our house we were friendly to Jews. Then I said, 'I think so.' Then he took me to one side. I and a couple of others had to go with him. Then we were in the back courtyard behind the school. He shouted, "Now march, and stand in a row with your backs to the wall. Now a doctor is going to see if you are healthy. Drop your trousers." A few of them weren't wearing any underpants. We laughed. But those who were wearing underpants had to take them off as well. The Doctor had two sticks, and he used them to stretch the skin on our willies back. A few of us could step forward and pull up our trousers. Elli, Joschi and two others had to go with the doctor." Emer looked at the floor. "But they came back to school?" Josefine asked. "No, they haven't been in our class since then. And I haven't seen them anywhere else." Josefine took Emer in her arms and pressed him to her. She kissed his hair, but, as always, he wanted a kiss on the mouth. Emer asked if he could now go out and play in the courtyard, drank his apple peal tea and left.

Gerdi tidied up as quickly as she could. She wanted to get this behind her. Josefine put the plank back in its place. She was thinking about Emer. He was an intelligent, hard working and good boy, but sometimes he was a bit too clever. In school he was the best gymnast. At home he practised in the courtyard on a trapeze, which Franz had fixed to a tree. He practised his stunts whenever he could. He had no fear, but he did have respect for heights. Emer also wrote poems and even when he was small he had loved operetta music. Josefine was very proud of him. When everything had been tidied up, Josefine went to the wife of policeman Presinschek and asked when her husband would be home. The first thing Mrs. Presinschek said, that she was very sorry that two men from the house had been taken away, but then she added, "If you are a policeman then it's not good to live in a house where people are arrested. I just hope my husband doesn't get into difficulties because of it." "I don't know why they have taken my husband away," Josefine said nervously." "Look, dear," Mrs. Presinschek said, giving Josefine an accusing look, "I'll have to explain something to you. Since you are not married with this man, you don't even have the right to know where he is or how he is. You should really think about marrying, even if it's just for the children." Josefine replied, "Yes! I have to go to the council and ask them, if we have got permission to marry. Oh! I'm so confused. I mustn't lose my nerve." Mrs. Presinschek said, "If anything happened, you wouldn't even get a widow's pension. But I don't want to summon the devil. My husband will be back at about seven for his evening meal. Come about a quarter to eight. I'll warn him of your visit. So, till later." "Thank you Mrs. Presinschek, I know you mean well. All right, a quarter to eight."

When the door closed Josefine had to lean against the cold wall. She felt very sick. She knew that something was coming up, held her apron in front of her face and vomited into it. The she gathered up all her strength and ran into her flat before she had to throw up again. Gerdi helped her off with her apron and held a bucket under her chin to catch the next bout. Josefine lay down on the sofa. I can't be pregnant again, she thought. No, for the love of God, please not. I can't and I don't want to bring a child into this mess. Please help me. She started to count back. Could it really be true? I already have three children. This child would really not be welcome. Please don't let it be true. I must be mistaken. I'm not pregnant. Thank the Lord I have Gerdi. She really is a pearl. In the meantime Gerdi had given the children porridge and got them ready for bed. There had not been time to cook anything else. Josefine ate a little from the porridge, because she remembered that the water from cooked oats was an old recipe for calming the stomach and the nerves. Gerdi said, "If Mr. Dorn wants something to eat, there's still some food left over from midday. It's getting late. I'm going now." Josefine knew that It was not all that late, but she let her go. Very soon Gerdi had more and more reasons for not coming and Josefine knew that one day she would stay away altogether.

In fact, Josefine had wanted to go down to the workshop, although she knew everything was going on as normal, but she did not feel like having to answer the questions which would surely be asked. She looked at the clock, put the children to bed and gave them a few toys to play with. That calmed her down. Erwin, Franz's and Luise's son, came up from the workshop. "They've all gone home and I've locked up. Here is the key," he said to Josefine, "have you heard anything from father?"

"Not yet. In a few minutes I'm going to Precinschek. Maybe I get something out of him. If you want you can wait until I come back. There are some left overs from midday. I can warm them up for you. Truth to tell, I'd be happy if you could stay. Who knows what else is going to happen today?" Suddenly she remembered, my God, Gerdi had kept the food back for Franz. How could I have forgotten. That is a bad omen. But I can't take it away from Erwin now. She secretly crossed herself. Erwin had not wanted to stay, but now he could not leave. The food was already on the table. And he did not want to deny Josefine his help. And of course he wanted to know where his father was and how he was. So he sat down and ate. He often came to his father's workshop to work for an hour or two. The he sat quietly in a corner and concentrated on painting the wooden figures. Sometimes one hardly noticed that he was there. But sometimes, when he started to tell his stories, it was really fun. He could make them all laugh. He was very cheerful and had a great sense of humour.

He was also a well brought up and pleasant chap. He loved his mother, Luise more than anything and he helped where he could. Later, when Josefine went to Mr. Presinschek, it turned out that he, although he was a policeman, knew nothing about what had happened, but he promised to find out where the Gestapo had taken Franz. 'Gestapo' meant the Secret State Police.

Late in the night there was a gentle knock on the door. Josefine opened it. A complete stranger stood in the doorway. "Switch off the light," he whispered and put his hand to the light switch. Then he forced her back into the flat. "I know where Franz is. We'll do everything we can to free him. We have sympathisers everywhere. It's best if you try to stay calm. See you soon." And he was gone. Josefine shuddered. More and more she realised what a terrible situation Franz was in. The next day Mr. Precinschek told her that Franz had been taken to a Gestapo interrogation centre and then somewhere else. He was trying to find out where he now was. Someone had denounced him.

When he arrived at the interrogation centre a powerful looking man wearing a black uniform pointed at Franz and roared, "He's for me!" Franz went hot and cold. What are they going to do with me? "I must go to the lavatory," he said. "What must you?" roared the uniformed man. "He has to go to the lavatory" he said to his colleagues and laughed loudly. The others also thought it was funny and they laughed with him. "Until number four comes, I'm taking him." Then he hit Franz so hard across the head that he and the chair on which he was sitting fell over.

Number four was a colleague who was not yet there to make up the card game. They always played a round of cards at that time. The man in uniform grabbed Franz by the collar and dragged him along the corridor into a room without windows. The walls were covered with large coat hooks. "I have here a list of names. If you know any of these people then it's better for you when you tell me. You understand?" He roared so loud that the room seemed to shake. He turned towards the door and clapped his hand a couple of times. It sounded as though someone was being hit, and then he made a strange whining noise. He struck the cushioned door with his foot so that it fell into the lock and he showed that Franz should sit on a blood stained chair.

He put on a glove and wiped blood from the floor under Franz's nose, on his head and on his chin. "Listen, Comrade," he said quietly through his lips and he said a password which Franz knew well. "Now you have to play along. I've already smeared you with blood. As soon as the door opens, I'll take you by the collar, pull you up and let you fall. You have to fall like a sack onto the chair. Understood! It's about both of us, you idiot. You've been caught out."

He took a list and read out the names on it. Franz knew some of them. "One of them has betrayed you. That›s why you are here" Then he took Franz by the collar and let him fall back on the chair, to show him how he should collapse. "Whine loud and miserably," he murmured, "and hold your head down to one side. Here is a tape with which you must later measure everything in your cell. I'll leave the light on so you can find the bucket to do your business, but then you must switch off the light and lie down on your plank." Then he grabbed him again and shouted, "Come on you son of a bitch."

That was when the door opened. The hold on his collar was strong. He was lifted up until he was on the tips of his shoes and then let fall. "The fourth man is here," someone called through the door crack. "The swine has had enough for the moment, let's leave him lying here," growled the uniformed comrade and kicked Franz's behind. "Now you can go to the lavatory," he laughed heartily. His colleague put his head into the cell and saw the captive lying on the floor, covered with blood. The heavy boots gave a loud echo. Slamming the door behind him, the comrade left the room.

Franz rushed to the bucket. After he had relieved himself he had to switch off the light. He stood next to the chair and the place where he should lie down. He counted the paces to the light switch, turned in the direction he had to go back in the dark. He switched off the light. His knees were trembling when he walked. He stretched out his hand, but could not find the chair.

In the end he lay down on the floor and curled up. He did not know how long he had lain there. His ears were buzzing and hurt from the blow to his face. He was thirsty and hungry. He tried to order his thoughts. When he tried to moisten his lips with his tongue he tasted dried blood and he knew that it was someone else's blood. That made him feel sick. He tried to concentrate and took a deep breath, trying to calm down. Eventually he dozed off.

In spite of everything that had happened he thought that he would somehow get out scot-free. The comrade, as Franz later called him, came again and whispered, "Don't move. Just let yourself be dragged out." The he shouted, "Come here, you know where to take him. Here is the transport paper!" "At your command! Heil Hitler!" was the answer. Two men took Franz by the legs, dragged him to a stretcher and threw him onto it. They pushed him into an ambulance with barred windows, got in and drove away. Franz realised that he was alone. He saw street lights flashing passed, but could not make out where they were going. About an hour later, he thought, they stopped. They put him on a hospital trolley and took him into a building. He kept his eyes closed and from all sides he heard "Heil Hitler!" Someone took him under the arms and turned him a bit. Then he heard a strong voice, "Wash room, prison wing, section two." "Yes, indeed, Professor," answered a woman's voice. A nurse pushed the trolley into a wash room with several shower units. She started to take off his clothes. He pretended that he was coming round. "So, how are you?" she asked, "Did they beat you up?" "Where am I?" Franz wanted to know. "You're in the Punti psychiatric clinic," almost joking. Franz lifted himself up slowly, "My sister was here after she had meningitis. She's physically well, but she doesn't speak like she used to." The nurse said, "I don't think you're so far gone. Apart from a nice hand print on your face, I can't see anything. Or is there something else?" Franz just said that his ear hurt him. "Can you undress yourself and go under the shower? Here is a towel and a long shirt, which you must put on afterwards. Here is some curd soap to wash with. You have also to wash your hair with it."

She took all his personal things and his clothes with her. On the floor he saw a pair of felt slippers. Apart from that the room was empty.

He slid down from the trolley and hurried under the shower, but there was no jet, it just dripped quickly. All the showers were the same. It took him a long time until he was really clean, particularly his hair and the smell was not exactly pleasant. He remembered the smell of curd soap for the rest of his life. It reminded him of the most difficult period of his life. "The soap back home smells better," he said aloud.

After this procedure, Franz stood there in a long, yellow striped shirt. His face, bottom and back hurt. And after the hard slap in the face, his ear buzzed constantly. The comrade had hit a bit too hard.

This idiot thought he hadn't hurt me, Franz murmured to himself. He lay down again on the trolley and went to sleep. As he was dozing he realised that he was being pushed somewhere, but he pretended not to notice. That's the best thing to do, he thought. I have to wait and see what happens. The comrade said that I should measure everything, but how can I do that without a tape. They've taken everything away. I'll have to pretend that I'm crazy. I just hope that I can do it well enough to convince them until I know how things are. Early in the morning the nurse and a warder came in. They looked at the beds, to see if anyone had wet them or so. They opened all the windows wide and aired the room. One nurse distributed medicine. Everyone had to swallow it. Franz asked, "What is it?" ""Just a sedative," was the short answer and the spoon was already in his mouth. When she turned away for a moment he dribbled it into his hand. Suddenly someone shouted, "Visits!" A few men in white gowns entered. "New admissions?" "Here, Professor and here and there." A fat nurse showed the men the people who had just been admitted. A man in a caged bed, started to scream and shake the bars. He was given a couple of heavy blows through the bars and after that he just whimpered. The men in white said, quietly what treatments were to be carried out and what must be done. One of them wrote this down in a notice book, an other hung a chalked slate at the foot of each 'patient's' bed. "What is wrong with him?" asked the

Professor. Franz had begun to take measurements with fingers, hand and elbow. "I have ear ache and my whole body hurts. And now I have to finish measuring everything." The Professor looked at his ear and looked inside with a cold instrument, and said, "It's probably a burst eardrum. We can't do anything about that. Mr. Hartseint, please look more closely at the injury. He's probably had a box on the ear. What caused that?" Franz was fully occupied with his measurements and pretended not to hear. The Professor went to the next bed. There were ten beds in the room and nine of them were occupied. Franz noticed how all of the patients were wary of each other. No one looked another straight in the eye. Most of them seemed to be sleepy and tired. That must be because of the medicine which they had all been given from the same spoon. The man in the caged bed was about forty and covered in blue and red marks. His face was creased in pain. Another was fastened to the bed with chains around his ankles. When he was sleeping his feet hit the iron bed frame which rattled the chains. When Franz lay down, he could feel every spring, because the mattress was so thin. As often as he could he stood up beside the bed. The windows in the room were barred and inside the doors did not have any handles. He remembered when his sister Senta was in the psychological clinic. You could talk to the people through the window. As often as he could, Franz stood in front of the window and looked out. But there was nothing going on in the street below.

The inmates, who were not chained or were thought to be not dangerous, were allowed to go into a neighbouring room and occupy themselves creatively. It was amazing what they hand crafted, drew and painted. One made a ship in a bottle. He drew up the most beautiful plans for a larger ship and Franz was really interested in building it. Franz managed to get together the material, bit by bit. Already with the first boat that Franz had built after two weeks, everyone was amazed. He gave the boat to the Professor, saying, "If the next boat is even better, then you can swap it." That was his trick to get better material. Everyone was afraid of Maria, the fat nurse who did the injections. Franz could smell her sweat a long way off. He also saw that the same needle was used over and over without being changed or disinfected.

Franz did not know how long he would remain there. He was worried. He had the feeling that no one outside knew where he was. He felt alone and forgotten. He soon began to throw little letters out of the window, hoping that someone would find them and tell Josefine. He did not know what else he could do. He did not address them to Josefine Dorn , but to Mrs. Pfeiffer in Vordersberg. He thought that would not be so dangerous. On the other hand, the people working there had always told him that Josefine new where he was. No one could do anything about the fact that she could not visit him. But he really wanted to know how things were at home. One time, Maria said, "Yes. That's the same for most of the people here, but we are forbidden to act as postmen. And anyway, the section was for deranged people. If, one day, you behave normally, then you'll be transferred to a normal prison or you'll end up in a work camp. You are a political prisoner and that's how it goes with people like you. It all depends on the Professor." "How can you assume that I am here because of my political opinions?" Maria answered, "I'm not saying anything more and you should forget anything I have said."

One day a German speaking Bulgarian brought Josefine a note. He was responsible for the garden area round the clinic and he had found it there. He had had the note for three days. Now that he had to collect saplings in the region, he thought that it was safe to bring it to her. He had got the address from the people in the milk shop. Josefine heard that he was going back to the clinic and that he had another Bulgarian in the comical three wheeled vehicle. She wanted to take the opportunity to go with him. At first the Bulgarian refused to take her with him, but then she persuaded him and hid herself on the trailer between the trees on jute sacks and under a brown blanket. When she reached the area around the clinic they stopped under a large weeping willow, where Josefine quickly got off the trailer. She hid the blanket under a bush and went to the clinic entrance. She had to show her identity card right away, but then she was told that there was no one there with the name Dorn. She did not trust herself to show the note and felt completely helpless. She went round the building, looked into every window and sat down on a bench. Then she thought of Alfred. He could certainly do more than her. She took the blanket from its hiding place, took a sip out of a small stream, to quench her thirst and left. As she was walking along the narrow road a Red Cross car overtook her slowly and she heard someone ask, "What are you doing here, Mrs. Dorn?" Josefine recognised Mr. Reisin. "Please tell me you are going to Vordersberg," she said, "then you have to take me there. As I see it, you are not in a hurry and you are not carrying any patients." But before Mr. Reisin could answer, his passenger said, "Come on, we have to drive on. It's forbidden to take private people with us." "Ah go on," Mr. Reisin said, "we're going home. She can sit on the bench behind and when the time is right, we'll drop her off. It will be dark then. She has children at home and they'll be happy when their mother gets back." To Josefine he said, "Hurry up. Jump up behind and make sure the door is closed." When they were not far from Alfred's house she knocked on the window. "Can I get out here?" "Yes, open the door quickly and close it after you. We'll stay in the car." "All right. Thank you." As soon as she got out, the car drove on.

Josefine knocked quietly on Alfred's door. "Who's there?" "It's me, Josefine." Everything whispered. People had got used to whispering. The door opened. Alfred poked his head out, looked around and quickly let her in. "What's going on with you?" he asked, "I've seen people taking things out of the workshop. Erwin told me that they took anything that was metal and I know that is all for the munitions factory. They've even taken all of Anderl's old beer mugs because of the metal lids. But it seems he had a few special ones at home. He'll almost certainly have to bury those. I'm amazed that Florenz has been spared." Josefine was shocked,

"I know nothing about all that." "But I know about you," Alfred said, "you disappeared and now you turn up here. You know I shouldn't even let you in, especially not in the evening when your husband is not here." Josefine's voice shook ,"That's what it's all about. Franz is in the Punti psychiatric clinic. I got a secret message from him and the person who gave it to me drove me to the clinic, but there they told me Franz wasn't there. There was no one there with that name." She handed him the note. Alfred said, "That is Franz's hand writing and it says here that the person who picks it up should say where he found it." Alfred looked inquiringly at Josefine, "but how did you get this note?" "That is not so important at the moment. What is important is that you go to the clinic in your smart uniform. That will impress them. Then they'll certainly tell you what's wrong with your brother. Please, do something. I have to rush home to the children." "Wait," he held her back, "put this helmet on and pull your jacket over it. We'll take the motorbike, that'll be quicker." They crept out of the house to the shed where he kept his motorbike, pushed it for a while and then rode off. In the courtyard in front of the workshop she gave him the helmet and the jacket and ran up the stairs. Erwin was with the children. The good guy had given the children something to eat. "Have you eaten?" "A little." "Come, you can eat some bread and dripping. Just eat. I have to go into the workshop. Have you got the key?" "Yes, it's hanging there." Josefine ran so quickly down the stairs that she almost fell. Only the outside door was closed. With beating heart she went in. "Oh! My God! What a mess! What have they taken?" There were no tools. Hammer, pliers, nails, brackets and the adhesive press, saws and planes, everything had gone. There was not even a piece of wire. All that was left was wood, paper and paints. The cast iron stove and the long pipe through the room was not there, even the tea kettle was missing. Josefine was appalled.

She locked up and climbed up the stairs, almost on all fours. Exhausted she sat on the bench. "Please, bring me a glass of water." Emer went to fetch water and gave it to her. She drank the lukewarm water slowly and told the children to go to bed. Little Fredi was already asleep. Erwin stood up and just nodded and, with tears in his eyes he went home.

Alfred went to the psychiatric clinic early. He was wearing his uniform with his uniform hat on his head and his thin leather case under his arm. In the clinic's entrance hall he marched briskly to the reception desk. His uniform and polished boots made an impression. "Heil Hitler!" he roared. He opened his case, took a few papers out, looked through them and said, "That's it, Franz von Dorn admitted on…" he coughed over the date and said, in a commanding voice, "we need a few important details. Bring him here immediately. I haven't much time. In which room can I wait for him?" "Yes, Sir…" "Don't bother yourself with trivialities. Just bring him here." He was taken to a light airy room. In the middle there was a large desk and two chairs. Could they offer him something to drink? Alfred declined. He stood at the window with his back to the door and listened carefully. After a while he heard steps and the door was opened. He leant down and made as if he was dusting his boots. A voice behind him said, "Here is the person you want." Without turning round he roared, "Are you Franz von Dorn? Leave us alone. The inmate may sit down." "Yes Sir. Thank you." That was Franz's voice. Once the door was closed Alfred turned round and whispered to Franz, "We don't know each other. Understood?" Franz stared at him in amazement and quietly said, "I didn't recognise you from the back." Alfred took a newspaper and a few pages, covered with writing out of his case and spread them swiftly on the desk. Then he looked in the desk drawer in which there was a photo camera. He told Franz to speak, but he did not want to involve him. He just told him how he arrived in the clinic and that he had no idea why.

Alfred looked closely at the photo camera. Then he saw that there was a door leading to a small fenced terrace. He opened the door, took a few paces outside and looked around. Quickly he came back into the room, took of his uniform coat and said to his brother, "Put that on and the hat. I'll take a few photos of you from the terrace. Then I'll take the film with me. Maybe we can do something with it." Franz did as he was told. He was a bit thin, but when he looked in the window, he thought he looked spruce. He had grown a modern Hitler moustache, which he knew would anger Josefine later, but right now it was very useful. Alfred used the camera like a professional. He took as many photographs of Franz as he could until the film was finished. Franz took off the coat and hat, put everything on the desk and sat down in his place. Alfred took the film out of the camera, popped it into his trouser pocket and put the camera back in the drawer. He put on his coat and made a note of all the names which Franz could remember in the clinic, including their positions. Then he became nervous and said. "Now I have to go, before they find out that I have no business to be here." He gave his brother a hasty farewell, wrenched open the door and marched to the reception desk with loud steps. He looked straight ahead, held his hand in front of his hat, like a greeting so that no one could see his face and then looked up to the ceiling and shouted, "Heil Hitler!". The warder stood to attention and held the door open for him. As soon as Alfred was outside he let loose a sigh of relief.

Franz waited until someone came for him. On the way back to his section he saw spittoons everywhere. On the wall behind the reception desk there was a large calendar. It was one where you could tear of the days and next to it there was a clock in a golden frame. Franz asked the warden who was accompanying him, "You, Warden, is that calendar on the wall right?" "Yes, it's right." A man wearing an armband suddenly appeared before them and shouted, "It is not permitted to talk to that sort of individual. He took an ink pen and a notice book out of his pocket, licked the pen several times and wrote down the warden's name. "Discipline! Have you heard the word before? Forwards!

March!" He waved his hands about and disappeared into one of the corridors.

The nurse, Maria, greeted Franz as he came back to the section. "Three days ago it was my birthday," he said, "I'd completely forgotten. How long have I been here?" Suddenly his voice started to tremble and his eyes were moist. "Shush," said Maria, in a friendly way, "don't say another word. Just go and lie down." Franz lay on his bed. His thoughts were all over the place. When Maria came with the medicine he waved her away. She offered him an apple, "Best wishes for your birthday," she whispered and bent forward over him, smelling of sweat. She placed the apple under his bed clothes and hurried away. It's a long time since I ate an apple, he thought as he crawled under the cover and took a bite. Mmm! That tasted good! But no! he had the feeling that his teeth were loose. From then on he massaged his gums regularly and chewed on a soft piece of wood to strengthen his gums. He also did some gymnastic exercises when there was no one in the room apart from the other inmates. He cut his hair as best he could. That was only possible in the occupational room, because that was the only place where there were scissors. Most of the new arrivals had had their heads shaved. Although they had no hair, they were simply sprayed with DDT to kill lice.

Franz began to notice how little time he spent in his room and also that there were often changes. Always new patients. The man in the bed next to him had been there from the start. He did not often trust himself to leave the room, almost never spoke, but he listened when Franz recounted or asked something. But he rarely answered. Now and again he shrugged his shoulders, more not. Maybe it was for the best. If someone knows nothing then they cannot say anything. Franz asked nurse Maria how long he would have to stay there. He was feeling much better. "You're here for political reasons, or have you forgotten? But hush now. Not a word. Ask tomorrow during the doctor's rounds."

The doctor started on his rounds. Franz sat very straight, smoothed down his blonde hair, pinched his cheeks so that they looked pink and smoothed his eyebrows with a little spit. When the Professor came to his bed he re-arranged his striped collar. "Can I go home?" Franz asked, "I'm feeling normal." "Yes," mocked the Professor, "we all want to go home," and opened his file. "Now who have we here? What is your name? Ah, yes, Dorn Franz." Then he read from the file, "His brain development is that of a ten year old: Sometimes confused: Weak memory, weak skeletal development, etc., etc,. Pure Aryan. Politics. Apparently not a member of any party." The Professor looked at him inquiringly, "That's suspicious... Well, I don't have to explain that to you. You probably know better yourself." He closed the file and grabbed Franz by the ear and whispered, "That with the measuring, already since the third I didn't fall for it." Then, aloud he said, "Until our examinations are complete, you'll be detained here. And another thing," his face went red, "talking to other inmates and the personnel will be punished. So hold your tongue." In the following days the Professor kept his distance from Franz, he did not even come near him. Franz did not take what he had said seriously. It's all rubbish, he said to himself and he almost had to laugh as he remembered; pure Aryan with an underdeveloped brain. What were they thinking? Probably Aryans are like that. Otherwise they would not do such stupid things.

Since Alfred's appearance, Franz looked more and more out of the window. He prepared a note to throw in case he saw someone he recognised. And then, one morning he saw Josefine standing on the road. He waved, but she did not see him. For half an hour she scrutinized all the faces she saw behind the bars, but she did not find Franz. From some of the windows people held out a hand and waved. She felt queasy. Then she heard a whistle. She recognised the tune and looked up where the melody came from. He waved a handkerchief and let the note fall. Josefine looked up and gave a short wave, while she took off her head scarf and arranged it again over her head. She waited a while before she picked up the note and through the corner of her eye looked around. Without attracting attention she picked up the note and disappeared into the nearby park. She read, "If the family is fine, put your hand on your heart and look upwards to the right. Otherwise look to the left. Business OK, hand on forehead and turn head to right, not OK left. Don't worry I'm more or less all right. I know you'll manage until I get out. With love, your future husband." Josefine understood that they were signs she should give him. She went back, made as if she had a headache and gave him the signs. Suddenly she saw the security man coming, wearing a Swastika armband. She waved up and walked a few steps further. She had put the note in her mouth. Alfred had warned her she should do nothing, or they would take her as well.

Alfred took the film of Franz in uniform to Otto, an acquaintance and a hobby photographer, who had his own dark room and could develop it. Alfred paid in advance, because he wanted to be there when the film was developed, but he did not see much in the narrow room. Otto grinned when he saw what was emerging. He clipped the photographs in reverse on to a string and said to Alfred. "When these are dry, take them down." Then he went on with his other work. As the photos seemed to be dry, Alfred took them down without looking at them. He put them into his bag, together with the negatives and went to his father, who was ill and lying in bed. When he heard that Berta and Senta had just left, he closed the door behind him and spread the photos out on the table. What he then saw, made him speechless. The first was a well dressed woman with two boys. Then the same two boys with a man, probably their father. But most of the photos were of two young women in obscene positions and always with the same man. It was the same man as in the picture with the boys. In the background Alfred recognised the room in the clinic where he had met Franz. The other photos were of Franz wearing the officer's coat and hat on the small terrace. But most of the photos showed the striped clinic trousers. Only one of the photos had really been successful. In that photo the trousers and felt slippers were in shadow and hidden by the ivy. The head was straight, almost in profile and the Hitler moustache could be seen clearly, the light coloured eyes, knitted brow with one hand behind his back and the other clutching the belt. Alfred put this photo into his breast pocket. He intended to take more photos of Franz in uniform. He wanted to throw the rest of the photos into the stove, but suddenly he had an idea, and only threw the bad photos of Franz into the fire. He put the others into an envelope. Alfred went to the hobby photographer and asked him for more copies of that one good photo. When that was done he went to Josefine. She was very depressed and wailed, “Everything is running out. Almost no one comes here. Anderl brought me a piece of bacon. That’s all we have to eat. I know a farmer who took the dogs. He probably has something to spare, but then you have to go over the pass. That takes half a day. Do you think you could arrange that?” Alfred thought about it. He could use something from there himself. “Do you have someone who could take care of the children?” “I’m sure I could find someone. Emer is still here. He could look after the children. Gerdi is afraid that she could also be taken away, because of Franz. She doesn’t come any more, even though I owe her money for the last two months. I told her that I couldn’t pay her right now. She said that was all right. I shouldn’t worry about it.”

Suddenly they heard a noise, “Shush,” she said and put her finger to her lips. She heard steps approaching the door. The children were all in the other room. Alfred jumped up, quickly opened the window and put the photos, which were suddenly burning a hole in his breast pocket, out on the window sill and placed a flower pot over them. He had only just closed the window as the door handle moved. Josefine, who had her ear pressed to the door, was shocked, but she pulled herself together. Who was there? It was her mother, dressed in black as usual. She had a large rucksack on her back and an enormous bag in her hand. It was the first time that Josefine had seen her mother carrying a rucksack. "Jesus! Mother, where have you come from?" she said, totally surprised, "You really gave us a shock." "Could this gentleman take my rucksack," said her mother and gave Alfred a stern penetrating look with her dark eyes. "Excuse me, I'm Alfred Dorn." "Well take it, before I fall over," she said, impatiently. Alfred jumped forward and took the rucksack. It was really very heavy. Mother sat down on a chair. Josefine brought her a glass of water and began to massage her shoulders. The straps had cut in, she could feel it through her clothes. "I've got some brandy in my rucksack. You can rub it in."

Alfred had waited, tactfully, but now he stood up, bowed to the mother, who had introduced herself as Mrs. Theresa, and turned to Josefine, "For the moment everything is settled. I'll go now." Then he remembered the photos, which he took from the window sill. "I have something for you, he whispered, "look. It's a photo of Franz. If anyone asks you how it was taken, then you must say that you found it in his things." Josefine handed the brandy to her mother, looked in amazement at Alfred and took the photo from him. When she recognised Franz, tears came to her eyes. "That's all right," she said, "I'll do that. God protect you." With a nod of the head he took his leave from the old woman and went out of the door. Josefine looked in her mother's rucksack. It was full of food. She took out some bacon and bread and ran after Alfred. "Here, take this. Mother has brought enough."

Then the children came from the other room and greeted grandmother. "Please, please, let's go back to the caravan today," Emer begged and fastened himself round her neck. "First we have to eat something," said grandmother and pressed her grandchild to her, "and first we have to wash our hands," she added when she noticed Emer's hands. "But first, give me a kiss. Reinhard and Emer, bring the pram. I want to say hello to Fredi." Emer rushed into the living room with Fredi, who was now six months old. Grandmother said, "My sweet little boy," and kissed him warmly. Josefine did not know what she should tell her and what would be better left unsaid. Reinhard had problems talking, he was very reticent. Josefine encouraged him to tell his grandmother about himself, but he became very excited and started to roam around the room. Then he ran into the other room and brought out his wooden toys to show his grandmother. "Those are very pretty things," she said in amazement, "I think your father made them. Anyway, where is he?" I suppose he's in the workshop." Then Emer blurted out, "No. Father has been taken away by the Gestapo." Josefine took her son to one side, "Listen, Emer. Let me tell her what has happened. I don't want you to tell her everything" "Yes, mummy, but everyone else knows about it. I haven't told anyone. They just know." "That's all right, son. You're a good boy." Josefine kissed his hair and told him to go and wash his hands.

Late into the night mother and daughter sat together and told each other what had happened recently. "Your sister Rosa wants to marry and move to Wienerneustadt," said mother, "I think she's expecting a child. He's called Kurt and he's a welder and a really nice person. When I told Kurt he should watch out for Rosa, because of her temperament, so that nothing goes wrong, he said, 'That's all right. I love her the way she is. Rosa has a good heart. I feel it and she loves me very much. That's the main thing.'" Mother continued. "Anna, Father and I are also going to live there. Our best friends and relations live close by. As you see, Josefine, we have stopped travelling and it's time we had an official place of residence. We always have to defend ourselves, so that people don't think we're Gypsies. We are entertainers and artists on tour and that is neither forbidden nor objectionable."

Gerdi stopped working there and only ever came to visit. So mother decided to stay with Josefine and the children. The children were happy to have a grandmother at home. Mother told them that Josefine's brother, Fritz, because he spoke so many languages, was often asked to act as interpreter for important people and was also driven around in chic cars. He had also flown in an aeroplane and almost died of fright. It was on one of these occasions he had met his pretty wife, Magdalena. "She is a widow. Some years ago her husband was found shot in a boat out at sea. He was supposed to have a briefcase with him, but that had completely disappeared. Magdalena had a small daughter and a pretty little house. Fritz had really found happiness. They seemed to have been made for each other."

After a while grandmother's travel lust returned and she could not stay there any longer. She missed her nomadic life and longed to return to the caravan. She understood Emer very well. After a few weeks she went to visit her husband and took Emer with her. She also visited friends and relations and came back refreshed and relaxed.

Franz was still in the psychiatric clinic. Alfred was able to meet him, using various tricks. Even Josefine trusted herself to go to the clinic again. When they did not want to find Franz on the list of inmates, she cheekily showed the photo of him in Nazi uniform. They then allowed her to visit him for ten minutes once a month. A comrade from the resistance worked in the clinic and advised Franz and Josefine not to try too hard for his release. Many fellow comrades had disappeared or had had a fatal 'accident' after their release. The safest place for Franz was in the clinic.

Because he was good at making things, Franz was liked and useful. In the meantime he built ever larger ships. He even got money for them that he was able to send to Josefine by post. He did not know that she never received it. She could not scrape the money together for the rent of the flat and the workshop. Nobody could work Florenz's machines, so there were no scraps of wood to be had. She was in arrears and, with a heavy heart she gave up the workshop. It was once again rented out as a flat and a new tiled stove was installed. Almost all the material which had been in the workshop had been used up and the little which was left was stored in the wooden hut. Josefine and grandmother had to search around for food and work. Josefine remembered the farmer, Mr. Katz and his wife. She managed to convince the inn owner Anderl to lend her the money for the journey. She set out almost at once and took Reinhard with her.

A lot had changed on the Katz's farm. The farm was often visited by special supply troops, which took most of their produce. As recompense, they supplied them with people who had to work on the farm. However, most of them had no idea about agriculture. The farmer had to plant as much as possible of his land with cereal crops and potatoes. That was an order from above, as he said. Josefine heard about many problems from the farmer's wife. They wanted to keep the German shepherds which Josefine had brought them, but it would be better to place them somewhere else, because otherwise they could not guarantee that they would survive. It had already happened that dogs had landed in the cooking pot. Josefine decided to take the dogs home with her.

Of course, the farmer's wife noticed that Josefine was pregnant and asked her about it. Josefine gave vent to her feelings. She was truly troubled with the idea of bringing another child into the world in these terrible times. "Then give the child to me," Mrs. Katz said and looked at her beseechingly, "little Ernst or little Christina, that's what I would call my children. Dear Josefine, whatever comes, I'll gladly take the child. Here with us, the children still have a good life." Then she turned to Reinhard, "And you, wouldn't you like to stay with us? Maybe just for a few days at first?" Reinhard said, "No…" and disappeared in the folds of his mother's skirt. Josefine said, "That sounds so simple, but first let's wait until the baby arrives."

They took leave of each other like two good friends, with tears in their eyes. "From now on we'll use the familiar form to each other. Do you agree?" "Yes," said Josefine, "I agree and I'll come again if I may. God protect you." Josefine was able to fill her bag with vegetables and fruit. "Come, take this with you as well, otherwise someone else will take it," said the farmer's wife and gave her flour, corn and other things in a rucksack. Fully laden, Josefine, Reinhard and the dogs set out on the journey home. In the bus she took Reinhard on her lap and held him tight. He slept throughout the journey. So now, for the moment, we have something to eat. I'll give Anderl the schnapps, as part payment for the trip money.

What does dog meat taste like? Can you tell the difference? What other meat does it taste like? Is it dark or light like veal? These were not the only questions going through her head. Both the dogs were lying quietly at her feet. One of them kept looking at her sideways with sad eyes, as though he could read her thoughts. Oh, no! thought Josefine, now I'm going to have to carry this stuff from the bus station to the house. How can I do that without anyone to help me? The bus drove passed the house, but, except in an emergency, no one was permitted to get off the bus anywhere else but the bus station. Ah, I can make use of my pregnancy. When they were almost there she shouted, "Conductor, tell the driver that he has to stop at the petrol station. I'm pregnant and I think I'm going to be sick." "It's only a kilometre to the bus stop. Surely you can hang on till then." She pushed the dogs to the door, and dragged her things with her. "I really feel sick," she whined, "let me off." The driver stopped at the petrol station, because he thought that if she vomited, he would have to clean up the mess. The conductor helped her down from the bus. A gentleman took the opportunity and also got off. He helped her with all her things right to the door. A woman came down the stairs and said, "Have you found some food?" Josefine was saying something to Reinhard and simply said, "Good day." She should have said, "Heil Hitler." Josefine coughed. Up to now she had got away without the Nazi greeting. But for how long?

The dogs barked. They recognised the place where they used to live. Grandmother was happy to see Reinhard with rosy cheeks and started to unpack what Josefine had brought. "We have to hide them," she whispered. Josefine took the bottle of schnapps out of the bag and went over to Anderl. There were only two men in the inn and they were consulting their diaries and some other documents. As Anderl was filling two glasses with the schnapps Josefine told him about the dogs and that she had heard they could also be slaughtered. "Is that true?" she asked him nervously. "Yes, there's some truth in that." "You know where the dogs come from. I had to bring them home." "Watch out that they don't go wandering out on the street. If they do, they will certainly disappear." "Look. It's like this," and she put on a worried face, "I can't keep them in the flat with the children and anyway, they need somewhere to run around. The courtyard behind your house would be ideal." She gave him an imploring look. Anderl said, "Yes you can easily salt dog meat in an oak barrel, for example from Florenz. He has one which is almost empty. Right now I've got a few litres of cider in it. Think about it. I know a good butcher and he knows what to do with herbs. No one knows what meat it is. And, by they way, the fat from dog meat is supposed to be a very good medicine for lung infections." "Ugh! Stop," Josefine shuddered. Anderl went on, "The neighbours have certainly not yet seen the dogs. Your washing room would be a good place to slaughter the dogs, because you can shutter the windows and apart from that, you have enough room in the cellar to hide the barrel. They make too many controls here. I've got enough problems trying to hide my own things. And by the way, thanks for the schnapps. Mmm! That tastes as if it's from a private distillery! But meat would be better." He grinned. Josefine said, "So, as far as money is concerned, we're quit?" "Yes, of course." He took the glasses away. Josefine had not quite finished her schnapps, because it was too strong. Anderl did not want to throw the rest away, so he poured it back into the bottle.

Josefine went home. Emer was standing there. He was afraid of the dogs. Reinhard liked them and gave them something to drink. The farmer's wife had also given them something to eat. But tomorrow and the day after? thought Josefine, what are we going to give them then? She told Reinhard that in future he should not use any crockery which the family used. She would find something just for the dogs. She picked up the dish from the floor and washed it in hot water and soda. The next day she went to the butcher, "Can I have remains and bones for two dogs, please?" A customer jokingly asked, "Have they got two legs?" and the other customers laughed. One customer said, "It must be for a soup." Josefine blushed and, in defence said, "No. It's for my dogs." "All right," said the butcher, "come back just before I close. Maybe I'll have something then."

She brooded on the way home. Bones and remains for dogs, in these times? No there are too many hungry people. Grandmother complained about the dogs. "They smell. Can't we find somewhere else for them? And why on earth did you bring them here?" she whined. Josefine grabbed the dogs, went into Anderl's courtyard and knocked on the back door. Anderl came out, "Jesus? You bring them here in daylight! Who saw you?" "I don't think anyone saw me." Anderl said, "All right. I'll tell you when we need the key to the washing room. You must get the key." Josefine nodded and left. That was hard. She had tears in her eyes.

What am I going to tell Mrs. Schorch, or even Mrs. Weisser when they come back? I'll just have to try not to think about it. Grandmother looked at Josefine, "You haven't just chased them out onto the street?" "No. I gave them to someone. Every thing's in order." Grandmother said, "That was quick. By the way, have you paid the last rent? I think the caretaker wants something from you." "Oh no, no. Not again. I don't know when I last paid the rent." Grandmother said, "He said he'd come back today." "Josefine said, "I'll have to give him some of the Franz schnapps, just to calm him down." "But, child," said grandmother, "he wants some money. You're going to have to ask Berta or Alfred, or someone else. I've got a few coins for an emergency in my pocket. If we put it all together it'll last for a while. "Suddenly Josefine listened carefully. "I can hear steps. Quick, hide everything."

Like lightning they packed all the food back in the bag and rucksack and shoved them into the other room under the bed. Someone knocked on the door. Grandmother sat down on a chair with her back to the door. Josefine straightened her hair and her dress and opened the door. It was the caretaker. "Hello, Mr. Gosch. I know that I'm behind with the rent. My dearest mother and I were just talking about it. I promise you that I'll pay tomorrow." Mr Gosch said, "I don't think it's right to demand the rent, when I know about your financial situation. Everyone in the house has money problems, but what should I do? I have to do my duty. Have you asked the council or the social authorities? Right now your husband is not here. Since you are the mother of three children and obviously in a certain condition, you should ask for support. I'll give you a paper. It shows how much rent you owe. I've already added the next two months. Please try to go to the office tomorrow morning." Josefine thanked him for his advice and promised that on the next day, she would be the first person waiting at the council office. "They'll give you priority," he said and looked at her stomach. "Just a moment," something else had come into his thoughts, "there could be another, additional solution. The family who recently moved into the former workshop are leaving. The head of the family had to join the army. His wife is going to her mother and her father is already in the army. So you could take their flat. The rent is 40% less." "I'll have to think about it, Mr. Gosch," Josefine said and thanked him for the well meant information. "At first, I'll try with the council and the social authorities. I'll let you know tomorrow."

Early the next morning Josefine went to the council and the social office. Both offices gave her an allowance, but it was simply not enough. Then she went to Berta, but could not bring herself to come to the point. Franz's father gave her a little something, but she was ashamed and just squeezed his hand, "Thank you father, but I'll have to find another way." When she got home she went straight to the caretaker. She put all the money which she had scraped together on the table. "Is that all?" Mr. Gosch asked. "Yes. All right, I'll move into the old workshop. But the flat is smaller and I can't take all the valuable furniture which Mrs. Schorch left behind with me." "We can leave Mrs. Schorch's furniture where it is," he said, "so she can find everything just as she left it when she comes back." Josefine was surprised, "I'm not altogether happy with that. I have the use of the furniture while Mrs. Schorch is away." "That's all right. Take the pieces you can find room for. But nothing must be taken out of the house." Josefine agreed.

The former workshop had two rooms, a sleeping/living room and another one where one could cook. There was a two burner gas stove. Then there was a large workbench in the corner. She could not take the bed with her, because it would take up too much room. Josefine took the work bench out of the cellar and put the three mattresses on it. That gave the children three, narrow places to sleep. Florenz offered his help. He shortened the legs on the workbench. That way they could sit on it during the day. The green, tiled oven was much loved, because you could sit on the surrounding tiles which were always warm. The children seemed to like it. There was enough place in the kitchen for the office cupboard and the chair. The only things left behind in the old flat were the heavy pieces of furniture. Grandmother packed everything which could be of use. Everything which she could not put in the flat, she put into the room in front of the cellar which Florenz barricaded. Mr. Gosch, had no idea, apart from the furniture, what belonged to Mrs. Schorch. Josefine wanted to look after everything, but grandmother was not so particular and used some of the things to barter for food. "It's the emergency, which makes us do this," she said. "Don't worry. I know that Mrs. Schorch will understand when she comes back and she will return." She said it with such conviction. And years later, she was proved right.

Franz was still in the clinic and the nurse, Maria, had fallen in love with him. In secret she brought him fruit and arranged that he could wear his own clothes, but he had to sew a strip on the front and back of his pullover with his registration number. He noticed that there were very few mentally ill people left around him. Where were all those people who he had so often heard screaming? He also noticed that hearses often drove up. He could see them from the barred lavatory window if he stood on the seat. "Today, very early in the morning they pushed four small coffins into a car," he told Alfred when he came to visit him out of uniform. He was always annoyed that Franz talked about such things in the few minutes they had together. "Now you're seeing ghosts. Don't start spying around. I've set everything in motion to get you released legally. Luckily, up to now no court processes have been started against you. We're trying to avoid that. Just stay calm. Don't lose your nerve. We know that this is a good time to get you out of here. It would be easy to escape, but until we can find a legal way to get you released, then it's better to stay here." After that Franz could not sleep peacefully. His heart started to beat faster whenever the door was closed from outside. The bars on the windows closed him in and when it was dark and the moon didn't shine he was afraid. Nurse Maria knew that he was unsettled, although he would not admit it. But he flattered her, whispered how much he loved her and how much he dreamed of being with her in freedom. She kissed him, admitted that she loved him too and almost crushed him with her weight. The smell of her sweat stayed in the air for a long time. Franz washed all the parts of his body which she had touched with the drinking water from his bedside table.

From that day on, there was no day without Maria. When she came, she placed his hands on her ample breasts, on her thighs and in other places… and she thrust her tongue so far into his mouth that he almost gagged. Franz overcame his inhibitions, did his part and drew a heart with an arrow for her, using nicknames rather than any give away letters. He had a plan. Little by little he discovered if Maria had access to the patients' files in the office. She said yes, but what did he want with them? she asked in amazement. If he had the complete list of names and there was no Franz on it, then he could live with her in freedom. "Many people leave here everyday," he said, "why not me? Why wait? I've got enough money stashed away. We could go to America or anywhere else where we would be safe and could start a new life. Without you, my darling, my life is worth nothing." He looked at her, kissed her and went on, "I'm a miner, almost an engineer. I can be self employed in almost any country. Just imagine. You and me. How romantic it could be. Our fate is in your hands. Please, darling, try. If you want something badly enough, then you will find a way. But, be careful, my angel, I don't want to lose you." Then the door opened and his bed neighbour came in. Luckily, because Franz was feeling very bad about his lies. Maria was just able to squeeze his hand and then she left the room. I have to get out, I have to get out, hammered through his head. The coffins were in his head. He no longer trusted himself to look out of the lavatory window.

Maria started, secretly to go through the drawers in the small office where the files were kept. She knew that she had no permission to be there, but this was not clearly written anywhere. Once she managed to look at the list of names for a few seconds. Some lines had been deleted with thick black ink. Some of them had a cross beside them and a date. There were various causes of death: inflammation of the lungs, heart attack, kidney failure, influenza, but also, shot whilst attempting to escape. Only two people were responsible for this office. Up to now Maria had never been interested in what had happened to the people when they left.

You never get a clear answer, she told herself in order to justify her indifference.

Then she had the opportunity to get a real look at the files. It was the birthday of one of her superiors and everyone wanted to go and congratulate him. Maria saw that one of the secretaries had hung the key behind a pillar. She waited until she heard the people laughing and singing a birthday song and then she acted quickly. She took the key, went into the office, unlocked the door and ran to the drawer. There she quickly found a file for Franz Dorn. She hid it under her blouse and still had time to conceal Franz's name on the list, which was hanging on the wall, with black ink. She locked the office and went to the door where the birthday celebrations were in full swing. With a happy heart and a smile on her face she sang, "May he live long". She looked around. The doorman was standing outside taking some fresh air and had obviously noticed nothing. The she went into the therapy room where Franz was, went to the only warden in the room and told him about the birthday celebration. Everyone had received a glass of wine. He should try his luck and anyway, it is often advantageous to congratulate a superior on his birthday. "You think so?" "Yes, of course. Go on. I'll stay here until you come back." Smiling, she adjusted his collar and pushed him out of the door. Hypocritically, she went to the patients and gave them a few encouraging words.

When she got to Franz she took the file from under her blouse and put it down on the table where his ship was standing. The ship was so big that nobody could see the file. He went through it, quickly. In the file were the names of the comrades who had denounced him – probably because they had been brutally tortured. Franz was accused of: "Suspicion of political opposition. No concrete evidence. Reason for admission – mental confusion." He had just spotted his identity papers when the door was opened violently. The warden marched in red in the face. To Maria he hissed, "He didn't even give me his hand when I congratulated him. He just looked down his nose at me and left me standing there as though I was in the wrong place." Maria thought about the files and inside she was like a pillar of salt. Then the warden went back to shut the door. She grabbed the files and hid them once again under her blouse. "I'm sorry,' she said feigning sympathy, "I thought you knew the birthday boy," and with an innocent smile, she left.

In the corridor she saw a group of outraged people coming towards her. Quick-wittedly she went into the personnel lavatory and locked the door. She put her ear to the door and tried to hear what was going on. Then someone knocked on the door and she was shocked. "Just a minute," she called and was suddenly afraid. I have to get rid of the files! Someone knocked again. Oh God! What shall I do? She stuffed them all into the lavatory bowl until her arm was up to the elbow. She pulled the chain twice and then pulled her sleeve down and opened the door.

There was a moment of tension and then she gave a very thin patient, who was standing in front of her wearing a striped shirt, a heavy blow in the ribs. He fell to the highly polished floor with a horrible scream and slid a few metres away. Two men from the group ran to Maria, who was out of breath. "What's going on here?" "She went haywire," the other said. They looked at the patient, who was still screaming, took him by the arms and dragged him into a room. When they came out, Maria was still standing there. The men joined up with the group, as though nothing had happened and Maria went back into the lavatory to retrieve the files, but without success. The files were gone. What should she tell Franz? Should she tell him anything? Then she went into the medicine room to disinfect her arm.

A colleague was sitting there on a swivel chair. He had a tray in front of him on which there were two hypodermics with yellow-violet liquid in them and alongside it there was a bottle containing the same liquid. He pulled a list of room and patient numbers out of a pocket in his white smock. Then he looked at Maria and said, "Where were you during the selection? I've prepared everything. We can start." Maria asked, "What do you mean? What can we start?" "Did you not meet the men? They have made drastic selections. Those who get the injection and those who don't. Here is the list. We have to do this together." Maria said, "What sort of vaccination is that?" "No idea. And I don't want to know. Someone put the bottle on my table." Maria took the bottle in her hand and held it up to the light. "It smells like petrol." "Stop! It is an order from above." Maria asked, "Can I see the list?" She grabbed the list and looked for Franz' room number. For a moment her heart stood still. Why was he on the list? "What criteria were used for the choice?" "No idea," was the answer. "Listen. I'll say it once more. I don't want to know. Come, let's get on with it. I want to finish my days work."

With shaking hands he wiped the sweat from his brow and picked up the list, stood in front of the first door and noted the time. Maria put the tray on the trolley and followed him. Her colleague called out the names of the men who had to lie down on their beds. As if in a fog Maria went from bed to bed and gave each one an injection. Her colleague filled the empty hypodermic for the next one. When she came to Franz's bed, she pushed his sleeve up, pressed her finger nails into his arm and injected the serum into his clothing. He made a grimace and said 'Ow!" He understood that that was the death injection! There had been some whispered rumours in the therapy room. I have to get out of here, went through his head. Now! No time to lose! Alfred was here yesterday. I saw his motorcycle on the other side of the street. Was it his? There was a blue cloth over the saddle. That's our sign. Couldn't he have contacted me?

Once Maria and the colleague were in the next room, a warder in a white smock came in. "Come" he almost dragged Franz out of the bed, gave him a pair of shoes and pushed him through the corridor towards the reception hall. He stopped at a coat rack which was full of jackets and coats, took off a leather coat with a Swastika armband, and held it out for Franz to slip on, grabbed a hat and pushed it on to Franz's head so that one could hardly see his face. At the exit there was a clinic warden who should have ordered a taxi. "So, where is our taxi?" he shouted and looked down the street. On the other side of the street there were a few black cars flying Swastika flags. He called again, "Taxi! Taxi!" Franz and his "warden" used that moment to run down the other side of the steps. There they found a taxi. They threw open the door, leapt in and the taxi drove off at top speed. When they had left the psychiatric clinic, the taxi driver said, 'That was a bit precarious."

Franz did not know in which direction they were going. Once they were in the car the "warden" took off his white smock and spoke to Franz using the German familiar form. "Now you can take off the coat but keep the hat on. But what is that smell of petrol? I don't even trust myself to light a cigarette." Franz realised that the man was not an enemy and, in a few words, told him what had happened. "As you can see, the nurse injected the liquid into my pullover. The man in the next bed was amazed that the injection didn't take effect immediately. He even said, "My God! You need an extra dose." The "warder", who said his name was Paul, gave Franz a horrified look, "What? They had already got to you? Show me. Oh yes, your pullover and shirt are full of the stuff. No, we didn't know anything about that."

The taxi stopped in a country lane in front of a small grass mound. Paul hid the clinic smock, the leather coat and the taxi sign together with the roof lights, in a hidden space under the mound. "That is your hiding place? Very clever, from here you can see nothing," Franz remarked. Then they continued on their way. Franz asked, "Where are we going?" "The comrades have freed you, now you have to disappear." "What?" Franz asked, "But I don't have any papers. Maria has them." The comrade asked, "Which Maria?" "Nurse Maria," Franz replied. She got my papers and showed them to me. All the documents are in a folder. We wanted to go away together. Maria had fallen for me and did everything for me. Probably today or tomorrow we would have run away. That's why she didn't give me the injection." The taxi driver shook his head, "Huh! That's how it goes in a mad house."

Franz said, "As far as I know, before someone goes on the run you get identity papers or at least false documents. Have you got anything like that?" The comrade hesitated. Franz was annoyed.

Paul said, "Now listen here, Comrade Dorn, we had no time. You would have been long dead if we had waited to get papers. And anyway, we were not sure that we could get you out alive. I'm sorry, but you have to understand. You'll get your papers." Franz calmed down a bit, "Yesterday my brother was there. I saw his motorbike from the window. I have no idea what he has done in the meantime. Without papers you're nobody. I won't get far like that. If they catch me or someone wants to check me out, then I am done for. And I can't go to my wife. If I did that, I might as well hang myself." Paul asked, "I thought you were divorced. Are you together again?" Franz replied, "No, not with her, with another." The driver started to laugh out loud, "And nurse Maria? You seem to have luck with women. Can you give me a few tips?" "Stop it. There's nothing to laugh about! My hard earned money is still in the mattress."

Franz took off his pullover, "Give me something to get rid of this inmate number." Paul gave him a pocket knife. "What are you really called? I don't know you from Adam and you're capable of anything. Who knows if it's good for me? But now everything's already screwed up." Paul said, "It's better if you don't know our names. Don't be afraid, we're all in the same boat." They drove up a hill. Paul got out and held his hand towards the brow of the hill. "On the other said, everything is quiet. Come, let's drive on."

Franz looked at the beautiful countryside; a few isolated houses; many fields. It looked so peaceful. "Can I get out for a moment? I need to relieve myself, but seriously." "Yes, just wait. We have to change the number plates. We have another hiding place close by. Just go a few steps. We'll see you then." Franz went into the bushes, squatted down and was almost finished when he heard shots and heard a voice, just a few meters away. "Examine them! Quick! Don't let them out of your sight." Franz's knees began to shake. He dared not make a move. His head was thumping. The veins in his temples were so swollen that his head ached. "Where have you come from?" the voice said, "and where are you going? Have you got identity papers? What's wrong with the number plate?"

Now Franz knew that his comrades were in danger. In fear he started to shake and sat down in his own business. "Shit," he said quietly to himself, and, although it was disgusting, he remained in there until he heard, "Everything's in order. Screw the number plates on properly. We'll drive behind you to the next junction." The car and a few motorbikes started up. The noise got quieter and quieter. Soon he could only hear the birds twittering. Franz cleaned his behind with grass and moss, pulled up his trousers and looked around. He did not know where he was. He heard a soft splashing sound coming from a small stream finding its way down the hill. All around it looked as though no human life had ever set foot there. He washed himself, cooled his brow with the fresh water and quenched his thirst.

He sat down and looked at his shoes. Whose shoes were they? They were almost new, he mumbled to himself; one size too big and the heel was a bit too high. He took the laces, which, because he had left the clinic so quickly, he had not fastened and tied them. The sun was shining. He had no better idea than to wait. Then he thought that you could also lie down to wait. The whole scene of his flight played in his head like a film. He had never imagined it like this. He was tired and fell asleep. He woke for a moment and saw above him the sky full of stars. Then he went on sleeping.

Early the next morning, he shook himself awake and went carefully down the narrow road. He came to a junction where the road went right and left. There was a road sign which showed two place names. He did not recognise either of them. Franz took the down hill road. There was mist hanging over the valley. The stars disappeared one by one and it was freezing cold. After a while he smelt a fire. He saw a plume of smoke rising. Looking more closely, he saw a plump women baking bread. I could ask her where I am, and went in that direction. But oops, she stood threateningly in front of him with raised wooden shovel and asked what he wanted. To show he meant no harm he raised his hands, "Yesterday I got lost in the woods and in the dusk I couldn't find my way, so I lay down until it was light. I have lost the people I was with. Where am I now? Where is the nearest train station, so I can get home?" "Well it's not just round the corner," she answered, "you're going to have to walk quite a way. Still, you're lucky that the weather is so dry and warm, otherwise you could not have slept out in the open." Franz stared at all the fresh bread lying on the two boards. The women broke a piece off one of the loaves and offered it to him, "Take this for your journey." To show her that he had no money to pay her, he put his hands in his trouser pockets. When he took them out he had the bit of material with his number on it in his hand. The women saw it, knew what it meant and stretched out her arm. Reluctantly he gave it to her. He was relieved to see that she put it in the oven, but not without a small ritual. She placed it on the wooden shovel and then in the oven. "Be careful," she said to him, sincerely, "go down through the beech wood. It's quite steep and make sure that you don't spoil your shoes. You'll see the train station after about half an hour. Wait until the first train comes. It's always full of workers. You won't be noticed, even though you haven't shaved. There is almost never a control, because the conductors are still half asleep. Maybe you should pretend to be dozing. Here, take the bread and good luck."

Franz followed her advice. He went down the hill. Because of the leather shoe soles he sometimes slipped. Finally he saw the train station. It was really only a guard house. He could not hear a train, cleaned his shoes, dusted off his clothes and took his time. There was no one around. He sat down and ate some of the bread which the women had given him. Suddenly crowds of people came and sleepily greeted each other. When the train arrived they forced themselves up to the edge of the platform. Franz was one of the last who was able to squeeze in. The train started. The conductor forced his way through the carriage. He wanted to stop when he came to Franz, but the crowd pushed him on.

Finally Franz saw a sign with the name of a village. Oh, now I know where I am, thought Franz. Only about 10 to 15 kilometres from home. The train stopped. People forced their way on and off. At the front and the back of the train two men in beige coloured coats got on, but Franz did not see them. Suddenly he heard, "Show your papers." Everyone looked for their identity papers. Franz put his hand under his pullover. The conductor thought he was also looking for his identity papers and waved him on. A stone fell from Franz's heart and he made as if he was putting his papers back under his pullover. Two stations later he got off. He knew that if he walked over the mountain then he would be close to Alfred's flat.

He wanted to visit his brother first. The church clock sounded the hour. From that he knew if it was time for the shift change and if there would be a lot of people around and then he would decide what to do. He crept into the wooden hut where his brother parked his motorbike. It was not there. He saw that through the gaps in the wooden planks. He asked himself how he could get into the hut. He shook each plank gently. One of them was not securely nailed. Probably somebody had already tried to get in there. He managed to move the plank far enough so that he could crawl in. Then he lay down on an old motorbike cover. The church clock rang every quarter hour. Time went by and he was thirsty and hungry.

In front of the hut there was an old metal barrel with rain water. Could you drink that? Just as he wanted to put his hand into the rain water, he heard the noise of a motorbike. It was his brother. Alfred stopped, shut off the engine and locked the chain. "Shush," whispered Franz, "it's me, Franz." "Oh! And how did you get into my wooden hut?" Alfred did not seem very surprised to see that his brother was free and said, "I was in the clinic yesterday. It's good that you got here alone, otherwise I would have got you out myself, today." Franz said, "I have no idea what you mean." Alfred replied, "Come on," he said, grinning, "you would certainly like something good to eat. Then I'll tell you a good story." They went into the house and Alfred placed an oven baked chicken on the table and a potato salad drizzled with the finest melon seed oil. Franz asked, "Where did you get that?" "Just eat and don't ask. Now I'm going to give you your release papers." Franz asked, "What have you got?" "In the psychiatric clinic it was said that your file with your documents and your identity papers had disappeared. I demanded a confirmation of the disappearance, which I have received. So now we can get new papers from the council. All I have is the original documents about your illness. The Professor gave those to me. Apart from that there was nothing more about your case and he said that when everything was in order, you were to be released today. That was yesterday." Franz was hungry. He ate without taking a break, but now and then he shook his head.

Franz said, "I don't know if Maria, nurse Maria has my papers in the clinic or if she took them home with her." Alfred asked, "What? How could that work?" Franz told him the story about him and Maria and that she had put the injection into his pullover. Alfred asked, "Do you think, that if that had not happened, you would have been dead when I came to collect you today?" Franz said, "What should I say. I don't know if Maria and I could really have run away. But I'm going to find those papers. Believe me."

So the brothers sat together and Franz told him about his adventurous journey. Then he wanted to know how Alfred had managed to get release papers for him. "That's not a long story," Alfred said, "Do you remember the photo camera which I found in the drawer? I got a friend to develop the whole film which was in it. Some of the photographs showed the professor with naked females. Compromising photographs like those were like a gift from heaven. I made good use of them. Very soon I had all the documents which were still to be found and your release papers on the table.

I just don't know, which criminal is responsible for the fact that I couldn't get you out immediately. I wanted to do everything legally. You must understand that. I only wanted your freedom. I could have come for you today." Franz could not follow him. "These swine wanted to kill me. The professor certainly had something to say about the selection. I told you, they are using a fatal injection. My pullover stinks of petrol. Just smell the sleeves. It still stinks after two days. In future there will be no mentally ill people walking around. Of course, that goes for normal people as well. They are going to kill everyone who stands in the way of their crazy National Socialism." Alfred said, "Hush! Not so loud. We have to be careful. Enemies are listening. Don't forget that. You are sitting on a chair, in front of me. You are well and free. You have to forget the rest."

They ate everything on the table and for a while, they said nothing. They had to collect their thoughts. After a while, Alfred said, "You know what, I'll get my colleague. He should come with me to the clinic. Let's see what Maria has to say. In the meantime, go home to Josefine and the children. Your "almost" mother-in-law, Theresa is there as well. Then we'll see what is to be done."

Franz took off one of his shoes, because it was making a clicking sound. The heel was not straight. "I'm sorry about Maria," he said while he was fiddling with the heel. "She saved my life and risked a lot for me. I made her all sorts of promises which I'll never in my life be able to fulfil. Now I feel so vile. She won't give you the documents. About six or maybe half past she should be in the clinic. Even without a watch, I'm sure of that. We didn't have any watches, but I got a feeling for the time and I still have it in my bones." Suddenly the heel came away in his hand.

"Oh! Holy Mary," he shouted, "Look Alfred. Look at this. Something is hidden in the heel." Alfred took the shoe from his hand and pulled out a small, black bag. It rattled and suddenly a golden rain of coins fell onto the table. Both of them grabbed for them, so they did not fall on the floor. Then they looked at each other, speechless. Alfred bit one, "I've seen them do this in films to check if it was real gold." He took a magnifying glass out of his old postage stamp case and both looked through it. "Wow! ... Wow! ... Wow!...," Alfred shouted, "I think I'm dreaming." Franz said, "I feel dizzy, but anyway people think I'm not normal." Tears ran down his face and he wiped them away with the back of his hand. He bent down and took off the other shoe, held it to his ear and shook it, "Is there something in it? Oh, Alfred, I don't know why I'm crying and my heart is beating as though it will burst..." Alfred took the shoe and fetched some pliers from his tool box. Franz said, "You won't be able to open it with those. Look it's like a three way lock, but because I've worn down one side, it's out of true. If you need something, you can open it by twisting it and then always close it again. That is a really clever idea. I wonder if it has been patented?" He laughed, "I'd like to know where Comrade Paul got these shoes." It took him a long time before he discovered the trick and released the heel. And it was just like the other one. Alfred pushed the money on the table to one side and emptied the second bag, which was also full of gold coins, but there was also a fine gold chain with a pendant in the form of the Star of David. Franz was appalled.

"I got out of prison wearing the shoes of someone who had been murdered," he said in a shocked voice and he wept. Alfred looked at the things and no longer trusted himself to touch them. "What are we going to do with them now?" he said and looked at his brother. Franz said, "Why are you asking me? I don't know either. But one thing is certain. We need a guardian angel, who's going to keep his eye on us and make sure we don't make any mistakes." Franz took the chain, removed the Star of David and hid it in one of the little bags. Alfred examined the shoes once more and tried to put the heels back on. While he was trying, he saw something unusual about the sole. He took one of his own shoes, which were also good quality and compared them. His sole was three times thinner. Then he took Franz's shoe in his hand again and drew his hand over the sole. It seemed to be rounded somehow. In the middle and at the toe it was a bit worn, but otherwise only a little scratched. He got a screwdriver and very carefully put it under the sole. The sole moved. There was a paper underneath, which he removed carefully. "An English bank note," he said in amazement, "look at that!" And in the other shoe, it was the same. And once again Alfred shouted, "Wow! ... Wow! ... Wow!..., "The shoes have been waterproofed. How did they do that? That's amazing," Franz was more interested in the technical aspect than the content. Alfred took a piece of paper and a pencil and started to count the gold coins.

Franz stood up to get some water. His throat was dry. Then he said, "Now I haven't got any shoes to wear. Your shoes won't fit. Your feet are three numbers smaller than mine." "Shut up," Alfred scolded, "now I've lost count." He got a tin and put the coins, the Star of David, which he put into the second bag, the English bank notes and the note into it. "What do you want to do with the gold chain?" Alfred asked. "You can take that to Maria. She has earned it. And tell her that I am very sorry that everything turned out differently." "Yes, yes. Forget your heart, sentimentality and pain otherwise I'll start to get tears in my eyes. If you need some shoes, there are some in the cupboard which are open in front. Apart from those, I've got nothing, you gold donkey." "Ah, now I have to wear something like this. Thanks very much," said Franz. Alfred said that he knew of a good hiding place and Franz asked, "Is it safe?" "Of course it's safe. Safe is safe." They laughed. Alfred stood up, "We've chatted too long. Come on, I'll take you to Josefine. When are you finally going to marry her?" Franz did not give a clear answer, he simply said, "Sometime."

Franz went up the stairs to the flat and tried the door knob. It was locked.

A woman, who he did not know, opened the door. He asked about his family. "They live downstairs now." Oh, no! He had forgotten that they had moved. But he was still in good humour. He went down the stairs and knocked on the window, using Morse code, which he had earlier taught his children as a game. Emer opened the door and shouted, happily "Daddy is here." That was the first time that Emer had called him Daddy. Franz took him in his arms, "Yes, I'm back." Theresa, the grandmother, came to the door and greeted him, "You're looking good, but I don't like your beard." What she really meant was his Hitler moustache under his nose. Reinhard and Fredi ran to him and clung to his legs. Reinhard stammered, "Don't you have a rucksack? Did you bring something with you" "You'll have to wait until tomorrow. Then I'll have a surprise for you." Josefine got up slowly, her stomach heavy with child. "It's good to have you back." She threw her arms around him and kissed him. "The cards were right. They showed that you would come home." Franz said, "Ah, yes, the cards." "Are you hungry? Do you want something to drink? Would you like some juice?" Franz knew that he was really back home. Grandmother asked the children to help her clear the table from all the crêpe paper, florist wire, scissors and glitter which were in a soup bowl and prepared papier-maché, which was in a larger bowl.

Then Franz had to tell them what had happened to him. He said that, by and large, it was not too bad, but that, of course, he would have liked to have come home sooner.

But, they wanted to know what he had done all day in the clinic. "But didn't I write you letters?" He told them about the boats which he had built and that he had been paid for them and that he had sent the money to them. Josefine asked, "What money? When should we have got that?" Franz said, "What? You got nothing? I don't believe you! Once a month we could send a letter through the post. The postman collected the letters personally." "Why didn't you give me or Alfred something?" Josefine asked accusingly, "you never said that you were sending money through the post." "I couldn't do that. You know that there was always a warden there who heard everything. I didn't trust myself to say anything about money, because it was given to me in secret and anyway, I never knew when I was going to get a visitor. And then there was this shameful examination before I was allowed to leave the ward." "Was it a lot of money?" Emer, who was sitting under the table, wanted to know.

Josefine told Emer to go into the other room, saying that when adults were talking then he should not be listening and he should not have hidden under the table. "But Mummy, you said that I was a big boy, because I can look after Reinhard and Fredi. That means I'm also a grown up." Emer was very dejected. Josefine took him into the other room and after a while she came back. "He always wants to know everything. He's very curious. That's good for learning, but these days it can be dangerous."

Franz sat there lost in his thoughts. "That band of pigs. Now I've done everything wrong. I should have known. On the one side you are always observed and controlled and on the other hand you can send letters. It's all my fault. I'm a complete idiot. And I had enough time to find a cleverer way. It wasn't completely hopeless." He was angry with himself and pressed his hands together until his knuckles cracked. "It was only a little amount, from time to time, to tide you over, nothing more, but in any case..." His bowels started to complain. Was it anger, or from the roast chicken he had eaten with Alfred? It was a bit fatty. I'll have to get used to fat again, he thought. Then, aloud, he asked, "How was it with you? During those ten minutes visiting time in a month, I didn't hear much, but nobody ever complained. I'd forgotten that you had moved down here. I think you did tell me once, very quickly." "It would not have helped if you had known more." Mother added.

Josefine told him that they made flowers from crêpe paper which they sold for various special occasions. Red flowers with glitter were very popular. At the cemetery she could exchange baskets of wired artificial flowers for other goods and they also liked wreathes with green oak leaves and 'real' paper roses and carnations, she joked. Apart from clothes, shoes and the like, sometimes they bring food. "We have a little store in front of the cellar and we try to barter our wares." In fact, Josefine spoke to everyone on the street, discreetly and only when she was sure they were not from the town. "That works quite well," said Mother. When Josefine saw that someone's shoes were falling apart, she would say, "I think we have a pair of shoes for you. Anyway, where are yours.?" "Oh, I left them with Alfred. The heel had come loose. He said he would repair them." Josefine said, "There is still some hot water in the wash room. You can have a bath and shave and if you want I could cut your hair. I'll fetch a towel and clean clothes. Come on. No one will disturb us at this hour." Franz was tired, but he did not want to say 'no'.

Josefine filled his bath and gave him a sliver of curd soap. "We haven't got anything else and you'll have to wash your hair with it as well. I'll bring you some vinegar water to rinse your hair with. That makes it shiny." She washed his back and laid out a sheet for him. After the bath she cut his hair. He watched her closely in the mirror and told her exactly how he wanted it cut. Then he shaved. Freshly washed and dressed, he came back. Mother was amazed, but said, "You should get rid of the Hitler moustache," and shook her finger at him. "Oh yes," said Franz, "I've got a feeling one day it might bring me luck."

In the meantime Alfred went to his colleague Arnold from the mine, who liked to go on motorbike rides. He asked him if he would like to come with him to collect a few papers from an acquaintance for his brother Franz. He did not want to go alone. In spite of his wife's protests, Arnold was eager to go with him. Alfred now knew where he could intercept Maria on her way to work, because Franz had told him. The journey was fast and dusty. They found a place where they could wait for someone without being observed.

When he saw a corpulent woman coming along the path, he asked her if she was Nurse Maria, he was to give her greetings from Franz. Undecided, she stopped. Alfred introduced himself as one of Franz's acquaintances and asked her to go into the park with him, just for a moment. Alfred spoke to her alone, while Albert acted as look out. Once he was back home, Alfred told Franz what Maria had said. "When I asked about your papers, she was shocked. She asked about you and was relieved to hear that you were still alive. Crying, she told me what had happened with the documents and your papers and how she had suffered in the last few days. Nobody could tell her what had happened to you or where you had gone or been taken. She also asked what would now happen with the pair of you. I had to lie and said that you would have to leave the country and that she would never see you again. It would, of course, be easier with papers. For the moment you had gone underground and it would be better if she forgot all about it. You don't want to make more problems for him." "What did she say about the gold chain?" Franz asked. "Oh, yes. She was very happy about it and said she would always keep it and always remember you. I said it was a parting gift from you and that you hoped she would soon find her man for life. Franz, I had to say that, otherwise she would have started to look for you. You must understand that."

Years later Alfred confessed to his brother that Maria had never received the gold chain. He had given it to his first wife as an engagement present. Franz was very angry about it.

Franz wanted to get work in the mine again and went to the labour office. One day, when it was raining heavily, he was called to a pipe break. He had to take charge and repair the pipe. Josefine was curious and wanted to see what was going on. She took the umbrella and went with him. Franz saw that the pipe had only slipped. Then he saw tracks of a heavy lorry, which had obviously caused the slippage. There was no one else there to help. He said to Josefine, "Somehow I'll have to push it back into place and then tomorrow I can seal it." He looked around and close by he found a stone and a thick, pointed haystack support. With Josefine's help and a great deal of effort they managed to get the pipe back into place. Now there was only a tiny trickle of water. Then Josefine held her stomach, "I'm losing water! Come on, help me! We have to go home quickly and you have to call the midwife." Franz held the umbrella over her and supported her. They had to walk about two kilometres. "We've made it. We're here. How can I get the midwife?" He pushed the door open and Mother came nervously out to meet them.

"There's going to be a war. I heard it from the caretaker. He shouted it out loudly so that everyone could hear." Mother was very agitated. Warily, Franz said. "I've heard that there is a plan to march into Poland, but then you hear many rumours." Mother looked at the pregnant Josefine. "What's the matter with you? Isn't it a bit too soon?" Josefine explained to Franz where the midwife lived. "Do you think I have time to change?" he asked, looking at his wet clothes. "I don't know. The pains are coming very frequently." Franz ran out of the flat. The children had to go into the kitchen and were told to be quiet. Josefine lay on the bed in the other room with sheets under and over her. Her mother put some water to boil on the stove. Josefine was very calm, even though the pains were already very strong. "Is Mummy going to die?" Reinhard asked, fearfully. Emer laughed, because he already knew more about these things. Grandmother said, "No. She's not going to die, but you are going to get a brother or a sister and that hurts your mother, until it arrives. She already told you why she had such a big stomach."

Emer said, "I want a sister. I told Mummy that. I've already got two brothers." Grandmother said, "God decides what it will be." In the meantime the water had come to the boil. Grandmother took it to Josefine. "I don't want this child. When it is born, war will break out. What's going to happen to us?"

"Don›t commit a sin," her mother scolded and felt Josefine's stomach, "this baby can do nothing about it. Almost certainly you are going to have a very pretty girl." Grandmother laughed. "No,"moaned Josefine, "please, not a girl. That will only bring problems with clothes and everything. She can't wear any of the clothes we have, because we only have boys. We'll have to buy everything new."

The midwife had arrived. Almost as soon as she was there, the tiny baby was lying on the sheets. "What a beautiful little girl," she said and examined the new Earthling from every side, "it seems that everything is all right even though she was in a hurry to join us. God protect you, you tiny little thing. We have to give her the warmest place so she can develop well." The baby started to cry without waiting for a smack on her bottom. Josefine began to cry bitterly. She refused to take the child in her arms or even look at her. Mother said, "She should be called Christine. I'll be your godmother and I'll look after you as best I can." Josefine looked at her mother in amazement. "The farmer's wife already said to me that the baby should be called 'Christina', if it was a girl".

Once everything had been tidied up Franz was the first to be allowed to take the new born child in his arms, and then the boys. The midwife had swaddled Christine so tightly that there was no problem holding her. Emer was overjoyed that it was a girl. His wish had been fulfilled.

Mother told Josefine to take the child to her breast. "The child needs your milk," she said in no uncertain terms, "that's the best you can give a new born child. Your breasts will swell and it will be painful if you don't give her your milk." Against her will, Josefine breast fed Christine for three months. Grandmother organised the baptism. On the way to the church Josefine muttered, "Another child born out of wedlock. That's the fourth." She hated everything around her. She even hated her own body. Had it not been for her mother, who was always cajoling her, she would certainly have harmed herself. She had only threatened to do that once. Franz comforted her, saying that he would marry her as quickly as possible.

He said, "If war breaks out and I have to die, then at least you'll get a widow's pension. They have promised that to every woman."

Josefine asked, "Where do you hear all this? I've heard nothing about that, even though I speak to lots of people. Are you an active member of the underground movement or are you working with the Communist party? If I find out, I'll denounce you. Do something decent, something which will be useful for us. You have enough ideas. Try to use them." "All right, all right. I just got home; let's see what I can do."

Franz often went into the town park. That was where people came to collect workers. But Franz preferred to win money by gambling. Sometimes he won and sometimes he lost; that's how it is when you gamble. The game was called coin flipping. He was very good at this, but after a while nobody wanted to take on Franz. Of course, playing for money was forbidden.

Because he was planning to marry Josefine, Franz went to the town hall. He introduced himself as Franz Dorn and was given three forms to fill in. The officer looked for his file and found nothing. "Look under von Dorn," a colleague suggested. Nothing. Franz was amazed, "There should be papers for my relations, "no 'Dorn' and no 'von Dorn'. That's very strange." "No, there's nothing here. Look, it's like this, the Gestapo, our secret state police, were here recently and they 'tidied up' the files. We'll have to ask them." He turned to a secretary and said, "Please ask the Gestapo about documents concerning Franz Dorn and tell them that it is about a marriage to Miss Pfeifer." Then he said to Franz, "For the moment, Mr. Dorn, you don't need to fill in any forms. We'll have to wait." Franz stood there, his mouth open, "What does that mean?" "Right now everything is being sifted through. Anyone with a clear conscience has nothing to fear. You will be informed." Franz wondered if he should say that his documents had disappeared in the clinic. No, it's better to ask Alfred for his advice. He only had the release paper, which had been obtained through blackmail and he had no identity card. He should have asked for a new one long ago. Alfred had advised him to be patient.

A month later the Dorn brothers, Karl, Alois, Alfred, Franz and their father Karl Dorn were told to come to the town hall. Father was ill in bed again and could not go. None of them knew that they would meet each other there. That was a big surprise. Karl, the oldest, lived rather secluded from the others. Mr. Kogler, the council officer, greeted them and asked them if they knew why they were there. They all said 'No.' Franz thought that it could not have anything to do with his marriage plans.

Mr. Kogler laid a few documents out on the table and said, "It's about changing your family name. We have to inform you that, as of now, no one in the family or even distant relations can use the name "von Dorn." An exception will be made for your father, because of his age, and also for Fritz and Gustav Dorn who have been interned in labour camp Dachau. It has been decided to give you the name Remi." The brothers looked at each other, speechless and then, all at once assailed Mr. Kogler with questions. Mr. Kogler defended himself, "The reason for this decision has unfortunately not been given us." "What do you mean? You have to give us more details," Karl shouted, "Who is this Fritz and the other one you say are in Dachau?" Franz asked, annoyed, "how are they related to us? That's the first time I've heard of them." "We are not rich aristocrats and that's why I haven't used the 'Count of' for years, the modest Alois said, rather quietly, "Our Father used it from time to time, but we are honest people. I'll get used to the name... what was it? Oh yes, Remi." He knew that he could not defend himself against the decision. Mr. Kogler said, "Aristocrats who come from other countries may keep their titles as long as they petition Vienna and include the necessary documents."

Alois preferred to stay in the background and was very undemanding. The most important thing in the world for Alois were his dearest wife, Ingried and his three children. Alfred was not yet ready to give his opinion, but you could see that for him the name mattered. He decided that he would do something later. Suddenly Mr. Kogler said, "Mr. Franz Remi, you can collect the papers for your marriage from me. Naturally we shall need your fiancée's agreement. Because it has taken such a long time, permission will be given immediately, if you wish." "Oh, so you're going to marry again. I didn't know that you were divorced." Of course, it was Karl who said that, because he never took any notice of anyone else. "Gentlemen," Mr. Kogler said and held open the door, "I have to go back to my office. We'll prepare your new papers which you can then collect from us. Until then, goodbye." Karl was outraged, "I'm not going to sit back and accept that. You'll be hearing from me." Alois said goodbye to his brothers, even though he thought they should possibly exchange some thoughts. Karl also took his leave. He wanted to take a look at his father. Alfred went a few steps with Franz. "For you, Franz, I think it's good. Now you can start again with a new name." "Now you don›t need to report the loss of your existing papers. You›ve come out of this well. And, Maria, who knows, won›t be able to find you so easily with a new name. "Umm – I'm not so sure. Who knows what papers the council or the police have? It would be really interesting to find out."

It was midday and Franz went home. Josefine asked if everything was all right. "Yes, yes. This afternoon we both have to go to Mr. Kogler. You have to sign about the marriage." Grandmother laughed, "If she still wants to marry you is another question." Josefine said nothing. She just thought about how often she had wanted a wedding. Now she wasn't so sure. If only I could find another way, she thought. She went to the stove and tears poured down her face, some of them into the cooking pot. She took her time laying the table and serving the meal. She was not in the mood for a wedding, even though she was the one who would have to organise it.

Only a photograph of the 'happy couple'. No photographs of the guests. That would be too expensive. We can make a good meal at home for the children and anyone else who happens to be there. Grandmother reminded her, "You don't get married every day until death comes between you. Believe me, child, that is what will happen. I feel it deep inside. We could have a celebration in the restaurant across the road. Of course, it is only a registry office wedding with your children! How can you explain that?"

Josefine wouldn't make her vows before God and all the saints. Anyway, Franz would never be accepted in the church. He had not been at any of the baptisms of his children. Even his first marriage had taken place without the blessing of the church. It must be said, that Franz had never objected when all the others went to church services. He just said, "No one knows if that's good or not." Josefine looked at the clock on the wall. "It's time to go to the town hall. We want to be the first in the queue otherwise we'll have to wait for ages." Grandmother said, "Go. The children are in school and kindergarten and Christine is asleep." Franz said, "It's still too early. We'll have to wait for ages." But Josefine insisted. She took his hat in her hand and stood in the doorway.

They were really the first in front of the town hall door. Franz felt uncomfortable. He sat down on a bench in the park opposite and smoked a cigarette. He still had to tell her about the change of name. Josefine knew nothing about it. He stood up and went to her. There was still nobody else there. "What I wanted to tell you … before we go in you have to know… as you know…" not coming to the point, "Alfred, Karl, Alois and I were asked to go to the town hall. They told us that our family name has been changed. We aren't called Dorn or von Dorn anymore, but simply Remi. What should I say? The whole thing stinks. Just what do these Fascists think they can do? And why? They couldn't or wouldn't give us any reason." "What? What did you say?," Josefine asked excitedly, "but they can't just take away your legal name! Who do they think they are?" Franz replied, "That's the way it is. Alfred and Karl are going to look into it later. We have found out that we are not the only ones this has happened to. We haven't inherited any land and there is no wealth involved. Maybe it's just envy. You saw how they confiscated the whole workshop. We're just poor, unimportant people. They can do what they want with us. Alois and I don't really care. The communists and the resistance don't use those aristocratic titles like 'von' and 'zu'. Karl was the one who was most upset.

Alfred was also thinking about it and neither of them will let it rest until we get our real name back. I have neither time nor desire to quarrel about my legal name." Josefine was angry, "Don't ever say again that you are a communist and a resistance fighter. You'll only make problems for us. Haven't you had enough? Obviously you had it good in the lunatic asylum. I thought that once you were free, you would come to your senses. Do you ever think about us, about your children? What is all this about?" Josefine was beside herself and could hardly catch her breath. Franz tried to comfort her, "Come one. We're going to be married and then we'll see how it goes. Up to now I haven't had any more political contact since I left the clinic. You can calm down or consider, if you really want to marry me," and he grinned. She shook her head. She could not understand. More people had joined the queue in front of the door, among them Mrs. Teller. After her husband had disappeared, she had joined the forbidden communist party and Franz and Josefine knew that. "Marry him," she told them after she had spoken to the pair, "you've nothing to lose." Josefine asked what she knew about Franz. Then the door opened. They went into the town hall without a word.

At first Josefine and Franz only talked about the most important things with officer Kogler. Franz read through the documents and said that his birth date was one day out. He told Mr. Kogler. Jokingly, he said, "One day more or less is not important. Here you are a day younger." Franz was angry, "I don't find it in the least bit amusing. Please correct it. First you annul my legal name and now you want to change my birth date from the 24th to the 25th. Just because someone didn't do their work correctly, do I have to accept it? Oh, no!" Mr Kogler said,

"But you can still sign. I can't guarantee how long the change will take. I'll look into it. So, please." He offered him a pen which had already been dipped in ink. Franz signed Dorn, scratched it out and, signed Remi, although it felt very strange. Mr. Kogler advised them to change the names of the four children from Pfeifer to Remi, "So that everything is regulated." Franz agreed, but Josefine said that they would first have to ask Emer if he agreed. "Isn't he a bit young to make his own decisions? You should be happy that Emer gets a father. Or would you prefer that he will grow up as – excuse me for the word - a bastard?" Josefine said, quite clearly, "His father disappeared and after five years he was declared dead. We were engaged and wanted to marry as soon as he returned. I can prove that in writing. Emer is a very clever and liberal minded young boy. He should decide for himself. Personally I don't think it's a good idea for Emer. As far as I know, if Emer is to be called Remi, then he will have to be adopted by Franz. Is that not the case?" Mr. Kogler replied, "Well, yes. That's correct, since Mr. Remi is only the biological father of three of the children. I suggest we wait and see what happens." Everyone was happy with this decision and they parted. Josefine was happy to be outside in the fresh air.

On the way home she asked who should be their witnesses. Franz had chosen Cooper Florenz and a good school friend who will come with his accordion which he can then play at the dance," he said, "that will put us all in a good mood and he's probably got the newest jokes to tell." What Franz did not say, was that he had met him while he had been playing 'coin flipping'. Otherwise Josefine would have told him what she thought even on her wedding day. However, she found he had chosen well, "But please tell them to behave respectfully and that they shouldn't tell any crude or political jokes," she warned him, "and no religious jokes either," she added. "Mother of God! That's doesn't leave much," Franz said. Josefine replied, "And while we're talking about the Mother of God, just wait until Mother hears about the change of name. She's not going to swallow that so easily.

Hopefully she'll have accepted it before our wedding day. My God! Excuse me when I tell you, but for her your name was the best thing about you." Franz grinned, ruefully. Back home he told Mother the date of the marriage. 29th September 1939. Josefine started, hesitantly, to tell her about it. With full respect she said, "My dearest Mother…" When she had finished, her mother felt anger and fury rising inside her. She stood straight as a candle and gave vent to her rage. She did not think about the children, who were shocked to hear her words. Josefine had never seen her mother like this. "You are not going to let that happen. With or without the Gestapo. You have to write to the government and fight for your name. When everyone this has happened to gets together and defends themselves, then they have to give you back the name you were born with. You have to take the best lawyer and if necessary go to court."

A deep wrinkle appeared above her nose. Her dark eyes glowed with rage. She clamped her teeth together so hard that you could almost hear them crunch. She stamped on the floor and made fists with her hands so that her knuckles cracked. Josefine said, Please, Mother, calm down. We're sure that Alfred and Karl will do everything possible." "And Franz? What about him?" He had gone into the courtyard to smoke a cigarette. Mother was exhausted and sat down, "I'll ask our priest. He has studied and he's a clever man. I want to ask him his advice." But first of all, she lay down, and exhausted by all the thoughts going through her head, she fell asleep.

She was so disappointed. At that moment she wished that her beloved husband was with her. She had always been able to rely on him. She felt empty. She had clung to the idea that her daughter was going to marry an aristocrat. And now this! Franz and Josefine left her in peace. Franz went out to 'do something', as he said.

When Mother woke up she went to Josefine and asked, "Have you thought about your dress for the wedding?" Josefine said. "Franz wants me to wear a traditional costume." "What? A traditional costume? We're not simple country folk! No, I can't imagine that. That's impossible. No one in our family has ever worn traditional costume. Am I spared nothing?." Josefine said, "I wanted to change his mind, but I couldn't. He will probably borrow a suit from Alfred. Then I said that he should shave off his Hitler moustache. That's annoyed me for a long time. He said that he would think about it. He might shave it off for the marriage, but then he would grow it again."

That same day Josefine and her mother went to a seamstress. The owner, Mrs. Hoppe, made them very welcome. Once again she had drunk too much. Every time her husband went away on a long journey, she turned to the bottle. Mother asked about samples of material for a wedding dress. Josefine interrupted her, "We should tell you that it should be a traditional dress." "Oh, so you're going to marry." Said Mrs. Hoppe, excitedly, "and who is the lucky man? Do I know him?" Josefine gave no answer, but looked at the sample dresses. However, Mother said, "My daughter is going to marry Count Franz von Dorn." "Oh, I'm honoured that you have come to me," Mrs. Hoppe, "So he wants a wedding dress in the style of a traditional costume."

Mrs. Hopp called her employee and asked her to bring a dress from the display. She had seen Josefine looking at a long beige dress. "This dress would be a little tight for you round the waist, but, ladies, just take a look at this burgundy red, sparkling traditional dress. We'll try it right now." She disappeared with Josefine behind a curtain. The dress was very heavy and the upper part was stiff and difficult to fasten with all its hooks. The skirt was ankle length. In the mirror, Josefine had a very pleasing waistline and the length of the dress made her look taller. Josefine said, "I'm only going to have to wear it for four to five hours. I think I can manage that, but after that I would never wear it again. I don't like traditional costume although it suits some very well." "And what are you going to wear in your hair? Have you already thought of something? While Mrs. Hoppe was speaking she was fumbling about in a drawer full of hair ornaments and placed them on Josefine's forehead. Mother stood by and gave her opinion about the most suitable. "Now we only need the shoes and stockings," Mrs. Hoppe said. Josefine replied, "I already have black shoes." They discussed the price. In the end they decided on a price for hire.

On the way home Josefine and her mother looked at a jeweller's display, particularly the wedding rings. Josefine said, "Mother, you still have father's broad wedding ring. We could have two rings made from it. Father never wore it because it was so broad." Her mother hesitated, "I know, but your father is a very kind hearted person, sentimental and very sensitive and tender. For years I have worn this ring on a chain and have never taken it off. I'm not happy about changing that." She took the ring lying on her breast, in her hand. "I'm sorry, mother," said Josefine, "it was just an idea." Mother said, "Let me sleep on it over night. I'll try to contact your father in my dreams. I'll give you my answer tomorrow." Josefine: "Thank you, mother dear."

The next day Mother went to the goldsmith and asked him to show her some wedding rings. She said that the groom would only wear his ring on the wedding day and she did not want to spend a lot of money. At the same time she wanted to give her daughter a ring which would not wear down too quickly. Neither ring should be too narrow. The goldsmith understood her very well. He showed her a gold plated silver ring for the groom and a nine carat ring for the bride. She looked at the rings and gave the goldsmith a piece of cardboard which had two different sized holes in it. Josefine's and Franz's finger sizes. While the goldsmith was looking for rings in the right size, Mother discovered in the display cabinet some delightful children's earrings shaped like forget-me-nots set with blue stones. Oh, they're sweet, she thought, with little Christine in mind. The goldsmith said that they were nine carat gold with semi precious stones and very well set." "If you give me a fair price, then I'll take them as well for my granddaughter Christine. She is still very small, but I'll keep the earrings until she's a bit older." Grandmother bought the two wedding rings and the little earrings and was happy to still have her husband's ring round her neck. On the way home she had to pass the church. She saw the priest going in and followed him. She called, "Father! Good day. I'd like to ask a favour. I've just bought two rings for my daughter and her future husband. I'd like to have them blessed. They can't marry in church because he's divorced. But at least we would like to have the rings blessed. I'll put a reasonable sum of money in the poor box if you would please do this for me." She held out the rings and the earrings to the priest. "In the name of God," he said and went into the vestry. He came back with a small, gold plate. "Put the things on this." He spread them out a bit, muttered a few words in Latin, dipped his finger in the holy water and touched the jewellery and Mother's forehead. He then asked her to say the Lord's prayer in front of the altar while he dried everything off and put the gold plate back in its place. Franz could have married in the church, because his former marriage had only been a registry office marriage. No one had told her this, because, given their situation, neither of them wanted to kneel at the altar.

The priest came back, gave the jewellery to Mother and took his leave, saying, "May God protect you and the bridal pair." He knew Josefine, and, in particular, the children, since he had baptised all of them. "The earrings are certainly for Christine. My blessing goes with you." Grandmother was so moved by his words that tears came into her eyes. Then she went home, floating on air.

In the meantime Josefine had gone to Anderl in his restaurant to arrange a meal for the big day. She also specified how much wine should be provided and insisted that there should be no schnapps. Anderl was quite certain that he would have to wait to be paid, but said that he was not too worried about that. He also promised to get a very presentable wedding cake from an acquaintance. "The flower arrangements will be my present," he said, smiling at her, "and if you still haven't ordered the bridal bouquet then I'd like to give it to you." Josefine said, "Now I'm happy about my wedding day. Everyone has been so kind to me. Thank you Anderl. Many thanks." "You don't have to thank me, it's an honour."

Franz asked Alfred for three gold coins for the wedding. He had already found out what these coins were worth. Alfred advised him to be very careful. He gave one coin to Anderl for the wedding reception. Anderl was amazed. Franz wrote down the value, in case Anderl wanted to change it at the savings bank. Anderl said, "Oh no. I'll keep it. Have you any more? How did you come to have gold coins?" "I'm saying nothing. Don't be annoyed with me, Anderl, but I don't want to lie to you and you know from our dealings up to now that I trust you. You know that, as things are at the moment it's better to 'see nothing, hear nothing and say nothing' just like the three wise monkeys. You can say that an unknown guest paid with the gold coin. That's possible, isn't it?" "Yes. That's already happened. It was exactly the same coin. The people have gone away. They said that it was a safe, international currency. I took it and sold it to the bank, but I got more for it than you have written here." Anderl looked at the note again. "For an aristocratic wedding feast one gold coin is not enough. No, without joking, you've certainly got more of these. You can trust me. I won't sell the coins now. These days nobody can find them. I'll pay you anything you have paid me in excess of the cost right away and I'll give you food ration stamps." Franz said, "All right, you can take ten percent off. I don't have to tell you why."

Franz went to the window. Looked out onto the street to see if there was any one around who could suddenly disturb them. Then he took off his hat, searched under the inner leather band and took out another gold coin.

When he turned round, the third coin fell out of his hat onto the counter. Anderl picked it up and started to make his calculations, taking his ten percent. Then he went into the lounge bar, took out the excess and handed it to Franz with the food ration stamps. In the meantime Franz hid the one coin which he still had in his hand back in his hat. Without saying a word, Franz checked the figures, nodded, counted the money and asked Anderl for a receipt with date and signature under the words 'Wedding paid.". Anderl poured out two glasses of quality schnapps and grinned, "Have you heard anything about gold coins?" Franz replied, "No idea what you're talking about." They swallowed the schnapps, laughed and took their leave.

Mother, Josefine and Franz got home at about the same time. Franz asked, "Where were you for such a long time?" Josefine told him. "Now we only need the money to collect the things." "Good," Franz said, "we'll go to the seamstress and collect them. I've got enough money on me for that." Both women looked at him in amazement. "Where did you get that money?" "I've been doing a bit of work. That's all."

Mrs. Hoppe was very pleased. It had been good business for her. "Turn round," she told Franz, who was grinning from ear to ear, so that he would not see the dress as she was packing it into a cardboard box together with the accessories. Then she gave Josefine a tiny bottle. "Real French perfume," she said and opened the door. "I wish you all the luck in the world."

On the day of their wedding, Florenz arrived in front of the house with a hay wagon, decorated with flowers and drawn by two horses. That was his surprise and his present.

He had even brought some steps with him. His friend, Horst played a song on his accordion. Everyone was happy and, for the first time in a long while, Mother laughed again. She looked at the decorated wheels and horses. She loved horses more than anything, because she had spent most of her life with them. Then Franz drove them to the town hall and afterwards to Anderl's restaurant. It was a happy company and they celebrated long into the night.

There was, however, one thing that had left a bitter after taste. Franz had not shaved off the Hitler moustache under his nose. Josefine and her mother were very dismayed. Josefine was so angry, that she later drew on the wedding photographs a very thick line under Franz's nose. From the beginning, she couldn't bear looking at the wedding photos and hid them in a box. The photo showed the pair sitting on a bench wearing traditional costume. The moustache was fashionable at the time, but when they had first met, Franz had sported a thin, pencil moustache exactly like the, Hollywood star, Errol Flynn. She abhorred the Hitler moustache. In time Josefine noticed that Franz, who had blonde hair and blue-grey eyes was colouring his eyebrows. Often it was obvious, since he'd had too little light to properly see what he was doing. When she told him about it he looked at her in amazement, "What do you mean, I'm using make up?" He thought that no one had noticed.

After the wedding, Josefine's mother went back to her husband and her other sons and daughters in Wienerneustadt. Josefine went on making artificial flowers, which she wove together with real ivy and other long lasting greenery. She also included green buds and coloured wood shavings which she got from Florenz. She put the bouquets in baskets which Father Dorn made from natural wood and willow branches. Mrs. Gasser from the general store gave her a small corner in her shop window where Josefine could display her bouquets. Sometimes they were sold and sometimes exchanged for other goods, but somehow they always came to an agreement. One day, in the shop, she heard an old woman complaining that she had to have coal for heating and cooking. She stopped the woman on the street and offered to give her some coal straight away. The women in exchange said that she had dried beans, bacon, preserved fruit, herb tea, acorn coffee and honey at home.

Josefine remembered that Franz had just managed to get hold of some coal. She found out the going rate for coal and promised to help her. She then went into the courtyard and saw the bicycle and trailer which Franz used all the time to transport the coal which he had collected at the mine. She knew that he was not in a hurry to unload the coal from the trailer. It was good that she knew Franz was with Florenz in the cooper workshop. No one saw her leave or return. It did not take her long. She let the coal fall into the cellar down a slide. Josefine laid the exchanged provisions in her apron, fastened them, put them in the trailer and cycled home. She took the goods into the house then put the bicycle and trailer back exactly as they had been before. She had also got dried fruit and she was happy thinking about how the children's eyes would light up and how Franz would react.

Yes, the bicycle and trailer, which had rubber tyres, belonged to Franz, He had got them from Alfred in exchange for something or other. The trailer was covered with a tarpaulin. He used the bicycle when he was doing odd jobs in the open cast mine and of course, sometimes he illegally brought some coal back in the trailer. So as not to be seen, he always took the difficult rocky road over the hill. On the way he went past a rubbish dump where he also sometimes found something useful. For example he once found horse hair from an old mattress. He could use that for one of his new ideas. He stuffed a beautiful horse and a swan with it, and mounted them on tricycles which he had built himself. He had some help. The seamstress Hoppe helped Josefine to make the covering for the horse hair out of strong linen. She had an agreement with Franz that she would get her share once he could sell or exchange one of these tricycles. At first they decided to make three. Florenz made the wooden legs with hooves made of barrel hoops exactly as Franz wanted them. The teeth were real. They were taken from slaughtered animals. Alois made the glass eyes in the glass factory, which normally just made preserve jars and he was happy to make something 'artistic' for once. Finally Franz painted the little horses. He did this very well. They were beige with black markings. The tails and manes were made from combed horse hair.

They became really luxury horses. They looked so beautiful that everyone wanted to keep one for himself. Emer and Reinhard were overjoyed when they made the test drive. The accountant Gosch calculated the price based on all the materials having been purchased and wages having been paid. "Oh, Jesus, Maria," they all said when they saw the price, "that's much too expensive. Who can afford that?" Mr. Gosch was not to be moved. He knew enough people who would buy anything for the children, or simply display such things in their entrance halls or living rooms if they were not mounted on three wheels. "Leave the sales to me. The best example will go into Frühwirt's windows, right on the main street, but we have to keep it as a sample. If anyone orders one, then they will have to pay a deposit of, let's say, 25%. But first we have to take a few photos. I'll get my camera."

Josefine dressed Emer and Reinhard in the best jackets and trousers. Franz spat on their shoes and polished them with a cloth until they shone. The boys had to stand next to the horse, then sit on it. Emer wanted to wet his hair and make a curl like a six on his forehead. "Mami, make me a six!" The photography session was very enjoyable. Everybody wanted to tell Mr. Gosch how it would look better and they all wanted to be photographed. The sunshine was so strong that for most of the time Emer was looking at the ground and all those who were standing around cast shadows on the picture. In the end Mr. Gosch chased them all away and only Franz could move the horse, millimetre for millimetre into the right position and then he too had to get out of the way as quickly as possible. When Alfred turned up, just by chance, he told them about his acquaintance, who could develop the film for them, but Mr. Gosch did not trust any one with the film until Josefine showed him the photograph of Franz in Nazi uniform. "His acquaintance developed that. I haven't shown it to any one else." Then Mr. Gosch agreed and Alfred took the film and rode off on his motorbike.

"Now someone has to put the two three wheel horses into the car so that I can take them with me and won't have too much trouble getting them out." Mrs. Gosch produced two suitable pieces of linen to cover the horses. However, only one of the horses could be fitted into the old Mercedes. Florenz looked at the way the passenger seat was mounted and said that if they removed the seat there would be room for both horses. "No," said Mr. Gosch, nervously, "that's out of the question and please don't touch the car. I've just polished it." He ran around the car with a soft cloth and here and there wiped off fingerprints. Then he thought about where he could sell the horses, calculated the kilometres and realised that driving that distance with just one horse would not be profitable. "All right then," he said to Florenz, "you can take out the passenger seat. It's 70 kilometres there and back." He trusted Florenz, because he knew that his work was very precise and that he would not damage his expensive car. "We'll make two cars out of one. You can be happy," Florenz joked and everyone laughed.

Josefine went back into the flat, but could still follow what was going on outside. As a surprise she put a large piece of bacon, bread and apples into a basket and went into the courtyard. "Now we're going to eat," and added unnecessarily, "you must be dying of hunger. Come on Franz, bring me that wide plank and push that tree trunk under it. Now we need something to drink. Florenz, haven't you got some cider hidden away somewhere? You can charge us for it when we have earned something. Until you get a new delivery, you can drink water from the fountain." Everyone laughed at the joke and Josefine realised that, in her excitement, she had used the familiar form to Florenz. She told herself that she would apologise to him later. "Yes, but not for the children," Florenz said and Mrs. Gosch gave the children some expensive raspberry syrup from her cellar. It was a happy crowd and everyone had a joke to tell. Josefine observed thoughtfully, "Today is a wonderful day. We should do this more often. I don't want to think of the future." Mrs. Gosch replied, "Let's enjoy it as long as we can," and touched Josefine's hands.

The men got up and went back to work. Soon everything was ready. Mr. Gosch was still unsure about the developing of the photos. The sun had been blinding. "I'm only going to start the journey when I have the photos in my hand," he said, "other wise we can't show that we have a selection." The third horse, which every child was first allowed to ride, was put into the shop window, decorated and illuminated. A large sign read, "Only to order. Price on request." It looked like a dream horse. Franz stood in front of the window with his hands in his pockets and it was easy to see how proud he was. Josefine's eyes were wet. Passers-by stopped and marvelled at it. "Come away, children. Other people also want to see it." That was Anderl, as he was passing. "You can make a horse for me, but without the tricycle. I'll display it in the bar." "There you are. The first order," shouted Mrs. Gosch and called her husband. "Get your order book. Anderl has just made an order." "My God, but that was quick," Anderl laughed. Emer wanted to know, "Have you got so much money?" and everyone laughed.

The next day Alfred came with the photos. He spread them out on the table and nobody was allowed to touch them. Of course everyone would have liked to take them in their hand, to see them better. When Mr. Gosch came, he looked at them very carefully, chose the best and left the rest on the table. He took the negatives from Alfred and went on his way. He sold one of the horses to the largest builder in the area and got an order, with special requirements from another customer. He was a good salesman and the business went well. They were able to pay the people who helped. Together with the flowers which Josefine made, they were well able to keep their heads above water.

One day Alois also had a fantastic idea for making money. This is how it happened: He took a photo of Reinhard and fixed it between a mirror and a plate of glass. Reinhard was not too happy about it. He wanted his name on it. So he took a nail and engraved his name on the picture side. Then he turned it round so that he could see himself in the mirror.

Excitedly he showed it to his mother, but she just scolded him for scratching the glass. "Stop," shouted Alois and looked more closely at it, "That's given me an idea. I could engrave the name on the back of the mirror. Have you got another photo?" he asked Josefine. She gave him two, one of her mother and one of Emer when he was a little boy. For my mother you have to bevel the edges and etch a few flowers in the corner, or around it and then write "With love from your daughter, Josefine."

That's how he got the idea of making pretty presents for someone you loved, or even for yourself. Josefine soon started to collect pictures and sayings which Alois could use. For example, for Emer he engraved a very presentable stag on the back of the mirror. Josefine agreed on a price from which they could both profit. Reinhard got a few pennies, because it was really his and his uncle Alois' idea. Franz wanted to patent it. "That costs a lot of money," Alois said and spoke to Mr. Gosch. He saw that there might be problems with the pictures, but asked Alois to give him a couple of samples. "I'll take them with me. Let's see if we can make something out of it." The he took other samples with photos of actresses cut out from magazines. He paid Alois for them and more than he had asked for. "Everything must have a true price," Mr. Gosch said, "otherwise someone will suffer and who knows how long we can go on doing this." Now Alois also had some work on the side which he enjoyed doing.

Until further orders came in, Franz often met up with a few men to play 'coin flipping'. His bets were so large that the others could not keep up with him. Josefine found out about it and also where he was playing. She took Emer by the hand and went there, hid behind a tree and sent Emer to them. Emer pulled on Franz's jacket until he went home with him. Once home Franz shouted loudly, "Don't ever send the boy after me. I know what I am doing." He slammed the door shut and went back to the gambling. It had been a while since he had shouted so loud. Josefine went to Alfred and asked for his advice. He convinced Franz that he should go to the mine as a casual worker. At first he did not accept the idea. "Alfred said, "There are many people who would be glad of the chance to earn some money." Josefine was happy that Alfred could take Franz with him to the mine.

When she saw Alfred's and particularly Franz's hands after work, she made a pair of mouse-grey suede gloves from strong leather for each of them. The leather which had been lying around for a long time was well suited. Alfred thought, "Can you make a few more? Proper mittens. I'll take them to the mine and I'll be able to sell them. Tell me how much you want for them, we'll agree a price and then we'll soon have another business." Josefine was very happy with the idea. She had found out that the leather factory only made thin, glossy gloves from the first layer of pig skin, so the rough leather underneath could be bought for a very low price.

Then, one day, Franz started to spit blood. His lungs were full of coal dust. Josefine was disgusted. He coughed all night and often spat beside the bed, even though she had put a bowl there. In the dark his spit often missed the bowl. Years later Emer spoke about the indignity his mother had to accept. He would never forget it. She told Franz to wear a cloth over his nose and mouth when he was working in the mine. "I can't be the only one there who covers himself," was his answer. "If you want to survive, you'll have to," was her reply. It got so bad that he was often too ill to work. He was very astute and soon realised that when he was on sick leave,

he received more money with all the other jobs he could do on the side. The main thing was he did not need to do this dirty, dusty work.

From then on he was more often 'ill.' Of course, he also took the opportunity to meet, secretly, with his comrades. Spending the whole day at home or even in bed was not his thing. People from the resistance carried out little sabotage acts. They put sand in the machines in the munitions factory and printed handbills against the Nazis. It was very dangerous! Any one with communist ideas was sought out and arrested. Franz was not afraid. He practised the art of speaking convincingly and soon became a spokesman. Josefine noticed, after a while, that something was going on.

On the one hand, she did not want to know anything about it, but her curiosity would not leave her in peace. At home she watched him out of the corner of her eye and looked everywhere for anything he could have hidden, but she found nothing. She followed him like a spy when he left the house on his bicycle with its trailer early in the morning mist. She watched the men who languidly hung around and she thought that they were either overseers or people looking for work. Then one morning, she got nearer to solving the puzzle. She had often followed him, wearing black clothes and a headscarf, but without success, because even with the trailer on the bicycle, he was quicker. But this time she knew that he was going to the place where there was coal. After about half an hour, he hid his bicycle in the bushes. He pulled the trailer further and hid it in a place close to the narrow gauge tracks, where the tip carts passed very slowly, filled to the brim with black coal. Franz looked around, pushed the trailer closer to the tracks and jumped between two tip carts to the other side. There he was able to release the safety catch. Because of the noise of the train, one could hardly hear that the coal had tipped out of the cart. Franz loaded as much as he could into the trailer covered as best he could and pushed it back to his bicycle. He took off his gloves and went to an abandoned mining gallery. Before he went in he dusted off his clothes and looked several times around. There was light in the gallery which could not be seen from outside.

From where Josefine was hiding you could just about make out the entrance. She waited a while, thinking that maybe other people would arrive and indeed, a few other people slipped in. The last one put a few planks over the entrance. Josefine crept closer. She listened, carefully removed the planks and pushed her way in. She took a few steps forwards and then everything went quiet. Suddenly she heard Franz's voice. "I welcome you all, comrades, ladies and gentlemen. Today we are going to choose a few group leaders who will have to carry out important tasks for us and our fatherland. Every group leader will be responsible for recruiting people from the surrounding area who are willing to carry out these tasks." Josefine felt shudders down her spine. She listened a while longer and then she had had enough. She would have liked to have known who the female comrades were. Who were these women? Do I know them? But it was time to go home.

When Franz returned, she was already in the courtyard. She said nothing, but she was surprised that he came back with the empty trailer. Where had he left the coal? She could not explain that, but thought that he might have sold it and searched through his clothes before she washed them. She found nothing. She looked in his hat and his shoes. Still nothing. Why was the umbrella hanging there, instead in its normal place? She opened the black umbrella carefully. Yes! There were bank notes hidden in it. She pilfered two, closed the umbrella carefully and put it back where she had found it. When she had the chance she would certainly ask him what was going on, but for the moment she did not know enough. After he had shaved Franz hastily ate his breakfast. "I have to quickly go into town. I'll be back soon," he said and rushed off. Lately he did not like it if anyone asked him where he was going. "Don't you trust me?" he had asked loudly a few days before, "Anyway, I'm only doing what you want." When Mother wasn't there, he often blurted out such things. Josefine's concern was to keep a peaceful household and protecting the children from these outbursts.

Franz left the house with the umbrella under his arm, crossed the courtyard and left by the large gate. Josefine pinched herself. She opened the normal entrance door. It's still so early and there's no sign of rain. She saw that he had taken the back road into town. She followed him, carefully and unobtrusively. Suddenly, he disappeared. She ran on, turned around several times and continued. Her pulse increased. At the corner she looked up and down the street. No sign of Franz. All right, she thought, I've lost him and decided to go back home when, through the early morning mist, she thought she recognised a woman. She hurried to overtake her. Then she saw the umbrella which the woman was carrying. Isn't that the umbrella Franz was carrying? But then there were many black umbrellas. She dropped back. Look! A car stopped and the woman got in. Josefine jumped to one side, so that the driver would not see her in the rear-view mirror and then ran back home by the shortest route. Five minutes later Franz came back, without the black umbrella! Her heart was beating so fast she was sure he would notice. She woke the children, because it was time to send them to kindergarten and school. Franz got himself ready to go to Florenz and started whistling on the way.

Later Josefine went to Mrs. Hoppe to bring her her share of the horses which they had sold. Mr. Gosch had divided everything exactly. Mrs. Hoppe greeted her with her first name "Oh, Josefine," she said, very distraught. "You're lucky that your husband is with you. My husband is at the front, probably in the north east, but I haven't heard from him for a long time." She sent a girl apprentice to bring them some wine. She had been drinking more and more and recently no longer in secret. Her pretty face was bloated and her figure was spongy, "Mrs. Hoppe, drinking isn't going to bring your husband home. You have to pull yourself together and get away from alcohol. It would be a shame if your husband comes home and finds you drunk." "I beg your pardon. I'm never drunk", said Mrs. Hoppe, "I still always know what I'm doing. He would have written to me long ago if he were still alive." She cried into her handkerchief.

Josefine sat down on a chair and said, "Give me your hand. I can read hands, but please don't tell my husband. He doesn't believe in it. But I have been right many times. So, sit down." Slowly she took hold of Mrs- Hoppe's hand, brought a lamp closer and after a while she said, very quietly, "Your husband is still alive. I can see that very clearly." She stopped and looked out of the window. "Look, he's rubbing his hands together. He's cold. There are other soldiers there. He is not dead!" Mrs. Hoppe took her hand away from Josefine and looked towards the window. She opened her eyes and mouth wide and thought, just for a moment that she had seen something, "Hermann!" She put one hand to her breast and the other towards the window and closed her eyes for a second.

"Oh! That does my heart good. What a feeling! It's as though a great weight has fallen from my shoulders. All those terrible thoughts have disappeared. How could I have fallen so low?" The apprentice came back with the wine. "Thank you. You can put it in the cupboard." To Josefine she said, "I don't need that any more," and she squeezed her hands.

Josefine felt a bit dazed, because reading hands took a lot of concentration. She leant on the edge of a crate which was close by. "Have you got bits of material in there?" "Yes and I've got a lot in the store room, but they're just small pieces." Josefine thought that you could sew them together and make funny fantasy little creatures out of the remnants. "Do you have any animal patterns? I'd like to try something out." Mrs. Hoppe looked through her shelves and found a pattern for teddy bears. It was very dusty, but Josefine was totally convinced that she could make something from it.

In the crate she also found brown bouclé material, which could easily be used as fur for stuffed toys. Mrs. Hoppe also found cutting patterns for giraffes, elephants and even for horses. "That's enough," Josefine said and she was as happy as a child. "Do you also have some thread?" "Well, I only have yellow. I've had it for a long time. I've got a whole box full. I had to pay the postman for it at the door. Then I realised it was not what I had ordered. It' not very good quality and then – well – the colour! You know that these days it's difficult to get hold of anything and certainly not good quality stuff" Mrs. Hoppe fetched an old cushion cover. Josefine stuffed the larger remnants into it and hurried home. Luckily she was always able to find a woman who was ready to do the housework, wash and clean, but also, if necessary, to cook and preserve fruit and vegetables when they were available. Right now she had Hilde.

One day Anderl had sent a woman to Josefine who was just looking for some work to get a meal. Josefine wanted to know what sort of work she could do. It turned out that Hilde worked in the castle close by. She had a roof over her head, but no money.

The count and his family had fled to Brazil, where the countess had grown up. Only the estate manager, two sheepdogs and a couple of other animals lived there now. In fact, she should not have told anyone about this, Hilde said, but people would soon find out. "That's not a problem," Josefine said, "Now you can help me with the cooking and then eat with us." Hilde agreed and it soon became clear that Josefine had been very lucky. Hilde always looked around and noticed what had to be done and she worked hard all day long.

Josefine said to Hilde, "The easiest way to work with these remnants would be with a sewing machine." "There was one in the castle. Maybe we could hire it. Should I ask the estate manager?" "Oh, yes, Hilde. Go there right now and ask him. That would be a great help." It was about twenty minutes to the castle. The path went through the park and then up a steep set of steps. There was a narrow road which led to the main door, but that was on the other side of the mountain. From there you could look over the river to the remains of an old ruined fortress. This way would take about three quarters of an hour. Hilde took the shorter path.

It was dusk. Franz came home earlier than expected. Suddenly he heard a horse drawn cart coming into the courtyard. He was shocked, wrenched open the door, ran up the stairs into the attic and hid himself. Josefine remained calm, looked out of the window and saw Hilde with a man at her side coming to the house. She went out to greet them. Hilde introduced the man as the estate manager. "Hilde said that it was urgent so we decided to put the sewing machine on the cart and bring it here. How long do you think you will need it?" "Well, I can't say exactly. For a few weeks." "All right, said the manager, "Hilde will tell me when I can collect it. Is there anybody here who can help us get it off the cart. It's on wheels, but it is very heavy." Josefine said, "I think we can mange it alone, don't you?" Hilde said, "Well, it only took two of us to lift it on to the cart even though it is very heavy."

Working together they lifted the sewing machine off the cart and pushed it into the flat. The children were very excited, crept into a corner and watched. "You don't have a lot of room here," said the manager, "the best place for it would be in front of the window, because of the light." Hilde asked if she could give the manager a glass of milk. Yes, of course. He enjoyed it. He had not drunk such good milk for a long time, he said. He thanked them and went back to the horse cart. "That's a wonderful animal," Josefine said, stroking its neck lovingly and remembering the horses that they had for the caravan. "There are still two of them in the stables," the manager said with pride, "the countess rode them every day. Luckily I can also use them to pull the cart." Josefine said, "Hopefully, one day, horses will no longer be collected. That's a shame. You should hide the animals. Right now they're collecting everything which is not nailed down. I'm amazed that the Nazis still haven't confiscated all the animals."

Josefine suddenly hesitated. She realised that she had said too much. Quickly she thanked him for the effort the manager had made and took her leave. Hilde drove back with him. Back in the flat, she remembered how quickly Franz had disappeared and she started to laugh about him. She laughed until she cried. She went to the children and they started to laugh as well. They stood round the sewing machine and laughed and laughed Oh, that's fine, now we have a machine! "Yes, but you mustn't touch it," Josefine said raising her index finger, "because it is very important for us. Do you understand?" "Yes," they chorused. Finally Franz had been really afraid, she thought and she did not bother to tell him that the coast was clear. He can stay in his hide away. He can't do any harm up there. But then, later, she called to him. "No need to shout," came the answer, "I'm not deaf." He came out of his hiding place and dusted down his clothes. "Have you got something to eat? I'm hungry." He said to distract her. He was angry with himself and was in no mood to start a discussion. "Look, we've got a sewing machine." "Oh! Leave me in peace! Am I going to get something to eat or not?" "Yes. It's all ready."

He started to eat, and said, in amazement, "Since when can you cook?" Josefine asked, "Does it taste good?" She had also been surprised at the herbs Hilde had put into it. It was really very tasty.

The bombs were coming closer. Bombers were flying over the large towns. Then you saw a glowing orange in the sky. It was gruesomely beautiful. You could almost think it was some sort of festival with rockets. The war had already lasted over two years. In Vordersberg, where Franz, Josefine and the children lived, no one had yet needed to take refuge in the cellar, but the blankets and emergency supplies were already there. There were little mounds of earth in the cellar, which had been stuffed with carrots and other vegetables. There was a barrel with preserved cabbage, jars of preserves with the owners' names on them and a barrel full of drinking water which needed to be replaced from time to time. The bombers flew by, a couple of kilometres left and right of the village. Obviously, this location was not strategically important. Now and again there were false air raid alarms but apart from that nothing happened. Up to now Vordersberg had not been touched by the war.

Little by little it became apparent from what Hilde told them that the castle estate manager delivered most of the stores to the old people's home. The count's mother was living there, with her own furniture, crockery and other things. She had not wanted to go to Brazil; not to a foreign country which she did not know. Hilde and the manager visited her regularly. She was content. She was writing her memoirs, read a lot of books, some even twice or three times. "That keeps her busy all day long and her mind is still intact. When she recounts something, everyone is keen to listen." Later it became clear that everything of value had been walled up in the castle fortifications. The valuable wine cellar had been sealed and the rooms in the lower floors had double walls. The electricity had been switched off and the switch box had been walled in. All the stoves had been removed or had been made unusable. The manager had his own little flat in the castle and always had a lot to do. He aired the rooms, looked after the animals and made sure that the surrounding land was cared for. But he had no privileges. He also had to live from his ration stamps. "Why has he not been called up?" Josefine wanted to know. Hilde had no idea. "That could happen," she replied "they are always recruiting new men. But then the manager is not exactly young." Then she looked at Josefine and said, "And anyway, your husband is also still free… Oh! Excuse me. Sometimes I say really stupid things." "That's fine," Josefine said to calm her, "up to now he's been able to get by, like a lot of other people in our little town, but he's already been in some tricky situations. I can't say anything else. I don't know exactly why and I don't want to know. That would only make me anxious."

The exchange business was doing well, but bit by bit everything was getting scarce. Sometimes Franz was already on his way at three in the night to get something. There were more and more spies and watchers around. There were people who denounced or betrayed others just to get some food. Early one morning Franz went down to the river to trap some fish with his torch. Sometimes he was lucky and could catch the fish with his bare hands. He knew a few tricks, but he could only catch carp. He did not like them very much. On that morning a few other people appeared wading through the river. They were carrying bundles on their heads. Franz immediately put out his torch so as not to be discovered. Suddenly he heard a shrill whistle, very close to him. "Come out with your hands up!" he heard someone shout, "forwards, march!" A bright light was scanning the water and the three people came to the bank. One man had raised one hand, with the other he was holding on to his hat. Suddenly he slipped, found his feet again. His hat had fallen in the water. He fished it out and put it back on his head. "Put everything down on the ground and take three steps back," a man in a brown uniform ordered. He searched everything and everyone. The man with the wet hat had something white running down his neck and face. He started to cry like a little child and looked into his hat. The white stuff which was now running down his face was sweetener; saccharine, which he had wrapped in newspaper and had dissolved. Saccharine was, at that time, very valuable. "Everything I have has melted away," he whined. In the strong light he was a picture of misery. Franz had seen everything and was deeply affected. Tears filled his eyes. After the man in uniform had looked at the hat, the two others grabbed their things and ran of in different directions. The man in uniform shouted, "Stop or I'll fire," but he did not know in which direction he should fire, and swearing he ran over the bridge. The man with the saccharin in his hat tidied his clothes and crept away.

Franz went on fishing until he had caught three medium sized fish but arrived home with his clothes covered in mud. "If your clothes were already stained by bilberries, then you could at least have picked some," Josefine said. "What do you mean? Bilberries? I hadn't noticed. It was still dark, but I'll go back and pick some." He went back. Saw the bilberries and cranberries all along the steep bank and wondered how he could pick them without slipping down. He went back and got a thick rope from the cooper. Then he made a narrow wooden shovel and covered it, on one side, with long nails. So, now he had a sort of rake with collecting shovel to gather the berries from the bushes. He grabbed a bucket and marched off. He fastened himself to a strong branch with the rope and harvested the berries to right and left. It did not take long before the bucket was full and his eyes glowed with delight. The children and Josefine will be amazed. Once again Franz thought he had invented something which he could make and either sell or exchange with the farmers round about. Now he had really got something which he could offer the farmers, but he had to promise not to sell the rake to private people, because they would destroy more than they could harvest.

One night someone knocked loudly on the window. It was on the side next to the chemist's courtyard. Franz went to look,

"What's the matter?" Someone whispered, "Can Mr. Dorn come quickly?" "My name is now Remi. What's it about?" It was the chemist, "Please make sure that you are not seen coming here. I've shut the dogs in. Don't come to the front. It's possible that someone is watching us. I've got a problem. I have to show you something." Franz knew that the children often went over the low roof to the cooper and then climbed into the pear tree and down into the neighbour's garden. "All right, I'm coming." He pulled on his trousers and a pullover and slipped into his shoes without putting on any socks. "Where are you going?" whispered Josefine. "Shush. The chemist knocked on the window. He wants to show me something." "Take care. Don't get dragged into something. You're almost certainly on the black list." But Franz had already left. She freed herself from Fredi, who had crept into her bed and went to the window grill. She could hear the water splashing into the water trough. Someone was washing. First her eyes had to get used to the darkness. She heard the garage door open and then close. Then, briefly, she saw a faint, nervous light from a torch under the garage door which was quickly put out. The door opened again and she saw two figures coming into the courtyard. Josefine assumed that it was Franz and the chemist. Two others crept over the courtyard to the garage, carrying a washing basket. Then they collected two buckets. Josefine smelt the scent of a fine soup. My, god, she thought, that smells good! Franz came back, put a few things into his leather briefcase, put on better clothes including a tie. Without a word Josefine gave him some food to take with him. She knew that she could not stop him. He kissed her on the cheek and whispered in her ear, "If anything happens, you know nothing."

Days passed. Josefine became nervous. She went to the chemist before it closed for lunch. The chemist waited until the last customer had left, looked at her nervously and then said, "What do you want?" Josefine asked, "Where is my husband?" The chemist went red and beads of sweat gathered on his nose. "No idea. How would I know? Now please go, if you don't need anything else. I'll leave a message behind the window grill if I hear anything." He wiped his nose with a handkerchief and opened the door for her. "God protect you," he said, before he locked the door. From then on she often found sweets, potatoes or other things behind the grill. Sometimes she saw the chemist crossing the courtyard, but he only shook his head and did not look in her direction.

Josefine did not trust herself to ask the policeman, who lived in the house, if he knew where Franz was hidden. But then, she thought, if he knew something, then he would certainly have told me. She started going to places Franz had often been to. Places where he had gambled, in the mine gallery and in other places. She even went to Berta, saying that she was just bringing a few sweets. Berta and Senta were, as always, in a good mood. Josefine smiled. "So you're doing fine. That's good. I'm happy for you. Then I am reassured. So I can go home. You know that I don't have much time. You know what I mean; with the children and everything." Berta said, "You don't need to worry about us. We've got enough to chew on for the moment." Then she added, quietly, "Since last week we have two war wounded here and we share their rations." She pointed to the end of the room which had been separated with a sheet. "They're from the city and they can't go back because of the bombing." Josefine came to the conclusion, that the way they were behaving, they knew nothing about Franz.

It was evening when Josefine left Berta and Senta. Then, suddenly, close by, a voice! A man's voice and speaking Bulgarian. "Don't turn round. I saw how your husband was taken away with other people. When you get the chance come into the garden." That was the gardener's voice. He knew Josefine and Franz. As silently as he came he disappeared. Josefine went on. Her heart was beating enough to burst. Just to calm down, she stood still for a moment and looked at a shop window. She pulled her headscarf a little forwards over her face and hurried home. Hilde was waiting for her, because she wanted to go. "See you tomorrow. Good night," and went out into the dark. "Yes. Until tomorrow."

The evening meal was on the stove. The children were playing. They had drawn a circle on the floor and were pushing little clay balls back and forth. "Hilde made clay balls with us. She baked them in the oven and coloured them," they called. Josefine took a glass of milk diluted with water and drank it down in one go. Her thoughts turned in her head. Just one question; what is going to happen now? She felt angry with Franz. If only I had no children, or at least just Emer, like before. She looked at Emer who was lying flat on the floor and rolling clay balls to Christine, who was sitting in front of him with her legs open. Emer lay his head to one side on the floor looked between her legs. Josefine ordered him to sit properly. A little ashamed, he did as he was told. From that day on Christine wore knickers with rubber bands on the legs.

What was that? They heard shuffling steps in the corridor and then the door latch was pushed down slowly. Who would come here at such a late hour? "Oh, dear Mother, it's you. That's a pleasant surprise," Josefine called when her mother put her head round the door. "I didn't want to knock. You know that everyone is listening." "No problem. Please, sit down," she said and kissed her mother's outstretched hands, "Can I take your things? Can I offer you a glass of boiled water? Oh, sorry, of course I've got some milk for you." "Yes, thank you child, a glass of milk would do me good after all the effort." Josefine got a glass, but she only had a little milk. "I'm sorry. I thought I had enough milk. Can I get you something to eat?" Josefine did not know what was on the stove, but it was certainly good. Hilde was a very good cook. But maybe it was just potatoes. And that is what it was. Mashed potatoes with yellow carrots and root vegetables. Dandelion roots and parsley. There was still just enough for one person and, of course, she gave it to her mother. All day long Josefine had only sucked three sweets. But there were also cooked forest berries in a pan. She took a cup full out. After she had eaten, Mother wanted to go to sleep, "Tomorrow is another day," she said, "and I don't have anything important to tell you." Josefine would have liked to talk to her; to tell her what was going through her head, but she did not know where to start. Her mother looked at the colourful stuffed toys which were lying around and Josefine told her how that had started.

Very early the next morning Josefine went to the gardener. She woke Emer and whispered in his ear, "I'm going to see if I can get some vegetables from the gardener. I'll see you later." She hurried and tried to avoid using the main street. At the garden she shook the gate which was fastened with a chain and a huge padlock. There was a drawing of a shepherd dog attached to the gate post. She looked through a gap in the fence and threw a stone in the direction of a home made mud house. It was a while before someone came. It was not the gardener, but a very small man who she did not know. When Josefine spoke to him in Bulgarian, he gave her a toothless grin and ran back to the little house. "Karel," he shouted and Karel came running out, dipped his comb into a barrel of water and combed his thick hair. He made an elegant gesture and invited Josefine into the house. "Tea?" he asked and gave Ismir, who had let her in, a sign. "Please, take a seat."

After a few more formalities, she started to ask some very searching questions. "About my husband," she said, "what did you see?" Karel told her that Franz had been pushed into a train with very small grilled windows. "Are you sure that it was my husband?" "Yes. I'm certain. You know that I have seen you both many times He was the last to be battered into the rail car." "In what direction was the train going?" Josefine wanted to know, "where was the train standing before it left the station?" Karel asked her to go with him and they went through the garden to a wooden fence which was covered with broken glass. "The tracks where the rail car was standing are right there and he pointed over the fence, "I was here, behind the fence. Look, here. Through this gap in the branches I saw what happened. There were at least ten people who were pushed into a wagon that was already full to bursting." Josefine hid her face in her hands. She wanted to run down the tracks. They went back to the mud house. On the way back Karel cut a head of cabbage and a few other vegetables and popped them into Josefine's colourful linen bag which she was carrying. Ismit got a flat loaf and put that in the bag. She thanked them. Then she suddenly started to swear loudly and let so many bad words out against Franz that Karel and Ismir were amazed. "Not so loud," they tried to calm her down, "otherwise you'll awake the devil in hell." She went into the little house and drank some tee. Ismir came with a cloth. When he opened it out he uncovered a golden, shining icon. He took it in his hands, kissed it a few times and crossed himself. Josefine was deeply moved. She excused herself for her outbreak, searched in her skirt pocket and fished out some coins. Karel took her hand in his and led her to the door. "Come and see us again. That is much more valuable than money. Nobody here speaks our language. Maybe by the next time you'll have had some news about your husband. Can I ask you to hide the bag in the folds of your skirt? I'm sure you understand." "Holy Mary, Mother of God protect you," she said. She took her leave from Karel and waved to Ismir. Karel looked right and left along the path to make sure that no one was close by and then gave her a sign that she could leave. She put the full bag under her skirt, held on to it through her pocket and hurried home taking a detour.

On the very same day information about Franz came from the police. There was a loud knock and the door and without waiting for an answer, a man came into the flat and disregarding any normal formalities started to speak. "Heil Hitler! Because of activities against the government Franz Remi has been interned until further notice. For security reasons I am not permitted to give you any more details until the case has been examined. Heil Hitler!" He put his hand to his hat clicked his heels. Bang! And he turned round. Josefine stood, there rooted to the spot. Reinhard came and clung to her skirt. “Come. We’ll close the door.” “Was someone there?” she heard her mother ask. “He knocked on the wrong door,” was her answer. What else could she say? She did not want to upset the family. As long as I can I’ll keep what I know to myself. I’ll say that Franz is travelling and that he did not tell me where he was going. That’s it.

Often, early in the morning, she found fresh vegetables in front of the door, hidden under the door mat. Josefine thought she knew where they came from and she would have liked to thank him. In the night she often listened at the door so that she could confront the person who was leaving the vegetables, but she heard nothing. She thought about it and fastened a string to the door mat which went to her bed. She fastened the other end to a child’s rattle. The first night she heard the sound of the rattle. She grabbed the torch and threw open the window. The light shone directly on Karel’s face. It was completely dark. Because of the war there were no street lights. She gave him a sign that he should wait, ran to the door and signalled that he should come in.

Pointing the torch to the floor, Josefine went to the cupboard and brought out a bottle of schnapps. Carefully she took two glasses from the shelf and poured out the drink. “Cheers,” she whispered, “finally I can thank you.” Very quietly she told him what she had, in the meantime, found out about Franz. “Karel tried to comfort her, “It’ll all turn out well.” A child coughed. Josefine listened, but then the child was quiet again. They were sitting very close to each other; whispered to each other and sometimes touched each other’s cheek or ear and her long hair touched his skin. She wears her hair loose, Karel thought. Karel smelt of earth, she noticed. Another cough. That must be Fredi. She crept to his bed, pulled the bed cover over him and stroked his head. Then she went back to Karel. In the light of the torch he could see her well shaped legs through her nightdress. She took his hand and led him to the door. “Round the back there is a room in front of the cellar. No one can see or hear us there. In that room we can talk to each other. Next time we'll meet there." She showed him the trick with the string and he promised to come back in three days. If he was late, then he should pull the string, but otherwise he should come at the same time as today.

As long as her mother was there and there was someone to look after the children, Josefine wanted to try to find out where Franz was. She went to Alfred, but he was not at home. She had thought that might be the case and had brought a pencil and some paper with her. She wrote, "Franz has been transported. Please get in touch." Without signing it she pushed it under the door. Then she went to the town hall and there she had to wait. There were women with children and old men sitting there. The younger men were in service on the front. Josefine saw a young office worker she knew going to the toilet and she followed her. "Is that you, Lotti?" the office worker asked from behind the closed lavatory door. "No. It's me, Mrs. Remi. You must remember me. I'm the interpreter. I'm looking for my husband. He was transported last Friday. I don't know where. I thought that maybe you could help to find out where he is. I know there are transport lists in the office. Please. I want to get in touch with my husband one way or another. Maybe I could even visit him." She heard someone rinsing the closet with a ladle and started to cry loudly. Miss Senger, the office worker, came out. "You know that what you are asking me is dangerous. Don't you know someone from the security people?" "Do you mean the Gestapo? No a courier told me that Franz had been transported and interned, but only that. Listen, Miss Senger, I'll pay you for overtime, or do you need vegetables, medicine or something else? Please help me." She sobbed deeply. Miss Segner thought about it for a few seconds and then she said, "We can't stay in the toilet any longer. Let's go outside. I'll see what I can do, but you have to promise that you tell no one about our conversation." "No, no, as God is my witness."

Josefine opened the door and asked a passing employee if there was a public toilet? I can see that this is only for employees."

"Why does everyone want to use the toilets here?" she asked, annoyed, "as if they didn't have toilets at home! If you don't have business here in the council offices then you are not allowed to use the toilet." "Sorry, it was only a question," Josefine said and left the town hall. She used the short time she had to walk down the railway tracks which she had intended to do. She went as far as the garden fence and looked through the gaps. There was no one around, but she had to be careful not to step on the broken glass. There were all sorts of rubbish lying near the tracks. She tore a strong branch from an elder tree and used it to turn over the rubbish, because she hoped to find some sign of Franz. She soon came to a place where the people had been pushed into the rail car. Right there the narrow path alongside the tracks came to an end. A little further on two tracks joined and became one. She looked around, saw no one and went on looking. She found a rolled up white handkerchief with ES embroidered in one corner, in a bunch of grass. Then, after a while, trampled into the ground, she found a single earring with a large tear shaped pearl on it. Probably silver, she thought after having wiped it. She wrapped it in the cloth and put it into her skirt pocket. She went on prodding the rubbish for some time and then gave up and went home.

There were no people queuing in front of the milk shop. It was closed. That is strange, she thought, up to now they had always had some milk, even if it had been diluted with water. She went on to the bread shop and there was no one there. Then she went into Anderl's restaurant. "Anderl, where are all the people? There's no one waiting in front of the shops." "Oh, you've missed something. A horde of soldiers arrived and, quick as lightning they loaded all the milk and bread and anything else they could lay their hands on in the shops onto their lorry and drove off. Anyone who stood in their way was threatened with their truncheons. They even hit a few people." "My God, she said and crossed herself, "but we have no milk at home and

Mother has come to visit us. I shouldn't complain. We still have some tea.

Anderl, have you any idea where Franz is?" She gave him a pleading look. Although she had only had a verbal report, she was not happy that only the gardener had seen anything. "So, you know nothing?" "Yes, but nothing exact." He answered, "Well, now they've caught him," he said sympathetically, "At first I couldn't believe it, but I can tell you this. On Friday, just as I wanted to close, the Station guard, who most of us know, came to me. He was already drunk. He banged his fist on the table and wanted to have one last schnapps. I poured it out and he drank it down in one. Then he started to talk. He said, 'They've pushed people into the rail cars like pigs. Women, children, men. All of them from round here. I recognised a few of them.' He mentioned a few names. Franz was one of them." Josefine went white. She was now one hundred percent sure that it was true. "I feel faint," she said and sat down. "It might not be so bad. There was a thick fog. Maybe the railway guard couldn't see clearly," Anderl, tried to comfort her, but then he went on, in a changed tone, "I'm going to tell you the way it is. The railway guard thought that the train was going to Germany; to the work camp in Dachau. I asked, why so far away? Then he said, possibly because of the Jews and started to swear like a trouper. 'These riff-raff,' he swore, 'these sub humans could have left. Their bloody money and property, of which they couldn't get enough, has brought us to the point of ruin,' and he went on like that. I couldn't listen to it any longer and I was glad when he drank his schnapps and finally left." Josefine put her hand to her mouth, "My God, holy Mary, Mother of God," she cried, "what else is going to happen to us? I can't think straight." "Come on. We're still alive. Everyone must carry their burden. Up to now we've got by. Tomorrow we will find out more. If I hear anything I'll tell you. And, I've got some milk from yesterday, but you'll have to use it today, otherwise it will go sour. Now go home and don't go crazy. Just wait. You'll certainly get some news." "Thank you Anderl."

She left the restaurant and went out on to the street without looking left or right and was almost run over by a car. "Stupid cow! Find another car to kick the bucket" the driver shouted at her. Oh God, and now that. Now you have to pull yourself together. Anderl told me to wait. I have to think of the children and Mother. I've got a lot to think about and do. She went quickly to the flat; greeted them all with the jug of milk in the hand and managed to conjure up a smile.

That same evening someone knocked on the door. Emer opened it, "Mummy, there's a woman here." Josefine went to the door and recognised Miss Senger from the council. "Oh, have you already got something for me?" Miss Senger looked at Emer, "Excuse me. Come with me" Josefine said and took her down to the cellar entrance and stood next to her in the light from the window. "Here is the number of the transport list and also that of your husband which I was able to quickly write down," Miss Sengeer said, "he's probably already in Dachau. I don't think that you can visit him there, but you can write to your husband. Now you have the most important details; both numbers and the address. Maybe you should write express." Josefine gave her her hand and thanked her from the bottom of her heart. "I need penicillin," Miss Senger said and gave Josefine a pleading look. "You know, you promised me. I'll come back tomorrow at the same time. Please, get me a few ampoules. It's for someone who has tuberculosis. He needs it urgently." She squeezed Josefine's hand and left. Tuberculosis! Josefine was shocked. Tuberculosis! That was infectious! She opened the door to the flat with her elbow so that fresh air came in. She was so afraid of this illness. Then she washed her hands with curd soap and scrubbed them with a brush.

Now she had to find the chemist. Once the shop was closed he often went across the courtyard to get goods from the store room. Not wanting to stand all evening in front of the window, she turned it into a game for the children. "Listen. The first one of you who sees the chemist crossing the courtyard will get a sweet, but you have to be very quiet and come to me quickly. Understood? Let's try." The children went to the window and pretended that they had seen someone in the courtyard. Then they ran to their mother. That was fun. "All right. Enough practice. Now you can do it. Now sit at the window and watch carefully." Christine's brothers pushed her away. She sat sulkily on Grandmother's lap and was cuddled.

And little Fredi was also not allowed to join in. That way Emer and Reinhard each had a window. After a few minutes Reinhard came running to mother, but he was so excited that he could only stammer. Josefine gave him a sweet and made a sign for Emer to come away from the window. She struck the window grill with a fork to make the chemist notice her. He looked around before he came close. "What is it?" "Please come to the cellar window." She went down to the cellar entrance and stood on a crate to get closer to the window. "Can you get me some penicillin? I owe someone a favour. It's for someone who has tuberculosis." "Penicillin? My God, that's very difficult to get hold of and very expensive. Who has penicillin these days?" he waved one hand in the air while he thought about it. His other hand was playing with the keys in his coat pocket. "Is the tuberculosis patient receiving treatment?" he wanted to know. "I don't know," Josefine answered, "the only thing I know is that I need a few ampoules by tomorrow evening."

The chemist wanted to say something else, but she interrupted him. "I've found out that my husband is in the concentration camp in Dachau. I don't know how he is." "Dachau concentration camp!" the chemist let out. He felt weak and held his head. "Hopefully he has not told anyone that I have hidden people in my warehouse." The dogs in the courtyard were becoming restless and started to growl quietly. "All right. I'll see you tomorrow," whispered Josefine and drew back from the cellar window. Grandmother had noticed nothing. "Take a look at Reinhard," she said as Josefine came back into the room. Reinhard had clamped the sweet between his lips and made his siblings mouths water. " What a rascal," Josefine said and laughed, "come here, all of you. I still have three. Emer gets the red one, Fredi the yellow and Christine can have the black one." The black sweet was liquorice. Christine spit it out on her hand and looked at Emer, who was standing close by. He grabbed her on the arm and pulled her behind grandmother's chair, knelt in front of her, took her face in both his hands and pressed his lips to hers. He spat his sweet into her mouth and started to lick the black liquorice from her hands. He licked them until her hands were clean. "What are you doing there?" shouted Josefine. She could still see how much pleasure Emer had licking his little sister's hands. "Go and wash your hands." She looked after him and thought, Emer is now a strong young man. I'll have to talk to him about the difference between men and women. He does things which I don't like. She had already found drawings of naked women in his trouser pockets and the photos of women in provocative underwear had been cut out of the newspapers which they used for toilet paper. Emer had certainly done that. Who else could have done it? He was the only "man" in the house.

Hilde came to soak the washing. "Tomorrow is washday. Not before time, because the children have got very few fresh clothes to wear. I keep having to wash the same clothes. Emer's clothes are almost too small for him and Christine is also growing out of her clothes, aren't you Christine?" She nodded her head and Hilde gave her a kiss on her cheek. "Don't coddle the child like that," Josefine complained in a rather loud tone. "Oh come on, it's not so bad," Grandmother interrupted, "that's no reason to shout." "Excuse me, Mother, but I'm with the children all day long. Sometimes I feel imprisoned in this little flat. Ah! I think I have a few clothing stamps. Come on Emer and Christine, let's see if we can get something suitable." It was not until she was standing in front of the shop that she realised it was midday. The shops would be closed for another hour. "The Red Cross is open. Come on, we'll go there. Maybe they have something for us."

There was almost no one on the street, but a group of teachers from the grammar school came out of the gate and approached her, "Mrs. Remi, it's good that we have met up. I wanted to ask you to come to the school. There's something we have to talk about." It was the head mistress. "Good afternoon," Josefine said, "can you tell me now what it's about? I'm alone with the children and it's difficult to get away, You must understand that?" The head mistress nodded and said to the children, "Can you go and play in the play ground for a while?" Then she said to Josefine, "Can we go into the school office for a moment? It's just here."

She went ahead, climbed a few step and asked Josefine to take a seat in her office. She took a file out of a cupboard and took out a written sheet. "Emer is very good in school, but you probably already know that," she said and paused, "but… how can I put this. Unfortunately we have been told that his father, that is your husband, has several times behaved in a politically unacceptable manner. You certainly have some idea about this." Josefine said, "I know nothing. My husband had been away for a few days and then a courier came to our house, probably from the Gestapo, and told me that he had been arrested. Why, how and where he is now will be sent to me in writing, after the case has been examined. But anyway, what has this got to do with the school?" "Well, your son will be sent back to the secondary school. That might not be too bad and he can always come back to us when your husband's case has been resolved." "My child won't be able to cope with that" Josefine said, "he won't understand why he should be punished. And in any case my husband Franz is not his father. You can see that from his name. So what is this about? Can't we appeal against this decision? Emer is an active member of the Hitler Youth and is proud to wear the HY badge. They can't punish him because my husband is supposed to have done something against the party. What am I saying? We don't even know if my husband is guilty of anything for which he should be punished. He could never harm anyone." The head mistress stood up, "I have made a note of everything and it will be discussed at the next meeting. Until then Emer should stay at home. I'll do my best for him; that I can promise you, Mrs. Remi. Goodbye."

Josefine wiped a few tears from her cheeks and took her leave. Outside she called both children. Of course Emer wanted to know then and there what the head mistress had said. "Oh, it was nothing. I'll tell you later. Come on, we were going to get some clothes for you."

Mrs. Reisin was on duty at the Red Cross. She got on very well with Josefine. But, what was that? A sign in front of the door said, "No distribution of clothes or food today." In recent times this sign was displayed often. Nevertheless, Josefine went in. "Good afternoon," she said to Mrs. Reisin, "well, whatever, I just wanted to say hello, even though I have apparently come on a wasted journey." Christine ran to Mrs. Reisin and held out her arms to her. "Ah, little Christine, how nice to see you again, my little darling." She sat the child on the table. "Heil Hitler, Mrs. Remi and Heil Hitler Emer. Isn't it good that there's no school today?" "I like going to school," Emer said, "because I'm the best in the class."

He looked proudly at Mrs. Reisin. "Well, that's great," she said admiringly, "I wish my children were a bit more ambitious. Apart from football and the HY they haven't anything in their heads. But tell me, Emer, last week you didn't come to the HY meeting. My husband brought your uniform back home. You can pick it up from us. You should wear it at the next meeting. All right?" Emer nodded. Josefine pointed to Christine, "You can put her back on the floor now." "Come little one, I'd like to weigh you and see how tall you are." Mrs. Reisin put Christine on the scales and then stood her against the wall where they had drawn a measuring scale. Well you could do with growing a bit and putting some fat on your bones, but you're a lovely little child and you look healthy as well." Josefine said, "Please measure Emer. He's got a lot of muscle in his arms and legs from gymnastics. He'll certainly be a great sportsman or acrobat one day. I can see that already." Mrs. Reisin said, "Yes he looks very good. But Mrs. Remi, tell me, what do you need. What can I do for you?" Josefine said, "The boy is growing out of his clothes and he needs new shoes as well."

Mrs. Reisin fetched a few sacks of clothes. In one she found a pretty knitted jacket, stockings and a nightdress for Christine and in the other she found something for Emer. "Look," she said, "here's a good pullover for you, Emer and a nice, white shirt. It looks a bit on the large size but you'll soon grow into it, if you keep on growing. Do you want these things?" "Maybe there's a pullover without stripes," Emer replied. "That's all we have right now. We have to be thankful for everything people can still donate. I've got some striped pyjamas for you. Blue and white, They're new." Emer was horrified, "Oh no! I don't want to look like someone from a concentration camp! Mr. Reisin said the criminals with those suits are called zebras. They're kept behind electrified barbed wire. He showed us pictures and a Jewish star and…" Josefine stopped him. "Don't talk so much." She turned to Mrs. Reisin, "We'll take the other things. You must believe me; right now we're happy and thankful for any help. Well, we don't want to detain you any longer. Have a good day and many, many thanks." "That's all right," Mrs. Reisin said, opened the door with a "Heil Hitler" and gave Christine a friendly tap on the rear. They both liked each other. That was clear to see.

The door was hardly closed as Josefine exclaimed, "Just look at that. If this cheeky little minx hadn't wound Mrs. Reisin round her finger we would have got nothing today." She hid the bag full of clothes under her wide skirt and went home with the two children. Her thoughts were all over the place: in the concentration camp; with the chemist, with the woman from the council; with Karel, the gardener. I have to put everything in order and collect my thoughts about who I can tell what. I cannot let any false word slip from my lips. I have to protect my mother the children and Hilde. The best thing is to distract them whenever possible. Give short, clear answers to difficult questions. I have to make it clear to the woman from the office that Franz is no longer able to support us. We need financial help and food ration stamps. I cannot wait until I have used them all.

In the distance she heard the air raid warning. The city was being bombed again. Our hospital here is full of wounded. Women help as first aiders and work in the fields until they are ready to drop. The war seems to have no end she thought. When she got to the house she told the children to go into the flat. She went to stand in a green, sheltered area in the courtyard. She ran her bare feet over the grass and freed in spirit the heavy burden from her shoulders. She raised her eyes to the sky, closed them and concentrated on taking deep breaths. She stood like this for a few minutes and then she looked down, touched the earth and put her shoes back on. After this ritual she felt strengthened and went into the flat. Grandmother and Hilde were there to examine the clothes. Josefine sat down and drank a cup of tea. Because everyone thought that Emer had received such a beautiful pullover, he put it on and gave his to Reinhard. "It's like Christmas," Hilde said and everyone rejoiced.

Josefine looked at the clock. It was time for the chemist to appear. She went down to the cellar, looked out of the window and saw white trousers and black shoes crossing the courtyard. She stood on a crate and opened the window. The chemist pulled a small box and a few unwrapped medicines out of his pocket and put them into her outstretched hand. "That's all I've got," he said, "tell the man who is sick that he must go to the hospital. I know someone who has even been sent to Switzerland in a clinic in Davos. I wish him a good recovery and lots of luck". Then he left. Josefine looked at the medicines: An ampoule, some herb oil and a few pills and all of them with instructions. She took out her handkerchief, wrapped the medicines in it and pushed it under a cupboard. In an hour and a half the woman from the office would be there to collect it.

In the meantime Josefine went to see how Hilde was getting on with the washing. The lye was steaming in the boiler and the washing had been separated into two buckets according to colour and material. Josefine had to again admit that she knew very little about washing and just stood there. Hilde checked the temperature and said, " For the washing in this bucket, we'll have to wait until the water is simmering. The clothes in that bucket can only be quickly squeezed in cold water. Oh, excuse me. I didn't need to tell you that." Josefine didn't react and simply asked Hilde to fill the boiler with water after the washing was finished so that they could all take a bath. When it was almost six o'clock, Hilde got ready to leave. Before she left she explained what she had done and what she would do tomorrow. This recital could be heard every day. Josefine normally agreed, but the constant explanation got on her nerves. However, Hilde kept to this ritual She was a simple quiet soul and had very good manners and she passed this on to the children.

Grandmother and the children were close to the garden fence burying a dead bird which they had found. So that's all right, Josefine thought, because Miss Senger would be arriving any minute.

She went into the cellar, pulled out the medicines and heard Miss Senger, wheezing heavily, because on that day she was having difficulty breathing. "Good evening, Miss Senger. Sit down here on the crate. You're not getting any air." Josefine pulled up another crate and sat down beside her. Miss Senger searched in her pocket and brought out an envelope. "Here. I've written a few lines with the typewriter. You only need to sign it, then I can send it tomorrow with the office letters and so it won't cost you anything. I'll read it to you, but first I have to catch my breath." In the letter, it was asked when Franz would finally come home; how he was and if Josefine could do anything for him. And then added: "We miss you and the children are always asking about you. We hope that you will soon be back home. With all our love, from your wife and the children.". At the top of the letter there was the transport number, his personal number and a sign for political prisoners. Josefine took the sheet, read it through again, signed it and then she looked at the envelop. To Mr. Franz Remi, IH/ PNR: …KZ Dachau, Grossdeutschland. "Oh, that's how you write it. I would have written it differently." "Yes, but I thought that was for the best," Miss Senger said, "every thing we know is there. Now we can only hope that your husband gets the letter, because it will certainly be read before it is given to him. I've written your address on the back and here is a note for you with the address on it. By the way, I've discovered that some of the people, who were caught then, had a visa to go abroad, but still didn't get an exit visa. Can you imagine that? How these people have been pushed from place to place? The only hope, for those who are still here is to escape to Italy or France, in the direction of Marseille."

She stuck down the envelope, put it in her pocket and looked hopefully at Josefine, "Have you got something for me?" Josefine said, "Yes. I've got the medicine. To be absolutely truthful I didn't think you would write the letter. There are still some honest people around. Here is the penicillin and also two other medications which the sick person should take following the instructions. The person who gave me these things said that the sick person should go to the hospital. The risk of infection is too high. As far as I know people with tuberculosis have to be isolated." Miss Senger started to cry, "That's not possible. I can't say anything. Please. Our conversation must remain between us two." She stood up, hid the medicines and left. Josefine did not have the chance to ask for a confirmation that she was now dependent on social money. All right, she had to postpone that until the next day. When she went back into the flat, Grandmother and the children were sitting at the table. There was a thick maize semolina made with milk which had once again been diluted with water, because otherwise it would have not been enough for all of them. The maize was nutritional and filled the stomach. They all liked it, but it was not a good idea to tell them that, in actual fact, the maize was normally fed to the pigs and was considered to be food for poor people.

XII

The night arrived when Josefine and Karel had arranged to meet. Actually she had wanted to cancel it, and then again she wanted to go. He provided her so generously with vegetables and the language brought them together. She set up the string, but this time she did not fasten it to a child's rattle but to her toe so that no one else would wake up. As the appointed hour approached, her heart beat faster, but still sleep overcame her from which she was suddenly startled when she felt her toe being pulled. She sat up abruptly and looked for the torch, but could not find it. In darkness she crept to the door then felt her way along the wall to the cellar storeroom.

There was a dim light shining through the window from the chemist's courtyard. Josefine and Karel sat down on the crates, went over everything which had happened and philosophised about what the future would bring. Karel held her hand and depending on what they were talking about pressed it, lightly or sometimes harder, but with so much feeling that she did not notice how cold it was in the storeroom. They both felt strong emotions. He ran his fingers through her hair and carefully untangled it; stroked her face gently and held his thumb tenderly to her lips. All the time he was speaking calmly and quietly and his face came nearer and nearer to hers. She did not move when he kissed her, because she had a tremendous longing for tenderness. Then she let herself slip onto the floor on which were laying some folded cardboard boxes and pulled him down to her. Karel took off his jacket and pushed it under Josefine's head. Then he felt her body. He kissed her and kissed her so that she was dizzy, but she let it all happen. It was heavenly… The experience was for both of them so immense that they could hardly wait to see each other again.

Time passed. Emer was allowed to stay in the high school. The fact that Franz was not his father and that his real father was registered as missing, made those responsible change their minds. Unfortunately it also came out that Josefine had only been engaged to his real father and was not married to him. "So! Emer is a bastard." This got around and from then on he was the target for badmouthing and scandal. He was teased by his school friends and they avoided him. Josefine was worried. Emer had never been a child with good friends. Of course she blamed Franz. If he had just stayed quiet and had not got mixed up in politics then Emer would have been spared all this. In school Emer's work was always down graded. Only the gymnastic teacher believed in him. She always encouraged him to achieve more. "If you want, you can visit me at home," she said, "then I'll show you the cup which I won in floor gymnastics."

Josefine was happy that at least the sports teacher took his part. "Of course you can visit her. Would you have anything against my coming with you the first time? I'd like to get to know her better." Emer said, "Come Mummy. We can go there right now." "Now? Is she at home?" "Yes," said Emer, "I think so." It was only about 500 metres away. On the door she saw, on the name plate, H. Slavic. Josefine knocked and Mrs. Slavic opened the door. "Ah! Emer, hello. This is certainly your mother. I can see the resemblance," she laughed and, a little embarrassed, invited them in. In the middle of the room there was a double bed and there was a small table in front of it where they sat down. On one side there was a small cooking area. It was a one room flat. Mrs. Slavic brought them some fruit juice to drink. Then she took some photos out of a colourful box, took a cup from a corner and put it into Emer's hands. Then she started to talk non stop. Emer was fascinated by her. He looked at her the whole time. This incessant chatter somehow disturbed Josefine. Although she felt that Mrs. Slavic was lonely, because her husband was away in the war, she did not trust the way the woman was behaving. She was hiding something, she thought and after a while she said, "Come Emer, we've been here long enough. You've now seen the photos and the cup. Thank Mrs. Slavic for the drink. Good bye, Mrs. Slavic. I'm pleased to have met you." Mrs. Slavic raised her hand in greeting, but only said, "Heil…" and ended the phrase with, "Have a nice evening."

When they got home Christine was sitting in a corner crying. Emer went to her right away, to comfort her. "Why are you crying?" She showed him her earlobes. They were crusted with blood and a length of yarn had been pulled through them, "Ugh. Who did that to you?" Emer asked, full of sympathy. Christine pointed to her grandmother. He went to her and on the table he saw a thick needle which was violet because it had been in the fire. "Hey! What's that?" Emer asked, horrified, "what have you done?" Grandmother answered. "I used it to make holes in Christine's ears. But before I did it I had to make it red hot to kill all the germs so that she wouldn't get an infection." Emer went red with anger, went to his mother and shook her. "Say something. Why did she do that? Tell her off." He went back to Christine and gently wiped away her tears. "Do you want something? Mummy has probably got a sweet for you." "I'm hungry and thirsty," she whispered. He got milk from the window sill, took a slice of bread, which he spread with jam. He took his little sister in his arms and let her drink the milk and take a bite from the bread. He cradled her. He was only there for her. He fetched a cushion and lay down with her. Exhausted from everything which had happened, they fell asleep.

It was three weeks before Josefine heard anything from Franz. The postman wanted to go straight to her, but unashamedly he looked more closely at the envelope. "A letter for you, Mrs. Remi. Heil Hitler!" Josefine looked at him without a word and took the letter. It had been stamped at the concentrations camp, Dachau and it was dated. She hid herself in the cellar storeroom and carefully opened the envelope. Franz's handwriting was difficult to read. He wrote, "Dear wife, don't worry. Considering my situation, I'm fine and hope that goes for all of you too. I have to be brief. Your Franz."

Later she found out that he was only allowed to write 25 words. She put the letter back in the envelope and went off to Karel, to show him the letter. She did not want to be seen going straight there, so she took a few stuffed animals to be sold in Mrs. Gasser's food shop with her. "Mother, I'm just going to Mrs. Gasser. Hilde will be here soon to do the housework. The children won't be back from school before 2 o'clock. You don't need to do anything. Go for a walk. Fresh air will do you good. See you later." Luckily there were a few customers waiting in Mrs. Gasser's shop, so she didn't need to get into a long conversation with her. "Excuse me, Mrs. Gasser, I just want to leave these with you. They're all labelled."

In front of the old people's home Josefine saw the empty vegetable carts from the garden. She looked around her and went slowly to the carts. Ismir was standing in front of the house door. He was holding something in his hand. When he saw Josefine he gave her a sign to pass by. She went on and heard loud voices. She wanted to know what was going on and bent down, as though she was fastening her shoe laces. She saw two men in brown shirts with Swastika armbands arguing with the director of the house in the garden, but she could not understand what they were saying. So she went on her way. Ismir disappeared into the house.

Only employees were allowed to go into the garden. Josefine opened the door, grabbed a watering can which was standing there and went to the water trough. She almost always wore a head scarf and she pulled it low over her forehead. The other workers took no notice of her. The watering can was not quite full and then Karel came, "What is it, dear?" he said without looking at her, "it's dangerous to come here today. We are being examined and have to give up our papers. Go behind the house," he told her and picked up some rubbish, so as not to be suspect. She said nothing. Picked up the watering can and went behind the clay house. It took a while before he came. She showed him the letter. "Can you read it to me?" Josefine read the few lines and then asked, "What do you think I should do now? Mother, the children – I can't just drop everything and go to find out what is going on, but I should still do something." Karel said, "Don't do anything hasty. I'll come and visit you this evening. Maybe we can think of something until then. Now go home."

When she got home she was in a miserable mood and she also felt sick. She vomited. "Are you pregnant again?" she heard her mother ask. Pregnant? When was the last time with Franz? No, that's not possible. Jesus! It can't be from Karel?! She went hot and cold. Beads of perspiration stood on her forehead. "What's the matter with you? Come and drink something." Her mother stood up and poured out some peppermint tea for her which Hilde had made and was still standing on the stove. She looked thoughtful and, a little tense, said, "I ought to go and have a look at Father. The last time I saw him he didn't look too good. He didn't say anything, but somehow he looked tired." Josefine said, ""Yes, if that's what you think. When do you want to go?" Mother replied, "I don't like travelling any more. It's just good that I don't have to go through the town. These bombs. My God, you can hear them from here. It's terrible. It's shocking that people always have to fight each other. I've seen so much misery in my life. I could tell you about it for days. Earlier, when we used to travel around, people were so friendly to us. We had some happy times. Do you remember?" "Yes, Mother. I remember." Suddenly, "I want to go now. Come on, help me. I'm getting really fidgety. I'll take the 3 o'clock bus again and, if everything goes well, in two hours I'll be with my bear." Hilde heard that and said, "That's a lovely nickname! Should I put some tea in your travelling bottle and get together some food for the journey?" "Yes, that would be nice. You know what I can eat and what not." Hilde took some bread and dripping from the cupboard. She cut the crust from the bread and spread some dripping on it. Josefine looked at it and shivered, because she was the only one who knew that it was not just any kind of dripping, but dog fat!

When everything was ready, they all went with Grandmother to the bus. When the bus came, Emer wanted to go with her. He started to gesture wildly. Josefine could hardly hold him back. "I want to go away as well," he shouted, "please Grandmother, let me come with you. Please, please." Passers bye stood still and saw how he was clinging to the bus door. Grandmother came to the door and said, "Come get on." "You can't do that, dear Mother," cried Josefine, "he still has to go to school." "You told me he was a model pupil. In that case he can certainly stay away for three weeks. Then we'll be back. As for clothes, we'll find something from his cousin. So, Emer say goodbye to your mother, sister and brothers." He hugged them all and said, "I'll come back soon." He whispered in Christine's ear "I'll bring you a present". Reinhard and Fredi were very calm. They didn't feel any lust to travel. They were happy to stay there and waved. Emer was smiling all over. He sent kisses through the bus window. Josefine was very wistful. "Emer still has travellers' blood in him," she said so loud, that everyone around her could hear, "he travelled around a lot with us." She held back her tears, drew herself up proudly and waved after the departing bus.

Back home she walked back and forth, disturbed. Hilde asked, carefully, if there was anything more to do. "Oh, Hilde. I don't know how to say this. My husband wrote to me and told me where he is and that he's fine. But he asked me to visit him for a few days," she lied, "but how can I do that? I want to see him again but who can look after the children?" Hilde looked at her, "If I may be so bold, maybe you thought of me, but I can't imagine staying here overnight. On the other hand, in my room in the castle I have only room for two." Josefine said, "If you could take two of them, I would be very grateful. Maybe we can think of something else. But before it's too late I'll go to the town park. There, they've built, three nice wooden barracks. That's where the social office is now and where you can get food ration stamps. I'll be back soon." She hurried off and met Mrs. Reisin in the social office. "Ah, Mrs. Remi, we seem to be meeting quite frequently recently. I heard that your mother has left and taken Emer with her. Hopefully not for long. He shouldn't miss too much school. It's important for him if he is going to get on in life." "No, no," Josefine said, "it's only for three weeks and he can cope with that, as you well know. But, I've had news from my husband. I don't know if you have noticed that he has been away for some time. He wants me to visit him, but I don't know who could look after Christine. The two boys can stay with Hilde in the castle." She was counting on Mrs. Reisin, because she had really taken to Christine, but she did not get the immediate agreement she had expected. "Haven't you thought about Berta? She's so good with children." "That's no good. She has two wounded men to care for which takes up all her time and then, she hasn't got an extra place to sleep." Mrs. Reisin said, "It depends on when you want to go. From tomorrow until the middle of next week I don't have anything special to do apart from a few hours each day in the field hospital. On weekdays Christine would be in the kindergarten and she could spend Saturday and Sunday with my family. That would be all right. When would you like to bring her to me?" Josefine almost wanted to hug her, because she was so happy. "If I could bring Christine to you this evening then I would be on my way tomorrow." Mrs. Reisin said, "Good. We'll see each other later. Let's hope it works out." When she got home Josefine asked Hilde to take Christine to Mrs. Reisin and to tell her a few things about food and clothes. She gave her some money and the rest of her food ration stamps. If she needed anything, she should go to Mrs. Reisin. She asked Hilde to take the children quickly, because she also had a few things to do. Once all the children had been taken care of, Josefine got out her rucksack and packed some dripping, jam, apples and a flask of tea. She cut some slices of bread and wrapped them in a cloth. I'll have to tell Anderl, she thought. Anderl was happy that she had come to him and gave her a half bottle of schnapps to take with her. She went to the chemist and asked him for bandages, healing ointment and pain killers. The chemist said, "You know what? I'll put all of that together for you. Do you need it today?" "Yes, today. I'm going to visit my husband and I'm leaving early tomorrow morning." "Oh, you're going to do that? All right. Just before I close up I'll have everything ready for you." She left the shop and wondered if Alfred might have some ready cash. She hurried to his house. "Who's there?" "It's me Josefine." He opened the door, standing there in his vest and military trousers. "I had just lain down. I've just got back. I've got a week's leave. I was going to visit you tomorrow." Josefine told him what had happened. He was shocked. "Are you sure that Franz is in a concentration camp?" She handed him the letter. Alfred read it and counted the words, "He has written exactly 25 words. Prisoners are not allowed to write more, but that depends on why he has been interned. Why is he there?" "I've no idea, Alfred. I've just come to you because I need money. I'm going to him early tomorrow." Alfred said, "He's got some money due from me." He took a piece of paper, wrote something on it and said, "Please sign here." Josefine was amazed, "How come Franz has money with you?" "Oh," Alfred said, "It's a long story. Just sign." Josefine said, "I'm walking around in shoes with holes in them just so I can put food on the table and he gave you money. Where did he get it from?" "Please, Josefine, just leave it. Right now you don't understand and the less you know the better for us all. Here, take the money. That should be enough for your journey. As soon as I can I'll sort it out. Right now I need to sleep, sleep, sleep. Greet him from me."

Josefine went up into the town. She was wondering if she could get some information from Berta. She knocked lightly on the door. "Who is it?" "It's me, Josefine." "Just a moment." It took some time before she came to the door. The windows were open wide. There was a smell of roasted chicken. Berta asked, "What brings you to me?" Jokingly Josefine said, "It could be just a visit, but it could be something more. Can I speak to you alone?" Berta said, "If you whisper, no one will understand us." Josefine saw that the curtain round a bed was moving and that she was being watched. Josefine said, "As you wish. Your dear brother has landed in the concentration camp in Dachau and no one knows why. Franz wants me to visit him. I think he expects help from us. Unfortunately the money I have is not enough. So now I'm asking you if you have anything to spare for your brother. I'm leaving early tomorrow." Berta said, "Oh my God, my God why? What a disaster. What should I do?"

Josefine mentioned a fairly large sum. "You need as much as that?" "Not me," Josefine tried to get her anger under control, "I'm trying to help your brother, who also happens to be my husband and the father of three of my children." Her stomach was churning and she felt the bile rising. Berta said, "Wait, I'll be back in a moment."

She disappeared into the dark corridor. After a while she called. "Come here. Here is your money and some packets of cigarettes, his favourites. Hide them in your bag. But you have to promise me something. If sometime in the future, it's better for you, then I'd like you to pay most of it back, possibly a bit at a time. Senta and I have really saved that money by spending less on food. "That's all right. I'll tell Franz. Close the windows, otherwise you and the chickens will catch cold. May God protect you from all the bad things in the world." Josefine hated herself for saying that. "But damn it", she said softly. I thought that the pair of them were just surviving, but then that smell of roast chicken and I really hadn't expected her to give me such a large sum. She stopped and counted the money. It was exactly the sum she had asked for. Where had she got the money, Josefine asked herself?

Then she thought that she should go to Mrs. Gasser; maybe she had already sold a few stuffed toys. The last time she told me that as long as she had a few, I shouldn't bring her any more.

But she had taken the ones she had brought that morning, so she must have sold some. But first I have to go to the chemist. The chemist asked her to come into the back room. "I've got your things ready," he said and showed her what he had put together. "Look; bandages, wound and healing ointments, pain killers, DDT powder for lice and also something for diphtheria. I've heard on the radio about outbreaks of this illness. I've also given you charcoal tablets for diarrhoea. I hope you get through to your husband. You do have a travel and visiting permit?" "Yes, yes," she lied, "I just have to find out how I can get there. I hope that a lorry driver will take me. I know the stopping places." "Isn't that dangerous?" "Josefine said, "Up to now nothing has happened. I don't have a great deal of experience, but I do have a good understanding of people."

The chemist was amazed at her courage. "You should take a map with you. First of all you should go to Salzburg and then on to Munich. Have you ever been in this region?" "No, but with God's help, I won't get lost." "I've got an old road map. I can get it for you if you want."

Just then the chemist's assistant came in, "Excuse me. Is this going to take long? Mr. Baumgartner is waiting for you." She was surprised that the chemist had served this woman for so long, 'behind the counter' as one might say. "Mrs. Remi, I have to go back into the shop. I'll put the map on your window sill and please, tell your husband how sorry we all are. Up to now I haven't any idea how I can help to get him out. I'll keep asking around amongst my acquaintances. I really am doing my best, believe me." "Well," said Josefine, "at least we now know where he is." She took a few bank notes out of her pocket, but the chemist refused. "You don't think that I want to take them. Go now and good luck on your journey."

Josefine took her leave and thought, today must be my lucky day. Let's see if I have some luck with Mrs. Gasser and she has sold something. And she had. Mrs. Gasser had made several sales. Josefine told her that she was going away for a few days and that Hilde would be collecting the food. She still had a few food ration stamps. She would settle up with her later. Mrs. Gasser thought that that was in order.

It was already evening when Josefine got back to the flat. She took off her shoes and then she heard someone knocking on the window. It was the chemist. "Here is the road map. Something else. Mr. Baumgartner is staying with Frühwirt overnight and I know that he is going to Salzburg early in the morning. I can ask him if he could take you with him. Would you agree?" Of course she agreed. He promised to leave a note on the window sill with the place and time of departure. He was sure that it would be all right.

Then, as promised, Karel arrived. He was amazed that Josefine invited him into the flat. "Where are the children?" he wanted to know and produced, among other things, four simple flutes and a little bird all finely carved from wood. "Something for everyone," he said and looked at her with warm eyes. Josefine said, "The children are not here. I've found good places for them. It's almost certain that early tomorrow morning I can go to Salzburg with an acquaintance of the chemist." While she was telling him this, she made some tea. Neither of them wanted to eat. "You should take a blanket with you, so that you don't freeze. Then maybe you can leave it in the camp." Karel knew what it was like in a concentrations camp. He had experienced many things; he had almost frozen to death and almost died of hunger. In the fourth camp, the last one he was in, they were looking for landscape gardeners for a new park in the town. He grabbed the opportunity. So he and Ismir were sent to the gardens where they had a little peace and even some freedom. But neither of them wanted to talk about the past. They only lived in the present.

"But it is so wonderful when you get some love back for everything you have lost. That is a true present," he said. And that was just what he found in Josefine's embrace. He understood that she still wanted to help Franz, with all her strength, in spite of all the anger she felt deep within about what he had done to her.

Josefine loved Karel very much. His care, warmth and consideration which he also showed to her children, even though he hardly knew them, meant the world to her. His eyes spoke volumes. They both enjoyed every moment that they were together. Just do not think about tomorrow. But Karel could not stay long. There were ever more patrols on the streets. All the windows had to blacked out. Before Karel left on that evening, he asked Josefine if he could do something for her. "Now you can only pray and wish me luck. My knees are beginning to shake, but I have to go to Franz. I could never forgive myself if I did not try to help him. I can't even think about whether it's possible, otherwise I would lose my courage right now." Karel said, "Take all your papers with you, including the letter. Put everything in your clothes. You have large hidden pockets in your skirt. That's good." He tried to joke and laughed a little. They hugged each other, as though it was the last time. Then he went along the wall to the courtyard gate, opened it a crack. She saw him jump over the fence into the neighbour's garden. Since he had worked in most of the gardens, he new a secret path back home.

XIII

In fact, the next morning Josephine was really able to travel with Mr. Baumgartner, a business man who brought goods to outlying chemists. He told her which route he was going to take. Stupidly, she did not know how much the chemist had told him. She had to be careful. She decided to let him do the talking. So she found out that that the chemist had told him that she wanted to visit someone in Salzburg. She was happy to hear that, hid her rucksack and put her blanket over it. "Keep your identity card handy. We're going to have to go through many control posts." Josefine said, "I've got my Aryan card with me. Do you think that is enough?" "Yes. That's excellent. We have to stop for petrol and then we can get on our way." Josefine wanted to know if he expected to be paid for taking her with him. "Can I give you something for your expenses?" "That's very kind of you, but everything is paid for by my company. Don't worry about it."

The journey progressed slowly, because Mr. Baumgartner stopped at every chemist and brought them goods, but always just small packages. When they came to a control he showed a special paper, got out of the car, opened the boot and without any further questions they were able to continue. Josefine was never asked to show her identity card. She thought that in this way, you could save many people from the Nazis. What was written on that paper? She took out her road map to follow the route they were taking. "Do you really need to go to Salzburg?" Mr. Baumgartner asked suddenly, "I only ask because many bombs have fallen on the town. Look, from here you can see many buses going to Salzburg, but I am going through this wood. It's a short cut and it's not as dangerous as the open road."

The track through the wood was narrow. Suddenly they heard shots, stop commands, dog barks and noise. Mr. Baumgartner stopped suddenly. Dogs ran to the car, jumped up and scratched the car. "Call off the dogs," Mr. Baumgartner shouted, "What's going on?" He jumped out of the car showing no fear of the dogs or the soldiers coming towards him. He took something out of his small breast pocket and held it up to them. They looked at it, clapped their heels together and stood at ease. One of them shouted "I have to inform you. A few prisoners have escaped from the quarry." Another asked Baumgartner, "Have you seen any?" "No," he roared, "now clear the way." He got back in the car and drove on. He seemed to be calm, but Josefine noticed that he was nervous. He apologised to her. "I'm sorry, but we're at war." Josefine began to feel uncomfortable.

He must be a high ranking official she thought. The way he had shouted chilled her to the marrow. "Oh, the shots really frightened me," she said, "and then the dogs. I hope they haven't scratched your lovely car. But, you know, you shouldn't be angry with the soldiers, they're only doing their duty." After a fork, the road went steeply downhill. "Dammit, now I've taken the wrong road. I hope I can turn round somewhere. Through the trees they could see long barracks and watch towers, behind several wired fences. As they drove on slowly they could see more and more barracks. They stopped on a hillside. There was a barrier in front of them bearing a notice with the Swastika and the words:

THOROUGH TRAFFIC STRICTLY FORBIDDEN – BEWARE OF LIVE SHOTS. Mr. Baumgartner swore, tried to reverse without success. He started to blow the horn wildly. Beads of perspiration were standing on his forehead. Soldiers appeared behind the barrier; guns at the ready. "Get out and come forward slowly with your hands up!" Mr. Baumgartner waved his special document. "Is nobody going to come and look at this pass paper?" One soldier came closer, looked at the paper and immediately raised his arm, "Heil Hitler! Excuse me Officer…", he did not get any further because Mr. Baumgartner interrupted him. "Clear the way. I'm in a hurry." Josefine raised her arms. Her whole body was shaking. She pressed her fingers against the car windows to try to stop trembling. She wanted to go and relieve herself behind a tree, but this was certainly not the right moment. Mr. Baumgartner lit a cigarette. A soldier said to Josefine, "All right. You can put your hands down now."

Relieved, she lowered her hands, but she really had to go behind the bushes. Somewhat ashamed, she said to the soldier, "I have to …." "Hurry up!" When she came back Mr. Baumgartner said, "Not very pleasant, eh?" He took his briefcase from behind the seat and put it on the bonnet. Then he took a small piece of paper, wrote a few lines on it and said to her, "Your Aryan identity card please." She got into the car, got her identity card and handed it to him. What was he doing, she thought, have I seen or heard too much?

Secretly she took a sip of tea out of the tee bottle which was hidden under her shawl. "You may continue," a soldier's voice suddenly said. But Mr. Baumgartner took his time. He took out a stamp and an ink pad, inked the stamp and then pressed it on the piece of paper which he had written. He then put everything away and sat in the driver's seat. He tapped his forehead with his hand and then drove off. "Here, take your identity card back," he said and handed it to her, "I've written a few lines so that you can get to your destination more easily. Soon I'm going to have to ask you to take the bus for the rest of your journey. Josefine thanked him warmly. She knew how important that could be, but she did not trust herself to look at the paper which he had put in her identity card. Hastily she put her identity card away. When she looked up again, she saw that they were not far from the wire fence. Then! It took her breath away. Behind the fence she saw people with shaved heads, thin as rakes, their eyes sunk deep in their sockets. It was difficult to speak, but she asked, "What kind of people are they?" Baumgartner said, "They're all criminals, if you like. The lowest form of human. The scum of our German empire. Don't look at them."

Josefine remained silent. Her whole body seemed to shrink. "Not a pleasant sight?" he grinned and felt in the glove box for sweets. He gave one to Josefine and asked him to unwrap one for him. It stuck to her fingers. He opened his mouth and wanted her to put the sweet in. She felt sick at the idea of touching his lips and pretended that she could not reach him. She put her tongue in her cheek and pretended to be unable to speak. Well, you do not speak with a full mouth. "You're in luck. Look there's a bus behind us. He put his hand out of the window, waved and sounded his horn. As soon as the bus stopped Josefine was ready to jump out. She grabbed her rucksack and the blanket and ran to the bus. He shouted after her, "Heil Hitler! Have a safe journey. She raised her hand and got on the bus. "Come on, and sit down quickly. This is not a bus stop," the driver said and drove on. She sat behind the driver and avoided looking out of the side window. She could read 'Salzburg' through a bullet hole in the windscreen. "How far?" she heard the driver ask. She leaned fore ward, "Sorry? Oh, excuse me, where are you going?" "To Salzburg, obviously." He told her the price and she got the money out of her skirt pocket, which was hidden by her rucksack. He was already holding his hand in the air. He looked at the coins and passed the ticket over his shoulder.

Soon after they came to a bus stop. People got off and a man got on and showed the driver a piece of paper. "So you're getting of after two stops? The travel permission is not valid for more." "I know," the man said and although the bus was half empty, he wanted to sit next to Josefine. She said, "Can't you sit somewhere else. There's plenty of room." Muttering, he went further down the bus, "Damn women. They›re worthless." She ignored him, bit by bit shoved some pieces of bread in her mouth and drank some tea from under her shawl. After a while she dozed off. Suddenly she heard the driver's voice. "Terminus. Everyone get off and don't leave anything behind. Take care, there are thieves in the town." A woman advised her to carry her bag under her coat. Josefine fastened the blanket to her rucksack as best she could, took it onto her back and held onto the shoulder straps. The street was full of rubble. There were ruins left and right. She felt fear rising. Her worst concern was how she was going to get any further. The driver was standing by the bus, smoking. Josefine asked, "Can you tell me how I can get to Munich?" "So. You want to go to Munich? Then you have to go to the other side of town, on foot. We couldn't drive any further. You can see what it looks like here." He left her standing there and got back on the bus. Josefine wondered if the train station might be closer.

A woman was sitting on her suitcase. "Can you tell me how I can get to the train station?" Josefine asked. "I'm waiting for my daughter," she said with an empty gaze. Two men in black uniform approached. Josefine spoke to them, "Excuse me, can you tell where I can get a bus or train to Munich?" "The curfew starts in five minutes. Where have you come from? Can I see your papers?" She took out her identity card. She had not realised how dark it was already. They gave her identity card back, spoke quietly to each other and then said, "Come on. You can't go on tonight. We'll take you to an air raid shelter. How long have you been on your way?" "We left early this morning. Someone I know brought me in his car and now I have to see how I can go on alone." "Come with us. We have to go over there. The entrance has not been properly cleared. It's only used in emergencies."

He helped Josefine over the rubble and broken tiles. In the distance she saw a light which seemed to be a long way below; the steps seemed to be endless. Somebody shouted from a platform, "There's no room left down there. It's packed full. Sit down here in the corridor." Josefine heard that one of the men with her was called Reiner. He explained to her how she could get further the next morning. "It's a miracle that you got as far as this today. What was it like on the journey?" "It wasn't bad. I think we were travelling at top speed, wherever that was possible. I took the bus for the last bit." Both the uniformed men took her into an air raid cellar. Suddenly Reiner listened. "Air raid warning! I have to go!" he shouted and ran off. His colleague stayed. Slowly Josefine's eyes got used to the dim light. She saw cardboard boxes on the floor, sat down on one, took her rucksack and spread the blanket over her feet. Then she allowed herself to take another piece of bread and an apple. After a while you could hear dull thuds; small pieces of masonry showered from the ceiling. The light went out. Her heart started to beat faster. She jumped up. "I have to get out!" she shouted, as if in panic. "That's not possible," a voice said, "stay where you are. It'll soon be over." And so it was. It was soon quiet again and the light came back slowly. She could not finish the apple. It was dirty. She took another sip of tea and tried to get some sleep on her rucksack.

The next morning she was woken by loud steps which came ever closer. Someone was leaning over her. His bad breath which she smelt and felt shocked her. "What is it? What do you want?" The person turned round and ran away. From the entrance two police voices shouted down into the cellar, "Identity control. Please get your identity cards ready." The ghostly voice went deep down into the cellar. One family let all the others go before them. "We have to go back down. We've forgotten our bag." People started to murmur, "Forgotten?" a woman said, "you don't forget something like that in this time of need. They probably don't have any papers. The police will go down there and then…?"

"Yes, well, what can you do? The best thing is not to look; to see nothing and hear nothing. I call that self preservation. As the saying goes if you help yourself, then God will help you." It was a portly woman who was almost talking to herself. She looked at Josefine, inquisitively. Josefine swallowed in confusion and said, "How can I get to the train station?" The woman said, "Yesterday I was still able to get over the rubble. The first streets to be cleared are the main streets. The train station had not been hit and the trains were still running." The woman showed her how to get further and then went in another direction.

It was 6 o'clock in the morning when Josefine arrived at the train station. It was crowded with people. She asked about the train to Munich. "The train to Munich should have been here a while ago," the man at the counter said, "I can give you a ticket, but I don't know if you will still get a seat. Look about you. Most of the people waiting here want to go in that direction. I don't know how far the train can go and any way, first it has to get here. Up to now I have no information." Josefine bought a ticket and went to look for a toilet.

A horribly stink greeted her; the water from the wash basin ran continuously because the tap was so dirty nobody wanted to touch it. Without sitting down she did her business, washed herself as best she could and put her hair in order out in the open. She felt hungry and took something to eat out of her rucksack. As she put a small piece of bread in her mouth she felt that people were looking hungrily at her.

When she closed the rucksack, there was a train employee with a signal disk standing next to her, smoking. She waved the smoke to one side and said, "You'll have to excuse me. I'm pregnant. Normally smoke doesn't bother me." "Where do you want to go?" he asked her. When he heard that she wanted to go to Munich he said, "Then you've got a long journey ahead. No one knows if the route is open all the way. If you want I can help you onto the train and make sure you get a seat. I'm going on the train." Suddenly there was a voice from the loudspeaker. "The train for Munich is approaching the station. Please step back." There was a sudden rush of people. "So, what have you got?" the rail employee asked, "have you got cigarettes? I don't do something for nothing. That's deadly." "Yes, all right," Josefine said.

"Make way," she heard him say and he pushed the others to one side and shoved her to the train. People were getting off and could hardly get through. "Back! Go back!" Everyone on the platform was shouting and screaming. The rail employee went in front and opened a way for Josefine to a free seat. She could not have done it alone. The train was full and people were still pushing their way on. She could not put her feet under the seat.

There were suitcases, boxes and bundles everywhere. She drew in her knees and clung to her rucksack. The woman opposite her wanted to get some air and put her hand on the window to open it. She was half standing when somebody forced themselves onto her seat. Now she couldn't sit down, but she did have an open window to lean out of. There was a stench of sweat, smoke and other undefined smells. Josefine pulled her shawl over her mouth and nose.

When the train finally left the station, somebody started to sing, "A journey is such fun, a journey is so nice…" And a few people were really enjoying it and joined in. Josefine looked out of the window. She thought that the train was travelling very fast; the countryside sped past. She was almost dizzy. Hours passed, or so it seemed to her. She managed to eat and drink something. Always hidden under her shawl. After many stops and stations, which at first, she had counted, the train stopped for a long time in the middle of no where. People got out, and asked what was the matter. A few men were called to the front of the train and helped to shift something.

It was almost 9 o'clock in the evening before the train reached Munich. Josefine felt completely exhausted as she dragged herself through the station. All the counters were closed. There were people lying on the floor and on benches. There was a dirty blanket lying on a bench. Josefine pushed it to one side, sat down and started to take stock of the situation. "Oh, just look at that," a well fed man said to her in a badly mimicked Munich accent, "do you want to sleep next to me?" "Don't pester me, or I'll scream for help," Josefine said and gave him a warning look. "Who's pestering whom, dear lady? You're sitting on my bed." "What do you mean? I thought that a bench was for sitting and can be used by all travellers." "Ah! So you're a traveller, but there will be no more trains tonight," he said a little more kindly, "may I introduce myself, before we get into a deeper conversation? My name is Haller, Erich Haller. I've been waiting for hours for someone to collect me." She hesitated to give him her hand,

and certainly not her name and she looked at him from top to bottom. His clothes were dusty, but they were good quality. She wondered why he had such a dirty blanket and where was his luggage? Finally she held out her hand and said, "My name is Remi and I'm passing through." "Pleased to meet you," he said and took her hand. He noticed that she was reluctant to make his acquaintance and said, "If you have any questions, then ask me. Maybe I can be of assistance." Josefine shook her head. Mr. Haller said, "I've waited long enough out here. They'll find me in the station buffet where I am going now. If you agree, I'd like to invite you to take a coffee with me. It's certainly warmer inside." "Thank you. I should be pleased to come with you, but I can pay for myself." "As Madame wishes." There was a notice on the entrance door: Open until 4 am.

There were hardly any free places inside. A waiter came and led them to a laid table. Josefine put her rucksack on the floor and pushed it under the table. The waiter said, "Good evening, Madame, Sir. Would you be wanting something to eat?" He listed things which made her mouth water. "No thank you," Josefine said, "just a coffee. Mr. Haller said, "Just give us a minute." The waiter nodded and left. Mr. Haller talked to Josefine and in the end they both ordered something to eat and drink. She worried about the money, but what else could she do? She told him about her journey and all her experiences until Mr. Haller asked her about her destination. Josefine's throat closed. Should she tell him the truth? What side was he on? Where is his pin with the Swastika? Probably under his collar. But he had not greeted her with "Heil Hitler!"

"You say nothing?" she heard him ask, as if his voice was coming from far away. "Oh, I'm sorry," she said after a while, "just for a moment my thoughts were somewhere else. What did you want to know? Where am I going?" She fixed her gaze on him for a moment and then, in a firm voice, she said, "I'm on my way to the concentration camp in Dachau." He stopped chewing for a second and looked around him. "What do you want to do there? Almost no one goes there of their own free will." She took Franz's letter out of her pocket and put it on the table. "Read it. After weeks of waiting and anxiety I got these few lines from my husband. What would you do? If you were in my position, you would certainly do everything to see him just once more."

He looked and she went on speaking, "Please understand me. I have four children waiting for me back home. I have to see him, because I need to know why he is there. He is not a Jew, a criminal or a wanderer." She avoided using the word gypsy, because she felt closely connected to them. The travellers.

Mr. Haller said, "Just a minute. Can you just go there to visit, or do you have a special permit?" "I've nothing like that. I'm just going to try. I've got this piece of paper." She handed the lines which Mr. Baumgartner had written, to him, but at the same time she was shocked about how much she was trusting him. She did not know this Mr. Haller. Why had she shown him that and told him everything? Hopefully it will turn out well. She could find out when the next train or bus was going to Dachau without him.

She felt that she had been stupid and incautious and took the letter and paper back. "What are you doing in Munich?" she asked him, "who is supposed to be picking you up?" In reality, I'm not interested, she thought, but it's better than sitting here and saying nothing. It's cold outside and the counters don't open until half past five. I have hardly slept for the last two nights. Suddenly sleep overtook her. She wanted to struggle against it, but it was no use. She rested her head on her elbows and with her feet on her rucksack, she fell asleep.

Mr. Haller asked for the bill, paid for everything and gave the waiter a generous tip, saying, "Take good care of her. I have to go to the telephone, but I'll be back soon." When she wakes up tell her to wait for me. The waiter agreed. If someone asks for Dr. Haller then that's me. He carefully placed the receipt under Josefine's sleeve and left. It was not long before he was there again. The telephone was not working. There were no taxis or other cars on the street. A curfew had been hung over the town. So there was nothing for it, but to stay in the station buffet. He asked the waiter if there was somewhere he could lie down. He said no, but gave him a second chair. He made himself as comfortable as possible, loosened his tie and tried to sleep.

The Station buffet closed at 4 o'clock in the morning. Without exception all guests had to leave. Josefine and Dr. Haller had been able to rest for a few hours. On the platforms everything looked grey. Dawn was breaking and the early morning cold crept into their clothes. Josefine saw that there was no where to sit. Dr. Haller tried to warm himself up by hopping from one leg to the other. "You wanted to tell me what you are doing here," Josefine said, "but somehow I fell asleep. "Yes. I thought that someone from our organisation was going to collect me. I left the group to visit an old friend and now I'm here and can't contact my people. I've forgotten what the hotel is called and the telephone number I have is useless, because the telephones aren't working. A colleague, with whom I share a hotel room, knows approximately when I'll arrive, but it seems that right now, nothing is working. Josefine asked, "What organisation are you talking about?" Dr. Haller turned his collar up. She saw the Red Cross symbol, but it was a little different from the one which Mrs. Reisin wore. "Do you know the Dachau concentration camp?" Josefine asked. "No, but I know the Theresienstadt concentration camp. We visited it a few days ago. We were invited to take part in a concert which was given by the inmates. I have to say, it was very professional. Afterwards we were allowed to ask the musicians pre-prepared questions. We learnt, of course, that, considering the situation, they were well cared for." Then he was silent. Josefine said, "I'm an interpreter. I've spoken to people who have been transported here from the east. They had no idea where they were being taken. They were encouraged to leave their houses because they had been promised work. Many were not even asked. They were simply loaded onto trucks." Dr. Haller said, "It's difficult for us to check if the conditions in the camps are fit for human beings.

There are many which we are not allowed to visit and in others we are only shown model barracks. But we still see the distress. As far as we can tell and according to the letters and reports which we have unofficially received, it must be damned different from what we have been told. We try to help by showing our presence and sending reports to the whole world. The outside world knows what is going on." While they were talking they were walking up and down the station. "Your identity cards, please." Suddenly there were two men wearing leather coats with Swastika armbands standing in front of them. As though they were rooted to the spot, they stood there, in front of Josefine and Dr. Haller, with splayed legs and their hands on their trouser belts. Dr. Haller showed his Swiss passport and his Red Cross identity card while Josefine took out her papers. "Heil Hitler, Dr. Haller," one of the men said and saluted, "what are you doing here? The curfew is not over. You have already come 150 meters from your hotel." Then he made a hand signal to the right along the street. "Are some of your colleagues also out on the streets?" "Not that I know of. I have only met Mrs. Remi, our interpreter here. She will accompany us." Josefine drew in a quick breath and then held her Aryan identity card in her hand. With the other hand she tried to hide her rucksack behind her wide skirt. Dr. Haller said, "Come, Mrs. Remi. I have to go back to the hotel." He took her by the arm. The men looked briefly at her identity card and left with a "Heil Hitler." "Heil Hitler," muttered Dr. Haller. Then they went in the direction which one of the men had indicated. Josefine was angry, "But I don't want to go into a hotel with you. Just what are you thinking? The station counters will be open soon and I should be in the queue." "Look, you trusted me with your story and now I know who you are. I want to help you. Right now the Gestapo will certainly be checking the people in the station."

He took her firmly by the arm and pulled her along with him. Josefine: "You didn't have to lie. What do you want from me? Now I can't show myself in the station. If they catch me, it will be very uncomfortable for me." Josefine did not know what to do. Dr. Haller: "Yes. I know and I shouldn't have tried to visit my friend, then I would not have lost contact with my group. But I could just left you standing here. What would happen then?" Josefine said, "What? How could you be so mean to me! You just wanted to save yourself, without thinking about me. That's what the Red Cross helpers are like!" Her blood was boiling. They went into the hotel and started to go up the wide stairs. A page boy came up to them, "What is your room number, please?" Dr. Haller said, "I've forgotten. My name is Dr. Haller from the Red Cross Commission," "Just a minute please." The page boy looked in his book and told him the room number. "That's a single room! Are you also staying here?" he turned to Joefine, "You have to sign in at the reception desk." Dr. Haller whispered, "She's accompanying me." The page held out his white-gloved hand. "If you want, I've seen nothing," he said quietly, but clearly. Josefine was on the point of collapse. She clung to Dr. Haller. Her knees were giving way. "Help me to get her on the sofa. Bring me a glass of water." The page disappeared and came back with a glass of water. Josefine swallowed it slowly. Then the page brought her the rucksack which was lying at the bottom of the stairs and left it there, saying, with a sneer "Your luggage, Madame." "I'm really sorry," Dr. Haller apologised, "don't take him too seriously. Are you feeling better? Just sit there for a moment."

He went to the reception, said a name and got a telephone connection to someone. While he was registering he asked for two cups of coffee. "The breakfast room is already open," was the answer. A man came hurrying down the stairs. He still had his jacket and tie in his hands. With pleasure he greeted Dr. Haller and gave Josefine his hand. Dr, Haller introduced him as Dr. Speier. "We were worried about you," Dr. Speier said, "where were you? And in heavens name what about this woman?"

They spoke French together. Josefine was able to follow most of what they said. She stood up, took her rucksack in her hand and wanted to leave. "Madame, give us some time. Please sit down again." Dr. Speier took her by the shoulders and pushed her back onto the sofa. A waiter came by. Dr. Speier stopped him, "Garçon! Un café et un croissant pour Madame, s'il vous plaît." "Oui, Monsieur, tout de suite," the waiter answered and took the money he had been offered.

The page, who had dropped the rucksack with such disdain, noticed that he had made a mistake and hid himself elsewhere. Dr. Speier said to Josefine in German, "Madame, I'll find a way for you to visit your husband. You don't need to take a train. We'll get a car with a driver for you. He will bring you there and back. Just have a little patience." His French accent sounded so charming and confident that Josefine promised to wait. She enjoyed her coffee – a real coffee – how wonderful! The smell of the croissant reached her nose and gave her hope. She asked if there was somewhere where she could freshen up. A page took her rucksack and led her through a hotel room to a bathroom. Josefine locked the door, quickly took off her clothes and stepped under the shower. Whush! At first the water jet was cold, but then she felt the warm water running over her whole body. Fantastic! It seemed that here everything was still working. When she glanced in the mirror she saw a freshened, contented, smiling face. She put on her clothes, dressed her hair and went down the stairs with her rucksack.

"The gentlemen are in the breakfast room. I'll tell them that you are waiting in the foyer." "Oh, leave them be. I'm not in a hurry." She looked around. Fresh flowers in gigantic vases, plaster mouldings and paintings on the walls and the ceiling. On the cold marble floor lay wonderful carpets. There were show cases with expensive porcelain and glass. Just like in the expensive shops in the large cities, she thought, but a bit boring. All luxury items. What can you do with them? Just look at them and nothing else. Maybe you could touch some of the things very carefully, just to find out what they felt like. I certainly wouldn't like to have to wash those long lace curtains. And the heavy satin curtains… She let herself dream for a moment. Oh, yes! A large flat. That would not be bad. But then you would have to be able to pay the rent. Hopefully this will not be bombed. The war should really stop.

But now, she thought and looked through the glass door into the breakfast room, now someone should come. A few men came towards the door, including Dr. Haller and Dr. Speier. "Ah, there you are." Dr. Haller said, "We can leave. The driver is already waiting for us" He took a bar of Swiss chocolate out of his jacket pocket and gave it to Josefine. "The driver knows what to do. You can trust him." He winked at her, taking his leave while he opened the rear door of the car. She got in. Leather seats, she thought admiringly. "Are you comfortable?" the driver asked and drove off. "Yes. Thank you." "Your husband must be an important person," the driver went on to say, "is he from the Austrian Government? As far as I know they have all been interned here. Even the Wittelsbachers are here, but with false names. Yes, yes. Our imperial monarchy has not been spared. Last time I was lucky enough to see some of these famous people close up. When you think of it putting such important people behind bars. Well, in these times it seems the impossible is possible."

"Do you often drive to Dachau?" Josefine asked. "To Dachau, yes, but I don't like driving to the concentration camp. I only do that when I get the order, like today. I don't want to know what it looks like there. I don't want to frighten you. But one hears things that you can hardly believe. Terrible things must be happening there. But people only speak about it by hiding their face behind their hands. You have to be careful what you say."

Josefine had heard enough and changed the subject. "Last night I hardly slept. When will we get there? Do I have enough time to close my eyes for a while?" "I can't tell you exactly. It depends on the road conditions. But you can rest for a while. I'll wake you just before we get there." She closed her eyes. They made good progress. The road was only closed once because of an unexploded bomb. They had to take a detour over meadows and fields. The driver swore, "The car will be dirty and the tyres are full of clay." Back on the road the car skidded close to a passing tank. "The tanks destroy the whole surface," he went on grouching.

"That's good for our tyres. Ha! Ha! People have to have a sense of humour."

Finally they arrived. Josefine wanted to get out. She could not see much from the rear seat. "Stay seated. Give me your papers." He added another document and blew his horn briefly. Two armed guards came to him. The driver gave them the papers. "We have been informed."

Then she heard a whistle and Franz appeared. "Visitor!" A high ranking officer told the driver, "You can take him as far as the post over there." To Franz he said, "You have to be back in half an hour, Remi. Take this warning seriously. Don't try anything. Now you can go. Open the gate!" Franz went to the car. The driver opened the rear door and Franz got in.

At first Josefine just saw his shaved head. She hid herself behind her scarf. When she looked again he was already sitting in the car. "Josefine! Josefine! Is it really you?" He cried and wanted to hug her, but the rucksack was between them. The driver drove to the post and stopped. "You can get out on this side, where you will have some privacy" he said, "I'm going to stretch my legs for a while. I'll leave you alone for twenty minutes. Then we have to drive back."

The driver walked a few meters away where he stood with his back to the car and lit a cigarette. They both got out. "How did you manage that?" Franz asked and went on, without waiting for an answer, "I had no idea. Have you brought something to eat with you?" She spread out the blanket. "Leave that. Give me something to eat," he said in a fairly strong tone. He opened the rucksack. Josefine took out bread and water from the bottle which she had refilled in the hotel. "Don't take such large pieces," she warned him and broke the bread into little bits. "You can take the rest, and the other things with you. Hungrily he pushed the bread into his mouth. He smelt the other things and stuffed them into his trouser pockets and into his underpants. He was chewing and swallowing like an animal. "Tell me what has happened," she demanded. "They beat us with canes when we arrived. My hands are still swollen, because I tried to protect my head with them. They beat us with rubber truncheons and rifle butts. But, all in all, I have faired relatively well."

With wide open eyes he stood in front of her. He grabbed her breast so hard that it hurt. Then he threw her on the blanket and lay over her. "I'm going to give it to you, so you don't go off with someone else." Josefine hardly trusted herself to breath. She did not want the driver to notice. Franz panted and wheezed. It was only a few seconds before he was satisfied. Tears ran down his face and his whole body was shaking. Josefine also had tears in her eyes. Laboriously she stood up, went behind the car door and brushed herself off as best as she could. Then the time was up. The driver came back and remarked, "Your suit looks as though you have been shot at." Franz said, "They don't have enough prison rags, so they shot at my best suit." On the suit were the letters K. L. D. (Concentration Camp Dachau). Franz took the cigarettes which Josefine had brought him and put most of them in his underpants. He took the bundle of bandages and medicines under his arm. In the car, Josefine wrapped some apples in her shawl and gave it to him. Then she put her hand into her skirt pocket and wanted to give him some money. Franz shook his head. "They'll take that from me. Put it away." The driver advised them to make their 'adieus' in the car and to Josefine he said, "It's better for you, Madame, to stay in the car."

She nodded and hugged Franz. "Write as often as you can. I'll leave no stone unturned to get you out of here," she said, trying to comfort him. "I know, Josefine," Franz said. "When you write send me an envelope with your address and stick some postage stamps on it. Now I'm going to get out. Drive off quickly. Don't wave. Tell everyone I'm fine and give them my best wishes. I'm sure I'll be home soon." He pressed another kiss on her lips. The driver opened the door and standing proud in his wooden slippers, Franz walked to the gate. Josefine looked at him and, as the car moved off, she started to cry bitterly.

A number on his suit which was full of bullet holes! His shaved head! He looked so small and humiliated! What have they done to you? I can only feel compassion for you. Her head was spinning. "Stop," she shouted and held her hand in front of her mouth, "I don't feel well." The driver stopped, pulled open the door and dragged her out. She vomited, but it was only mucus and bile, because she had not eaten much. She knew that was from the pregnancy. After a while her stomach calmed down. She went back to the car and took a sip from her water bottle. Then she felt the chocolate in the outer pocket of her rucksack and popped a piece in her mouth.

"I'm all right now," she said and leant back, closing her eyes for a moment. I really liked that scarf, she thought. Mother gave it to me. She always liked my wearing it. Now Franz has it. Maybe I can find something similar from somewhere. After a while she heard the driver say, "I'll give your papers back to you," and she opened her eyes. She took the papers and put them into her skirt. Then she felt hungry. "Aren't you hungry?" she asked the driver. "I can wait until we get to Munich," was his reply, "You won't get anything worth eating on the way and the prices they ask are ridiculous. You're all right. You can eat in the hotel with the elite and the committee." Josefine did not want to ask what he meant by that and leaned back on the comfortable leather seat. Suddenly she remembered the blanket. "Oh" she shouted, "I left my blanket there," as though it was something very valuable. The driver, who could not know why it was so valuable to her, simply said, "I've put it here on the front seat." She replied," I wanted to leave it for my husband. Maybe he doesn't have enough bedclothes." "You can take it to him next time," he said in a calming voice. "Ah, yes," she sighed taking the blanket in her arms, "the next time." Then she dozed off.

It was late afternoon before they got back to the hotel. The driver had had to take a few detours. He took her rucksack and opened the hotel door for her. He went quickly to the reception desk, signed something and received an envelope. To Josefine he said, "The page will bring you the room key and take you to your room. As you know, you can have your food brought to your room. I have to leave you now and I wish you a good journey tomorrow." "Adieu" she said, clumsily. He bowed and left the hotel.

Josefine pushed her rucksack between two armchairs and went to the reception desk. "Excuse me" she said, speaking like an actress in a film, "Have the people from the commission already left or is someone still here?" The concierge looked at the key board and then in a large book. "I'm sorry, all the gentlemen have left." Then he said to the page, "Heinz, have they taken their suitcases?" "Yes. About half an hour ago they took them to the car." "This is for you, Madame" the concierge said to Josefine. An evening meal with drinks has been reserved and paid for as well as a room and breakfast. Actually, the same room you used early this morning." "That's for tonight and everything is paid?" she asked. He said it was so. "Can I see the receipt? I don't like surprises. "Here. This is a collective bill with today's date. Here is your room number and here is the half board. Everything is in order. I wish you a pleasant stay and if I don't see you again I hope you have a good journey tomorrow." Josefine thanked him, collected her rucksack and followed the page to her room.

She locked the door from the inside and pushed a heavy upholstered chair against the door. Then she lay on the bed and thought hard about everything which had happened . One question after another. An international Red Cross committee had paid for all of this. Why? Why would any one pay for such luxury for me? How did this happen? As they say, only death is free. There has to be something behind this.

A film played out before her. Women and children with Red Cross collection boxes on the road and knocking on house doors. "Help us! Every penny counts!" she heard in her thoughts. Or, she suddenly thought, are the Nazis paying for all this? She stood up and washed her face in cold water, went to the window and saw elegant people in the hotel park. She decided to go to the train station while it was still light and buy her return ticket.

In the station, there were long queues of people standing in front of the counters. She joined one. A woman came up behind her with a lap dog. She whispered to the dog, "Tonight you have to be very friendly. Barking is forbidden. I hope that there will be no smokers or drinkers in our compartment." Then she asked Josefine if she was going to take a couchette or a sleeper. "Neither one or the other," she said. Then the woman's voice was shriller, "Can't you read? You've been standing here for half an hour," she exaggerated, "in the wrong queue and you're blocking my way to the counter." Josefine was irritated. She lifted her head and saw the bed sign above the counter, "Oh! Pardon," she said and had to get right to the back of another queue.

As she was standing in line she noticed a young woman, wandering nervously back and forth and offering her coat and one of her two travelling bags for sale. She was wearing a very nice scarf on her head which she had skilfully fashioned into a turban. She was wearing a matching scarf round her neck and elegant shoes. Josefine wanted to know what had happened to cause this young woman to sell her coat and travel bag.

When she finally got her ticket, she saw the woman with the turban leaving the station. Josefine followed her. The woman went round the corner of the station building. Josefine caught up with her and was amazed to see a large group of people selling their possessions. Some had even laid things out on the bare ground. There were many beautiful things, but even more junk. Everything was very cheap. The temptation to spend every last penny was great. Josefine picked up this and that and then saw, quite close, how the woman with the turban was dealing.

"I'm in a difficult situation. I need money urgently." "Nobody buys such elegant things these days. I couldn't sell that as long as I live." "Let me have a look," Josefine interrupted and took her to one side. "What do you want to sell?" "This coat, these travel bags, a pair of shoes and if I can, this scarf." Josefine asked, "What do you want for everything?" The woman named a sum which was way over what Josefine wanted to spend. She asked, "What's happened that you want to sell all this?" "That's a long story," the woman answered and took of her turban.

Her wonderful red hair fell down to her shoulders, long and silky. She looked up at Josefine from her squat position, while she tried on the coat. What a blissful feeling! And the perfume which rose from it! She would have loved to have closed her eyes and pirouetted. It fitted! The woman stood up and reduced her price, even though Josefine had said nothing. Then Josefine held a dress in front of her and put her foot into a shoe. "That's a bit small," she remarked, "How much do they cost? No, wait a minute. If I take the coat, the bag and the turban, how much would that be? Oh, and then the dress and the scarf?" "Well, how much money have you got?" "I have to go home early tomorrow morning. That means I have to sleep somewhere over night, so I have to keep a little back." Josefine took her money out of her skirt pocket. The woman counted it and said, "If you give me all of this, then I'll give you everything." She packed the bag, quickly shoving everything in. She took off her scarf and put it over Josefine's shoulders and held her shaking hand. Josefine gave her the money and grabbed the bag with all the clothes. She was still wearing the coat. Tears of joy filled her eyes. She had not bought anything for a long time and now she had so many elegant things.

She went up to the dealer who had tried to trade with the young woman before, who said, "I've already seen that you bought everything from the addict. She comes here often, but for the people who come here, the things are much too elegant. What did you give her?" Josefine told her. "My God! I'm not saying a word more. Look in the shops where all that comes from. Then you can think yourself lucky."

Josefine wanted to get back to the hotel as quickly as possible. Expectantly, she tried on the elegant dress and the shoes, put on the turban and then took it off again. She looked at herself in the mirror, fixed her hair in an elegant knot and put the scarf around her neck. Then she pinched her cheeks and bit her lips a little, because she did not have any rouge or lipstick. Clothes make the person! Now I fit in here. She tidied everything away and put the rucksack to one side, because it really did not fit in with her new look. With head held high she went down to the hotel foyer. She knew very well how beautiful and elegant she looked. The hotel guests turned to look at her.

The door to the dining room was open. "Would you like to go to your table?" she was asked. "No. Not yet." "In the meantime you can sit over there and take an aperitif." She thanked him and went to the table with the drinks. She felt like a film star, but she still did not feel completely comfortable with all these rich people who were standing on the terrace, talking and laughing with a glass in their hand. Some steps led to the hotel park and she decided to take a look at the park after the meal. She was nervous when she thought about having to sit alone at a table in the dining room. And anyway, her elegant shoes were pinching her feet. She went back and said to the waiter, "I'd like to eat in my room." He asked for her room number and took a list from under his arm. "I see that today's menu has already been ordered for you. Would you like something else, or is that in order?" "No that's fine, thank you." She went back to her room. She had no idea what was on the menu. She sat down and did not dare to take off her shoes. There was a knock on the door. "Your evening meal, Madame."

A waiter pushed a small table, fully laden, into the room. Much too much for one person, Josefine thought and only ate the soup, the vegetables and the potatoes. She put the meat, bread and fruit into her newly acquired travelling bag and she poured the drink into the bottle that she always carried with her. Then she went out behind the terrace into the park along a narrow path. She walked on tip toes, because otherwise her heels sank into the gravel. Along the path there were chairs and tables. She sat down on a chair at the far end of the park where there was a little pond surrounded with flowers. She enjoyed the view, made a few relaxing breathing exercises and felt as though she was in heaven.

As she stood up in order to go back to the hotel, she heard rail cars rolling over the tracks. The station was close by. There was a loud grating sound and the train stopped. Josefine heard someone shout, "Locomotive uncoupled." She could hear the locomotive making a loud noise as it moved off. The rail cars stayed where they were. Then everything went quiet again. But wait! What was that? People were shouting. Josefine went closer to the voices. "Water. Give us water! Can nobody hear us?" She couldn't get any closer. There were thick bushes and then a high barbed-wire fence, but she could see the rail cars and she saw that they only had small barred windows. From behind them, she could see hands clinging to the bars. Some waved. "Open the hydrants," someone ordered. There was some fumbling. A hosepipe was taken from window to window and for a while water poured into the rail cars. When it flowed out of the cars it stank bestially.

Josefine was fixed to the spot and did not hear the foot steps behind her. A man's voice asked, "What are you doing here?" There are people in those rail cars. They're asking for water." "But they're getting water. Go back to the hotel. There's a terribly stench here. Come on," the voice said, "they won't be here long." The voice belonged to an employee from the hotel. Probably very high up when you looked at his suit. "Is that a transport to Dachau?" Josefine asked without thinking. "Ah! You know about that! Probably. Recently they've had to wait here on the way. The camp must be very full. For many it's just a transit camp. I can't help wondering why the tracks have not yet been bombed. That would be better; then we wouldn't have this filth in front of our doors."

Josefine's heart was beating fast. She thought of Franz, but tried not to show her feelings. She walked beside the man and was happy when they got back to the hotel. Politely he opened the door for her. As he left her, he whispered, "Tell no one what you have seen. You never know who you are taking to." She nodded and sat down in the nearest armchair. "Can I get someone to bring you something to drink? Tea or a glass of red wine? Then you can sleep well." "A glass of wine would do me good. Yes, please." Then she noticed that her dress and shoes were dirty. She tried to dust off her dress without being noticed and hid her feet under the chair. But no one was looking at her. Most of the guests were already in the restaurant. A waiter put a small table by her side and served the red wine.

The wine was light and sweet. As soon as she had taken a couple of sips the waiter came and filled up her glass. Soon she felt her cheeks glow. She looked at the people going in and out of the bar and found it very entertaining. But it was difficult for her to put together the two very different worlds; here inside and out there on the tracks. Suddenly she accidentally brushed the wine glass from the table and it fell on the floor. She wanted to pick it up, but her head started to spin. A waiter rushed up and picked up the broken glass. She excused herself and wanted to stand up, but she fell back in the armchair. "Ow! I can't feel my legs. How am I going to get to my room?" "With your permission I can accompany you."

He presented his arm and she took it. When they got upstairs he said, "Don't forget to lock the door. Good night." She locked the door and lay down across the bed. When she woke up it was 4 o'clock in the morning and her head was throbbing. She had drunk too much wine. She filled the bath with steaming hot water and added some bath salts, which the hotel provided for its guests. She lay in the water for a long time and afterwards felt as though she had been born again. She put on the elegant dress, set the turban on her head and put the new scarf around her neck. Intending to take breakfast in the restaurant, she went into the corridor. The floor waiter came to her, "Good morning, Madame. Your breakfast is already on it way. Just a moment. I'll bring it immediately." "That's all right. Then I'll wait in the room."

She was not sure that she had said the right thing. Oh well! You have to live in hotels like this for a long time before you really feel comfortable. She tried to imagine what she would do all day long, but she soon realised that she was not born for such an idle life. That must be lonely and boring, she thought. The breakfast table which the waiter pushed into her room was overflowing with good things. The coffee smelt very good, but she only ate and drank the things which she could not take with her. She wrapped the rest in newspaper which was also on the breakfast table. When she had finished she went into the corridor. The breakfast tables which had been pushed out of the rooms were standing along the wall. There was a lot of bread and fruit on them. Since there was no one about she crept to the tables and collected everything which had not been eaten. Now her rucksack was very useful. She took the soap and the rest of the bath salts from the bathroom and there were also candles. Then she went on her way to the train station. Surprisingly, the express train which she had to take arrived on time.

A man, who had seen Josefine the previous evening in the hotel foyer was sitting in the same compartment. Fortunately she had a window seat, so she could look into the distance and still observe the other passengers mirrored in the glass. "Identity cards and luggage control." The compartment door was slid open and a conductor demanded to see their identity cards and tickets. Another checked their luggage. The man from the hotel also had to open his large travel bag and unpack everything. And there were hand towels, bath towels, silver cutlery, glasses, a coffee service, light bulbs and even bedside lamps. They were all from the hotel. Josefine was shocked and hardly dared breathe. She showed her identity card and her ticket. The conductor was amazed what he had managed to pack into his luggage, but only gave her luggage a quick look. He did not even punch her ticket. The man was told to pack everything up and come with them. After a while he came back with a contented face, lit a thick cigar and filled the whole compartment with smoke. Josefine started to cough and pointed her finger at her stomach. He was not in the least impressed and went on puffing. Suddenly the door opened again and the conductor was there again asking for her ticket.

"I don't think I punched it," he joked, "Please come out of the carriage." Josefine was happy to leave the smoke-filled compartment. "Look. This is not a ticket for this class. You must go back four cars. Do you want to do that with all your luggage?" Josefine hesitated. "You can pay a supplement, or we could come to an arrangement" he grinned. "I'm sorry," she said, "but I only have a little money left. It's only enough for the bus which I have to take." "And I'm supposed to believe that? You in your fine clothes and that travel bag? I can guarantee that the next conductor will throw you off the train." Josefine said, "All right, then I'll go into the class I have paid for." The conductor said, "It's more than full. Do you not want to think about my offer?" He named a sum, but than quickly went lower and lower. Josefine said, "Excuse me, I have to get my things." "Maybe you've got some cigarettes? Then I'll let you sit there." "No. I haven't got anything like that and anyway this compartment is full of smoke."

She thanked the conductor, put on her turban and wrapped her shawl round her head. The new shoes were beautiful, but they were very painful. So she changed them for her sturdy shoes and made her way back through the four cars. She could see through the glass doors how full the cars were. The toilette door was banging opened and closed. Josefine looked in and saw a rubbish bin. With the tips of her fingers she lifted the cover. The bucket was empty and still clean. She looked around, pulled the bucket into the corridor, took some newspaper out of her bag, placed it over the bucket and sat down. She kept her luggage close to her Then she took her blanket and covered her feet and everything else around her with it.

Just before Salzburg the train stopped for a few hours. Somewhere in the distance you could hear the air raid sirens. You could feel the detonation of the bombs in the train. A few women in the compartment started to scream with fear, but luckily nothing happened. Josefine stood up and took a few steps. The toilet started to stink. The people were using it although it was forbidden when the train was stationary. Nobody trusted themselves to get off the train because it could start again at any time without them. Josefine held her scarf in front of her nose and opened the toilet window. Finally the strain started to move again. She had to change trains a few times and then, finally, the next day she was home.

She opened the flat door. Before she took off her coat, she took care to put all the food carefully away after eating a little. Since she was still alone she lay down on the furthest bed, pulled the blanket over her head and fell asleep.

Later she met Karel and told him everything she had experienced and heard. He comforted her warmly.

Daily life went on, but it was some time before she could recover from the rigours of her journey. The children had had a good time and were eager to talk about it.

In the Dachau concentration camp Franz got to know the strict catholic, Father Lenz, who, daily wrote down everything which happened, even though this was very dangerous for him. Many inmates asked him tauntingly, "Where is your God? Why does he allow this to happen?" But he had to let the worst profanities go over his head. Father Lenz said, "It's the people who are cruel and not God. God is love. If you believe strongly in God then you can receive His love and give it on to others." Father Lenz knew that Franz also wrote down many things and also made drawings. He said that Franz should give him everything, because otherwise they might be discovered and burned. "We have someone outside the camp who keeps such documents," he said to Franz, "and he can put your drawings in his book which he is going to call

'Christus in Dachau'." Written pages were secretly passed to the outside world through the garden kiosk. Belonging to the concentration camp was a large plantation. At the kiosk, people from outside could buy seeds, flowers and all sorts of vegetables with their ration stamps. There were many Christian believers amongst the customers and some of them were able to smuggle the written pages out of the camp. On the other hand, medicine, cigarettes and other things which were needed also came into the camp. Franz gave everything which he wrote to Father Lenz, but he was careful not to tell him his personal ideological opinion. He thought the father was obstinate, shifty and outrageously cautious. He creeps his way though, Franz thought and that's how he is going to save his life. There was also a bishop in the camp, but he died in the first typhoid epidemic. Everything which the so-called clerics, who were also called 'blacks' did in the camp was done in secret. They could not even cross themselves. They were also not allowed to have a cross or anything which looked similar. But there were crosses which were not visible to the unbelievers. And then there was a chapel. What a contradiction, Franz thought. Like the other clerics, Father Lenz had a large black 'X' on his back. Otherwise you could not tell him from the other inmates, apart from the fact that he got a large number of parcels. He had many friends in and outside the camp.

Before he came to Dachau, Father Lenz had been in Giessen and Mauthausen. He told Franz that in Mauthausen the 'greens' had the power. They were called this because they had green labels sewn on their clothes. They were criminals. Concentration camp inmates were categorised by the sewn on codes. Those with a green code on their chests were criminals, black was for the anti social, pink for homosexuals, brown was normally for gypsies. Franz had a red code, which meant he was a political inmate. The Jews wore a yellow star, and so it went on.

The "greens" are murderers and criminals, Father Lenz told him, they are very dangerous and unpredictable types. He gave Franz a few tips should he ever land up there. Father Lenz knew all the vagaries and dangers. But Franz also had his own tricks to survive. In particular he held fast to his powers of concentration. For example when all the inmates from his barrack were ordered to leave the barrack and stand outside for hours, he would fix his gaze and concentrate on one point. That made the standing more bearable.

Or, if they were forced to watch other inmates being tortured, then he could look without seeing anything. He could even take control of his hearing, so that he thought he was hearing something a long distance away. If it was cold, he convinced himself, through his powers of concentration, that it was not cold. Of course, he did not overlook the barbarity. Once he saw how the SS henchmen ran ice cold water over two naked men until they were just blocks of ice, collapsed and died. Later it was declared: cause of death, cardiac arrest. The emaciated naked bottoms which were thrashed until only flaps of skin were hanging down. Then the people whose hands were tied behind their backs and then hung by their arms from a tree and left in this position the whole night long. Father Lenz told him about a forest, where hundreds of people had been hung like this. Their cries of pain could be heard for many miles in the countryside. Mockingly, the people spoke about the 'singing forest'.

The selection commission separated those who could still work from those who were no longer able to. Those not able to work were sent to the gas chambers.

But there were people in the camp who were not subjected to such brutality. Franz heard that they were members of the higher aristocracy and politicians.

Early one morning, about 4 o'clock they heard, "Everyone out! Quick! Quick!" A certain number of people had to get into each rail car.

Franz found his place (if you could call it that?) under a small barred window. His face was pressed against the wall and he could hardly breathe. He supported his body against the wall and pushed as hard as he could against the others, so as not to be squashed. There were loud cries for help. "Bugs! There are bugs everywhere. They'll eat us before we arrive." Franz saw the vermin in the cracks in the wood and squashed them with his finger nails which became red from the blood.

The journey seemed endless. First of all it started to stink of urine. Some of them fainted from thirst and hunger, but there was no room for them to fall down. Finally the train stopped and the sliding doors were opened, but a barrier held the emaciated bodies back. "Stand back, otherwise you'll all fall out." Slowly the rail cars were emptied. The people could hardly put one foot in front of the other. They had been standing for so long that their legs were swollen and stiff. Those who were unconscious were put to one side, until the medical orderlies took them to the camp in Flossenburg. It smelt of burning flesh. The new comers were horrified. Some of them already recognised the smell from Dachau. Somebody, who had not quite understood, looked into the sky and cried, "It's snowing. Look! It's snowing". He did not yet know that these 'snowflakes' were the ashes of people who had been burned. They were 'bone flakes'.

Franz came into a very long barrack, where naked corpses were stacked up to the windows. Although the ovens which burnt the dead were working day and night, the mound of corpses did not get any smaller.

Franz was not in this camp for very long. The SS did not want any political prisoners there, the block leader told him. He was moved to a prison, in the Landsberg Fortress. He heard that Adolf Hitler had once been imprisoned here. In 1924 Hitler was released early. Franz thought that if this bugger got out of here, then I also will not be here for long. But, as luck would have it, he had to stay there until just before the end of the war; together with murderers and criminals. He soon noticed that there were very few Jews there. People said, "They kill each other to entertain the SS and the Gestapo; even women watch" The prison warder, who sometimes spoke more than was allowed, told Franz, "I've seen it myself. Franz and the other inmates were forced to be present at these "entertainments". Two Jews were standing thigh deep in a pool and were told to get stones out of the water. To do this their faces went under the water, which the wardens used to piss in. Then they had to hit each other on the head with the stones. It was said that the one who survived would be freed, but that was a lie because what it really meant was, 'one Jew less.' Franz could not believe that the men hit each other on the head with the stones. But the truth was that they did it. Blood ran down their faces, mixed with the filthy water.

The SS men and some of the inmates cheered on the fight until one of them did not come up. An SS man shouted, "You filthy pig! You've just killed one of your own, in front of us all. You are a murderer!" Then he took his pistol and shot him in the head. Two catholic priests, who were also inmates, had to drag the corpses out of the pool, strip them and spray them with clean water. They were buried somewhere outside the prison. Inmates who had not shouted their support for the 'game' were punished in a special way. For the next three days, for each meal they only got an onion. Franz was also one who had to eat onions and the guards made sure that he ate them. He was given almost nothing to drink and his stomach started to burn and hurt.

In the meantime Josefine had given birth to Charlotte. Karel was over the moon about his 'schwarzen Murl', which is what Josefine called her because of her black hair and dark skin.

Josefine visited Franz twice in the Landsberg prison and she was allowed to bring food with her. On the second visit he hardly greeted her, unwrapped the things she had brought him and looked at her long and hard. "Is that all you've brought?" He was very disappointed that she had not brought him any cigarettes. When she saw Franz like that, she could not imagine how it would be when he finally came home. She just felt sorry for him. It had taken her hours to get there. It was so difficult to get food and she had not even thought of cigarettes, even though she knew that you could exchange them in the prison. Franz's feet stank of sweat. No one had told him that he was going to get a visit. He had simply been called and taken into the visitor's room. She asked him if he was not allowed to wash. He explained to her that from early to late he had to sit in a pit and take apart dirty, worn leather shoes. In some of the shoes the imprints of toes were so deep that you had to accept that they had been worn for a lifetime by someone who had no socks. The leather was sent to the munitions factory for recycling. From some of the shoes the uppers were taken off and better soles would be fitted. That's how Franz learnt to be a shoemaker.

Franz also told Josefine about a fellow inmate, who had to serve the soup into the prisoners' tin bowls and gave the top of the soup to those he did not like. For others, he went deeper with the ladle and they got more than just the liquid. Franz had told the warden with whom he had spoken before, carefully picking his words. From then on Franz had to stand there and stir the soup. If he did not pay attention, he was the last to be served and only got a half portion and sometimes an even smaller portion. When that happened, the man serving the soup grinned. He was a gangster through and through.

Josefine and Karel often heard, on forbidden foreign radio stations, that the war would soon be over. They wondered what would happen to them when that happened, because they did not want to separate. Karel wanted to go back to Bulgaria and establish a garden centre. Josefine wanted to go with him and as the end of the war neared, this feeling became ever stronger. However, she would have to find a solution for the children. She was prepared to give them up to follow the one man she really loved. The children and she had been helping out in the garden centre. The children worked well and Karel always gave them a little something. After the work they sat on padded quilts on the floor in the clay house and Ismir gave them something to eat. They often stayed there overnight. One night a rat bit off a bit of Fredi's ear. He screamed and wanted to go straight home. Ismir disinfected the wound with alcohol, which burnt like mad. He looked around to find out where the rats had come from and found a nest with new born rats behind the thick wall paper.

Then the time came, when Josefine wanted to leave the children.

First of all she met Mrs. Slavic, Fredi's gymnastic teacher. By now Emer was a well-built young man. With Mrs. Slavic he did regular acrobat training and often visited her privately, almost too often. But, in her situation, Josefine did not want to worry about what the pair of them did or did not do together. Emer seemed to be happy, that was, at the moment, the main thing. Josefine and Mrs. Slavic agreed that Emer would move in with her and that she would help Emer to find an apprenticeship. There were opportunities as a plumber or carpenter. So she handed over Emer's papers and asked her to apply to the council or social office for financial help. Mrs. Slavic promised to look after him like her own son until she returned. Josefine had told her some story about having to help her husband. She could not take the children with her, because she did not know how long she would be away.

She gave away Reinhard and Christine to the farming family Katz. They were happy to take them although they did not have much for themselves, because all agricultural produce could only be exchanged for ration stamps. Everything left over was collected regularly by the council and that's why Mr. Katz had to work at the mine to earn something extra. Josefine took Christine's forget-me-not earrings. She was not honest with her, saying it was so that she did not lose them. Christine used to remove the earrings every evening and wrap them up in the handkerchief in which Grandmother had given them to her and then lay them under her pillow. She was sad to give them up, but she did not protest. When they got to the farmhouse, Mrs. Katz showed them where they would be sleeping. While she was doing this Josefine crept out of the house and ran down the hill. The farmer's wife was shocked, when she realised that she had not even said 'goodbye.' She comforted the children, "She'll come to visit you soon." But the children did not seem to be worried. They ate some bread and sat down happily on a bench in front of the house. Unfortunately the SS often came by and took with them whatever was to be taken. In the end they even took the sacks of seeds.

Josefine simply stood Fredi in front of Alfred's door with his things, but first she made sure that Alfred was at home. She told Fredi that he could stay with Uncle Alfred for a while and promised to come and collect him as soon as possible. Leaving Fredi was the worst. She heard Alfred calling, but ran off with tears in her eyes.

Then there was only Charlotte. The child she had had with Karel and who had inherited her father's darker skin. A love child as they say. She wanted to take her with her. From that moment on she stayed in the garden centre and did not let herself be seen by anyone from the town. Karel sometimes doubted if Charlotte was really his child, because Josefine had also been with Franz. But he loved the little one and Josefine so much that he did not ask any questions.

It was strictly forbidden to talk or give food to the foreigners who were working as forced labour everywhere. In the garden centre it was a little easier, because there were no overseers there, and controls were rare, but you still had to be careful.

Karel tried to convince the council to release him. Everywhere you heard, "It'll only be a few days before the English get here." He went to various departments, but nobody wanted to have anything to do with him and Ismir.

Only Miss Herzig from the office had the courage to fill out a release document and she did it without asking anyone else. She even convinced a colleague to sign it as well and, without any money changing hands, to put a stamp on it. She had had enough of all the chaos and was glad not to see the pair in the office again. In the council offices Ismir met Bulgarian women who had worked in the munitions factory. There was very little material left there and those who were against the war had carried out sabotage acts. They had thrown sand in the machines to disable them. The women were simply allowed to go free. Some of them had only recently been brought from Germany. A few had orange hair. This came from breathing in the powder with which they had had to fill the bombs and bullets. They had not been given the required protective masks.

One woman, a bit younger than Ismir asked him for help. Her family had warned her that she should not go back to Bulgaria, because, since she had worked for the enemy, she would be shot. It did not seem to matter that she had not gone to the enemy of her own free will. She had been taken forcibly from her parent's house, along with many others from the village. They had then calmed down when they had been promised a job by which they would earn some money. So they had received just enough to pay for their food in the factory canteen. They even had to pay for the soap which came from Italy and which, they heard later, had been made from human bones. Ismir listened to all this and hesitated for a while, but then he took her to the garden centre, although the clay house was already quite full. But it was no longer as dangerous as before, because the controllers had not been seen for some time. Even some of the SS men had fled or hidden themselves somewhere or other.

Ismir decided to stay for the time being at the garden centre with Pirscha, the young woman he had taken in. He was attracted to her and showed it. As for her, she never let him out of her sight and worked side by side with him everyday.

Karel spoke to Josefine. When the time came, they only wanted to take with them what they could easily carry. The journey to Bulgaria would not be easy. Then Josefine went to visit Berta. Making the excuse that she wanted to get Franz out of prison, she once more asked Berta for money. Berta gave her something, which she thought was acceptable and wished her luck. She had also heard that the war would be over in a few days. One had heard, on Radio London, that SS people had called on inmates to join up of their own free will in order, at the last minute, to send them to the front. Now they knew that the end of the war was just days away. But in some parts of the country, youths were still being called up. It was terrible to see how they had to follow the order and leave their mothers. The youths were sent to a training camp for a very short time and then they were in action.

Karel and Josefine wanted to leave! To go to Bulgaria as quickly as possible. They considered how to do this and discussed it with other Bulgarians, because the war was not yet over. But none of them wanted to wait any longer. So they arranged a meeting place in the main station in the town. Some of them went off in various directions. There was some hope that they would get through. Some suggested that they could go by ship down the Danube flying a neutral flag. But then, suddenly, for Karel and Josefine everything turned out very differently from what they had planned.

Franz was released. He had to make his way from the prison on foot. As he passed a half bombed church, he smelt good food. He looked around and saw a fat cook standing by the stove. "Good day," he said, "I don't want to beg, but I'm on my way home and I haven't eaten for a long time." The woman said, "You startled me. You look as though you have risen from the dead. We haven't got a lot, but I can certainly give you some rice." Franz took it thankfully, but almost choked, because the rice was so dry. Even though she had poured some hot stock over it, he still found it difficult to swallow. "Take your time," she warned him. When he had finally finished it he stood up, but immediately fell back, screamed with pain and pressed his hands on his stomach. Later he found out that his stomach had slipped down from the heavy rice. Still holding his stomach he thanked the cook, took his leave and went on his way. Days later he arrived at his flat in

Vordersberg. No one was there. Then he went to Bert who greeted him warmly. From Berta he found out that Josefine was on her way to him in the prison. She did not know where the children were. Alfred had also not been to see her for some time. Franz decided to go to Alfred, but let his sister give him something small to eat before he went. While he was eating he told her what had happened to him. Berta saw that Franz's head had been shaved and that his cheeks were sunken. But he was wearing good shoes and a passable brown suit with a grey shirt, which he had got from the prison on his release. But he did not have any socks, hat or tie, which he had always thought were important. It was also what he asked Berta for, before anything else. Berta still had a hat and tie from their father. Then Franz went to Alfred to ask him about Josefine and the children.

"Josefine wanted to go somewhere without taking the children," his brother told him, "I've no idea where she went. Fredi told me. During the day he's with a neighbour, but every evening he comes to sleep here. I haven't had time to find out more about the whole business." Franz said, "Berta told me that she was on her way to the prison to get me out or collect me. So she'll surely be back in a few days." Alfred gave him some money for food.

When he went to Mrs. Gasser to ask about food, she sent him to the council to ask for ration stamps. She said that she could not just sell food over the counter. The rations were smaller and smaller. So he went down into the town to the council office. But they sent him to the town park, where, much to his surprise, he found the distribution centre for food ration stamps and social assistance established in a beautiful new wooden barrack. Franz went in and registered that he had returned. By coincidence, Ismir was, at that moment, in the same office. "I need your release papers," the woman said and when she saw them she thought she knew him. "Ah! Mr. Remi, your wife will be very happy that you have come back home. We have so many women in the town who are still hoping for their husbands' return," Ismir heard this and the name Remi went through his head. Isn't Josefine's name Remi? He slipped out of the office and hurried back to the garden centre. "Karel! Karel! Come here! I've got something to tell you." When Karel heard that Josefine's husband had retuned, he knew immediately what he had to do so that he did not lose Josefine. But first of all he had to know for certain that Ismir was right and see for himself if Franz was really back. He told Ismir to say nothing to anyone. Late that evening he jumped over the fence, as he had often done when he visited Josefine in secret. Since the clay house was too small, Karel and Ismir had cleared some space in the garden shed so it could be used to sleep in. The two women and little Charlotte slept in the clay house which every evening they had had to check to make sure there were no mice or rats. That's why Josefine did not notice what was going on.

Karel crept to Franz's flat. There was light. Carefully he went to the window, squinted through it and saw a starved man with a shaven head washing himself in an enamel bowl. He squatted down for a while. When he looked through the window again he saw Franz take something long out of his black trousers and put it beside him. It was a rubber truncheon and the inside was made of steel (but that he found out later). He had 'let it come with him' from the prison. It had been used to beat the inmates. Actually it was only a bit of rubberised wire that had one end wound with elastic plaster which you could see had been often used. Karel went back to the garden shed and lay down. "And?" Ismir asked, "is he there' Say something." "Yes, you're right. He's there." "And now what?" "Josefine has to go to the city. She can leave the children here. Her friends can look after them. But she must leave the town. She shouldn't know that her husband is back. Come on, let's sleep."

The next morning, very early, Karel spoke to Josefine. "Listen. We have to do something to get out of here. It would help us all if you went to Graz to find out a way to get to Bulgaria. I've got the feeling you are very used to such things. Let's say that in about two days you'll have found a way. In the meantime Pirscha will look after the little one." Josefine agreed. She was happy that Karel trusted her to do this. So she packed her travelling bag and went behind the garden centre along the rail tracks to the station.

A woman sat next to her in the train, who said she knew her. She started chatting and asked her where she was going. "I'm going to meet my husband," she lied, "we have to sort out a few things and then we're going home. May I ask you who you are? I can't remember ever having met you." "Oh, excuse me. Edita Petritsch. I'm an actress. We had to settle in Vordersberg, until everything quietens down. We have parked our caravan under the little Murbridge over the Graz and we've got a swing boat there and parts of a children's roundabout. Our father has stayed there to keep an eye on them. We have hidden everything under planks, covers and bushes. From time to time, like today, I go to check them out.

The Murbridge is still standing. More or less. It hasn't come under direct fire." She stopped for a moment and looked at Josefine inquisitively, "I know that you used to travel around as an artiste, or whatever you call it. I've never trusted myself to introduce myself to you. I've been told that artistes are so sensitive. That's why I never spoke to you on the street." Josefine, started to listen more closely and asked if she slept in the caravan, how much room there was and who was living there now.

"Right now only Father is living there," Mrs. Petritsch told her quietly, "but he prefers to sleep out in the open. Well, to be more accurate, he sleeps in the swing boat where he has made himself comfortable. He is really looking after the things that we have saved especially since we heard that the war is coming to an end". Then Mrs. Petritsch went on to say that there were other caravans there, closely packed together. Josefine said that she would like to take a look, because she and her family had also once travelled around in caravans, very elegant ones, and her son, Emer, still dreamt of living in one. Mrs. Petritsch said, "If you are in the area, just pop by. If you're lucky I'll also be there. I always stay for a few days and try to keep everything in order."

When they got to the main station, Mrs. Petritsch was greeted by a woman who wanted to go to Vordersberg. "This is Mrs. Remi," Mrs. Petritsch said and introduced Miss Semmel, "If I'm not mistaken, you know a Mr. Remi." "Oh yes, he once worked for my boss." She offered Josefine her hand, but Josefine had both hands full and exclaimed that she was in a hurry. She left with a short "Adieu,", turned around but did not know in which direction to go. What do I do now? A little lost, she wandered through the station to the exit and suddenly stood in front of a dreadfully bombed out town. All the walls which were still standing were pock-marked with bullet holes. She saw Red Cross women doling out soup, but you had to have your own soup bowl.

She went back into the station hall and tried to find some Bulgarians who might be able to help her, but she only saw pitiful faces. One came up to her, begging. She fended him off, "There's a soup kitchen outside," and went to the information counter. "Yes, please?" the employee asked. "I want to go to relatives in Bulgaria, but I don't know what route I have to take. Which train should I take? They live a bit north east of Silistra on the Danube plains. I want to leave in the next two days." The employee said, "If you look at the map the shortest way would be through Yugoslavia, or you could go through Hungary and Romania. But we're still at war and I can't guarantee that you'll get through. If I were you I'd wait or, if it's possible you could take a nice trip down the Danube, because the place you want to go to is on the Danube. That would not be bad, but it costs quite a bit more than other forms of transport." Josefine said, "But I don't want to wait. If I wait, I might be dead. There are still bombs falling out off a clear blue sky." There were many people behind her who also wanted information. The employee leaned forward, looked left and right and said, "You know what? I'll finish work in three hours. Then we can look at the map back at my place. In the meantime I'll find out which way is the best. You can think about it. Right now I can't do anything for you. Goodbye. Next please." Josephine was pushed to one side. She was outraged, "What is he thinking of? Go to his place! What a nerve!". She went out of the station hall and sat down on a pile of rubble and thought about how, as a young girl, she had got to Bulgaria with her family. In a caravan, she remembered, but she no longer knew what route they had taken. She had vague memories of the capital city, Sofia. Of, large, beautiful buildings, packed closely together and many golden domes with high pillars.

In the meantime, Miss Semmel, Mrs. Petritisch's acquaintance, had arrived in Vordersberg and, as it can happen, she met Franz on the street. She would not have recognised him had he not spoken to her. "Hello, Miss Semmel." Miss Semmel almost screamed and held her hand in front of her mouth, "Jesus, God. Is it you, Mr. Remi. I wouldn't have recognised you. Where were you? You have changed so much." "Franz asked, "Is it really as bad as that? Up to now the people I have met have said nothing except that I am thin, but then I'm not the only one. It'll get better, Miss Semmel, you'll see," he joked, "I'll soon be my handsome self again." "I met your wife at the train station," she told him, "but only briefly, because I had to get my train and she was also in a hurry, so we could only say good day." "Did you say in Graz? When does the next train go there? Maybe I can find her before her train leaves. I heard that she wanted to collect me. But it's not easy to get to where I've come from. I don't think there are trains going there." The train to Graz goes backwards and forwards. If you hurry you will catch the one I came on. Franz was lucky. He managed to get on the train just before it left.

During this time, Josefine had gone into the station toilets and looked herself in the mirror. She could not understand why the man at the information counter had treated her as a common harlot. She thought she looked respectable. She tidied her hair and went back through the restaurant. There was a trolley standing in her path with an empty salad dish on it. Quick as a flash she took the dish, hid it in the pleats of her skirt and walked calmly out. She hurried to the soup station. She wanted to save her money. The enormous pan was almost empty when she handed out her dish, but it was enough for a small meal and she got a small piece of bread with it. She sat down on a nearby stone and drank the soup. She did not have a spoon. She kept the bread for later. She saw that the people from the Red Cross were washing their hands at a water pipe, so she did the same. She washed the salad dish and hid it away.

An old rusty bus stopped next to the train station. It was very dirty and must have come a long way, she thought. The people getting off the bus were laden with bundles and bags. Josefine heard many different languages. She went up to a woman and asked, "Where are you all coming from?" "I've come from the suburbs," she answered, "I don't know where the others have come from." Josefine asked the driver if buses were going to Yugoslavia or Hungary. Because, she explained, she wanted to go to Bulgaria. "Oh!no. There's no way I'm going to drive to the partisans in Yugoslavia and the Russians are about to march into Hungary. I have no idea how far I can still drive this bus. Somehow people get through. You'll find out more when you go to the kiosk over there."

He shut the door, because he had to make way for another bus. Josefine went back into the station hall, hoping to find some other solution. She saw the same pitiful people from before standing around. Even the man who had tried to beg from her was among them. But she still asked people from the group if anyone knew how she could get to Bulgaria. A man with wise eyes broke away from the group and said to her, in broken German, "I'm Hungarian. Why do you want to go to Bulgaria?" "I don't have the time to tell you my life story," she answered in Hungarian, "do you know a way?" "The easiest would be over Budapest and then through Romania." Somewhat annoyed she said, "I already know that, but I wanted to know how I can get there." "With the train, bus, donkey cart, horse drawn carriage, on foot. Just go. Avoid the bombs and don't let the enemy catch you. It's war time and there are many bad men around. Maybe you'll get through and maybe not, who knows? Maybe God knows, who has left so many bad people on this earth? In the ammunition factory the war is over. They have no more material. The bullets don't work. Now it's only a front. We have to work there day and night for many hours and all we get is a piece of bread and some bad soup. Recently we've had better food, because they have stopped bringing more workers. They keep us alive. Work means freedom! Have you already heard that?"

Josefine understood that this person wanted to tell her his story, and stopped listening to him. Her target now was the kiosk. But as she walked through the station, someone came up from behind and covered her eyes. "Who am I?" She recognised Franz's voice. His rough fingers stank of cigarettes. She was just able to turn round before her knees gave way. Franz held her up and with one hand searched in her travel bag for something drinkable. He knew that she always had something with her. He gave her a sip from a bottle and helped her to stand up. No one took any notice of them. They had seen worse than someone fainting. Franz took her into the fresh air and sat down next to her on the stone she had sat on before. She did not trust herself to look at him. Her eyes might betray what she intended to do. Only then did she notice how many war wounded cripples there were. People without legs; with bandaged heads; with an arm missing; a bandaged eye. Franz said, "Come. We'll go home. It's not so bad there." And that's what happened. They went back to Vordersberg with the local train which stopped at every pile of rubble. Franz pushed her into a corner seat by the window and slept next to her with his mouth wide open and his hat pulled down over his face. Josefine looked out of the window and cried all through the journey.

Back home she took of her shoes and laid on the bed without undressing. Franz lay down next to her and wanted to kiss her, but she shoved him to one side. That made him angry and he fell on her, but she was stronger and angrily asked him if he had only come home for that. He hit her hard on her cheek with his bony hand, punched her in the ribs and hit her in the stomach with his foot. She started to scream. Then someone hammered on the door. Franz put one hand over her mouth and held her throat with the other. She should be quiet he hissed and slipped into his shoes, grabbed his hat and jacket and opened the door.

It was Florenz who had seen both of them going into the flat. He was a little deaf from the noise in his workshop and had heard nothing of what had happened behind the door. Josefine heard them greet each other warmly and both men decided to go to Anderl to see how he was doing. Franz locked Josephine inside and took the key with him. She could not get out through the barred window and if she called no one could help her.

Franz came home late. He was drunk and wanted to vomit. He wanted to go to the toilet, but he did not make it and threw up everywhere. Josefine held a bucket in front of him, but he pushed it away. It started to reek of urine, so she opened the windows. He wailed that everything hurt and he was thirsty. She should bring him something to drink. She brought him a glass of water to drink, a bowl full of water with which to wash and a towel to dry himself. Then she set about cleaning up the vomit. It disgusted her and she put a cloth with some lavender oil over her nose. She wept softly. Franz pealed off his urine soaked trousers and threw them into a corner of the room. Still unsteady on his feet he washed his back side and legs and crept under the bed cover. "Close the window," he groused, "otherwise I'll catch pneumonia. You can't send me into eternity with these concentration camp tricks." Then he went on muttering the meanest things until he finally fell asleep. Josefine cleaned up everything, washed his trousers, hung them up and decided to run to the garden centre.

It was three in the morning. She thought there would certainly be no one about. But, just to be careful she climbed over several garden fences before she went onto the street. She got to the railway tracks, crept through the hidden hole behind the bushes and went first to the garden hut, knocked lightly on the door and called Karel's name. It did not take long before he was standing in front of her with a torch in his hand. "Are you back already? What happened?" She told him that most of the people were still afraid of the war and she had been advised to wait a while before she made the journey. It was too dangerous to go through Yugoslavia or Hungary if you did not know the way and had to ask people. You could easily fall into a trap. Karel said, "I understand that. It's better to wait."

Then she told him about Franz. Karel admitted that he had known of Franz's return and confessed that he had acted the way he did because he was afraid of losing her. "You can't stay here with me any longer," he went on, "for the time being you're going to have to go back to Franz with Charlotte." He took her face gently in his hands and, thank God, in the dark he could not see the hand mark on her cheek. He wiped the tears away with his handkerchief, kissed it and said, "You can take that with you." Then he kissed her and pointed to the sky, "Look, our stars are already on the journey. Now I'm going to fetch our little one." He disappeared and came back with a bundle and the child, who was still fast asleep. He accompanied her to the gap in the fence. "Take care of yourselves, I'll be in touch. Please, be patient, our fate will surely bring us where we both belong." He gave her another long kiss, hugged her gently and then Karel turned away and disappeared in the bushes. With the child and the bundle in her arms Josefine ran back to the flat, opened the front door, which she had blocked ajar with a cleaning cloth, quietly and crept in. She put Charlotte on Emer's bed, took off her dress and drew the covers over herself and the child. So she avoided having to sleep next to Franz. She buried her face in Karel's handkerchief and fell asleep. The next morning Charlotte woke her. She was hungry and needed a fresh nappy. Josefine was in pieces. She had not had enough sleep and hurt all over from the beating. The day before, Franz, who was still fast asleep, had managed to get milk and bread, so she could give the child bread soaked in milk.

Josefine wanted to contact Emer, who was with Mrs. Slavic, before school began and hurried there with the pram. She knocked on the door and Emer opened it. He was eating his breakfast. Mrs. Slavic disappeared behind the curtain where she could wash and dress. Emer was amazed. "You're back already? Or are you about to leave?" He noticed immediately that she had a black eye. Josefine said, "Come into the corridor, I've got to tell you something. If you want to, you can tell Mrs. Slavic about it later."

When Emer found out that his step-father was back and had beaten his mother, he wanted to rush off to him and show him his fist. "I don't want you to get mixed up in this," Josefine told him, "I just wanted to say that after school you should come back home." He put on his shoes and said, "Yesterday the Nazis came to me. At noon I have to go to a training camp on the Croatian border with the Hitler Youth. We have to meet in the main square." Josefine was horrified, "For the love of God, I've heard that the partisans are fighting there and they're fighting relentlessly. I won't let you go. I can hide you. Now, when Radio London reports that the war is as good as over. It's completely stupid that they are still recruiting young men." Emer took it very calmly, "I'll look after myself. You know very well that I have never taken a weapon in my hand, so I can't shoot anyone. I'll defend myself somehow. Come on, there's still some tea on the table and we have a very good apple tart." He pulled his mother, with Charlotte on her arm, into the room. Mrs. Slavic, from behind the curtain, excused herself and said that she still needed a few minutes.

Emer packed his things and went home with his mother. But Franz had already left. He had even made the bed. Emer took out his uniform. There was a knock on the door. The door opened and Fredi came in and behind him was Alfred. "Hello, you two", Alfred said. He had not seen Charlottte. "Now it's my turn. A couple of those men came to me yesterday. I have new marching orders." "What, you as well?" Emer asked, amazed. "Yes. I've heard that anyone who can still walk must go to the front. It's good that Franz is back, because now Fredi can come home." Josefine took her son in her arms and kissed him. Tears ran down her cheeks. Elmer told Alfred that Franz had beaten his mother and pushed him towards her so that he could see it with his own eyes. She also had bruises on her arms. "Oh, no," Alfred said, "what has happened to him? He's passing on what he experienced in the camp. I'll talk to him and convince him that in future he has to get himself under control. I'll tell him that when I get back, I'll often come by to see how things are going." Emer said, "I'm going to punch him on the nose as soon as he comes through the door and that's the truth." At that moment the door opened and Franz appeared with a smile on his face. "So you're here, but a few of the family are missing." Emer stood there rooted to the spot, held his hand in front of his mouth and stuttered, "Is that you, Father?" Tears came to his eyes. He cried loudly and hugged Franz, who still looked pitiful with sunken eyes and cheeks, even though he was correctly dressed and had the beginnings of a moustache on his lip. His teeth seemed to stand out of his mouth, his throat looked as if it were only veins and tubes covered with a thin layer of skin. He was as thin as a rake. The shirt and tie stood away from his neck and his black suit looked as though it was hanging on a coat hanger. He clapped Emer warmly on the back and said, "Come on. It's all right." Emer forgot everything he had intended to do. Then Franz told them that he had been to Alois. "Alois and Karl have to leave the mine and go to the front today. I don't understand this at all. I was released because they said that the war was coming to an end. So what is this now?" Alfred said, "We all have to go to the front. Every available man. Now you are the only one in our family who can stay here. Visit the others from time to time while we are away. And behave yourself. We're going to end the war and when we return we want to live in peace." He stood very close to Franz, "Up to now Josefine has been very brave. We all have the greatest respect for her and that should go for you too, my dear brother. Don't ever forget that." Josefine stroked Emer and thanked Alfred for the kind words. Emer and Alfred left the flat. Franz promised to be in the main square at mid-day so that he could see Alois and Karl again before they had to join the troops. Josefine: "I'll be there too." Then Charlotte started to demand attention. She was wet and hungry. Franz looked around. "How is it that I have never seen the child? I must have been really confused." Josefine was changing the child's nappy. Franz looked at Charlotte and tried to amuse her. "That's my little Charlotte," Josefine said and reproached him. "Since you got back you've only been interested in your friends and relations. That's why you didn't notice the child and didn't even ask about her. Franz had no doubt that she was his daughter. He did not want to upset Josefine so he held his tongue.

Now Josefine had foisted a child on him. What else could she do?

When the child was born she could not claim the forced labourer Karel as the father. They would have shot him immediately. How would Franz react? She did not want to think what sort of life Charlotte would have if the truth came out.

Of course she felt wretched about it, tried not to think too much and sorted out some food. Then she went into the cellar. There were still some carrots under the heaped up soil, but that was all. She lit her torch and looked into the neighbour's cellar and although inside it was hung with jute sacks, she could still spot eggs in a preserve jar, jam and a large jar of vegetables. Using all her strength she tried to break through the planks, but it was no use. They had been well nailed down. She went back upstairs and asked Franz if he could go to Florenz or Anderl to see if he could get something. "Tell them, you'll give it back to them later." Franz went out and Josefine went back into the cellar with some tools. She managed to prise free the two rearmost planks and noticed some potatoes and three apples which she had overlooked. She thought for a moment if she should leave something there, but then she took everything she could find and nailed the planks back in place.

Josefine cooked three potatoes, two eggs, made some tea and poured it into a bottle which was half filled with cold water. Then she put everything into a pouch. Franz came back with a nice piece of hard Tyrol bread which you had to slice very thinly. He cut off half of the loaf, wrapped it in a cloth and put it in the pouch. Josefine was ready to set off with Fredi and the pram. There were not as many people in the central square as expected. She saw Alfred, Alois and Emer.

Josefine reminded Emer not to play the great hero. Whenever possible he should stay in the background and protect himself as best he could, He should only fight back if he was really in danger. "If you kill someone or hit them with a truncheon it will stay with you for the rest of your life. You can't undo it. Don't forget that." She gave him the pouch with the food and she had also hidden a neutral, blue shirt in it. Emer promised to be careful and hoped that he would not have to take a weapon in his hand.

"Have you seen Karl or his wife?" Alois asked and looked at his watch, "there's no sign of his children either. Franz, go and have a look. I've got a bad feeling in my stomach." Franz said, "They'll come at the last minute." Alois said, "No! No!" "Come on Franz," Alfred, who was already wearing his correct uniform, said, "run as fast as you can to Karl. You should meet him on the way, if you go up the alley." Franz said, "What's the use? Maybe he ran away last night." "No! No, I don't believe that", Alois said again. "Just go," ordered Alfred. "All right. Come back safe, all of you," Franz said, hugged them all and ran off.

Panting, he arrived at Karl's house, knocked on the door which Herta, his wife opened. She was alone, the children were in the school. "Well, look who's here. Franz?" she said in amazement, "but why are you so out of breath? What's the matter? My God, you look awful." Franz realised that she knew nothing. His heart was beating fast. "Can you give me a glass of water?" Herta invited him in, pulled up a chair and brought him a glass of water. He took a sip and asked about Karl. "He's gone to the mine," was her answer, "he's on the early shift. He'll be back in about two hours. Should I tell him something? He knows that you are back and he was happy when he heard that you are still in one piece." Franz tried to calm down. He did not trust himself to ask if Karl had to go to the front. "You know what," he said, "I'll come back later and then I won't be panting like an ox. So, goodbye, until then." He had hardly taken his leave when, as soon as the door was closed he ran off like crazy. He did not trust the situation.

When he got back to the central square, the last army lorry was driving out of town. People were standing around and waving hands and scarves. He ran gesticulating towards Josefine and caught up with her totally out of breath, "I don't know if Alois has misunderstood something. Karl's wife said that he was in the mine." "In the mine?" Josefine slowly remarked, but her thoughts were elsewhere. She was holding Fredi in her arms. She put him down slowly, went to a shop window and stared at it. But she wasn't looking in the window. She was looking at the reflection. She saw a male figure slowly disappearing. Franz took Fredi and the pram and stood next to her. He was embarrassed in front of the people, a man did not push a pram. That was women's business. Josefine was standing in front of the shop window. She put her hands over her face. Then she turned round slowly, lowered her hands and opened her eyes. Franz asked, "What's the matter? Are you not feeling well?" Josefine said, "After we've eaten go back to Karl's wife. She needs you. I can't see anything more." "Why all the drama? Of course I'll go to her. I already promised I would." He sighed and pressed his hand to his forehead to clear his thoughts.

Back home Josefine served up the preserved vegetables and the potatoes. Franz only ate a small portion, because of his stomach problems. It tasted wonderful. But he was nervous and he kept looking at the clock. "I'm going now." He stood up and left the flat. As soon as he was gone Josefine put Fredi and Charlotte in the pram and made her way to the garden centre. She used the normal entrance, where she was met by Pirscha. The young woman greeted her warmly and took her to the clay hut, but was shocked to see the bruises on Josefine's face. She wanted to know what had happened, sat Josefine down on a chair and poured out some herbal tea for her. Josefine did not give her a direct answer. Pirscha did not insist and changed the subject "Karel got a letter today. That's the first time that he has had an answer to all the letters which he has sent home since he was abducted from Bulgaria. Now finally a letter has got through from his family. There was good and bad news. His father has died, but his mother is doing well, in spite of all her worries. She is praying that he will come home soon. His son has just had his tenth birthday. Look, she put a photo of his birthday party in the letter. That's Karel's wife, that's his son and that's his mother. Both the women are wearing festive head scarves." While she was talking, Pirscha had not noticed that Josefine was physically shaken. She realised that Pirscha had no idea about her and Karel. The men had never told her about it.

According to National Socialism law, relationships such as theirs were strictly forbidden. Women who were found out were severely punished. They had to go into the central square, in front of all the people and take off all their clothes down to their underwear. Their heads were shaved and then covered with pitch, and then spread with chicken feathers. Some of the women were hanged with a written slate hung around their necks or were stood against the wall and shot.

Pirscha put the letter on one side, looked in the pram and wanted to take Charlotte in her arms, but Josefine stopped her. "I came here because I have to look for something to eat. We've got nothing at home." She did not let it show how shocked she was. She had no idea about Karel's wife and son. Why did he not tell me?

Pirscha went on chattering and chattering, trying to cheer Josefine up. She took some vegetables, put them in Josefine's bag and hid it under Charlotte's blanket. "I'll go and fetch a few potatoes," she said and for that she had to go into the garden hut. As soon as she left Josefine broke down in tears.

She looked around for things which were hers and looked at Ismir's icon and the letter from Bulgaria which was lying beside it. She took the photos out of the envelope and looked at them once more. The round peasant faces of the family seemed to stare at her. She quickly put them back. Ismir came. He looked her in the eyes and understood what had happened. "Karel has gone to the council again. He'll be leaving tomorrow. I don't know if it would be good for you to see him again. It would only break your hearts. Please, keep a good memory of him and try to forgive him. Circumstances brought you together and then tore you apart." Pirscha came back and saw Ismir's arm on Josefine's shoulder. He went to Pirscha, put his arm round her waist and kissed her on the cheek. "Thank you that you went to get the potatoes. Pirscha you are truly my precious little wife." He gave Josefine the potatoes and promised that he would always put something on the side for her. Ismir and Pirscha did not want to go back to their home country. They had permission to stay in the garden centre for the time being.

Josefine wiped her nose, thanked both of them, collected Fredi, who had been playing with some water and set of on her sad way home. Fredi wanted to sit on the pram. Josefine picked up a plank of wood and placed it across the pram so that Fredi could sit on it. "Don't cry, Mummy," Fredi said as she lifted him onto the seat, "I'll sing you one of Alfred's songs: Hop, hop, hop! Rider gallop! He sang it all the way home. When they got there Charlotte needed her nappy changing and to be fed. Then Josefine took her dark skinned little girl and pressed her close. Her tears started to fall again. Then she lay down for a while. She was totally exhausted after this ordeal.

During this time Franz had waited in front of Herta's door. "Come in," she called through the window and Franz entered. "Karl should have been back by now and his food is getting cold. I'll have to put it over hot water to keep it warm. Would you like a cup of tea?" Franz nodded, took the hot tea and mixed it with some cold water before he drank it. "Do you know what?" he said to Herta, "I'll go to meet him. You just have to show me the way." He was worried and nervous. "Well, I can come with you," Herta said, "he's never been so late before. We wanted to go into the garden. But now it's a bit late for that." She looked out of the window again, took her husband's food from the stove and locked the door. They had only gone a few steps when one of Karl's work mates came towards them. "Good, afternoon" he said, "I just wanted to ask if Karl is ill. He wasn't in the mine today." Herta said, "That can't be true. Are you sure?" "Yes, I'm certain. I asked everyone if he had been told to work somewhere else or something, but there was nothing on the work plan. He's normally so dependable. I hope he hasn't had any accident and is in the hospital or somewhere." Franz said, "We can ask the colliery. They can telephone the services and the hospital." They went to the works office and asked about Karl. The hospital was contacted, but no new patients had been registered in the past two days. "His brother, Alfred showed us his marching orders and said that he had to go," the man in the works office said.

Franz said, "But now I have to tell you." Herta said, "In the name of God! What is it?" Franz replied, "Karl got his marching orders too, just like Alfred and Alois. All of those who had been called up had to go to the central square. When Karl didn't turn up Alfred sent me to you. That's why I was so out of breath when I came to you at mid-day. When you said that he had gone to the mine, I thought that he had not been called up. I didn't want to upset you so I thought that I would wait until Karl came home and told me himself what had happened. When I got back to the square Alfred and Alois had already left. All I saw were the army lorries leaving. Emer also had to go." Then the tears started to fall and his chin started to tremble. Herta said, "But he told me nothing." The man from the works office started to telephone around. Miners started to gather round the hut and wanted to know what was going on. They talked about it together and agreed that they should all go looking for Karl. One of them got out a map. Franz wanted to go with him, but they sent him home. His work mates would deal with it. A good colleague of Karl was ordered to accompany Herta home and not to leave her alone. Franz went home with a heavy heart. Josefine realised something was wrong, gave him some herbal tea and put some food on the table. He said nothing and pushed the food to one side. "Come on, eat something," she said trying to encourage him, "You should eat. It will make you feel better and then you can lie down for a while." It worked and apart from that he saw the vegetables which were still in the pram and that calmed him down a little.

After a while Franz told her what had happened and that the miners were looking for Karl. Josefine wanted to say, 'the face in the window', but she knew Franz did not want to hear something like that. So, without saying a word she went out and went to Florenz, because she knew he had a pendulum. It took him a long time to find it. Florenz had always been interested in the pendulum, but had never had time to get to grips with it. She asked him if he had a map of Vordersberg. He said no, but she should go to Mr. Gosch. "He needs such things for his work. He's certainly got a map of some sort. But why do you need it?" Josefine answered, "I'll tell you later. And, by the way, I thought we were on familiar terms?" "Yes, of course. Excuse me." There was no one at home at the Gosch house, so the only person who could help her was Anderl. "They've all gone to look for their dog," Anderl said. "It wasn't there when a small grenade exploded in the courtyard. No one was injured and no one knows where it came from, but since then the fat poodle has disappeared," he told Franz, grinning "You haven't thrown it in the pan, have you?" and gave him a piercing look. "No. Unfortunately not,"

Anderl said, "he didn't come to me, otherwise he would have already been on the way there. A really pretty, spoiled animal." "Keep your fingers off the poodle," Josefine said clearly, "the poor animal, I hope they find it soon. And now, where is the map I asked you about?" "It's here, but what do you need it for?" "You are all curious to know, but no one believes in it. For you it's just hocus-pocus, so I'm saying nothing. Goodbye." She took the map and left.

Franz asked her where she had been and if she had told anyone about Karl's disappearance. When she said that she had told no one, he said that it would have been better not to show her black eye to everyone. Josefine said, "That won't go away so quickly." "Put some powder on it. You must have something like that lying around from your tinsel times," Franz said, provoking her, "I'm going to tell people about Karl. If anyone asks for me, I'll be back soon." Josefine was quite happy about this, because it meant she could use the pendulum without being disturbed. She hoped she could find out where Karl was. The map showed all the streets and pathways in Vordersberg and on the other side it showed the surrounding area. The children stayed quiet, as though they knew that Mummy needed total silence. Completely concentrated Josefine let the pendulum swing over the map. She turned the map upside down and let the pendulum swing again. Then she let the pendulum swing over the local section. Most of the time the pendulum showed the same place. Deep in thought she folded up the map, wound up the pendulum string and put her head in her hands. After a few minutes she took a piece of paper and wrote, "Karl, Wallgasse between house numbers 8 and 12." She had never been in this lane which was on the edge of town. Her head felt hot. She washed her face with cold water and looked out of the window. She said to herself, "Karl is no longer alive. His soul is in heaven. She looked up at the clouds.

The chemist came out of the house and crossed the courtyard. Josefine used a spoon to knock on the bars. He heard it and, after looking left and right, he came to her at the window. "Good afternoon, Mrs. Remi. Is there any news?" he asked. "My husband is back home and is more or less healthy, but he needs some care. Could you support him a little?" The chemist's face showed his relief. He had always felt somewhat guilty on Franz's misfortune. "What were you thinking of? Does he need vitamins?" "No, but he needs something to eat; something for headaches; maybe a sedative and something to help him sleep, preferably in liquid form, because otherwise he won't take it. And have you got some cocoa powder or something similar? Franz really needs to gain weight. He looks so emaciated. I would really be pleased if you could help me build him up and calm him down until he has his feet back on the ground." Otherwise, everything is as it was before. The chemist had seen Josefine's face and understood why she wanted calming medication for her husband. "Come to the shop in an hour. I'll get something for you." Josefine said, "It's for him, not for me. Thank you in advance for your kind help." When the chemist had left she was annoyed that she had said, 'for him, not for me,' because when he had now and again put food in front of the window, it was clear that it was for her and the children. She could have slapped herself in the face and thought about excusing herself.

Then Franz came though the door. "What did you need the pendulum and the map for? You don't listen to what I'm telling you. You should stop all this nonsense." He went to the table where the map and the pendulum were lying and saw the piece of paper with the address written on it. "Who gave you this address with Karl's name on it?" "I found it out with the the pendulum," she said, defensively. "Don't tell me such rubbish," he shouted. "Your brother is in one of these three houses which all have even numbers," she said, and stuck by her words, "his work mates should look for him there and search from the cellar to the attic. You should keep out of it. It's not going to be a pleasant sight." "God damn it! That's enough," he shouted, beside himself with anger, went out and slammed the door behind him. The children clung to each other and started to scream. "Shuss!Shuss," Josefine said, trying to calm them down and gave them something to drink.

Then she set off with them to the chemist also taking with her the map and the pendulum. On the way she visited Anderl and when she retuned the map, the piece of paper with the address fell on the floor. He picked it up and read it. "What have you done now?" he wanted to know. "I'll tell you later," she said and continued on to Florenz, who asked her the same question. But Josefine asked him if he knew anyone who lived in Wallgasse between the houses 8 and 12. He scratched his head. "Herta a friend I knew as a youth, lives there. I don't think I know this Karl, her husband who you're looking for. Just imagine. I only just found out from Franz that Karl is his brother and your brother-in-law. Strange, I never paid much attention to family names and I always thought that in such a small town everyone knew everyone else."

Josefine said, "As far as I can remember, I have only met them once and I only found out that they lived there by using the pendulum." "There you are! I believe in the pendulum as well." He took it from her and looked at it.

Josefine got a whole load of things from the chemist. He had written exactly how Mr. Remi should use them. Then she bought some acetone, which she normally used to remove varnish and glue, but also to make her almost dried out nail polish liquid again.

The chemist gave her a very small bill. When she looked at it with wide open eyes, he winked at her and pressed a few sweets into her hand. She thanked him, paid him, went back home and unpacked everything. But what a surprise. She found some ointment made of acetate of alumina for the bruises on her face! A small tin containing skin coloured cream to cover the marks was also there. She was really happy for his thoughtfulness and for just a moment found herself smiling. As she sat there lost in thought, she suddenly remembered Christine and Reinhard.

She had told Franz that she had taken them to the farmers to recuperate.

When she realised that Fredi was no where to be seen, she called his name and heard a "Hereee," coming from the cellar. She found him sitting on the floor playing with Mr. Gosch's poodle. "Oh! There he is," she said, "poor little dog. They're looking all over for you. Fredi, just look how sweet he is. Give him some water to drink. His tongue's hanging out. Don't you think he's thirsty?" "Yes, we both are very thirsty." Josefine gave them both something to drink and then said, "I'll just go round and see if his owner is at home. They'll be really happy to know their dear little dog has been found." However, she found no one there. When she got back she said, "There's no one at home. You can play with him for a bit longer." Some time later there was a knock on the door and someone called, "Franz." It was Anderl's voice. Josefine thought to herself that he had never before left his restaurant at this time of day so it must be something very important. She opened the door. Anderl was very flustered, "Heh! They've found a body on the rail tracks, so horribly disfigured that it's almost unrecognisable. I thought about your brother in law. Is Franz here?" "No, Anderl, Franz is not here. But it can't be my brother in law. Thank you for coming. I'll tell Franz as soon as he comes home." "Yes, please do." He went off in a hurry but then turned and came back to the door. "Didn't I see Gosch's dog back there?" "Yes, Fredi found it in the cellar, but his master is not at home." "He's in the restaurant. Come on, give me the dachshund," he grinned. "Oh he's there? He'll be very pleased to get his dog back. Come on Fredi bring the dog here." Anderl took the poodle under his jacket and hurried off across the courtyard. After about half an hour he came back. "You won't believe this but the dog ran away from me on the street. Don't tell Gosch anything, otherwise he'll blame us all and say that we turned the dog into a tasty goulash. I've got to get back to the restaurant. Tell me if you hear anything new" Josefine was not sure that she should believe him. She could not believe that he was not capable of controlling such a fat poodle.

A few days later, when Mr. Gosch asked Anderl if he knew anything about the missing dog and had already downed a few glasses of schnapps, Anderl served him up a very expensive "Wienerschnitzel". It smelt fantastic. "Come on, Mr. Gosch, I put one on some bread for you. You can't just drink, you also have to eat. Enjoy it, we don't get meat everyday. Of course Gosch did not know that it was his poodle on the bread and that he would also have to pay for it. "So, is it tasty? You are really a gourmet." "It's very well seasoned. My compliments to the cook." Anderl went into the kitchen and laughed wickedly until his sides ached.

Franz wandered along the main street. He was very uneasy and then he saw two policemen who were busy checking identity cards. "Is this really necessary when you can see how chaotic everything is?" he heard one of them say. It was the policeman Precinschek. Franz called out, "Mr. Precinschek, I haven't seen you for ages. He looked round and said, "Ah, Mr. Dorn." Franz said, "I'm not allowed to call myself Dorn any more. Don't tell me that the word has not reached you." "Yes, but first I'll have to get used to Remi. How are you?" "Well," Franz said, "life goes on. Right now I don't know what to do, we are looking for my brother, Karl. He's disappeared without trace. I wonder if anyone has searched his house, or the neighbouring houses. Do you know anything?" "No, we've heard nothing. How long has he been gone?" Franz said, "It's like this. He didn't turn up for work. He did not say anything to his wife and in addition he had got his marching orders, but didn't report for duty. He's always been so dependable. I don't want the Gestapo or the SS to find him. They don't know him and they could do something to him. You know what can happen. Two of my brothers and my son were taken to the front at mid day. I think Karl panicked and has hidden himself somewhere. If we could find him, we could say that he had forgotten or something else. I can't go searching in other people's houses." Precinschek said, "So, what you really want is that we go looking for him. We'll have to think about that. There's not a lot going on here, so I reckon we could break off for an hour or so. All right, we'll have a look. What's the address?" Franz said, Wallgasse 10 and possibly 8 to 12." "Come on," Mr. Precinschek said to his colleague. Have you made a note of that? We'll take our bicycles and you, Mr. Remi; you should stay out of this." Franz went down to the river and for a while he looked at the waves. And then he felt the urge to go home.

Herta was surprised when she saw two policemen standing at her door and wondered what they had to say. "Good afternoon. Have you any news about your husband?" Herta said, "No, up to now, nothing." "My name is Precinschek and this is my colleague, Hauser. Has anybody looked in the house for him? Do you have a cellar or an attic?" Herta said, "No, nobody has looked in the cellar and you can only reach the attic by the steps outside." Precinschek asked, "Do you have anything against us having a look around before we ask you any more questions?" Herta replied, "My husband is not here, but you're welcome to come in and see for yourselves." She let the two policemen in and they looked everywhere. They also opened drawers and looked under everything; they knocked on the walls and the floor. In the rubbish bin they found a torn up note. They put it together like a jigsaw puzzle and read, "My dearest Herta. I hope you can forgive me. I know what should…" There was nothing more on it, but for Precinschek the message meant a lot. He put the pieces of paper into his pocket. They then searched the cellar, but found nothing. In the meantime, Hauser had taken his pistol in his hand. They went into the attic up the outside stairs. "Look at that," Precinschek said, "the key is in the lock and the door is open. Is anyone there?" It was dark inside and he could not find the light switch. "Should I go and ask for a lamp?" Hauser asked. "Yes," Precinschek said, "a torch would help," and felt his way to a half covered roof window, which he wanted to open. On his way he stumbled into something soft. "Wait, there's something here," he called to his colleague and stumbled over a torch. He switched it on. The beam danced around and lit a stool which was lying on the floor and when he raised the beam, he saw trouser legs, a body and finally the head, hanging from a rope. Both policemen were deeply shocked. It was the first time either of them had seen a hanged man. They stood there like pillars of salt. Hauser said, "We have to cut him down. I've got my bayonet here." They stood the stool back on its feet. Precinschek had to hold the corpse while Hauser climbed on to the stool and cut through the rope.

And then, there was Karl, lying lifeless on the floor. Precinschek and Hauser had a quick conversation and then they left the attic, locking the door behind them. Hauser went to the next shop which had a telephone, called his colleagues at the police station and told them what had happened. Then he called for a doctor and a transport car. Precinschek stopped a man who was on his way to Herta. "Stop! Who are you?" "Möller, I'm one of Karl's work mates. We're looking for him. Do you want to know if we have any news? But aren't you Precinschek? What are you doing here? Are you on duty?" Precinschek pulled him to one side and his face was very serious, "We've found him. You can stop looking." A miner, covered in coal dust, stopped his bicycle in front of them and looked at them both questioningly. Möller whispered that he should go back to the works office and tell them to break off the search for Karl, because he had been found. The miner asked, "Is he dead?" "Yes," Precinschek answered, "he's dead. The miner peddled off furiously. Möller was white as a sheet, "Did you say 'dead'?" "Yes," Precinschek said, "dead, but stay calm, here's my colleague. He has informed the doctor. Hauser, go to his wife and hold her back until the body has been removed. "How did he die?" Möller wanted to know, but did not wait for an answer and said, "I live close by. I'll get my wife." The doctor came with two other men in a Red Cross lorry. Precinschek went up with them into the attic. "Death from hanging," the doctor said, and, turning to the other men, "you can take him away, but don't change anything. We still have to make a more precise examination." Karl was wrapped in a white cloth. Precinschek put the rope with it and the corpse was driven away. In the meantime Hauser had gone to Herta and asked her countless questions so that she did not look out of the window. When her neighbour, Mrs. Möller arrived he could finally tell her what had happened. "No!" Herta cried, "I don't believe it. Why? Where is he now? I have to see him." Hauser said, "Your husband has been taken to the hospital. You'll be told when you can see him." Mrs. Möller took Herta in her arms and sat down beside her. "My God! The children will be home soon. How terrible."

In the hospital it was clearly suicide. They found a farewell letter in his trouser pocket, which they brought to his wife along with all his other things. Weeping, Herta unfolded the letter and read:

"My beloved wife, my Herta, my most beloved children!

Please forgive me that I take my leave from you for ever. I can see no other way out. It was unthinkable for me that I should go to fight in this useless war. I would have been a bad soldier. I am not capable of killing another person, even if he is the enemy. I thought about this and if I did not go to war, then I would anyway be executed because I was a conscientious objector. If I went into hiding I would have been constantly on the run until they found me. I don't want to do that to you. So it's better that I end my life myself and quickly.

Please forgive me. I can't help it.

Karl"

There was no priest at the funeral, because in the Catholic church suicide was a deadly sin and the priests were forbidden to give someone who had committed suicide a Christian burial. There was even a special part of the cemetery, divided from the main area by bushes. Josefine refused to go to the burial. She hardly knew the family, who had always lived apart. And she was also worried that Franz's first wife Luise would be there. So she decided to take the opportunity to go to the Katz family and take Reinhard and Christine back. She told her housekeeper Hilde, about it and took the post bus over the pass to the farmers.

Just as she got to the place her children came running towards her. "Mummy, Mummy. It's good you've come. We have run away. We wanted to come home," Reinhard stammered. Christine said, "They didn't bite me. They don't like me." "Who doesn't like you?" Josefine asked, "who hasn't bitten you?" "They've bitten Reinhard. The bugs and fleas like Reinhard." Josefine put down the milk can which she had brought with her and looked at Reinhard's face, throat and the rest of his body. They were covered in bites and scratches. Christine lifted her dress and wanted Josefine to look at her as well, but Josefine just scolded her and said, "Pull your dress down. Everyone can see your knickers. A girl doesn't do that. Do you understand?"

The farmer's wife had run after the children, but when she saw Josefine she stopped dead. "So there you are, you runaways." She shouted and went back to the farm. Josefine and the children followed her.

"The children have smeared all my pine furniture with blood," Mrs. Katz complained. "With blood?" "Yes. Look!" She opened the bedroom door and pointed to the bed frame, "A Romanian who was forced to work here made this very fine piece of furniture," she said, almost in tears. Josefine said that you could paint it with pretty colours and saw the bugs in the joints, which Reinhard was trying to squash with his finger nails. All his fingers were dark red with blood. "Stop that," Josefine cried, "that's disgusting." She pulled him away from the bed and turned to Mrs. Katz, "I'm taking the children with me. It's for the best."

Then she looked through a window and saw the farmer eating from a bowl. Suddenly she felt hungry. The farmer's wife wiped her face on her apron and went into the living room. The children went outside and looked at the farmer with hunger in their eyes. He gave each of them a spoon and left them the bowl with something left in it. They sat down on the floor almost hitting their heads together and, greedily, ate what remained.

The farmer's wife said, anxiously, "The fleas and bugs came into the house with the last batch of starving workers and we can't get rid of them. I've already bought something to kill them, but it doesn't seem to work." Josefine said, "I'll bring you something more effective as quickly as possible. I think that our council or the Red Cross are handing out something which works. Otherwise I can ask my neighbour, the chemist. He certainly has something which will get rid of this plague. If you can give me milk and food, then it would be a good exchange. I know that nobody is having a great time right now, but thank God we can still help each other."

She looked up at the cross on the wall and held out her milk can and rucksack. The wife gave the milk can to her husband and disappeared into the bedroom with the rucksack. While she was waiting Josefine undressed the children and looked for vermin. After a while they both came back. "I'm going to miss the children," Mrs. Katz sighed and wiped some tears from her eyes, "bring them with you if you come back."

Josefine promised she would do that, looked in the rucksack to see what they had given her and thanked them. "May the lord God protect you. You are good people. I thank you for everything and I hope to see you again soon" The farmer's wife said, "Until then, yes, please come back again." She hugged the children. "Hopefully it will soon be better. I've heard that the war is almost over. Then things will start to improve". "Yes," Josefine said, " That will be so, there will be better times ahead. I've read it in the cards, but we need to have a little patience, hold on and look forward. Who would want to give up now? Everything will turn out for the best. God has put us to the test and He will help us." She shook hands with Mr. and Mrs. Katz, took the rucksack on her back, the milk can in one hand and Reinhard in the other - she had already tied the bundle of clothes from both children on her back - and set off on the return journey. Christine had to walk in front, so she would not get lost, but she kept a close hold on her brother. They never returned to the farming family. It was too far away and because of the bugs, they did not want to.

Rosita, the sixth child came into the world. Three months after her birth Josefine was pregnant with Isabella.

XIV

In the south the war was already over. But the air raid sirens were still heard in Vordersberg because the British bombers were flying north over the small town and releasing their bombs. The reason was that it was too dangerous to land with the bombs still on board. Time and again the people had to take cover. So Josefine and the whole family were forced to sit in the cellar with the other house residents. They waited, ears alert for the all clear siren. So almost no one spoke, and if they did speak, only in a whisper.

Suddenly! A loud motor noise in the sky. The plane seemed to be flying directly over the house. They all squeezed themselves into a corner and squatted down from fear. There was a huge explosion. A bomb had dropped on the park in front of the castle, killing several people and injuring many more. In the cellar the small window broke and glass splinters flew around like bullets. Screams and wounded. Blood flowed from Fredi's throat. Christine had glass splinters in the left side of her forehead and chin and her nose was covered in blood. Both children were lying there as if they were dead. The other's only had superficial injuries. "Bandages over here," Mrs. Gosch commanded in her deep voice and, once the all clear siren sounded, added, "Stand back, first the wounded into the open." Franz ran out to get help.

Josefine, with Charlotte in her arms, screamed over Fredi and stayed with the children until they were carried up out of the cellar. Cooper Florenz put Fredi into a newly made low wooden trough which was standing in the courtyard. Mrs. Gosch felt their pulses. By Fredi she felt nothing. Christine still had a pulse, but it was feeble. A Red Cross lorry sped into the courtyard. And then, suddenly some stacked barrels started to roll. The implosion had shifted them. One barrel rolled over the trough where Fredi lay and grazed down a side of Josefine›s back. Everybody started to shout in horror.

The rescuers leapt out of the lorry and bent over Fredi, "There's nothing we can do." His jugular vein had been severed. His eyes were half-closed. They closed his eyes lids and said, "Someone from the family should come to the hospital later. We can send a car to collect the boy if you want. We'll take the little girl with us. Nurse Sonja will stay here and bandage the boy and give you some help." They could not get Josefine away from the trough. Nurse Sonja pushed her a little to one side so that she could not see her son's wide open wound which had almost cut his throat in half and she bound his head so that you could only see his face. Then Florenz told Josefine that Fredi could now be taken into the flat and took him in his arms. They removed his little jacket which was soaked in blood.

In the flat Florenz laid him on the table. Nurse Sonja washed away the blood, asked for a clean jacket and put it on him. She placed him under a woollen blanket and the little boy lay there. Franz, who kept wiping his tears away, sat on the bed with Charlotte and Reinhard clung to him. With great difficulty he tried to calm the children. "I'll go and ask about your daughter," Nurse Sonja said to Josefine, "I think she's called Christine." Josefine gave no answer. Franz said, "Yes, her name is Christine," and his voice broke down in sobs, "I'll come to hospital as soon as I can." Josefine, overcome with pain, held the still warm little hands of her most precious child and stroked Fredi from head to foot until the hearse came and took him away.

Hilde came and excused herself, for coming so late, but there had been a lot going in the castle. She had seen the hearse driving off and was shocked when she was told that Fredi was in it. "Oh my God," she cried and had to sit down. Franz reminded her that no one had eaten and that she should make some tea for his wife. She gave Josefine some tea and tried to get the children to the table so that they could eat something and then go to bed. Then she reported that at the castle one side wall had been broken, that a few valuable windows had been destroyed and that there was a huge bomb crater in the park. Franz was not really listening and said that he had to go to the hospital because of Christine and all the forms. With his hat already on his head, it occurred to him that he might need the birth certificates, collected them and left the flat. Charlotte drank her bottle. Reinhard did not want to eat. He also wanted a bottle. Josefine nodded and said, "Today you can have a bottle too. Come here and hide yourself under the cover with it." Hilde put all Fredi's belongings in the bottom drawer of the large cupboards and took his bed away. In the courtyard Florenz and his helpers had already rearranged and secured the barrels. They also brushed away the blood from under the fountain spout with water from the trough, collected the glass splinters from the damaged window and spread sawdust on the blood stains.

Three weeks later Christine was still in the hospital. Her wounds had almost healed, but she was in a coma. Nurse Sonja took care of her as though she was her own child. "Can you imagine?" she said to her colleague, Mrs. Reisin, "Mrs. Remi, the child's mother has not yet been here to visit her." Mrs. Reisen implied that Josefine did not care too much for her daughter, Christine. "I'll go and see how she's getting on," Mrs. Reisin said, "the poor woman has just buried her favourite son. He was really a treasure. But her other children are also very nice, but whenever I see her pushing Christine to one side, I want to take the child in my arms. She really should pay her more attention even though, as it appears, the little one doesn't seem to mind."

Every day people returning home arrived at the station. Women, who were waiting for their husbands stood there with photographs and cards with names written on them in large letters. They asked if the returnees had seen their husband or their son, or if they had some news of them. There were tears of joy, hugs and disappointments whenever the troops arrived. Franz's second oldest son, Erwin came home with shrapnel in his legs. However, right up to the end of the war Emer was able to hide from the partisans. When he returned to Vordersberg he went first to Mrs. Slavic, but she was very nervous, because she was expecting her husband to arrive any day. A half starved soldier had come to her and told her that he had met Mr. Slavic and that he was on his way home.

She had written the name of the soldier on a piece of paper. "Ah! Rudi! He's crazy," Emer said, "you can forget it. At the beginning he was at my side the whole time when we were in Yugoslavia. Then I escaped from the group and went into hiding. I only went back when they started to bring the troops home and I said that I had been surrounded by the partisans and did not have any ammunition. Of course I had thrown the ammunition away. In the evenings we talked about what we would do when we returned to civilian life. That's how this idiot got to hear about you and your husband and that you are my trainer. Imagine, at the last minute he jumped on a train which was already full to bursting. He wanted to get to you. That much is clear. It was several hours before I could get a train. Was he here for long?" "I gave him some soup and then he went for my skirt. Thankfully I'm strong and I soon pushed him away. He realised that he had no chance, apologised and left. I'm so angry when I hear that he lied to me. My God! Now I'm going to cry."

Emer comforted her until she calmed down. Since they were both standing, she asked him to sit down, because she had something to tell him. "I'm sorry, Emer, but I must tell you something. A single bomb which fell on the castle park caused many injuries and some deaths. One of those who died was your brother, Fredi." Emer looked at her, horrified, "What! Is Fredi dead?" "Yes, Emer, I believe so. He was buried about three weeks ago. Your sister Christine was seriously injured. She's in the hospital and has been in a coma ever since." Emer jumped up, clung to the chair and stared into nothing. It was as if a film was running in front of his eyes. "Tell me it's not true," he cried in pain. But Mrs. Slavic said nothing. Instead she brought him a glass of water. Then she took him in her arms and kissed him gently on the neck.

"I want to go to the cemetery. No, not to the cemetery. I'll never go to a cemetery again, never! That brings back too many bad memories; back then when we had to hide a whole night in a cemetery. I can't get those pictures out of my head. But I want to go to Christine in the hospital. Will you come with me? Right now." Emer's chin quivered and he could no longer hold back his tears. "Emer, it would be better if you changed out of your uniform. You still have some clothes here. Maybe something will fit you, even though you've grown a lot." Mrs. Slavic brought him a shirt, trousers and a jacket, but saw right away that the trousers and jacket were too small. Without further ado she took some of her husband's clothes. Emer put them on without realising that they were not his clothes. She then said, "Put this coat on." "But that's your husband's coat," he protested, "I don't like that idea." Mrs. Slavic ignored what he said. "Come on, let's go," she said, "are you sure you don't want to go to your mother first?" "No," Emer said, "we'll go to Christine first of all."

Josefine had heard that Emer had arrived at the station and wondered why he had not come home some time ago. He did not knock on the door before evening. Josefine said, "My God! You're in mufti! Have you been to the Red Cross? Then you must have heard about everything which has happened here." She took the cloth which she had in her hand, wiped her eyes and took her son in her arms. "I don't think I'll ever get over it. My Fredi has left us for ever. He must be in heaven, looking down on us. It all happened so quickly. He couldn't have suffered. He was, quite simply, suddenly dead. I still don't believe it to this day that he's there in the cemetery."

The whole time they both wiped tears from their eyes and did not notice that Reinhard had been standing by them for some time. "Have you brought me something?" he asked Emer, and pulled at his trousers. Emer bent down, “Hello. No, I haven’t brought you anything, but next time I come I’ll have something for you.” “Promise?” “Promise. Emer looked at Charlotte and Rosita and then asked his mother, “Why have you not visited Christine?

Someone told me that the whole town knows that you have not been a single time to the hospital”.

Before she could answer, father came back home. Still very thin, he stood in front of Emer, hugged him and said, “You’ve already heard everything?.” Emer nodded “I’ve already asked Mum why she has never gone to the hospital to see Christine.” Josefine said, “Who told you such nonsense? I’ve been there many times, but not during the visiting hours, because there are too many people around then and the doctors are always busy answering all sorts of questions. And with all these war wounded they have a lot to do. So I always crept into the room where she is lying without being noticed. Then I talk to her and leave. I’ve been there almost every day.”

While she was talking she was messing around at the stove and avoided looking at Emer and Franz. She then asked if it would not be better to eat something than to repeat the gossip spread around by people who think they know better. Franz said, that at the beginning he had been there a few times because he had to fill out forms. “Christine just lay there with her eyes closed,” he said, “I’m sure she doesn’t know what is going on around her. The doctors don’t know how long it can go on and, as you have just heard, your mother is always there.” Emer asked himself why his mother was lying. “Tomorrow we’re all going to go their together,” he decided, “and during the visiting hours in the morning.” Josefine knew that she could not avoid it and Franz agreed, because he wanted to stop the malicious rumours in the ‘village’. “What? Tell me! Did you go to the hospital before you came to visit us?” Josefine asked and looked defiantly at her son. Emer said, “Yes. I visited Christine, my little sister and I spoke to her.” He stressed that so hard that the parents looked at him in amazement. "But she couldn't answer," he went on, "she has been in a coma since all that happened."

Then Reinhard stammered, "Tomorrow we'll bring Christine home. She can lie here in coma. It's not infectious." Franz said, "My God, boy, you could be a lot brighter at your age and stop stammering. Josefine, as soon as we have been to the hospital tomorrow morning, you must go to the school and talk to the teachers." Josefine said, "You should look after him. His exercise books and marks are all right. Hilde told me." Franz said, "That's a surprise, but then it's all right."

The next day Josefine, Franz and Emer went to the hospital, but Christine was not in her room. Emer looked at all the beds. They feared the worst. The nurse Elisabeth came into the room. "Are you looking for someone?" Josefine said, "Christine should be lying there." "Do you mean the little Christine Remi. She's been moved into the nurse's room. Unfortunately we can't let her go home for a while, but don't worry, nurse Sonja is taking great care of the little one. We really have a great deal to do! If it wasn't for Sonja… who knows! She gives up all her free time to massage the little one and move her limbs, so that her joints don't stiffen and she doesn't get any bed sores. That means she has to keep turning her, day and night. She also has to change her nappies and make sure she is being fed and getting enough liquid. You are going to have to do that back home and the whole family is going to have to work together, because no one can do that alone. None of us have given up the hope that one day she will wake up. Many of us are praying for her. The little one is our darling. She looks so sweet. Come, I'll show you where she is now. Unfortunately nurse Sonja is not yet here, but you'll meet her next time. She never stays away too long."

Nurse Elisabeth went on ahead, opened the door and led them to a bed saying, "So, Christine, how are you today? You've got a lot of rare visitors." She stressed the word 'rare'. "Wouldn't you like to open your eyes? You've got such lovely toys and a pretty musical box full of music. Look, your Mummy and Daddy and your brother are here. You must be happy about that. I'll leave you alone with them, till later my little angel." She straightened her pillow and left the room. The three of them stood round the bed and did not know what to do or say. They had been surprised how the nurse had behaved. They had never imagined something like that. Emer touched Christine and stroked her, He could not speak. Just seeing her lying there like that with the crossed scars on the left side of her forehead seemed to close his throat. Josefine just plucked at the duvet and looked at the lace edged cover.

Franz whispered, "She's lying there like a little princess. Just look at her face. Such a beautiful shape. You could imagine she was only sleeping." Then he shook the bed and called softly, "Hey! We're here!" But Christine did not move. "How long can this go on?" he brooded, "but they are really taking good care of her; you can see that right away. Look at the expensive toys they've put around her. Are they hers or are they from the hospital?" The he stood up abruptly and said, "Right. It's time to go. Anyway, we can't do anything. We'll just have to wait and see what happens." Josefine said, "Come on Emer." Emer kissed Christine once more on the mouth and tearfully whispered, "I'll come back soon." Josefine just touched the duvet again.

Nurse Sonja fought for little Christine's life. She was seriously worried that, if she was allowed to go home, only Emer would look after her. Josefine was against it. She said that she was not a competent therapist and that she had to sleep at night. If you thought about her work with the other children and the housework then you might be able to understand Josefine's attitude. Truth was that she had no desire to look after Christine and be bound to the house. Not least, she was in a certain condition. She was expecting her seventh child.

Alfred and Alois came back from the war safe and sound. Most of the time they had been working as medical orderlies close to the front. They were deeply shocked about what had happened while they were away. The thing which shocked them most was that their brother Karl had hanged himself. They could not understand that. Alfred soon went to visit Christine in the hospital and he carved a wooden cross with a curved metal roof for Fredi's grave. He planted forget-me-nots and pansies from his garden on the grave, which flowered every year.

When Emer finally persuaded his mother to go to the hospital again, she took Reinhard and Charlotte with her. In the room they met the nurses and the doctors who were very excited. Christine had opened her eyes a little and then closed them again. That is why they had made the room a little darker. She had also made some sounds and twitched her fingers and little feet. After 82 days she had woken up. There were tears of joy from everyone. They let Emer, Josefine and the children into the room and waited for more signs. Nurse Sonja infused Christine with a yellow liquid and then started to massage her body. Emer carefully stroked her light brown hair back from her forehead. Someone gave Josefine a chair. She sat down and wiped away her tears. She was deeply moved by the emotions which the others were showing. When she bent over Christine to look at her more closely her head scarf, which she almost always wore, fell back and her raven black hair was uncovered. What a noble face; a classic beauty; the dark tinted skin and high cheek bones. In spite of the fact that she was heavily pregnant, she had an attractive body and very beautiful legs.

Finally Franzi, the oldest son of Franz and Luise, came home. He was the one who had been in the war the longest. With other soldiers he had taken part in a relentless hunger march in the freezing cold from Russia to Finland. He and his comrades had been cut off from the rest of the troop. When they got to Finland they heard that the war had ended, but it was months before they came home. Franzi came home without any notable physical damage, but he was somewhat psychologically disturbed and suffered from paranoia. He could only sleep if he had a pistol under his pillow and he tried to forget his experiences during the war by drowning them in alcohol. He never told anyone what had happened to him before his march to Finland, where he had been deployed and what he had done or not done. When he was drunk he sometimes sang a song in a foreign language, Once Josefine said to him, "That's Polish, isn't it?" He was totally confused and said that it was Finish. However, Josefine understood Finish quite well, because it is related to Hungarian, her mother tongue. So she went back to her clairvoyant skills and assumed that Franzi had been in a Polish camp as a warder. That would explain his behaviour. What had really happened or where he had really been never once passed his lips.

Christine's recovery progressed, slowly but surely. She had to learn to speak and move again. They took her into a ward with several children. The chatter and visits from other children at her little bed did her good. But the toys started to disappear. Nurse Sonja tried to tie them to the bed, but that was not much help. She took the music box away and told Christine, "You'll get it back when you can go home, all right? Say 'yes.' Little one, you have to start speaking." Christine was not a great speaker and had never been one, but she had been asked to repeat, she said clearly. As soon as she could eat for herself she was sent home. She had to come to the therapy centre once a week.

When Christine did not turn up for her appointment the next week, nurse Sonja was informed. She made her way to the family and was surprised at the friendly invitation to come in to the flat. Hilde had opened the door and called Christine. Nurse Sonja saw Josefine sitting at the sewing machine and Christine crawled on the floor to her. She took the little one in her arms and said, "Christine missed her appointment today at the therapy centre. You really shouldn't miss these appointments otherwise there could be lasting damage." Josefine said, "Yes, her brothers and sisters sometimes help her to her feet, but otherwise she is quite independent. She was never very talkative. Just look at what

I'm doing here. Even though I'm a heavily pregnant woman I still have to make sure that there is something to eat. As long as my husband has no real work I'm the one who has to make sure that there's something on the table. Luckily I have Hilde, who helps me, but otherwise we get no help. The money we get from the social office is no way enough. There are too many people who are starving even though things have improved a bit. The Protestant Church have a soup kitchen, but they have threatened that very soon they will only be giving soup to their own church members. The English are also helping there. So now we have to be Protestants. Something is being done, but for the time being I have to work harder so that the situation improves. My husband is trying to be self employed again, but right now he's got problems with the authorities."

Nurse Sonja listened and looked at what Josefine was sewing. They were stuffed animals and they looked very quaint. She had already put Christine on a blanket to train her leg muscles and joints. She also stood her up and practised a few steps with her. One knee was still a bit weak, but otherwise she was making good progress. "So, my darling, now tell me something," Sonja said, "now come on. I'll help you. What have you eaten today?" Christine said, "Jam bread." Hilde added, "But today you ate more than before. What else did you eat?" Christine frowned and looked at Reinhard "Reinad, you say," she said. Stammering, Reinhard told her what she had eaten. Sonja shook Christine gently, "But Christine, I want you to tell me. Come on, Christine." Then she seemed to have an idea. "You know what? I'll come and take both of you to the next speech therapy session. Then maybe Reinhard can speak better and Christine can exercise her vocal chords. Do you agree?" Josefine said, "It's all right with me. I'm happy to have your support. You've already done so much for the child." Once again Josefine avoided calling Christine by her name. "I think otherwise she would no longer be here." Nurse Sonja said, "Yes, but I only did my duty as a nurse. Well, all right, maybe I did a bit more for my darling. Is that right?" She looked tenderly at Christine and got a kiss from her. Sonja said, "Thank you. That was very nice. Now say, 'See you again soon'." Christine shook her head and only said, "God you" which should have been "God go with you." "Yes, and God be with you." Nurse Sonja arranged another appointment and left the family.

When she had left, Hilde wanted to know why Mr. Remi had problems with the authorities. Josefine said, "Oh, Hilde. It's probably the same as last time, about the trade licence or something similar. They've always got something, but this time he'll have to sort it out for himself. I'm not going to get involved and certainly not in my condition, otherwise I might lose another child." Josefine thought of Fredi and wiped her nose. "You know what, Hilde? I'm going to go to the cemetery. It'll do me good to stretch my legs and take some fresh air. I'll take Reinhard and Charlotte with me." She did not mention Christine. "Put Charlotte in the pram for me." Christine had been watching everything with wide open eyes. She slid under the table. There was a cardboard box there with pieces of paper and crayons which she had received from the hospital so that she could practice writing and exercise her fingers. Once they were alone, Hilde joked around with her for a while, then sat her on a chair and put the paper and crayons on the table. Christine occupied herself with the drawing utensils until she was tired and fell asleep. Hilde picked her up and laid her on the little mattress which was lying on the floor.

On the way to the cemetery Josefine met Mrs. Berger who had hidden her two mentally impaired sons from Hitler's euthanasia programme and had been able to save their lives. You could see that she was happy to be able to talk about it now. Josefine found that the story was more and more gripping and this time she lent her an ear. Then Mrs. Berger said how sorry she was about Fredi's death and finally she said, "It's hard to believe that your husband is suspected of wanting to increase his wealth because of your son's death." Josefine said, "What?" Mrs. Berger said, "You seem to know nothing about the whole thing. That's a bit embarrassing." Josefine: "Tell me what you know. Come on, talk!" "Well, it's like this; your husband and his colleague Lanegger, who everyone knows is a Communist, have accused the cooper of being responsible for the death of your son. He hadn't secured the barrels properly and that's why they rolled down and killed your injured child. Yes, that's how it was supposed to have happened. Mrs. Remi, you look very perplexed. And now you and your husband want compensation, which everyone understands." Josefine asked, "Where did you hear all this?" "My husband is a secretary with an arbitration committee. Mr. Lanegger asked them how your husband should go to get justice." Josefine: "And then?" Mrs. Berger: "I don't know anything more than that and I shouldn't say anything until the case has been cleared up. But the investigation is already under way. Have you not had a visit from an investigator? You seem to know nothing about it." Josefine: "Mrs. Berger, I'm already late. I have to go. I'm going to the grave."

Josefine left hurriedly. Her pulse was racing and when she got back home she was out of breath. She had great difficulty sorting out her thoughts. Hilde was standing at the door, ready to leave. "Oh! Mrs. Remi. You have to take care of yourself. You shouldn't walk so fast. Sit down. I'll get the pram. I'm not in so much of a hurry." But she kept looking at the clock. Josefine held her hand over her stomach. The child was boxing fiercely. Hilde gave her and Reinhard tea and wanted to go, but Josefine held her back, "Hilde, please stay for a moment. I just want to sort something out with someone in the house," and she left.

Suddenly a veil fell from her eyes. Recently some people in the house seemed to be in a hurry when they met and avoided her. Even Florenz had not spoken to her for some time. Why had no one said something to her? She ran to Lanegger and knocked on the door. His son opened the door. "Is your daddy here." Jokingly he called back into the flat, "Daddy, are you there?" laughed and added, "Come Mrs. Remi. I'll take you into the best room. You'll have to excuse me. I have to go out." "That's all right," his father called from the sitting room and when Josefine entered the room he said, "Please take a seat, Mrs. Remi what's the matter?" "You ask me what's the matter? I›ve had to hear from strangers what has been going on behind my back. First tell me your version. I haven't had a chance to ask my husband, because I hardly ever see him. Why do you want to make Florenz guilty for the death of our son? Why did you have to pick such an honourable man to pillory? You›re totally crazy. You think you're true Communists. On your pamphlets you write 'Truth and Justice? And what do you do? You›ve turned into a band of money-grubbing gangsters."

Josefine had to take a breath, "You've got it wrong dear Comrade." "I'm not your Comrade and I will never support this sort of imputation." Mr. Lanegger said, "Just listen for a moment. What has happened is very sad, but we mustn't lose sight of the reality about how and why it happened. Only Mrs. Gosch felt Fredi's pulse. The others came after the barrels had rolled over him." Josefine said, "That's pure conjecture. I don't believe that the barrels killed him. The whole time he lay there just where Florenz had placed him," crying she went on, "His face wasn't damaged, but his throat had been pierced by a splinter of glass and that's what killed him. The barrels rolled over half my back." She stood up and left. She could not go on. When Josefine arrived home Hilde was waiting in the doorway with her bag in her hand and did not know if she should go or stay. Josefine told her, "Thank you Hilde, till tomorrow."

Franz came home late and saw that Josefine had been crying a lot. "What's the matter?" he wanted to know. Josefine told him, briefly that she had been to Lanegger. "Couldn't you leave Florenz in peace?" Franz was angry and he stank of alcohol. "We wanted to protect you from the whole thing, but you had to do something different. We have to find out the cause. I came later, because I had to call the medics. I know nothing else. Lanegger told me about the insurance after the funeral. I don't care about the money, but the guilty party must pay. That's life."

Josefine lost control. "The air pressure from the bombing loosened the retaining supports. The first barrels started to roll when the ambulance braked close by".

It was Florenz, poor thing, who put Fredi in the trough and he hadn't noticed that something had broken free. The barrels didn't kill Fredi!" she hissed at him. She did not want to be too loud. Her anger rose, "You didn't even look at Fredi, because you can't see any blood, you cowards. That's also why you didn't go to war and didn't defend your family or your country. Your sons were all there, two of them have come back almost crippled. Karl left his wife and children behind and he did that out of pure cowardice." Franz was furious, he kicked and punched her, "What's got into you, god dammit?" he shouted. At that moment the door opened and Emer rushed in. He gripped Franz's arms strongly to stop him throwing a few more punches. Franz wanted to give him a few, but Emer was stronger. He pulled Franz's arms behind his back, led his step father to a chair and sat him down. Franz started to cry.

"You destroy everything because you are out of control. I don't know what to do," Josefine, bent double, went to the toilet. Emer did not know what to say. He was breathing heavily. The whole thing unnerved him. "I'm bleeding. I'm losing a lot of blood," Josefine said as she came crying back from the toilet. It was already dropping on the floor. Emer laid his mother on the floor and pushed a pillow under her. Franz jumped up, "Should we call a doctor? I'll go to the chemist. He should call a doctor or the hospital." Emer said, "Wait. I'm quicker. Cover Mum with a blanket." Long minutes went by before the ambulance arrived and Josefine was taken to the hospital. Emer was allowed to go with her and when he got home he reported that Mother would probably have to stay in hospital until the child was born. Franz said, "Well, it's all for the best. She can build up her strength. Everything which has happened was simply too much for her." Emer said, "Why were you fighting? What was it about?" Franz replied, "Your mother said that Karl and I were cowards and other things. I couldn't take that. I shouldn't have hit her, but she provoked me. At first I thought that a slap on the cheek would bring her to her senses. Luckily you arrived. Otherwise I don't know what might have happened. I completely lost control. How can something like that happen? Something so stupid? As if we hadn't suffered enough." Emer stayed with him over night.

Franz knocked on Lanegger's door. He could not sleep. He suggested that it might not be better to drop the whole thing. But Lanegger said, "Our town is going to be in the Russian zone. The English have gone to the west. The Russians themselves are gathering all the animals and everything edible. They'll be providing stews for everyone. They don't ask who you are or where you were. They work on the idea of collectivity." They were now in the middle and should not give up. He had a great deal of influence over Franz and read him a long speech which Franz should read out in the central square when the time was right.

"Communism must win. Truth and justice for all, Comrade. We now have our own newspaper. The title is 'The Truth!' We have to distribute it. I let you have a few copies. You'll see that it will influence the people. There has never been a newspaper like this."

Shortly after, Josefine gave birth to another girl. She christened her Isabella.

A Communist meeting took place on the central square. Franz handed out a few felt shoes, which he had made himself, to barefoot children.

Josefine let herself be persuaded and presented a puppet show in the restaurant hall while Franz was standing on the platform and giving his speech. He spoke louder and louder and shouted until he was hoarse. It was his first and last public speech.

Thirteen months after Isabella, Josefine brought Hermine into the world.

She had Franz's blonde hair and blue eyes. When the doctor put her in Josefine's arms she was very happy with the little, pale skinned girl. "Now you have seven children Mrs. Remi. That should be enough, it would not be very sensible to have more." Josefine said, "To whom are you saying that? I would have stopped long ago, but you men can't leave it alone." "Yes, yes, Mrs. Remi, but it always takes two." "Is there something to stop my having any more children? Or what should I do?" The doctor replied, "I'll make an appointment for you, so you can get some advice, if you agree." Josefine agreed, but forgot to keep the appointment.

Straight after the birth a man and a woman from the court came to the hospital, showed their identification cards and asked her about Fredi's death. Josefine protected Florenz and said that Lanegger had persuaded Franz, because he would not have done it on his own. He was not capable of doing something like that. He would never have joined the Communists if Mr. Lanegger had not persuaded him. He should leave her husband in peace.

Then Lanegger and Franz were arrested, came to court and were found guilty of fraudulent dealings. Franz got six months and Lanegger eleven months in prison. Both men thought that they had received a punishment which was harder than normal because of their Communist leanings. That only strengthened their political opinion. In the newspaper "The Truth" it was made clear that they were innocent Communists. The people were fired up with paragraphs like, "What has happened to justice and the right to freedom for the common people! We will continue the fight!" The result was that their imprisonment was reduced by one third. With that and other, similar actions, the party gained strength. When Josefine heard this, she lost her sanity and wrote to the prison, that they should kill him right away. These idiots get mixed up in everything. She had to get by with seven children… and so on and so forth. She knew all these sayings about collective ideology. Everybody had the same treatment and the same rights. But there had never been equality and there would not be equality in the future. She just had anger in her stomach. The letter arrived in Franz's hands in a small prison and when he was released he gave it to his sister Berta and asked her to keep it safe.

One evening, when Josefine was sitting at the table with the children, Christine pointed at the window. "There! Look!" They all looked. Josefine said, "Oh my God! Look, my father is saying goodbye. Come on, wave to him. Wave! Father! Please don't go! Father! Father!" The man at the widow waved, turned round and waved again. Then the picture disappeared slowly. Josefine crossed herself and started to cry. "It's so long ago since I last saw him." Reinhard said, "I didn't see Granddad." He went to the window and looked out. Emer said, "It's all dark outside." But he knew about Mother's and Grandmother's clairvoyant gifts. Joesefine was amazed that only Christine had seen the apparition. They soon got news that Father was dead.

In Anderl's restaurant the train track controller, who was already a little tipsy, explained that a goods wagon had been standing in a siding for a long time and nobody seemed to be concerned. He thought, from the smell of it, that it contained already mouldy wheat or something similar. The wagon had no windows and was not sealed as usual but had a chain with a huge padlock linking the sliding side doors firmly together.

"Do you think we can look to see if there is anything useful for our starving people in the town?", thought Anderl. The track controller: "If you wish, I'll look away and won't see anything. Between 2 and 3 am would the safest time since no one will be around". Anderl: Not to-night but I think tomorrow we could take a look." Franz and Florence came for a glass of wine before going home. "Now the three City Musketeers are back together." expressed the track controller. "You mean the three of us?" laughed Florence. "Yes, who else?" Anyway, I don't think I can take another drink so I better go home. Until tomorrow! ". He staggered out the door.

Anderl told Franz and Florence what he had learned from the train track controller and where the wagon could be found. Franz: "You know what, afterwards I'll creep along the track and look what's there. Florence, leave a few tools in front of your door to break the chain which I think must be pretty thick, but it will be easier to tackle a link than trying to open the lock. If it looks as though there is something useful I'll round up a few colleagues and we'll take what's there. Franz's son Erwin came in and said that tomorrow he would come later. Franz: "You've come just at the right time, you can quickly come with me to check something. Come Florence, you can give me the tools now to take with us, maybe us two can manage alone." They drank up and left.

Franz and Erwin who did not really want to, checked the tools before setting off. They very soon found the wagon which had been hidden with overhanging branches. Erwin: "That smells like stale bread or something. No one can see us if we work on the chain. But still we have to watch out." Franz: "Wait a few minutes then we can be sure that nobody's seen us". They sat down on the hidden side and from time to time looked through under the wagon. Erwin: "I'll try now". With all his strength, using the tools they had brought with them, he tried to prise open a chain link. Then together. It only budged a millimetre with all of their efforts. Franz: "We need to use the hammer but that make a noise." At this moment a goods train approached and they hammered as hard as they could. At last they could just about remove one of the links. Erwin lost his fear: " Now it will be exciting". He reacted quickly and carefully slid open a chink in the door so that he could slip in. Using his lighter he was able to look around and stuck his pocket knife into the full sacks to see what was inside. Franz was becoming impatient. He looked under the wagon and then on both sides. Everything was quiet and not quite completely dark. Erwin found a spade in the wagon, collected samples from a few sacks and held the spade under his father's nose. Franz: "Not mouldy as far as I can see". Dried beans, peas, lentils, wheat, corn ears and strange yellow white cereal that they had never seen before. Erwin: "It says rice on the sack. So now we know what's there. We'll close the door and replace the chain. We must decide how best to fairly distribute the stuff among the people." Franz was very surprised that Erwin did not want to immediately take something with him.

Franz arranged a covered truck and an older acquaintance who knew how to drive it. Erwin cleaned the truck load area, took an extra spade with him and informed Anderl that they were going now to load the goods rather than waiting. Anderl asked spontaneously two strong young men if they would help to load a truck. He knew he could trust them and they agreed immediately even though it was almost midnight. Erwin and his father considered how they could drive as near as possible to the Wagon. Because of the overhanging tree branches there was very little space to manoeuvre. The two young men noticed immediately that they had to work quickly. Erwin had already pushed the wagon doors aside before they had finished parking. Franz ordered, that as soon as a sack was on the truck, it should be opened and where necessary slit with a pocket knife and the contents emptied and mixed together so that everyone had a little of everything when the goods were distributed with the shovels. It took longer than expected to transfer the goods. The wagon was closed and the chain re-linked. Then they drove through the courtyard to the workshop and rested there until daylight. There was only tea, jam and bread to eat but it was enough for the moment. Franz went outside, climbed onto the truck and filled a sack with two shovels full of provisions for each of the two young men, the driver, Anderl, Florenz, Erwin and his own family and also for the neighbours in the house and his relatives. The next morning they drove the truck through the town. They stopped a few times and called out "Free food!". At first the people looked at them strangely until Franz said to a women "open your bag" and filled it with a shovel full of food. After that, the other people reacted by holding up aprons, skirts and hats. After the third stop, so many people came that they could not continue and took it in turns to shovel the food until they had distributed everything. Overcome with emotion, dusty and tired they returned to the courtyard. Everyone took the sack Franz had prepared for them, took their leave and went home.

The Russians occupied Vordersberg. The English had gone further south. Franz and Lanegger had been released. Franz and Josefine watched the Russian tanks roll into town. Josefine shouted out a few words of greeting in Russian. The Russians waved at her, chewing on sunflower seeds, and accepted the flowers that she had quickly picked by the side of the road. The Russian flag with hammer and sickle was raised over the church tower. In the central park the three wooden houses were cleared out for the Russian commanders. That was the end of the Nazi era. The National Socialists would be brought to book. Many were arrested, including the house administrator Gosch and his wife; Precinschek, the policeman; Mr. Frühwirt who was Mrs. Weisser's manager and Mr. Gasser from the general store.

Franz, Josefine and Lanegger decided to go together to the Command post and ask for the release of their neighbours, who had been members of the Nazi party, but had done nothing wrong. Josefine greeted them in Russian and presented their case. Franz and Lanegger showed them their party membership card with the hammer and sickle on the red cover. The Commandant could not understand everything. He spoke a strange dialect, but he did speak some German. "You Communists?" he pointed to the men. Josefine said, "Da!" "Now everyone Communist, now Russians good. Fascist good, SS good!" His eyes were just slits in his round face. After a few tense moments he stood in front of them, his legs planted wide apart, looked at all of them, one after the other and shouted, "Njet! dawei!"

With a hand movement he showed them the door. Once they were outside Josefine said, "Well you're fine Communists! Your party card with the hammer and sickle didn't count for much. And now what?" No one answered. They were broken and went back home. Those who had been arrested were taken to a train that evening. Mr. Gosch, his wife and Mr. Frühwirt were able to escape between two rail cars. Around midnight they came home, but they had to go into hiding for a while. It was amazing that nobody asked about them. Precinschek spent many years in a prison camp in Volgograd. When he returned home he said that Gasser had died during the transport to the camp.

It was gruesome. They stripped the clothes from those who had died and threw them into the last rail car. The rail car for the corpses. Precinschek said, "I still can't believe that he's dead. But he is. All of us, including the personnel in the train almost died of cold and hunger. They didn't have anything to chew on either. Sometimes we got a slice of stale bread and some water, but nothing else. We got our first cabbage soup in the camp and that was like a banquet, a gift from heaven. Afterwards I crossed myself and thanked God for this gourmet meal. I won't forget that as long as I live."

Time passed. Christine and Reinhard made great progress in therapy. Reinhard learnt to speak more slowly and in a controlled way. Christine developed into a normal child. She only had some small scars from her injuries. On the left of her forehead she had a scar which had grown together like a small cross. Both children loved going to school. Now that Reinhard had stopped stammering, he was finally accepted by his school colleagues. Christine was left handed , but she had to write with her right hand, otherwise she would have her knuckles rapped. She had problems with letters and numbers. She inverted them and towards evening, when she was tired, it got worse.

She also had problems with capitals and small letters, but the school director was not too severe, since overall she was above average in her class. No one noticed or said anything about dyslexia.

Then came the years after the war. Many crazy things happened and many dangerous youthful escapades.

At dusk Reinhard would go into a seat which he had built for himself in the crown of an old tree above the surrounding young forest and watched the young lovers who thought they could not be seen. Sometimes, although it was hard to believe, Reinhard hid his school bag in the school! He then went with others who were also playing truant and they fished war material out of the castle pond. After the war, many people who had things at home that could be incriminating threw them into the pond or buried them in the surrounding area and this included a great number of weapons. Obviously it was very dangerous to dive and bring the things out of the water, but it was an adventure and the money which they could get for the copper, lead and iron was too enticing. Pans were made from helmets. The cartridges which they found were taken apart, very carefully and the gunpowder used to make little 'bombs'. They used these when they went fishing. They exploded the things above the waterfall and below dozens of dead fish could be netted. Unfortunately many young fish and other animals were killed in this way. But that was their playground in those difficult years after the war. Even weapons which they found were restored and once again made ready to fire. With these weapons they shot birds in the woods and even the neighbour's cats were targeted. They set up a storage place where they piled up helmets, complete uniforms, badges, guns, ammunition etc. The store was set up in a neglected store room in the family home of two of their school friends, which was below the ruins of the old castle. Christine was also allowed to go with them to the park or the ruins, but only when she had no school. Hilde made sure of that but she had no idea what was going on there.

And of course, what was going to happen, happened. Walter, one of those who played truant, wanted to open a cartridge and take out the gunpowder. He was the specialist and was the least afraid. His father, who had formerly worked in the munitions factory, had shown him how to do it and how you could then go fishing. Of course he had never let his son get close to weapons. They were safely locked away. Walter chattered and laughed, as he 'carefully' as always, knocked the cartridge. Suddenly there was a loud bang! Blood on the walls, on the clothes; even on Christine, Reinhard and two other boys. There were bloody bits of skin. They all stood around and wondered who had been injured. First of all they looked at themselves. Walter was white as a sheet and held up his hand. He had lost three whole fingers and half of another. The explosion brought the mother of the two boys, running to the store. She saw the children covered in blood. She was horrified. Walter screamed and gripped his hand. "Come out of here. Quick, quick!" she shouted, because when she saw all the war material, she was afraid there could be another explosion. She asked Walter if he could walk. She sent his brother off on his bicycle to get help. Then she took off her headscarf and bound it tightly round Walter's hand. Reinhard tried to wash the blood off Christine's clothes at the well in front of the house. His own clothes did not look too bad, but he held his head and arms under the water. Christine saw something in Reinhard's hair, took it out and gave it to him. It was a finger nail. He threw it away in disgust. Then they heard a motorbike coming. It was a road worker. "I heard an explosion. Has something happened?" "We have to go to a doctor or to the hospital. Walter has a serious hand injury." "I'll call the medics, but it will take them about a quarter of an hour before they get here. In the meantime he should lie down and keep his hand up. I can't take him on my motorbike. Right! I'm on my way." The son came back with the bicycle. Christine and Reinhard wanted to go home, but Walter's mother kept them there. "You're staying here until I know what has happened." The ambulance came. Walter was put on the stretcher and pushed into the car. The medics asked what had happened and how. One of them trusted himself to go into the room where the explosion had happened and locked it. "I'll give the key to the police. We have to notify them. Is there anyone else in the house? If not I'm going to seal the house and take you and your son with me. Hurry up!" Then he turned to Reinhard and Christine and told them to go home. They ran off straight away. When they got home Hilde looked at their blood smeared clothes. "What do you look like? Is that blood on your dress?" Christine nodded. Reinhard said that he had had a nose bleed and that was why they both had blood on their clothes. Hilde could not spend any more time with the children because she had something on the stove. "Take your dirty clothes off and wash yourselves well with soap." She gave them clean clothes and Reinhard threw the blood stained clothes into the wash basket.

All the children involved had to go to the police station, accompanied by at least one parent. Walter gave his statement in the hospital. The parents argued in front of the police. It was a question of who was guilty. Walter had lost four fingers from his right hand. They were charged with not watching what their children were up to. The teacher had also to admit that the children were often absent from school. The district council should have known how much danger lurked in the pond and the river. The firemen cleared out the store. Warning notices with a skull and a red X were put up along all paths to the pond: "Fishing and bathing forbidden." But the youngsters were still there, even Charlotte. One day when a police control team came by, she came out of the water with red eyes and a military helmet on her head. Cheekily, Charlotte said, 'It doesn't say diving is forbidden." After a while the council decided to drain the pond and clean up the river bed. They used unemployed people for the work. With time, there was a wonderful, neat recreation ground established including a little fisherman's cabin built by the Fisher's club and a small garden restaurant with a place to sit outside and look out onto the water. They put carp, trout and eels in the pond. Later it was possible to buy a licence to fish for a day. That was valid for 2 fish per day and the fish had to be of a certain size. The income was used for the upkeep of the area.

XVI

One day people from the Red Cross came to the school and inspected the 4th class which Christine was also in at the time. The children were restless, because it normally meant that they would be vaccinated or their heads would be powdered with DDT because of the nits. But this time the Red Cross only picked out children who were very thin. "Now, children, you have been selected for a holiday in beautiful Switzerland, which was not in the war." The children who had been selected were happy and they cheered loudly, with the exception of Christine. She started to cry. She was 9 years old and the youngest in the class. "I don't want to go to Switzerland. I don't know anyone there." One of the men bent down and said to Christine, "Look. If you go there, you'll have enough to eat. You have to put on some weight. You're very thin." Christine said, "We have enough to eat at home." He went on to say, "Which of your chosen school friends do you want to be with you? We can arrange that." Christine looked at her friend, Schilla and nodded happily. Christine went to her, took her by the hand and they both smiled. Everyone was given a form which the parents had to complete and also say whether they agreed or not. For Josefine it was not a problem, but Father was against it. They had just moved back into the larger flat where they had lived before the war and the workshop next to the cellar was also in operation. Franz had started up a shoe and leather bag production. He needed everyone to help him. "You don't send young girls away, because something could always happen to them. There are so many criminals around. You can't watch them enough." Emer heard this and he knew the real reason why his father did not want Christine to go. Like all the other children, after work Emer, a joiner's apprentice, had to help at home and he knew that when it came to riveting the parts of bags together, Christine was the fastest. Father had timed them, behind their backs! Much to the chagrin of the other employees, with their coarser fingers, who were expected to work at the same rate.

Emer filled out the Red Cross form and put it in front of his parents for their signature. "You would also like to go to recuperate in Switzerland, if you were in her place. Now write here, now!" He held out the pen. Franz hesitated, but in the end he signed the form. Christine and her friend handed in the forms and got a list of things which they had to take with them. They read: 1 small rucksack, 1 pair of underpants, 1 vest, 1 warm waistcoat, pullover or jacket, 1 head covering, one pair of stockings or knee socks, a toy, 1 handkerchief, 1 toothbrush (if available). Anything else was rejected. The parents had to make sure that the children did not have head lice and were in the best of health when they came to the meeting place.

But before the journey each child received a square piece of cardboard which was hung around their necks. On it was a large Red Cross, name, date of birth, weight, home address and their Swiss address was written on the back. Schilla compared the addresses. Her address was with a doctor and Christine's was a guest house. Only the place was the same. Emer, who had gone with them said, "It looks as though you won›t be together every day, but you'll certainly meet each other often." The two friends held each other by the hand. Emer said, "The school holidays will soon be over. You're only going to be there for three months. What are three months in your whole life?" Schilla said, "When it's nice then three months is short, but when it's not nice it can be very long." All three laughed and were excited. The meeting place was a bomb crater in front of the train station. Only the Red Cross team and the children, with their cardboard around their necks were allowed to go down. Some people were angry that they had not found a better meeting place; their shoes would be dirty. Down there was milk for the children, two slices of bread spread with sausage paté and an apple to take with them. Before they got onto the train, their rucksacks were checked. Emer managed to kiss them both on the mouth. Christine quickly wiped her lips on her sleeve and then Schilla did the same. She looked very cute with her twisted ringlets which her mother had made. Christine loved her plaits with the pink ribbons. They waved out of the window when the train set off. Emer stayed there until the train disappeared in the smoke from the locomotive.

Then Emer sauntered through the town. There was not a single house which did not have bullet holes. Most of them were bombed out. People, mainly women wearing head scarves, piled up the bricks and the buckets full of rubbish were handed from one to the other until they were loaded onto a lorry and taken out of the town.

Emer met a colleague from the war coming towards him on crutches. They embraced each other and sat down on a bench which was almost broken. They had so much to tell each other. Heinrich, that was his name, had not been wounded in the war, but in his parent's house, half of which had been destroyed. His family had been warned about thieves. So, with a few friends he tried to get into the living area, but soon a batten fell down and with it came a lot more, as he tried to run away he had dislocated his foot. He worked with his father as a simple labourer in a welding shop every day after school. He could have started an apprenticeship there, but he was not interested. "Would you like to be a welder?" he asked Emer, "you could start right away, but you have to show them a permanent address, otherwise you won't get the job." Emer said, "For a year I've been employed as a carpenter's apprentice, but I don't like the atmosphere there. I've learnt a lot, but I have to admit that bastard, my boss is very strict and I don't get much money."

Emer looked at his colleague and asked, "How much does your boss pay?" Heinrich gave him a figure. "As much as that? In the hand? I can't believe it. Then I'll start there tomorrow. Have you got a small corner in your house or flat for me?" Heinrich said, "I'm sorry, but with the best will in the world, I'd like to help you but we share the kitchen, toilet and bathroom with three other families. All the families only have one room for themselves, stacked with mattresses with a table in the middle." Emer: "That's a pity." Heinrich: "I've got an aunt who was able to go back to her flat. I don't know if she's already there, but come with me, we've got time. We can have a look. It's not far from here."

And his aunt, Mrs. Geller was there, busy with arranging the flat. "I'm glad you've come," she said, "and it looks as though you've brought a nice friend with you. I'm going to take a break. Come on, I'll show you where you can sit down then we can chat for a while. I'm hoping that before evening I can move into this room where we're sitting. The kitchen is finished. Well, you can call it a kitchen. It's really just a corner where I can cook. I still have to find a bath and of course, you know how it is, I'll have to share a toilet with the others. The other rooms are not yet suitable for living in. They've just been propped up. Luckily this room here is very big."

Heinrich and Emer looked at each other. Mrs. Geller had bread and sausage for them all. Heinrich said, "Aunt, we want to help you, but first I have to ask you something. My friend, Emer, can work where father and I work. He could start an apprenticeship, but he has to prove that he has a residence. Don't you think you could give him a corner? Just for a while until we find something else. He really wants to be an apprentice welder. Can you help us? You must know that it is very difficult to get an apprenticeship." The aunt said, "I think it is very good that you want to help your friend and that both of you can find some time to help me is even better. I have to say, that right now I'm a bit taken off guard. It's all a bit too quick for me."

She looked thoughtful. "All right, let's think about it. You could start the job at the beginning of next month, but you must have a contract and your parents have to agree. Well, we could put a place to sleep here, but you'll have to give me a hand and agree not to loaf around till late in the night. We can listen to the radio together if you want. Naturally Heinrich can come here whenever he wants, but you can forget any visits from girls; no alcohol and no smoking." Emer thanked her warmly and Heinrich said, "But first of all we have to introduce Emer to my boss." He would return when everything was arranged. "Good. I understand, but don't come back without an apprentice contract." She laughed and wished them luck.

Josefine was very happy when she heard that Emer had a new apprenticeship that paid better. She did not mind that he would move out. Even his chances to succeed in gymnastic competitions would be much better in his new place. Mrs. Geller looked after him well. She cooked and washed for him as though he was her own son and he helped whenever he could. They were both happy with the arrangement.

XVII

Christine and her group were on the way for two days and one night and arrived at the Swiss border in Buchs. They were very tired. They all had to get off the train and they were taken to a barrack. Schilla held on to Christine. She wanted to stay with her as long as possible. Women received the children in the barrack. Christine and Schilla were led to the fattest woman who was wearing a white apron and a white bonnet held in place with elastic. She took their things from them and put them in a wire mesh basket. Then they both had to take off all their clothes. They resisted. They did not want to take off their knickers, but there were only women and a lot of girls in the room, some of whom were already completely naked.

The women searched for lice, took a pair of scissors out of her apron and snip, Christine's long plaits, with the pink ribbons were on the floor. Christine was shocked when she saw her beautiful plaits on the floor. She started to scream and thrash out and sat down on the floor next to her plaits. She was pulled onto a bench and her remaining hair was drenched in DDT. She went on screaming. The woman put her hand over her mouth and told her to be quiet otherwise she would be put into a dark room. Schilla hugged her and whispered in her ear, "Hey. Your hair will grow again." She put the pink ribbons in her hand and they also went into the basket. Now it was Schilla's turn. One ringlet after the other fell on the floor. Schilla closed her eyes and pressed her lips and hands together. Christine watched, shivering all over and cried quietly. Why are they doing this? And she was smiling as they did it. She had such beautiful curls! Schilla sat down next to Christine and DDT was also spread over her hair. They cuddled up close to each other, crossed their legs to protect their modesty and held each others hands firmly. Schilla wiped the tears from Christine's face, smiled at her, brushed some powder from her forehead and tried to comfort and console her. "Look, now we both have the same colour hair and the same hair cut," she laughed, but she was still crying and her whole body shook.

Then all the girls had to go under the shower one after the other. A woman wearing a black bathing suit and swimming cap scrubbed the girls. In the meantime the baskets with the clothes in them were disinfected. When they got their clothes back they were very hot. The girls were allowed to take their under pants out of their rucksacks and put them on. Then they went into another room where there was a large X-ray machine. They were pressed into the machine and their chests were X-rayed. Then put on their clothes, which were still warm and went into a room with tables and benches.

They were given a thick soup and bread and for afters they were given chocolate cream. They were given cordial to drink.. A few of the children had already been collected by their holiday parents. Schilla and Christine with a few other children had to travel a bit further. Finally they could get down and were collected by Schilla's host father with a car. Christine's host mother was not there. She was waiting for her in the restaurant.

The doctor checked the Red Cross labels which were round their necks. "Ah! Schilla and Christine, that's right. Well! Gruezi, that's how we say 'hello' in Switzerland. He laughed and they both said, "Grüzi". In the car they tried out some Swiss dialect and the girls were happy. The doctor was very friendly with them. They hoped that the woman from the restaurant would be just as pleasant and whispered a few things to each other. The doctor said, "You won't be living too far apart from each other. You'll certainly see each other on Sundays in the church. Christine can also visit us if no one is against it." Schilla said, "Oh, yes, please! Thank you!" Christine pressed Schilla's hand to her heart. The doctor said, "It's getting dark and you won't be able to see much.

Try to sleep. You must be tired. It'll only take about an hour." Schilla leant back against Christine. When they finally arrived, they were both asleep.

The woman from the restaurant said, softly, "Come on Christina, you are now in your new home. Say goodbye and thank you to the Doctor. Christine said goodbye to Schilla with a kiss and said, "She's also very nice." Then, shyly she gave the woman her hand, looked thankfully at the doctor and was stuck for words. He gave her his hand and said see you soon, 'Uf, Wiederluege" in Swiss dialect. Christine waved at the car and her heart started to race. She was taken up to the first floor. "You can get undressed and get into bed. I'll bring you some warm milk with honey. That will help you sleep. My room is just next door. If you need anything then just knock on the wall and call me. For you I'm Mother Marieli, all right?"

Christine put her hands to her head, "They cut off my plaits and Schilla's ringlets. I haven't got any nits." She got her rucksack and showed her lovely hair ribbons. Mother Marieli said, "Tomorrow we'll see what we can do with your hair. You're a pretty girl. I'm sure we can do something with your hair. All right?" Christine undressed and sat down on the bed. Mother Marieli brought her the honey milk. "Drink it up. Do you want to take the ribbons to bed with you?" Christine nodded and held the ribbons firmly in her hand. Then she laid her head on the pillow and closed her eyes. Mother Marieli whispered something and made the sign of the cross on her forehead, mouth and chest. "Tomorrow we'll pray together. Sleep well." Christine was happy that the street lights were shining into the room and fell asleep peacefully.

In the night she woke up once. She heard the wooden floor creek and knocked on the wall. "What's the matter?" Christine said, "I have to go to the toilet." "There's a chamber pot in the little cupboard next to the bed. You can use that and then put it back in the cupboard." But then Mother Marieli did come into the room and helped. "This evening, go to the toilet before you go to bed." She covered the chamber pot with a piece of round cardboard and put it away. Then she left.

The next day a young Italian girl came into the room, early in the morning. She woke Christine and brought her fresh clothes which Mother Marieli had given her. "Come, Christina, eat breakfast. My name Rita. You put on, nice dress." Christine looked at the thick grey material covered in little crosses, which Rita pulled over her head. There was a bib front and back. The material was coarse and felt warm. Under this she had a multi-coloured, hand knitted pullover. Then hand knitted grey stockings with each two buttons and were fastened to her knickers by two elastic bands on each side with buttonholes in them. "Here. Felt slippers for in house."

Rita opened the window wide and hung the bedding, very precisely over the window sill. She took a wet face cloth and washed Christine's face. She brushed Christine's hair with a coarse hair brush. Christine took out her pink ribbons and held them out to Rita, who did not know what to do with them. "Come. Now downstairs. After we make hair pretty." They went into the small guest room. Mother Marieli was sitting there at the table with her son Beatli, who, she found out later was 36 years old. "Come, there's a place for you. But first say 'Good morning' to everyone."

Christine sat on the chair and looked all around. She saw a labourer and Rita sitting at the next table with their hands folded in prayer and looking down at the table. Then she whispered, so softly that she could hardly be heard, "Good morning" and held tight to her chair. Mother Marieli looked at her and gave her a sign that she should also fold her hands and look at the table. Then she prayed for a while and afterwards picked up a knife and made the sign of the cross over the bread with it. Rita stood up and used a bread cutter to slice the bread. There was butter on a plate which was painted red and had an edelweiss design and a matching cover. There were two different jams in glass jars and coffee with milk. Christine was only given milk with some sticky red mixture in it. Later a guest claimed that it was chicken blood and that it was very healthy.

From then on Christine only wanted milk. This breakfast they had every week day. On Sunday there was also a special bread, which looked as though it had been plaited, honey, a chocolate drink and a slice of cheese. Every day at exactly 9.30 she was given an apple from a basket. The midday meal was served at 11.30. Usually they had potatoes cooked in all sorts of ways and often there was a piece of braised meat and a brown sauce. Sometimes they had pasta with vegetables in the sauce. On Fridays they always had fish, usually served with a potato salad. Every afternoon she was given a home made fruit juice or fruit tea, a slice of bread with mustard, cheese and pickled, sliced gherkins. Sometimes there was sausage instead of cheese. The evening meal was a soup made from bread and everything else which had been left over. Or they had Birchermüesli made from oat flakes and all sorts of fruit, soaked in milk and with a spoonful of whipped cream on the top. Christine liked that most of all.

Because there was a lot of fat in the food, with the full cream milk and the butter, Christine's stomach was not used to it and she almost always had diarrhoea and lost weight.

She was also upset that before every meal, every morning, every evening and before she went to sleep she had to pray to God to protect all the relatives and not to forget those who had died and were in heaven. There were many in this family who she had never known.

The sheep's wool pullover and stockings irritated her skin and she was always scratching. Her skin was always bleeding. Apart from the grey dress, she also had one in burgundy red, which was exactly the same as the grey one, but the red one was a bit longer, came over her knees and did not stand out as much as the grey one. She had to wear a bonnet made from the same sheep's wool as the stockings when ever they went to church. In the meantime Rita had cut her hair evenly and, having soaked the pink ribbons in sugar water to strengthen them, put two bows on either side of Christine's hair.

The first Sunday in the church was exciting. Schilla found Christine and they were really happy. Schilla had a blue dress made of velvet with a white collar. She was wearing black, patent leather shoes with black bows and a little blue hat with white ribbons hanging down the back of it. They both had to sit on the left with the other girls. The older women sat behind. The men sat on the right. Schilla and Christine joined them and joined their fingers together in prayer. They understood very little. It was anyway mostly in Latin. It was very boring for both of them, having to sit, stand up, kneel and cross themselves for one and a half to two hours.

The sermon from the high pulpit seemed endless. So they sat on the hassock and whispered to each other about their experiences. Schilla was wearing white gloves, which were soon dirty and her white stockings had black stains on the knees. Her patent leather shoes squeezed her feet and the organza collar scratched. Christine was plagued by her sheep's wool clothes. They giggled and scratched like hell. "I often have stomach ache," Christine complained, "and sometimes headaches." "You have to come to us. I've already got some medicine from my Doctor. Shall I ask if you can come to us?" Finally the Mass was over.

Schilla went straight to her guest mother and asked if Christine could come with them. When she hesitated, she added, "Christine has stomach and headaches." "All right, I'll see what we can do." She greeted Mother Marieli and said, "If you want, I'll ask my husband to have a look if there is anything wrong with Christine." Mother Marieli was not too pleased and said, "I think it's the food which she's not used to." Christine showed her blood smeared arm. "The pullover and the stockings make me want to scratch. My stomach and my head hurt." The doctor recommended that she should stop wearing the sheep's wool clothes, until her skin had calmed down. Otherwise, just bread but no other dairy products. Leave out fatty meat, sausages, bacon and butter for a while. Just cook some oat flakes in lightly salted water and add a little honey. You can give her potatoes, vegetables, pasta, rice and eggs." He turned to Christine, "There is enough food which you can take, "so you don't have to go hungry. We'll see each other next Sunday in the Church. Until to then, bye, bye."

Christine had not forgotten anything which the doctor had recommended. When she got home she took off her stockings and pullover. She only ate what he had listed. Soon it started to get better. The scratch marks left light scars on her skin. Instead of the woollen bonnet she should wear a head scarf when she went to church. This she definitely did not want to do. Rita found a solution. She put one of her lace handkerchiefs on Christine's head and let her look in the mirror. One corner fell over her forehead. She liked it. Instead of the woollen pullover she wore a light blue flannel blouse and the jacket which she had brought with her. Instead of the stockings she had thin socks which came over her knees and were held in place with elastic bands. She looked very colourful; white handkerchief over her dark blonde hair, hair standing up a little with the pink ribbons; light blue blouse, burgundy red dress; brown shoes and yellowish socks. She had freckles scattered over her nose, doe coloured brown eyes and only her two front teeth had grown completely. Most of the time when she smiled she pressed her lips together. People thought she was both funny and charming.

Schilla had a prayer book from which she had to read a chapter at the table. She was happy to do this. She also went to the Bible class in the Convent with the nuns. Christine asked Mrs. Marieli if she could also go to the Bible class. She was very happy with this, because she already noticed that Christine had problems praying. She had also understood that Christine did not want to address her as 'Mother.' After the first Bible class, Christine told them at table what Sister Kathrin had explained to her. "She told me that if I don't want to pray, then I can read something from the Bible. That is also good." Mrs. Marieli looked at the others, "All right. Read something to us and then today we'll only say the 'Lord's prayer'."

Christine read a long chapter. The labourer and Rita understood nothing and started to yawn from boredom. Only Mrs. Marieli was really listening, and now and again she said, "Amen. Holy Mary, Mother of God and Jesus, show us your mercy now and in heaven," and so forth. Beatli cleared his throat and asked, in his dialect? "How long do you want to go on? The soup's already cold. Come to a stop." Christine put a beer mat between the pages and closed the Bible. The others crossed themselves and then they ate.

Christine promised that next time she would read something shorter or perhaps just half a chapter or maybe even less. "It's all right," said Mrs. Marieli, "I've got a present for you. You can have it later," So when Christine was the first to finish eating she helped to clear everything away and stood in front of Mrs. Marieli expectantly. She took her by the hand, led her into the other room and held out a brightly coloured money box. "Look. Do you know what this is?" Christine said, "You can save money in it." "That's right. You've got a few cents in you drawer. Now you can put them in this. When you save enough coins you'll soon have a franc. We'll put it on the counter in the bar and when you go home you can take it with you." Christine hoped that by then the box would be full and said, "I'll give it to my mother. She'll be glad that I've saved some money for her."

There were now only 14 days left before the recuperation holiday was over. Christine could hardly wait to get home. Unexpectedly, two Red Cross workers came round to see if Christine had made any progress. They were very pleased with Schilla. She had put on a couple of kilos and had rosy cheeks. They wondered if Christine should stay a little longer. She still looked pale and she had not put on any weight; not a gram. She had actually lost some weight. "She should go out in the sun more; in the fresh air.

She should go walking. But no one had time to go for walks with Christine. She also did not have the chance to play with other children although you could hear children's voices from the other side of the convent wall.

Rita helped with the ironing in the convent and was paid for her work. When she heard that they wanted to put Christine with the children on the other side of the wall she objected. "Not good other children there; not normal; all crazy. Christine very, very sensible. No! No!" The convent was cut off from the outside world. Sometimes the nuns crept through the gate, but you could not see what happened inside. Rita had to go through the delivery gate into the cellar where she did the ironing with other women. Of course, Mrs. Marieli and the doctor knew that in the convent there was a psychiatric clinic where handicapped and abnormal children lived. But no one spoke about it.

From the attic Beatli could see when new patients arrived. He made a hole in the tiled roof and looked through a telescope which he had hidden there, into the courtyard. Christine often went up to the attic. She had found an old music box there. When you turned the handle a ballet pair danced on the round top to soft music which was a bit scratchy, but still lovely. She could not watch them enough.

Once she crept up behind Beatli and hid herself. He was talking to himself but she could not understand. When he left she looked into the courtyard and the convent gardens through the telescope. To do this she had to climb up on a small library stool, which was standing in a dusty corner.

She saw a young woman with a very long tongue who was walking up and down. A small body with a giant head was fastened to a high chair. Then Christine saw something which, at first she thought was an animal on two legs, but it was a person covered with so much hair that you could not see the eyes. Then she saw people with open mouths just sitting there and swaying backwards and forwards. A nun held up a young man repeatedly onto his legs and constantly cleaned his mouth with a nappy.

Several children were sitting sideways or forwards on chairs fitted with wheels. She could see that there was a chamber pot under some of them. When she had seen enough, she went back down the steep steps. But she forgot to put the library steps away so Beatli knew that someone else had been up there and closed the hole in the tiled roof.

Now Christine was allowed to walk along the river bank with Rita. They did this every day, except when it was raining. The first few times they were alone but, after a while, Rita met other people from her home country. Then they sat under the bushes, spoke Italian and gesticulated. One of the Italian women could speak a bit more German than Rita. She often talked to Christine and told her that she went ironing with Rita. Christine admitted that she had seen everything through the hole in the roof. "Oh, my God!" she said in Italian, "many sick people. I know." Christine asked if she could come with them once, when the went to iron. "Yes. Once. I'll see." The same evening when Christine had been sent early to bed, she pretended to be sleeping until someone came to check up on her. Then she jumped out of bed, dressed and arranged the pillow under the cover and her pullover so that it looked as though she was still sleeping in the bed. She heard loud voices coming from the bar and rushed past the open door into the garden. She hid behind a garden chair until she saw Rita and her friend meet up.

When they left the house she ran behind them to the rear door of the convent. "I'm coming to see how you iron." "Christine, what you do?" Rita asked. Her friend took Christine by the hand, "It's all right. It's my fault. I promised her." They argued with each other, but quietly. Then they put Christine between them. Rita in front and her friend close behind. They went into a cellar room with no windows. It was very stuffy. They hid Christine behind a large laundry basket. "Now here wait," Rita put her index finger to her mouth. A door opened and a nun came in. She unlocked and opened another door. They were overwhelmed by a wall of hot air, although the barred window in this second room was open. After a short greeting the nun left the two women alone.

They stripped off almost all their clothes and opened another door with a crowbar which they had brought with them. Comfortable, cool air came into the room. In the room there were two tables over which they each laid a blanket and a cloth and started to iron. Most of the laundry was white or blue. The two light bulbs on the ceiling were not very bright. Christine crept out from her hiding place. Her cheeks were already red from the heat. She looked at the oven which was glowing red and which was covered with small irons. Each women took an iron out of its fixings, slid it over a cloth to make sure it was not too hot and then started to iron quickly until the iron was cold. Then they put it back and took another. And so it went on until the oven was also cold. By then almost all the laundry had been ironed. While they were ironing the two women chatted in Italian, without giving a thought to Christine. She saw some wrap round blouses with very long bands stitched to the closed sleeves. Christine asked a lot of questions, even why some of the large trousers had a gap between the legs. She had only ever seen that in children's trousers. Rita said, "You know. Here is hospital. It is so," she twisted her finger on her temple and looked at Christine, "here everything special." She held up other strange pieces of clothing and laughed.

Christine slipped through the door through which the cold air came. Steps led to the upper floor. She went up slowly, along the corridor for a few metres and suddenly she found herself in front of a large room with lots of beds, some had bars. These contained children a few of whom were tied to the beds. In the grey light of dusk there were thin curtains waving around like ghosts. There was a strange smell in the room. One child saw Christine, rattled the bars, heaved a rasping sound, pulled his hair and became louder and louder. The other children started to move about and suddenly they all started to scream at once. Rita came into the room before a nun appeared and pulled the terrified Christine back down the stairs and locked the door behind them. The two women gave up their ironing, pulled on their head scarves and left the convent as quietly as they had come with Christine hidden between them. At the restaurant the two women parted company. Rita sent Christine to her room without a word. Christine undressed and lay down on her bed, but she could not sleep. The evening had been so upsetting. Now Rita was really annoyed with her.

The restaurant owner Marieli received a message from the Red Cross that they wanted to take Christine home with the second group, so that she could recuperate a little longer, put on some weight and get more colour in her cheeks. In the meantime she drank the creamy milk without problems, mostly with cocoa powder and a lot of sugar. But when she heard that she could not go home with Schilla, she threw into a rage and refused to eat anything. "Come on, eat. That's not going to help. That's only making it worse." But Christine remained obstinate and wondered how she could get to the station and go home on her own.

She went into the bar and shook the money box. It was only about half full. Mrs. Marieli had always encouraged Christine to go to the guests and hold the box out to them, so that it would be full before she went home. But up to now Christine had not had the courage. Now it was urgent, because she hoped that she might get enough money to pay for her ticket home. She held the box out to all the guests, sometimes twice. Some of the men sometimes gave her a smack on the bottom. She even held out the box to passers by. One evening she packed all her things into her rucksack and crept out of the house.

At the station she asked when the next train was leaving for her town. Was she travelling alone? The rail employee asked. "No," she lied, "someone is coming with me. I just want to know if there will be a train soon." The man asked her to wait and went to his colleague. "That's the little one from the restaurant. She'll go back with the Red Cross. Maybe she wants to go home now. I'll take her back to Marieli." He came back to Christine and said, "Just wait a moment and I'll take you back to the restaurant." Christine did not wait, but ran along the river bank until she came to a wobbly wooden hut. Inside she lay down, exhausted on a pile of hay. It was getting dark, but the moon was shining brightly. She was very thirsty. There were tools hanging on the wall and among them a long pole with a metal bowl on the end. I could get water from the river with that, she thought. But she didn't have to go so far. Outside there was an old bath full of rain water. There were leaves and beetles floating on the surface, but that did not bother her. She pushed the leaves and the other things that were floating around to the side, slurped the water from her cupped hands and went back to the hay. With her rucksack under her head she fell asleep.

Eventually they realised that Christine was not in the house. Marieli sent Beatli to look for her. When he could not find her he thought of Schilla and went to the doctor. He rang the local policeman, but he was in the neighbouring village. So he gathered together a few men. It was early the next morning before Beatli found her in the little hut. She was fast asleep. It smelt so sweet that Beatli wanted to lie down on the hay beside her. He was so tired from the search, but instead of that he carried the little runaway back home. When they put her in her bed she woke up. The doctor spoke softly to Christine, "Christine, I'm just going to check that you are all right." "I don't want to stay here. Please, I want to go to my mother," she sobbed. "Where is your doll?" he asked, "or have you something else which you take to bed with you?" Christine searched in her rucksack and took out a small, colourful dog which Hilde had put in. Then the money box rolled out. The doctor picked it up and put it on the chest of drawers. "I can't open the box. It's locked. Can you open it?" she asked "Marieli will open it. She's certainly got the key."

"I want to go home with Schilla. Please, please. I don't want to stay here. Over there, there are bad people. I've dreamt about them. All of them come into my room in the night. I've seen them. They have bars round their beds and some of them are fastened to their beds. They must be very bad." "All right," the doctor said, "I'll make sure you can go home with Schilla. So don't run away again and you must eat, otherwise you'll be ill. Now you can come down with me for breakfast. Is that all right?" He wiped the tears from her face and wondered what she had seen and what she had dreamt about. He requested Marieli to send Christine to him in the afternoon after she had slept and explained that there was no point in keeping her there any longer. He would send a report to the Red Cross. Marieli agreed. It seemed clear to her that Christine was very homesick and missed her siblings and parents even though she hadn't talked about them very much. Christine was happy. She ate a large breakfast and then went peacefully back to bed.

She enjoyed the afternoon, because she played with Schilla. There was carrot cake with a lot of whipped cream and warm Ovaltine to drink.

Then came the departure day. Christine's money box was full. She begged repeatedly for the box to be opened. A guest told her that you had to take the money to the savings bank and change it to Austrian currency. Marieli said "Yes! Yes! It will be all right. Just be patient." Christine did not let the money box out of her sight. Her rucksack was packed. She checked what was in it. She did not want to take the thick dresses, the scratchy pullover, the woollen hat or the scratchy stockings with her. "Anyway, I'll never wear those again," she said and started to take them out. Marieli said, "Look, I've put a whole block of good chocolate in there. If you take those things out, then the chocolate stays here." Christine asked, "Where is the money box?" "You'll get that at the last minute, otherwise you'll lose it." "No, please. I'll put it right at the bottom of my rucksack. Then I won't lose it." Marieli said,

"All right. I'll pack it like that. Your clothes will be on the top. But now go and drink your milk. You'll get something for the journey. Beatli is preparing everything." Beatli packed apples, nuts, a cheese sandwich and a small bottle of water with raspberry juice and, secretly, another block of chocolate wrapped in newspaper. The doctor was close by and asked about Christine. She heard his loud voice and ran up to him. Marieli was in the kitchen. "So, Christine," the doctor said, "Where is you suitcase? I can take it now. We're going to the station by car and I've promised to take you with us." She got her rucksack. At the top was the wrapped block of chocolate. She went right down to the bottom of the rucksack searching for the money box. "Marieli won't give me the money box," she explained, "but it's full." "Maybe she'll give it to you when you leave. I'll come to collect you in about an hour or maybe a little later. See you then."

Doctor Giger put the rucksack in his car and drove home. When his wife heard how Christine was feeling she asked her daughter, Susi to take the rucksack out of the car and put it in her room. She did not want Schilla to know about it. Mrs. Giger unpacked the rucksack, "Just look at that. Those are all the things which Christine was allergic to. Just one block of chocolate and the things which she brought with her. The poor thing. You can't send her back like that. What do you think?" she asked Susi. "There's another block of chocolate wrapped in newspaper. Mummy, we'll take my pink suitcase and fill it with anything we can find. Marieli is not so poor. Why does she take guest children when she can't afford it? And she didn't have any time for her. We should tell the Red Cross." "Yes, we'll do that, but now we have to hurry," thought Mrs. Giger, "I know where we can find clothes. In the attic there are things from you which I didn't want to give away, but now's the time to bring some happiness to someone."

They brought a box down from the attic. They found a good selection of clothes in Christine's size and some a little larger. Most of it they packed, even shoes which were a size too big for

Christine. They looked round the room. There were a couple of children's books, a little cuddly hare, children's jewellery, bags, purses and other things. Now the suitcase was packed full. They only needed the name plate.

Doctor Giger thanked both the women for what they had done and asked if they had found a money box. "A what?" Mrs. Giger asked. "A metal money box." "No, there was nothing like that in the rucksack. We've put everything back, just in case the restaurant owner meets us." "Do we have any Austrian money? Please have a look and we must have some chocolate. The Swiss would be shamed to send a child back with only this rubbish from the restaurant owner." Mrs. Giger found a few bank notes and blocks of chocolate. Susi opened the suitcase, took the little purse out and put in it the same amount of money which Schilla had been given. She put it into a small handbag and put everything back into the suitcase. Susi said, "I think I also would be really happy with all these things, especially as a surprise. My heart would burst with joy." "Yes. All right," the doctor said, but now I have to go. Bring Schilla to the car. I'll take the pink suitcase." He carried Christine's rucksack and the small pink suitcase to the car. Schilla got in and Mrs. Giger and her daughter said their 'good byes' with tears in their eyes.

Christine was already waiting in front of the door. She said 'goodbye' to Beatli and Rita who had made a present of the lace handkerchief which Christine had worn to church and also gave her some sweets wrapped in shiny paper. Then Rita sent her into the kitchen to say 'goodbye' to Mrs. Marieli. Then she sadly got into the car, which then drove off. Schilla waved enthusiastically and held up Christine's hand to wave. She tried to cheer her friend up, stuffed sweets in her mouth and held her hand firmly. But there was no smile on Christine's face. "Christine," the doctor said, trying to cheer her up, "we've packed a surprise for you." "It's the box; the money box!" "No Christine , we've put some money in your luggage. Now you have the same as Schilla. "Just the same? Thank you, thank you, thank you! Now Marieli can keep my money box, maybe she didn't have any more money. I'll give almost everything to my mother. She likes money." Then they all laughed. "All right. Now both of you, try to sleep. You've got a long way to go." Soon he heard nothing more. Both girls had fallen asleep.

At the meeting station there were already some children waiting there with Red Cross labels round their necks. Schilla and Christine put on their rucksacks and took their food out of the car. Doctor Giger took the suitcases and put them on the luggage trolley. Then he hugged both the girls and warmly took his leave. They had to wait behind a barrier.

Doctor Giger went to a Red Cross helper who had two medals on her chest. He introduced himself, gave her two envelopes and explained about the pink suitcase, about which the girls knew nothing. "One letter contains a statement, why no more guest children should be housed with the restaurant owner," he said, "What?" she said, amazed. "She has no time," the doctor went on, "and she didn't think about the food. Christine had problems with the food and during these three months she has lost rather than gained weight. And then she is very pale. She was almost never out in the fresh air. Even the clothes made of old material for old women and the coarse sheep's wool pullover were not suitable for children. The poor child had sometimes scratched until she bled. That is why my wife packed some clothes in the pink suitcase, which she will certainly be pleased to wear."

Then he gave her the second letter, "This letter is for Christine. When you give her the pink suitcase, then please read it to her. She knows nothing about the pink suitcase. I thank you already for doing this. Believe me, she is a very grateful child. Schilla will write to us and tell us what happens. She has promised to visit us again, later. We'll organise it somehow, when the time comes. Maybe through your organisation." The Red Cross worker was very moved that Doctor Giger took so much interest in Christine's fate. We need people like him in our organisation, she thought. At the next conference I'll make a proposition. The control before they got into the train began. Those accompanying them had to wait until the train left. The suitcases would be distributed to the children later.

Christine and Schilla sat opposite each other. They could wave out of the window until Doctor Giger was no longer to be seen. Christine started to unpack her food. She wanted to know what was there. She was overjoyed to find the chocolate from Beatli. Schilla also looked at her food. Both of them sorted out what they could take home and also left the sweets in their rucksacks.

Soon Christine took the clothes out, but she did not want to show them to anyone and turned her back on the others. Christine and Schilla whispered together and then they opened the window. One piece of clothing after the other was thrown out. It was huge fun watching the horrible clothes flying away in the wind. Schilla made sure that no one saw anything. Christine laughed, "Now I don't have any clothes." "You can have some from me. I've got sooo many clothes," Schilla said and made a large pile in the air with her hands. Then the person who was accompanying them came and handed out the suitcases and other luggage to the children. The Red Cross worker with whom Doctor Giger had spoken stood in front of Christine with the pink suitcase. "Is that your suitcase?" she asked Christine. "No, I don't have a suitcase," she answered calmly. "But your name is on it and I should read this to you. So listen." And she read:

"Dear Christine!

You have spent three months with us in Switzerland. You have won our love, just as Schilla. We hope that you will like the things we have put into the pink suitcase and have good memories of Switzerland. We wish you all the best for the future and send you our warmest greetings.

Your Doctor family, Giger."

"So, are you happy?" the Red Cross worker asked. Christine just nodded and looked at the suitcase. Schilla said, "Come on. Let's see what's in it." They put the suitcase on the seat and were amazed at all the things which they took out of it. When Christine found the money she counted it and her whole face lit up. Then Schilla wanted to open her suitcase. On top was the satin dress with the organza collar. "Ugh," she said, "I don't like that at all. Do you want it? Maybe the collar won't scratch you as much as it scratched me. Come on. Try it on." Schilla turned so that Christine was hidden while she changed. Christine looked at herself in the window. She really liked the dress. Schilla went on looking through her suitcase, found the money and was pleased with her things.

"How much money have you got? Don't you want to know?" Christine asked. "We've got the same," they laughed. "We'll hide it in our rucksacks and we won't let anyone else get their hands on it." They went on looking in Christine's suitcase and laughed when they put the children's jewellery round each other's necks.

Later on they were given tea and the train carried on through the night.

When they got to the station at the end of their journey, Schilla's sister was there, waiting to collect Schilla and also Christine.

The relative picking up each child had to sign the label which the children had round their necks and hand it over to the Red Cross. Reinhard should have collected Christine but he was glad that Schilla's sister could collect Christine as well. He saved the price of the ticket and he was afraid that he would not find Christine in the big station. But he was waiting at the new bus terminus in the centre of Vordersberg when she finally arrived. Back home, Christine was so happy that she could not contain herself. Josefine unpacked the suitcase. Christine took her small purse and the chocolate blocks and started to hand it out. "You can give me one block and we'll put it on one side," her mother said. "No," Christine said in a strong voice, "I'm going to give that out today. You'll get another present from me. Just wait!"

She took her little purse, went into the adjoining room, took out two of the three bank notes, hung the purse round her neck and went back to the others. Without saying a word, but with a big smile she handed the two notes to her mother. Her brothers and sisters said, "Ah!" and "Oh!". At first Josefine said nothing and then she said, "Have you got more, or is that all?" Emer, who was also there, could not stop himself, "Mum, that's no way to say thank you." But Josefine found it difficult to thank her daughter. She put the money in her pocket. Then, finally she said, "God's reward."

Changing the subject she started to explain what had happened in the family while Christine had been away. "Aloisia has a fourth child. She's just come back from the hospital." Charlotte said, "And when you were away we got another little sister. She's called Hermine. The flat is getting a bit small for us." Reinhard pushed the pram forward. Charlotte said, "Now we are four girls and two boys. And father has 5 girls and three boys." Josefine said, "Charlotte, don't be so impertinent." Reinhard wanted to go to Aloisia. "Come on, Christine, let's go and take a look at Aloisia's baby. They live close by and are always glad to see me." Christine picked up a chocolate block and went with him.

They knocked politely on the door and waited until someone opened it. Christine did not know her half-sister, but she was enchanted by her smile. "Come in, both of you," Aloisia said, "you must be Christine. Is that right? You're very pretty! Reinhard told me that you were in fairytale land, in Switzerland. I've heard that chocolate grows on the trees there. Is it true?" They all laughed at the joke. "You look like a princess in your royal blue velvet dress and you walk like a princess." "Here," Christine said, "look! I've brought you some chocolate which I picked from the tallest tree. We can have it right now. If you close your eyes and let a piece melt on your tongue, you can really enjoy it. Try it," and she laughed. Aloisia unwrapped the chocolate and broke into ten parts. Everyone could take one piece. "Now! Close your eyes and let it melt on your tongue." Every one said, "Mmm, mmm." One of Aloisia's sons said, "Oh! I could eat that until I made myself sick. Their dog wagged its tail and wined. So Reinhard gave it a piece. That pleased Christine and she was so happy that she slid backwards and forwards on the sofa. Aloisia took the last piece for her mother, Luise. They all remembered that moment for years and sometimes asked each other, "Do you remember when…?"

In the school in Vordersberg they tried to teach the children about saving. So Christine took the last bank note, which the Swiss doctor had given her, to the school and put it into a savings book. "You are a very bright child," the teacher said. "Most of us don't have a lot of money, but we have to try, when possible, to put something into a savings account instead of spending it on sweets or other things we don't really need. When you leave school, you'll see that all these small amounts add up to a larger sum. That is our aim."

Christine considered how she could make more money. Then she remembered her grandfather who had made a windmill out of newspaper. She wanted to implement this idea using stronger paper on a long stick. It did not take long for her to find material from old colourful magazine covers which were thick enough. She cut straight sticks from bushes by the river. She needed a piece to separate the paper in the wheel. For this small elder branches were ideal since the inside could be removed leaving a hole in which to insert the wire. There was wire in the flat left over from binding flowers. She tried first with newspaper to find the optimal way to cut the paper so that even a light wind could turn the wheel.

She also collected small pieces of left over wood from the cooper, smoothed the edges with sand paper and painted them with different colours. She made, out of four different coloured clay, small balls which she backed in the oven to produce marbles for children to play with.

When Christine had enough goods to present on two upturned empty fruit cartons and a bucket full of windmills, she set them up for sale, on a sunny Sunday, near the swimming pool entrance.

A small boy in swimming trunks sat on the ground because he was not let into the swimming pool without paying. He approached Christine: "I would like a windmill but I don't have any money". Christine: "You can take one and wave it in front of the people to show them what we are selling. Then when everything is sold I'll help you to get into the swimming pool. Agreed?" The boy, beaming all over his face, fanned the windmill backwards and forwards in front of the people, especially the children. After almost four hours, when everything except two windmills had been sold, a security guard came by, pointed out to Christine that it was not allowed to sell goods on the street without a permit and sent her away. She put the two cartons together, took these and the bucket and left. The small boy ran after her with the windmill. "Can I now go into the swimming pool?" Christine: "Yes, we'll first take these things back to my place which is just across the park. You can keep the windmill and when someone else wants one send them to me and we will share the money." At home they drank some water and ate some bread and an apple. Christine then showed him the way through the stream to the back of the swimming pool and helped him to walk across. The low water level made it easy for them. Before he went through the bushes into the swimming pool, Christine warned him never to do this alone and not to tell anyone about it. She gave him some money for an ice cream and put her hand on his shoulder. The boy thanked her cheerfully before they parted.

XVIII

Then came a day when Hilde packed all the clothes and everything from the house into boxes, sacks and bedsheets. She was helped by Viktoria, who, as an ethnic German had been driven out of her Yugoslavian homeland and had recently found a job with the family. Everything was done in secret. Everyone was sworn not to say a word and to tell no one about what was going on. "You'll soon see. Don't ask so many questions," the children were told. This evening you'll all have to sleep in your clothes on bare mattresses. Then at about 2 o'clock in the morning everything was taken out of the flat. The small children were the last to be carried out and they all walked down the back road past the girls' school to the town. They went through a small courtyard into the back door of Frühwirt's clothes shop. Frühwirt, who had managed a shop for the Weissers, had arranged two years rent for the clothes shop in the central square since the Weissers had informed him from Palestine, to where they had fled, that they were coming back. But now he had moved to Graz, because both his daughters were studying there and the building containing the shop was scheduled for demolition. So the Remis were the first to take possession of a house in the town, so that they could force the local council to give them a larger flat. As an active Communist, Franz was not exactly welcomed by the Mayor, who did not share his political opinions. Frühwirt was grateful for Franz's support when he had been summoned before the court during the denunciation of the Nazis, and that was why he had given him the second key to his business premises. He advised him to hurry up with the move, because workers had already been engaged to knock out the windows, so that no one could live there. Two windows already had holes which had been hacked out under the frames.

After the move Hilde did not want to come any more. She had no idea how she should behave. And she did not want to belong to either party. She wanted to marry her friend and start a family. That was her goal.

Viktoria had come from a camp in the north of Yugoslavia. Everyone from her village had been driven out. Her whole family settled around Vordersberg. The so-called "Volksdeutsche" kept close together. In time they created a whole village on the edge of the town. The houses were mainly built of wood and they were fenced in to protect themselves from outsiders. They were religious, simple, hard working people. Most of the time Viktoria sang melancholic and sad camp songs which had a glimmer of hope. Christine liked to listen to them and she could soon sing one of them by heart. It went like this:

Oh that sad camp life
How could I ever forget
Dear God, if you spare my life
I'll gladly return to my home.
If an abuser would have his way
God›s justice will he have known
He may take my body
But he will never get my soul.

Viktoria often worked late into the night and she was the first to get up in the morning. Josefine did not really like her because she was so sad and was waiting for her Hans, her fiancé, who was also her cousin. She hoped she would find him again, but up to then she had no news of him.

No one had worked in the house like Viktoria, although she was paid less than they had paid Hilde. She made sure that the children went punctually to school, and helped them with their homework. Her cooking was simple, but good and she did the washing. She gave her mother any clothes which needed to be repaired and also lengthened the girl's skirts with suitable odd pieces of material, if they had become too short. She made sailor suits for the girls from remnants which she dyed blue and decorated them with white strips. Reinhard got blue trousers and a white shirt. One Sunday she dressed the children in their new clothes. Franz and Josefine were so surprised that they had them photographed. Viktoria was also allowed to be in one of the photos. That was one of the few photos which showed the children during their young years.

On Sundays Viktoria went to early morning Mass. She had noticed that the Remis were often blasphemous about the Lord God; where he had been when the people were suffering; why he had allowed and still allowed this to happen. But she did not let this influence her. She held her tongue, because in the camp many, out of desperation, had been of the same opinion. "Do you know, Christine," she said, "God gives us love and staying power. If you believe in him you can feel it deep in your heart. We must pray for the people who do bad things and have strayed from God's path, because, when they die they will come before the Last Judgement. No one can escape this. We must all stand before it. The good people are let into Heaven and the bad people go into purgatory. Some will be taken into Hell by the Devil." Christine liked to listened to Viktoria when she had something to recount. She, herself, often went to the ten o'clock Mass. There was a lot of singing and she also met her school friends there. After the mass many men went to the restaurant and the women went home. The older children were allowed to stay in front of the church for a while and meet the others. They mostly had fun together. Christine's family started to call her 'the Holy one'. She did not mind it, in fact she rather liked it. It was strange that no one made any attempt to keep her away from the church.

The council promised to rent the Remi family a part of the two wooden houses on the central park. Up to now the Russians, who were a part of the four occupation powers in Austria, had been housed there, but they had been assigned to a new area, so the houses were free. Franz and Josefine wanted to look at it a little closer. Erwin went with them, because he hoped that he might find a place in the upper floor for himself and his future wife. There were a lot of boxes standing around and a man was sweeping the wooden floor, which had been smeared with old oil. "Because of the vermin," he told Franz. He had caught a rat. "They come out of this hole," he said and pointed to a hole in the wall which he had stuffed with steel wool. In the meantime Josefine had had a look around.

Surprised, she said, "There are really eight rooms in this house." "Actually that's two flats," she heard Mrs. Reisin say, who had just come in. She was at the fire brigade which had its station to the rear of the building. "You can have the larger," she said in a firm voice, "and the three rooms on this side are mine." Then Erwin came down from the first floor. His eyes were bright, "And then I can live upstairs." All the rooms were large. In the entrance hall there were two toilets. There were two stoves with a heating system in each of the flats. "Yes, Mrs. Reisin. I don't think that we would get the whole house just for us. Do you really want to move in here?" "Oh! Yes! Our flat is damp. My three children can't live there any longer and here it's dry. Anyway, wood is healthier."

Mrs. Reisin went on, "All right. Then we have to go to the flat authorities. Who's coming with me? We have to go right now otherwise someone will come with a prerogative or something. Erwin, Franz and Mrs. Reisin hurried to the council offices. Josefine and the cleaning man stayed behind. "You could turn the boards over if you want," he said, "I've spread the oil very thinly. On the other side the wood is probably as if it had been freshly planed." Josefine asked him if he could turn over a plank so that she could see it for herself. He got his tools and carefully removed part of the baseboard and then a floor board and turned them round so that Josefine could see them. She was amazed at the beautiful wood. "But now we have to be careful not to stain the wood with oil soaked fingers. Maybe we should use some newspaper."

Then she looked at the outside walls and the windows. The wide, overhanging roof had protected everything very well. She went to the green varnished water trough, which was a few metres away from the house, pumped it a couple of times and checked the water. The cleaner said, "That works well and the water doesn't freeze in winter. You only get a few icicles. You can drink the water. The mayor gets his water from the same source, but he has a pipe into the house." Josefine found a mouse hole. "Oh, no! How do you get rid of them? Have you seen many mice?" "Yes," said the cleaner, "in the other houses we sprayed DDT and closed the holes with steel wool. Then it was all quiet for a while. Yes, also the wood lice just fell out of the joints. You wouldn't believe how many corpses we found on the floor." "Yuck," Josefine cried, "are there still some bugs?" He took out his pocket knife and pushed it into a crack in the wooden facing. The knife was smeared with blood from the wood lice. "Then, first of all, something has to be done about that," Josefine said and shivered, "we certainly can't move in when it's like this. That's a pity. What are you going to do when you no longer have to clean up here?" "Well, then it's going to be difficult for the Huber. I'll just have to look around. Something will turn up." Josefine said, "So, Mr. Huber, I'm Mrs. Remi." She held out her hand. "Pleased to meet you." "You could help us to make the house liveable. You know best how to do it, My husband and Ms. Reisin would be pleased to have your help. I'm sure you can get DDT and sprays from somewhere." She looked at him in anticipation. He gave her an address where she could get the things and said that she should send the bill to the property owners, in this case the council. He could clear up the matter and get all the necessary materials. "If you want, I'll ask my boss. He can do that for me. That shouldn't cost you anything." "All right, but now I'd like to see the upper floor. And is there a cellar?"

Mr. Huber showed her the other rooms. Upstairs there was only one large room with a stove. The rest was the attic. There were steps down to the cellar. The floor was just earth and there were various wooden compartments which could be locked. The keys were still in the locks. Of course, it had been cleared out, the stove, the toilet and everything else. Josefine said, "Tell your boss that he should leave the stoves where they are and the toilets should be left in place. Only the floor boards should be turned over. Thank God nothing has been oiled in the upper rooms." Mr. Huber promised to do what he could and he was glad, that he would still be occupied. Josefine promised him that later he would also get work, but first she would have to speak to her husband.

They managed to get the rent contract. The house was completely sealed and all the bugs were killed with gas. It was scrubbed and cleaned and the floor boards were turned over. At the trough there was someone there pumping water to spray the leached doors and windows. After that, there was only the smell of clean wood. Frühwirt had left behind his kitchen stove with it's water bath and they made good use of it. In the last few days all of them had had to move from the business premises into a camp and they made the best of it. Viktoria had been ill for a week. She had inflammation of the lungs and had to go to the hospital. Her mother had told no one that she was ill, because many people would have thought it could be tuberculosis.

Her mother came and did Viktoria's work for her as well as she could, but the provisional house was too much for the old woman and Josefine was always complaining. She did not hear Viktoria's mother running around, because her straw soled shoes with the black cloth uppers made no sound. She soon started to sweat in her long black skirt, he blouse closed to the neck and her hand knitted woollen stockings. So she often sat down and wiped her face and arms with a wet cloth. When she was again sitting down, Franz also thought that it could not go on. "We don't pay anyone to sit around. If you aren't capable of staying on your feet, then it's better that you don't come at all."

Emer heard those harsh words and saw the old woman weeping. "She only wants to help out until Viktoria is well again. And anyway, you're paying her a miserable wage. How much more do you want?" Franz was angry, "Don't get mixed up in this. She should go." Emer said, "But at least you have to pay her up to now." Josefine also had something to say, "Now I know what is wrong," she said and she shouted at the old woman, "you're daughter has TB!" "No, no! That's not true," she said in defence, "She just has a shadow on her left lung. She'll soon be well again, my poor Victoria." "She's never coming into this house again. She'll infect all of us, and worst of all, the children. Make sure she leaves. Get out!" and she pushed the old woman to the door. Emer went to his mother, stood in front of her and said, "I don't know you like this! What's the matter with you? Just how are you behaving? Have you lost your decency? Now give the poor woman her money. Apologise and let her go." Franz said, "What money? She has already had what she has earned."

That was too much for Emer. He pushed his step father against the wardrobe, which was standing in the middle of the room and that almost fell over. Franz wanted to hit Emer in the face, but Emer grabbed his hand and twisted it outwards. Franz was shocked that it hurt so much. Viktoria's mother begged both of them to stop. Josefine just stood there and did nothing. Emer, red in the face said, "Mother, give her a reasonable wage. Now! Right now! Otherwise something bad is going to happen!" Then Josefine was afraid, gave the old woman her wage, looked at Emer and since he did not look satisfied, she added a few more bank notes to it. "I owe Viktoria that," she said as she gave them to the old woman. But Emer was still not satisfied. He let Franz go on whinging and demanded that his mother apologised politely. "Oh, my dear!" she said, "that just came out of my mouth. Please don't be angry with me. Come on, now you can go home."

Viktoria's mother did not say a word. She took her things and let Josefine open the door for her.

Slowly Viktoria recovered. Reinhard and Christine wanted to visit her in the hospital. The Mayor had beautiful flowers in his garden. Reinhard suddenly decided to creep through the fence. Christine had a whistle and stood guard. Reinhard soon had a lovely bouquet, but at the hospital they were not allowed to see Viktoria. A nurse took the flowers from them. "I'll show her the flowers through the window and then put them in the corridor, then we can all enjoy them. She can't have any flowers in her room. I'll give her your warmest wishes. Is that all right?" She went up to the last door. The upper part was of glass and on the way she wrote Reinhard's and Christine's names. The window was too high and she could not see Viktoria. Christine read the notice on the door, "Isolation room! Entry strictly forbidden!" And then the name: "Stättele, Viktoria." The nurse looked at them both, "She'll get well, but it will take some time. Now go home." Hand in hand and without a word they went home. In the last minute, Reinhard said, "You know what? It's probably better that we don't tell anyone that we wanted to visit Viktoria." Christine agreed.

Very soon two young women were engaged to do the housework. Inge and Irma. They spoke what they called a 'secret language', so that the children could not understand them. They did the work which Josefine gave them. They did not have much interest in the children, they just made sure that everything was in order. Since they also spoke with their hands and mentioned names, it was not long before they understood that their favourite theme was 'Men and love.' Charlotte and Rosita often hid behind their chairs with wide open ears until they blushed. They whispered to each other and were highly amused.

Rosita was a happy, obedient and willing child, but she had no interest in school. No one bothered about how the children were getting on in school like Viktoria had done. They had to get on as best they could. Josefine expected that they would be as self sufficient as Emer had been. With Viktoria and Hilde they could ask if they did not understand something, but Inge and Irma did not know very much. They had had very little schooling. Because of the war they had only been in school until the fourth class. And the children did not respect them.

One year they learnt Russian and then they learnt English as their second language. Charlotte was better than Christine in German, because Christine still turned the letters round sometimes and had problems with putting words in the right place in a sentence. Strangely enough, she did not have this problem in foreign languages. She was very interested in other languages. One day Christine asked her teacher if she could stay behind in the school. She wanted to do her homework in the school, because at home she had no time to do it. Charlotte was allowed to stay longer in the school almost everyday and that is why she could write better and did not make so many mistakes as she did. The teacher said, "But Christine. Staying longer in the school is a punishment. Your sister disturbs the others because she is always chattering. You don't do that. You don't want to be picked on because you have to stay behind do you? You already have a problem because you are left handed. In England and other countries children are allowed to write with their left hand, but here it is not allowed. I think that's why you don't write so well. Well, sometimes you write letters and numbers backwards and you could be better in grammar, but maybe that's a result of your head injury. We take that into consideration. Otherwise we are very pleased with your performance, which is above average." In this way she tried to comfort Christine, but the little miss had tears in her eyes. "Oh! You look so sad. What can we do?" "I really want to do my homework in the school. Please!" she sobbed "I have to do so much work at home because I'm the oldest of my sisters. Please, let me stay here, just like my sister. Please! Then I'll be happy to work in the workshop, because I'll have already done my homework. Later on in the evening I can't concentrate. The light is not good and my eyes keep closing." "Do you want to stay here today? I mean, do you want to do your homework here in the school today?" Christine nodded excitedly, "Oh! Yes!" "All right, but we have to find another way in future." Christine was taken into a class room where there were children of all ages, including her sister. Charlotte crept under the bench. She did not want Christine to see her. The teacher spoke quietly to the supervisor, but she was not satisfied. Christine's teacher said that she would speak to the directrix and find another solution. Charlotte saw the teacher waving friendly to Christine and that they smiled at each other. Charlotte thought this strange, because normally the children were angry and the teachers very stern. When they got home Charlotte was very happy to tell them that Christine had also been kept in detention this time. Christine said nothing and no one asked her. The next day the teacher asked Christine how it was. "My sister told everyone at home, but apart from that, no one said anything." "Today you can stay in the class room with me if you want. You can do your homework while I'm correcting the exercise books, but without any help from me. Just as you do it at home. Otherwise people will think that I am giving you extra lessons and that is not allowed in the school. There are other people for that and they are paid separately."

Christine nodded and stayed in her place in the front row. With complete concentration she did her homework which she had to give in the next day, just like all her school friends.

This went on for some time, until Franz noticed that she did not always come into the workshop regularly. "Why is that?" he asked Christine one day. "Because… because… I'm doing my homework in the school. That's better, and I don't have to stay up so late." "And nobody says anything about it? That's homework and it should be done at home. What is going on? Are there some new rules which the parents haven't been informed about or what?" He turned to Josefine and in a loud voice said, "Josefine, tomorrow you must go to the school and get things sorted out." Christine defended herself, "Charlotte does her homework in the school, why can't I?" "She has to say behind because her teacher is stricter and she abides strictly to the rules. She was also a strict follower of the Nazi Party. That's where it comes from," Josefine said, dramatically.

That night Christine could hardly sleep. She got up early, crossed her teacher on the way to school and told her what had happened and that her mother would be coming to the school. The teacher said, "It's all right, Christine. I know how much you like going to school. We can put things right."

Josefine came in the middle of a lesson. She knocked on the door and then opened it immediately. She had not even thought that she might have taken off her dirty work pinafore. "Excuse me, I've come straight from work to speak to you Mrs. Hofer. You can't keep our daughter in the school without any reason. All our children have to do their share of the work at home." The teacher said, "Höfer, please; not Hofer.

Just a moment please. Who are you anyway?" She asked Josefine to leave the classroom, pushed her into the corridor and closed the door behind her. "Who should I be? Mrs. Remi,of course." "Please wait outside. You are disturbing the lesson." "I don't have any time to wait. I have to go back to our shoe factory. That is more important." Josefine's voice was suddenly whining, "what do you think? Do you know how hard we have to work simply to survive?" "Then you will have to make an appointment with the director," Mrs. Höfer said, "It cannot be done like this."

She opened the class room door and said to the children "carry on." Then she went down the corridor with Josefine.

Many wanted to know who she was, but Christine ignored them and concentrated on her work. After some time, Mrs. Höfer came back into the class room. Of course she noticed that Christine was embarrassed about her mother's behaviour. After lessons the directrix wanted to see her. Christine knocked on the office door. She heard someone say, "Enter!" opened the door and stood there. "Come here, Christine. It seems as though your mother, like so many others, can't do without your help at home. You must be very diligent. She praised your deftness and your sense of responsibility."

A stone fell from Christine's heart. The Directrix asked, "Do you want to say something about that?" Christine said, "May I do my homework in school?" "Is that all you want?" "With Mr. Bernhard, the music teacher, I could learn to play the cello for very little money, and I could pay that myself. Or Mrs. Schönberg would give me free piano lessons. She even suggested it herself. Can you persuade my parents to let me learn to play an instrument? Please?" The directrix was amazed, "Do your parents know that you want to learn to play an instrument?" Christine nodded. "Your mother used to be an artiste. She would certainly agree. What about your father?" Christine said, "He always wanted to learn to play the accordion. He says that you can earn money if you can play an instrument." The directrix said, "Well, for the time being if want to go on doing your homework in the school, that's all right as far as I'm concerned."

Christine nodded eagerly. The directrix said, "You are one of the best in gymnastics. Maybe you could take some time from that to do your homework so that you get a good final report which will please your parents. Your mother told me that you, your sisters and your brother have put together a real circus programme. Your brother Emer is the seventh best gymnast in the whole of Austria and you have had an offer from a large circus." "I'll never go to the circus," Christine said vehemently.

"Later I want to study archaeology or geology. That's what I really want." "Oh. You have big, interesting plans," the directrix said admiringly, "then we'll have to see. In the meantime you can do your homework here when the class has gymnastics. The other days will stay the same. You'll have to find another solution for music lessons. Maybe one of your relations will help you. Think about who might be ready to support you. So, that's all for now. Go and do your homework. Or are you going to go straight home?" "I don't know yet. I'll have to think about it. Thank you and goodbye," Christine closed the door behind her. Deep in thought she walked down the corridor and then she went home.

Her father decided that Christine must learn to play the accordion. It was not the instrument she wanted to learn so she was not very good. Christine liked the instrument and then father said, "Then Christine should learn to play the zither and Charlotte can learn to play the accordion". Christine begged to be allowed to learn the cello or the piano with Mrs. Schönberg. That would cost very little or even nothing. But Father wouldn›t change his mind.

Charlotte stayed in the primary school until the eighth class. Christine got into the upper school and took her final exams.

When Christine left the school, the reports were handed out in the presence of the parents and the Head Mistress gave each child who had saved something their savings book and the advice to be careful with the money. Christine got nothing. She found out that it had already been given to her mother who had come to the school and asked for it. Christine took her report and happily showed it to everyone at home. She had got better marks than the others, Erwin told her. "No wonder. You spend most of your time in the school," she heard her mother say. A few of her siblings did not show their reports.

Christine really hoped that she would be allowed to go on with her education at college. The school had already registered her for the entry exam.

Christine did not trust herself to ask her mother about the savings book. She also wanted to know if the forget-me-not earrings she had got from her grandmother were still there. She searched around, found the secret place and looked for them. There was a casket with a lot of costume jewellery in it, some of it gold plated. There was also a bent earring with a tear-drop pearl on it, but there was no sign of the earrings from her grandmother. Upset and with shaking hands she put everything back in its place. She must wait till Emer got back. He had the courage to face up to mother. They were all agog to see Emer's report as metal work apprentice. His reports were always the very best. But Emer didn›t come home quickly. He took his time.

At the festivities marking the end of the school year, Christine had a small part in the first act of a two act comedy. It was just a short sentence. She only had to say, "Madam asks you to enter." When she was standing on the stage, the prompter, who poked his head out of the prompter's box at the front of the stage, whispered the phrase so loudly that Christine was irritated for a moment, but she managed to say it in time.

Her school friend Sylvia had to sing a song. Christine helped her to learn it. Sometimes they sang very skittishly. The music teacher, who was accompanying them on the piano heard, for the first time how Christine sang with joy and verve. "Oh. You sing really well. I hadn't noticed that up to now." "I've been practising with Sylvia. That's why I can sing it too," Christine said, "but on stage I would certainly lose my breath. I don't think I could do that." "There's always a first time. You just need a little courage and, as I know you, you've got that."

Then came the moment for Sylvia's performance. She was very nervous. "Have you got stage fright?" the music teacher asked, "as soon as you're on the stage, everything will be automatic. Just concentrate on me. I'll give you the sign. Nothing can go wrong."

Sylvia got stomach ache. She felt sick. A stage hand grabbed a cardboard box and held it under her. "Come on, Sylvia, we have to go on stage, "the music teacher called. She stood stock still, "I can't," she started to cry. Christine cleaned Sylvia's dress. "Go on, Sylvia. Just like we practised it. I'll keep my fingers crossed. I'll give you the note." Christine gave her the note, but Sylvia ran off. Then the teacher called, "Come on, Christine. That is your chance," she said and pushed her in front of the microphone, "just look at me. I'll give you the entry." He sat at the piano and gave her the note. Then came the entry. "Louder," he whispered and looked straight at her and she sang to the audience:

"Wenn ich ein Vöglein wär und auch zwei Flüglein hätt, flög ich zudir.

She hesitated, briefly…

"Weil›s aber nicht kann sein, weil›s, aber nicht kann sein,
bleib ich all hier".

She sang and sang to the end of the song. Applause out of the darkness. Then she was aware of all the people, including her mother, who was sitting directly behind the school directrix and the Mayor. "Christine Remiii," she heard the music teacher trumpet. "Curtsy," he whispered to her. Christine made a rather shaky little bob.

The teacher took her backstage. "Bravo. Although that was your first time, you did very well." He left and then Sylvia came back. She was upset that she had not got the applause. Christine wanted to look again at the audience. She went to the side curtain, pushed it a little to one side and looked for her mother. She saw her wiping a few tears from her eyes, but she was looking right and left and leaned forward to say something to the Mayor. Christine was amazed that she was sitting in one of the front rows, which were reserved. When the stage show was over she wanted to ask her mother if she could stay for a while. It was already ten o'clock in the evening.

She pushed her way though the crowd to follow her mother to the exit, but her mother did not notice her, and announced, in a loud voice, "All of my seven children have artiste's blood in their veins. Soon my eldest son will be performing his acrobatic feats in a large circus. You must see that. He'll show you Vordersbergers what he can do. You will just be astounded." She spoke louder and louder and started to wave her arms around in the air. Ashamed, Christine remained in the background and without asking, stayed there longer.

Now came the fun part of the evening. There was loud music and people started to dance. Christine was asked to dance many times and she enjoyed flirting with the youths. She thought Hans was especially likeable. The way he put his arm round her wast and pulled her close to him. They drank wine together and laughed. He was continually giving her compliments, so that she had to tell him to stop, because she found herself in a permanent state of embarrassment and she should have gone home long ago. Hans asked if he might accompany her. "But it's not far. We live right here in the central park. Someone might see us, and I don't want that." Nevertheless, he still walked next to her.

"Tomorrow we could meet at the swimming pool. I'll wait for you by the river. Shall we say tomorrow afternoon at 2 o'clock?" "No," Christine said, "that's too early. I can't come before 5 o'clock." "But it closes at six." "I'm sorry. I can't come any earlier. I'll be lucky if I can come at five. Then I'll walk through the river to the swimming pool." Hans said, "Isn't that dangerous?" "I've often waded through the water and up to now nothing has happened. I know the river and I can swim." They stood next to a tree in the park. Hans held her round the hips and then held her head and he kissed her gently on the lips. She leant back against the tree, until she was dizzy. Then she freed herself and ran the short distance to her house, crept in and looked into the dark through a gap in the curtains. She saw the light from a cigarette lighter. Hans showed his face in the flame and sent her a hand kiss. She went to bed and slept well with a pillow in her arms.

Early the next morning she was woken up. "Come on. Get up. We're going to buy leather," she heard her mother shout. "Put on some good clothes and make sure you look a bit like an adult." In the last few months Christine had often gone to buy leather and had even delivered completed goods. Mainly leather bags which she had taken to stores and received checks in return. Up to now she had always gone on her own. She knew the different types of leather and their quality. Only once had her father sent her back with the heavy load, because a seller had mixed bad pieces with good because she had not paid enough attention.

Christine had learnt her lesson. The leather was heavy and she had to bring it back to the workshop with the tram and the bus. If Emer was around he met her at the bus stop. The goods were normally divided into two parcels and often she was lucky to find someone who helped her carry them. On this morning Josefine went with her to a leather warehouse, which she did not know. "Be nice to Mr. Bauer," Josefine told her, "Come on. Put on a bit of lipstick, and don't look as pale as a sick chicken." Christine did not want to do this, but Josefine handed her a lipstick and insisted. "I haven't got a mirror." "Don't be so stupid. You only need to colour your bottom lip and then you press both lips together. Even a blind person can do that." She did as she was told. "What do I look like?" "That's all right."

A secretary welcomed them into the warehouse. She called for Mr. Bauer. He seemed very pleased to see them. Josefine introduced Christine. "This is my oldest daughter. She looks a lot younger than she is. From now on she'll be buying leather from you. She knows the trade. Take time with the selection. We only want to take good material with us." "Does your daughter have a name?" She sat down on a chair facing the secretary and let Christine say her name.

Now she was alone with Mr. Bauer in the warehouse. He put his arm round her shoulder and pulled her to him. "Your mother is a brave woman. She knows about these things." Christine did not feel good and ducked to get out from his embrace. They had soon selected the pieces of leather and they could have left, but Mr. Bauer had something else in mind. He said that they could sit down and chat for a while. He showed her to a chair, but she did not want to sit down. "Surely you're not afraid of being alone with me?" he said, took her chin in his hand and pressed his lips to hers. Christine defended herself and ran back to her mother, who was sitting with her back to her.

When the secretary saw Christine she stood up and showed her the toilet. She could see in the mirror that her lipstick was smeared. Her anger rose and she stayed in the toilet for some time, trying to calm down. She washed her face and drank from the tap. Josefine had not even looked at her when she came back into the office. She only said, "Go and see if all the leather has been packed up outside." Christine went out. She saw Mr. Bauer standing there with the packs of leather, smoking a cigarette. "I'm sorry that I frightened you. I apologise." He placed a bank note secretly into her cardigan pocket. "Please don't tell your mother."

With those words he disappeared behind the warehouse door. Christine felt the bank note and did not know how to react. She had the strange feeling that her mother knew what would happen. When she went to up to her, she could see that her mother was still bombarding the secretary with her stories. "Hold on," she said, "I want to finish what I was saying." And she talked and talked. The only thing the secretary could say was, "Please don't be angry with me, "but next time you can finish telling me everything. So until next time, Mrs. Remi. Have a safe journey". "That's fine," Josefine said. With that the secretary opened the door for both of them.

They dragged the leather to the bus. Josefine sat next to a woman and again started to involve someone in a conversation. Christine sat behind them and looked at the landscape flying passed. She dreamt of once travelling, all on her own, anywhere, to get away.

During the journey she remembered Hans. No, I don't want to meet him again, she thought, we're both too young. I think he's about three years older than me. My feelings for him could be too strong. Don't even think about it before I burn my fingers. So she did not go to the swimming pool as arranged.

Emer was expected to come home, as usual, on Friday evening. Christine waited up for him. When he finally arrived and only the parents were still awake she opened the door quietly and listened to what they were talking about. Recently he had often said things and then contradicted himself, made excuses and changed the subject when he did not want to talk about something. Josefine: "Where have you been all this time? Have you brought your diploma with you?" Emer: "My boss didn't give me one, because I was very often not there, because of my training for the championship and also because I took time out to work on the circus number. He resented that, so I stayed away completely. Then the aunt, where I was lodging also got annoyed. They think that anyone who has anything to with a circus is a gypsy.

They've got no idea about the background and how much training and discipline it needs." Franz asked, "Why didn't you tell us? We could have talked to your boss. Have you, at least learnt something which we can use? We need leather punching machines and the properly shaped knives to go with them. I was counting on you. I already have plans and I've also collected some material together. It should be enough for three punching machines and the knives. We'll start tomorrow." Josefine: "But the aunt was a nice woman. Only during the last visits, she acted a little strange. Was there something?" "Yes, well. One time I hugged her a bit too hard. It can happen, but the silly cow thought I wanted something more." Emer laughed awkwardly. Josefine felt that something had been going on. In any event, she and Franz had often visited Emer when they were in the area and had secretly given him money or other things. They never told each other about this, so Emer had received double and therefore much more than his half sisters and brothers. Franz rolled out his plans and studied them with Emer until late into the night.

The next morning Christine waited until Emer got up. He washed his muscular upper body and flexed his pectoral muscles for her. "Why are you up so early?" he asked her. Christine said, 'I don't know how to tell you this. Mum took my savings book from the school and said nothing to me about it. I didn't trust myself to ask her. You know how she treats me. Then I looked for my forget-me-not earrings which grandmother gave me. They're not in her jewel box." Emer said, "Just wait. We can find that out with a trick. Let me think about it.

You know what? In front of you, I'll ask her for money and before she can answer you say that you want to lend me some from your savings book. Or you can say that you want to sell the forget-me-not earrings because, anyway, you're too old for such childish jewellery. You'll see. Then we'll find out if everything is still there." Christine said, "Can't you just ask her outright instead of playing around? I don't know if I can play out such a scene". "That's called diplomacy. Watch out, she's coming," he whispered and then louder, "Mother, I need a large some of money for a few props and costumes for rehearsals before we appear in the circus ring. I've got an address where I can get them cheaply, right now." He looked at Christine, but she did not open her mouth. "That sounds expensive. You'll have to wait a while. We'll talk about it," mother replied.

Christine said, "Maybe my savings book from the school would be enough. There's quite a bit in it and I could lend it to you, Emer. Mother, give him the savings book." "What are you talking about? I know nothing about a savings book." Christine started to shake, "The headmistress told me that you had tak…" Emer interrupted her and in a masterful tone said to his mother, "Mother! Give me the savings book now!" "Wait. Now I remember something. You didn't give me time to think. Where did I put it?" Suddenly she produced it from somewhere, put it in Emer's hands and sat down. He looked at it. "Everything, apart from a few pennies, has been taken out a few days ago. Wow! Christine, you have really been saving. Don't worry. I'll make sure you get it back." Then he turned to his mother, "So have you any money left, or what?" Christine's eyes filled with tears, which she tried to wipe away secretly. "We could sell the forget-me-not earrings," she said, "I haven't worn them for years. They're like new and now I'm too grown up for them." Emer said, "Thank you Christine." She was shocked. Emer went on to say, "It's good of you to help me. Where are they? Maybe we could get a good price for them." Christine could not say a word and pressed her lips together. Emer kissed her on the cheek and, without looking at her asked his mother, "Have you flogged them?" "Yes. Maybe I had money problems. Otherwise they would still be there."

She was annoyed about all the questions. She fetched the jewel box and fumbled about in it. Trying to distract them, she showed them the bent earring with the tear-drop pearl and told them the story about it; how she had found it next to the rail tracks. Since the earring looked like silver and the pearl was very big, she did not think that it could be worth much. Christine took it in her hand. The pearl was really heavy. Josefine closed the jewel box and put it away. Christine wanted to give her back the earring, but she waved it off.

Reinhard came in and Emer left. He could do nothing else for her. Christine looked at the earring and thought she saw a stamp on the silver. She pulled Reinhard by the sleeve and asked him if he still had the magnifying glass which he had once brought home from the glass factory. They took the earring outside and with the magnifying glass saw a number on the silver. Reinhard compared the stamp with that on his genuine silver cross which he wore around his neck. "Look! That must be some other material. I've heard of white gold. In any case, it's not the same stamp as that on my cross. How can we find out, without raising suspicion? And if the pearl is also real…! It's certainly not glass or plastic. A jeweller would know immediately. He though about it for a moment, "Grandmother always went to the same jeweller in town. She also bought my cross there. Come on. We'll go to him. Now that grandmother's dead, you can say you got it from your grandmother."

Christine told him the true story. That mother had found it by the rail tracks, where people had been transported to the concentration camps. Reinhard said, "Most of them are now probably dead." On the way, Reinhard showed her a plaque on the church wall. "Look that is a memorial to the people from this town who died either in the war or in the camps." When they got to the jeweller's they also looked at the display in the window and they saw a notice in the corner. "We accept jewellery from private people for sale on commission." Reinhard said confidently, "We're at the right place."

He opened the door and after saying "Good morning" he started off, "Our grandmother – you must remember her – often came to you. Her name was Mrs. Pfeiffer. She has died." The jeweller said, "Oh, my God. Dear Mrs. Pfeiffer. I hope she didn't suffer like my mother. That was terrible. My condolences." He shook Reinhard by the hand. Christine let the pearl earring that she had been holding drop into the jeweller's hand. "This is from our grandmother," she said. "It's a little bent, but it's a beautiful piece." Reinhard began to understand that it must be valuable and lying, said, "She gave us the earring the last time she visited us and said we should bring it to you. The pearl is very valuable. Anything which we get for it should be paid into our savings book." Christine was amazed at the story Reinhard had thought up.

The jeweller fetched a magnifying glass and a tiny set of scales. "Let's see. It's certainly a very fine pearl; high carat white gold, which bends easily as you can see and then the small blue star… Did she say how much you should get for it?" Reinhard answered, "No. She just said that it was very valuable and that we should show it to no one but you. We've kept our promise." The jeweller said, "Really nobody? You must have shown it to your parents?" "No," Reinhard said, "nobody knows about it. That's what grandmother wanted. We promised to keep it until she died," he exaggerated. "All right. I have to reckon it up exactly and right now I have only got some small change in the shop. We can meet in front of the savings bank in the small park. I'll go there as soon as I have closed up in the afternoon. Bring your savings book with you then you can pay the money in right away." Christine took hold of the earring. The jeweller gave her a tiny bag to put it in. "Don't lose it."

Back home Christine found her plundered savings book and put it in her pocket. Reinhard had deposited his at the bank under a code name. He had some money on him. It was just enough for two nut rolls which had been reduced in price because they had been made with yesterday's dough. They went to sit in the little park in front of the fountain and enjoyed the nut rolls and waited for the jeweller. After a short time he stood in front of them. He gave them both an envelope. Christine had the little bag with the earring in her hand. "If you aren't happy with the amount then you can keep the earring. I'm sorry, but I can't give you more, but I don't think you'll get a better price elsewhere. So, think about it. I'll give you time until this evening. But you must keep this a secret between us just as your grandmother wanted."

He took both of them in his hands and looked into their eyes. Reinhard said, "On my honour, of course"

The jeweller took the little bag with the earring in it. "I have to go back to the shop. If you ever want to buy anything from me I'll give you a discount price, just like I did for your Grandma; God bless her. Goodbye, to you both." Christine wanted to count the money right away, but Reinhard stopped her. "Not here. Somebody could be watching us. Let's go into the savings bank. There's a small table there in the corner." They went to the savings bank and Reinhard sat down at the table. Christine stood next to him so that no one could see.

She gave him the envelope. He emptied it and counted the money twice. Then he wrote the amount on the envelope and put the money back. Now he counted out his amount. It was the same. He added the two amounts together and counted it again. Then he took a bank note out of his envelope and gave it to Christine. "That's for you for what you have lost because of our mother, and a little more. Do you want to put it all in the bank, or do you want to buy something? Think about it, but be quick." Christine was dizzy. "Did you really think it would be so much?" she asked Reinhard. He answered, "Truth to tell, I didn't think it would be half as much." They smiled at each other. Reinhard went to the counter and Christine to another. She kept back a little money and handed the savings book to the cashier, who counted it all over again in a loud voice, wrote the amount in the savings book and signed it. She showed it to Christine and wanted to return the savings book. "I'd like to leave it here with a code, if that's all right, please." "Yes, that's all right. You only need a code word which you can remember easily." She gave Christine a piece of paper and a pen and pointed to a line. "Write it here and then write your signature underneath." The cashier knew Christine from their school days.

Reinhard was already waiting for her. "Now I'm going to buy something for going out. We have to celebrate. Are you coming with me?" Of course she went with him. He bought a pair of black trousers and a matching jacket, which was a little too big but had been reduced and still suited him. Then he bought a modern nylon shirt and a leather tie. The young shop assistant said, "That's great! You'll look like a real young stag when you go out. Heads will turn." Reinhard said, "Do you think it's a bit flashy? I like it very much." He was looking forward to Friday which was the evening to go out.

Christine was not allowed to go out; not even until ten o'clock. It would not have been a problem if she had gone with Reinhard, but her parents were strictly against it. But the two of them still practised dancing to the newest Rock 'n Roll music. Christine was not heavy and could be thrown around easily. In secret, she also had a petticoat made; a stiff underskirt with three flounces with a black satin bell skirt over it.

The very skilled seamstress, Mrs. Kratz was a refugee from Jugoslavia. She worked for the 'Shoe and Leather ware company of Franz & Josefine Remi'. They had given her a Singer sewing machine which she had at home. It was a treadle machine meant for sewing leather.

Christine often had to collect shoe uppers from her and she had the idea of asking her to sew her skirt. Of course she wanted to pay her for the work, but Mrs. Kratz did not take the money. "Just bring things to me when you need something to be sewn. You mustn't tell anyone, otherwise they'll take the machine away and I'll be out of work. Your parents are very strict with me and they don't pay much, but with the machine and finer, normal needles I can sew things for our people, so that's good." "Oh, of course that's good," Christine said and promised to say nothing.

Hans did not let Christine go so easily. He kept on trying to see her and at the very least hold her hand. Most times he knocked on the window and asked for Christine. Once Charlotte looked out of the window and said, "Are you looking for Christine?" Hans did not want to admit it, but Charlotte laughed, knowingly, "She won't be back for a half hour or so." She went out and saw Hans going across the park, caught up with him and talked about a new building at the far end of the park which she wanted to see. "Do you want to come with me? You can still go into it. It's going to be a very interesting building when it's finished. Come one, I'll show it to you; we still have time." At first Hans did not want to go, but she showed him the building. She saw that there was no one else on the building site and pretended to have hurt her foot. "Oh! That hurts. Can you see if it's bleeding?" She lay half down on a broad plank. Hans knelt down and wanted to remove her shoe. "I think it's a bit higher up," she said, showed her knee and pulled up her skirt so that he could see her pants. She looked at him and pulled him down on her, kissed him furiously and started playing in his shirt and then in his trousers until he succumbed to her. Afterwards he ran way and was suddenly standing confused in front of the open window. Christine looked out and waved to him. "There's no one else here," she called to him, "we can talk to each other at the rear window."

She went into the back room and opened the window. Hans slowly came closer. He looked at her forlornly. "Has something happened?" she asked anxiously. "Christine! I've spoilt everything! Your sister Charlotte seduced me. We did it." He put his hands over his face and cried. "I don't know why I let it happen." Christine closed the window slowly and sat down on the bed which was close by. She was shocked and ashamed that her own sister could do something like that. With tears in her eyes she watched Hans leave the square. After a while she heard the front door creak, quietly. A few footsteps to the toilette then she heard the key turn in the lock. Christine opened her cupboard, pretending to tidy it up, but Charlotte did not come into the room. Then the front door slammed to and Christine saw, from behind the curtains, her sister leaving the house. Now she really felt pain in her heart.

Reinhard came home and Christine just had to tell him everything. He was not very surprised. "Come on, forget it. Pull yourself together. Get your new clothes before someone comes. Tonight we're going to make a big entrance. I know where there is a really fantastic rock 'n roll band. Then we'll show them our Rock number. As far as I'm concerned, nobody can do it like us. We can change our clothes in Aunt Bertha's corridor."

She pushed everything into a bag and had to jump out of the window because she heard someone coming. She changed her clothes in the park. It was already fairly dark. Reinhard knew a place where they could meet people who had a car and would gladly take others with them if they contributed to the petrol costs. They were in luck. They met a somewhat older jovial guy in groovy laid back clothes. He was driving a pale blue Thunderbird. "Hey, where are we going this evening?" he asked Reinhard. "Well, I've heard of a place where a crazy rock 'n roll band is playing, but it's about ten kilometres from here. Is that OK? They have giant plates of Wiener Schnitzel and it's not expensive." "I've heard of it, but there's hardly any room to dance. It's always very overcrowded." Reinhard said, "Well, we'll just have to find a way to get the dance floor for us." "Are you crazy? How are you going to do that?" Reinhard answered. "I just have to fetch something from the wooden hut near the workshop then you'll see. We'll have a ball."

He held a bank note under the nose of the fun-loving guy. "That's fine," he said, "I'm Benni." Reinhard: "Look over there, the chick with the big breasts. We'll take her with us. I've seen her dance and she's good." Benni: She seems to be alone, I'll chat her up". Christine interjected, "Why don't you tell him straight that that's Lilli from our neighbourhood?". "Shush. We have to make it exciting for Benni. Do you understand?" Lilli looked at Reinhard. He gave her a signal that she should not say they already knew each other. Then a blonde appeared. "Lilli, is there room for me?" she asked, "please take me with you." She was not the most beautiful girl in the world. Benni and Reinhard looked at each other. Reinhard shrugged his shoulders and Benni asked, "Have you got some money for petrol?" "Yes," Frieda said, "but I have to be back by midnight, other wise I'll be stroked with the belt. You wouldn't want that to happen to me, would you?" Christine said, "Don't worry. That is the absolute latest time we have to be back"

Benni added that he could not stay there long because he had the early shift the next day. Reinhard fetched a metal box with holes in it and a wooden box from the wooden hut. Benni asked, "What have you got in them?" "You'll find out soon enough." He gave the boxes to Lilli and Frieda to hold and told them not to open them. Christine smiled at her brother. She knew what was in the boxes. Reinhard said, "I'll sit in the middle. I feel comfortable there." He was grinning all the time. They were already enjoying themselves. Lilli painted her full lips with a very red lipstick which she passed on. Frieda played around with her hair and sprayed so much hairspray that there was a regular concert of coughing. Christine made her cheeks look a little fresher with some of Lilli's lilac rouge. Frieda had mascara in her bag. She spat on a black block and, with a small brush, mixed the spit into a thick, black paste.

When she was trying to spread the eyelash dye on her eye lashes, Benni had to break suddenly. "Ow!" Frieda yelled as the tiny brush went into her eye. She had a red eye for the rest of the evening which she tried to cover by a lock of hair. Christine and Lilla also spat on the block of dye and coloured their eyebrows and lashes. Benni's torch and Lilli's powder compact mirror did the rounds. Frieda made Reinhard's hair stand up. Benni had a quiff right down to his forehead. They thought they looked fantastic.

Benni was a real gentleman. He stopped in front of the dance hall and helped the ladies out of the car. Reinhard got out. Someone said, "Great car." Benni was very proud of his pale blue Thunderbird. Engine screaming he drove into a parking space and left a stink of petrol behind him. That reminded Lilli of her perfume and she sprayed all of them with it. After they had looked at each other and all agreed that they looked fine they went to the dance hall. There were so many people already there that it was a bit of a tight squeeze. Reinhard held on to his boxes and at the entrance asked if there was still room for five people who wanted to eat. He did not know that he was speaking to the owner. He asked them to follow him, moved a couple to another table and fetched another chair. Reinhard put the boxes on the floor and put his feet on them. The owner asked, "What can I bring you? I can recommend our excellent house wine." Benni said, "OK by me and bring us a bottle of fizzy water as well." "Shall I bring you a litre of our red?" They all agreed.

There were men on the stage who were setting up their instruments. The red wine went straight to Christine's head. She was glowing. The others were very amused. Frieda said, "You should have eaten something before." She laughed and Christine also thought it was funny. Suddenly four crazily dressed musicians sprang on to the stage, grabbed their instruments and the show began. Small lamps blinked on and off. The young people started to scream hysterically and ran on to the dance floor. Most of them moved wildly and jumped around crazily. Reinhard and Christine though that most of them could not really dance. The music became quieter and some of the couples started to dance enraptured together. The dancers were pushed and pressed together. Benni winked and found it extremely enjoyable. Everyone except Reinhard was dancing. He was afraid that the boxes under the table might open. After the band had played a few numbers they started to play rock music, which got all of them moving. Reinhard said, "Now it's our turn, come on Christine."

They took the boxes to the door and found a quiet space. "Come on. Tie your blouse up like I'm doing with my shirt." He took the corners of his shirt and tied it up loosely. "I'll take the mice and you take the snakes. They're just harmless slow worms. We'll go right into the middle of the dance floor. I'll open my shirt and shake the five mice out. Then you throw the three snakes into the crowd. Benni has promised to collect them up right away. Then we'll both shout, very loudly, "AaaaH! Help! Mice and snakes! You'll see. As soon as they realise that they are really mice and snakes, then they'll leave the dance floor and we'll have room for our show." Christine was a little sceptical but decided to put the snakes in her skirt. Then they pushed their way on to the dance floor. Christine threw the three snakes into the crowd. Reinhard emptied the mice onto a chair and moved the chair around. People started to scream. Everyone left the dance floor. As arranged Beni was ready and put the mice back in the metal box and the snakes back into the wooden box. Reinhard clapped his hands in the air and shouted to the musicians, "Come on! Let's Rock 'n Roll!" The musicians complied. Christine was in her element. Reinhard threw her over his shoulder, wrapped her round his neck, grabbed her through his legs then over his back and back on the floor. The people formed a circle round them and encouraged them. When the music finally stopped, there was loud applause and shouts of 'Bravo'. Breathless and happy, they went back to their table. Somebody bought them a bottle of sparkling wine, which the owner served to them. He was obviously pleased. Reinhard said, "It went just as we had rehearsed it at home. I told you it would be a hit." Lilli said, "My God, Reinhard, can you dance like that with me? That was really sensational." "I never thought that such a stiff stick like you had such swing," laughed Benni. Reinhard: "Come on. Let's eat a fine Schnitzel. Then we'll dance again until we have to leave." He stood up, raised his glass of sparkling wine and shouted loudly, "We thank the person who gave us this. Long may he live! Cheers!" From all sides they heard people shout, 'Cheers!' Frieda said, "This is going to be an evening I'll never forget as long as I live. I don't think it can get better than this. Super!"

Benni had not drunk much alcohol and drove them all safely home. Reinhard and Christine changed their clothes, which stank of smoke and perfume mixed with sweat, before they crept into the house.

In the night Reinhard worked, secretly, for a few hours in the glass factory. After the first night, he told Christine how it was. He had to carry the hot, ready blown glasses on a wooden shovel to a conveyor belt. Back and forth, the whole time. Then the cooled glass was transported into another room. If anything got broken, one of his former school friends had to pick up the pieces right away, so that no one was injured. Since most of the time nothing happened he hid in a corner and slept on a pile of wood shavings. The two of them swapped jobs and so they did not get too tired. Nobody really bothered to check the night shift and, apart from that, it was better paid than the day shift. Every evening Christine helped Reinhard to climb out of the window. She put a chair against the outside wall and as soon as he had gone, she brought it back inside. She put a black brush on his pillow and scrunched up the bed clothes, so that it looked as though Reinhard was at home and sleeping. Normally he came home just when father's alarm clock was ringing. Christine, prepared sandwiches for him to take and kept his clothes in order, so received a part of his wage that they had agreed. Reinhard was happy to give it to her. Things all went well for a surprisingly long time.

Until one night when Reinhard was half asleep, he tripped over some hot glass which had fallen off his wooden shovel and ended up in hospital with serious burns to his legs and hands.

His parents were informed and the whole business was no longer a secret.

Mother wanted him to pay her money for his board for the time he had been secretly working. Luckily his sickness benefit was paid directly into his savings account. "I didn't work there very long, and the little money I earned I used for clothes and now I won't get any more," he conned her.

The ambitious Emer trained with the best gymnastic club. His speciality was floor gymnastics. In competitions it was called 'Parterre Akrobatik'. He held on to his position as the seventh best in Austria. After that he concentrated on his acrobatic programme which he wanted to show in the circus. Naturally his half sister had to accompany him and her parents thought that was good. They thought that it would be a nice little source of money on the side, which they would earn when giving shows.

Christine was keen to do the training, but still continued to say, "I will never appear in a circus or on the stage as an artiste." She did not want people who knew her, to see her perform. And she certainly did not want a kiss on the lips from Emer in front of all those people. Charlotte objected to any of the exercises and she demonstrated this in a very decisive way. When Emer lifted her into the air she emptied her bladder. So he gave up trying to include her in his performance. The few spectators who always turned up by chance when they were practising found it highly amusing. Charlotte was not in the least embarrassed, "Serves him right, because he never leaves me in peace." Rosita was a good and willing partner. She allowed him to spin her round in the air and was not in the least bit afraid that something could go wrong. If she had any pains she hid them skilfully. Isabella, the youngest sister in the group, was always pleased to be the centre of attraction, even though she was the least talented. She also did not mind when Emer hugged and kissed her; just on the cheek, of course. She defended him by saying, "That's the way Emer wants it. It's just part of the show."

As father wanted, Christine started to play the zither. She thought that this was one way to learn the notes better. But she did not make much progress. In the first place she did not really like the instrument and secondly, she did not have enough time to practise. When she was not in school her time was occupied; acrobatics in the morning and afternoon and between the two, sincc she was very good with her hands, she had to do whatever work came up. Studding bags; stamping out leather uppers and soles; cutting out shoe linings. When necessary she even stretched the leather uppers for special shoes over the shoe last. Father bought her special tools for left handed people. Her knees could not take this particular job for long. The protection from the hard shoe last was not good enough.

Lilli, her best friend, came every Friday and helped where she could so that Christine could finish the work she had been given and then go out for the evening. When a delivery date approached all the children had to work late into the night. So as not to disturb the neighbours, all noisy work had to be finished by 10 o'clock in the evening. Because Christine was the oldest girl, she felt more responsibility than the others who, one after the other, crept away.

Emer never went out, did not dance, smoke and never drank a drop of alcohol. He preferred to help Eva, the attractive book keeper, who Franz had employed, but he did not show any personal interest in her. He was just interested in the book keeping. He was very impressed by her extensive vocabulary. He tried to use all the foreign language words which she used. She had been in prison for a while. She had been accused of being a swindler, which she was not, but she had had no chance against her former boss. So she had to look for a new job for a long time and finally the Remis employed her for a low wage. She always wore very tight fitting dresses with low necklines, which her sister sent her from America. In these clothes she did not look exactly common. She was, in fact a very refined woman, who knew all the tricks. She was self confident and smart. She even wrote a letter to the government, requesting that the Remi company should not pay any taxes for a few years. She also had many imaginative suggestions for the work flow.

It was not long before Franz Remi trusted her with all the office work and, in addition, paying the wages. When Eva heard about the sand quarry, she was very interested. She spoke to Mr. Dvorak who was responsible for the building sand and for the employees. She soon realised that he was dishonest. When he was eating with the Remis one mid day, she had a look at his car which was parked in the courtyard. There was a thick briefcase on the rear seat. The window on the driver's side was not quite closed. Eva looked around and acted very quickly. She pushed the window down until she could reach the inside door handle and could open the door. Then she grabbed the briefcase and went straight back into the office. There were account statements which she checked quickly and soon discovered that there were some forged payments among them. She made a few notes. She also found applications to travel to the USA and Canada; tax accounts and payment receipts. For the moment that was enough to tell her boss that there were a few problems. Mr. Dvorak was paying very little tax and would soon find himself in trouble. She managed to put the briefcase back in the car without being noticed and pull the window up.

Later Eva looked for the contract conditions and shook her long blonde curls. "How can anybody be so stupid," she said to Emer, "if something goes wrong then your father will find himself in deep trouble." Then she looked at him, grabbed his muscular arms and said, " The sand quarry is a goldmine. You have strong arms. Why don't you take it over? If I were as strong as you I'd leap at the chance. There's a lot of money to be made."

She knew that the only thing in Emer's head was the circus. "After a while you could start your own circus. Come on. Think about it. Be clever. We'll look over it all once more. First: Inspect the sand quarry, without Mr. Dvorak. How would it be next

Sunday early in the morning. I know someone who can drive us there. We'll speak to your father afterwards. What do the Amis say, 'OK. Give me five'. She held up the palm of her hand and Emer had to clap it. He started to get interested in the whole thing.

Every day after work Eva went to the Café Varia and drank a "Verlängerten". That was a milk coffee which she liked very much. The café was frequented mostly by business men. She knew that she would meet the salesman Sivacek, who worked for Remi there. He had a car and apart from using it for shoe sales, he also offered driving lessons. He had even installed a second brake pedal and a second rear view mirror on the passenger side. Unfortunately very few people were interested in driving lessons, so he also offered a taxi service, although at first, he did not have the necessary licence. He enjoyed driving around in his car. It always brought him a little money. Eva saw him drinking his favourite Turkish coffee. "Hello, Mr. Sivacek. How's the sales business going?" "Hello, Eva. Tomorrow I'm going to pull up my socks and knock on a few business doors. Do you have any stock? I'd like to take a few shopping bags with me as samples and if you've got any in the warehouse, I could take them with me and sell them there and then. Goods for cash is the best way. You have to know that I'm a good salesman." Eva sat at the table next to him so she could continue the conversation. She did not want to sit at the same table because of the other people in the café. It was bad enough that she went there alone to drink coffee. A woman didn't do that. She managed to convince Mr. Sivacek that he should drive Emer and herself to the sand quarry the next day.

They met at 5 o'clock the next morning. The journey took exactly forty minutes. Sivacek looked at the conveyor belt and saw that it was damaged. A cut which was almost halfway through the band had been held together with wire. The sand sieves which had large holes in them were also unusable. There were rusty shovels in the work hut, which was not even locked.

Eva made some notes and told Emer that he should work with them for a while to see what was going on there. "You can learn something and also earn something. You can find out how the tools are used and how they can be better used effectively. I've already prepared a new contract." Emer: "I don't want to do that for ever. That's not for me." Sivacek: "What does the lorry look like? The building sand here is top quality as far as I can see, and I worked with my parents when they were building our house." He ran the building sand through his fingers. "Dvorak is certainly doing some good business with this," he said, "who is he supplying? Has he got a lease contract? What is the arrangement? That would really interest me. And it wouldn't be bad for me to deal with the master builders, for example. Who's working here? Dvorak is certainly not doing this on his own."

On the way back they talked about many things. Eva made notes of what would concern Mr. Dvorak and Mr. Remi. "We have to get both of them round the same table," she said, "You, Mr. Sivacek and Emer must be present, because you know how it is. Think about how you can improve things. You have to bring written suggestions with you. Both of them have to understand that we are serious and ready to get on with the job. We'll agree on an appointment. Let's say the day after tomorrow at 2 o'clock. Up to then we have to be well prepared, but that's our secret. When I get the chance I'll tell the boss today. I'll tempt Mr. Dvorak with some sort of pretext. Don't worry, I'll think of something. Otherwise I have the feeling he'll escape. From what I have seen, that would be no surprise." Sivacek asked for Dvorak's address. He wanted to look at the condition of the lorry.

Aloisia, Franz and Luise's daughter came to the workshop. She wanted to speak to her father alone. Josefine said, "We don't have any secrets you can say what you have to say in front of both of us." Aloisia, just stood there and looked at her father. "OK, then we can talk in the courtyard." Outside she asked if he could not give her husband, Willi, some work. He was unemployed until he could find another job at the glass factory, because the work he had done up to now had attacked his lungs. So it would be better if he could have another job for a while, preferably in the fresh air, but he could not find anything suitable.

Franz promised that he would think about it and said, "We'll find something suitable. I'll let you know. It shouldn't take too long." He went to Eva and asked her how it was going with the salesmen. "Willi is a strong young man, but I can't see him working as a salesman or something similar. What about working from home? Could we do something there?" Eva said, "Mr. Remi, it's good you asked me. I think your son-in-law could do something in the sand quarry." "Yes. That's a good idea. Maybe that would work. I know that he can drive a lorry. I've seen him drive a military lorry through town. I think he learnt to drive in the army." Eva said, "Good. Dvorak is coming this afternoon. I've taken the liberty of writing a new contract between you two. If you could just read through it now, then I can show it to Mr. Dvorak. Emer and Mr. Sivacek are also interested in what is going to happen with the sand quarry. Now I can tell you that we were there and have looked at everything. We couldn't imagine how everything has fallen into disrepair and that they have to work with broken tools. Mr. Sivacek is going to take a look at the lorry before Mr. Dvorak comes." "What, you went to the quarry without telling me? I don't like that at all." "It was Emer's idea," she lied in defence. "And since when has he taken any interest in anything but the Circus? He's got nothing else in his head. So Sivacek is going to look at the lorry? No harm in that. Then I only need to get Willi here at the right time and we can come to an arrangement with Dvorak. But in future don't do anything without telling me. Don't forget that!" Eva said, "Yes, boss." She did not want to talk about anything else and left the office. Franz was able to read the draft contract in peace.

Later Franz, Eva, Emer and Sivacek met in the office. Sivacek said that the lorry tyres and brakes were worn out; there were oil leaks and badly repaired holes in the exhaust pipes. The driver's hut looked like a rubbish tip. He had not seen Dvorak early in the morning. Sivecek asked, "Franz. When was the last time you got money from Dvorak? Isn't he supposed to pay you rent on a regular basis or something like that?" Franz knew that he had been very slack and had not checked the bank payments carefully. At the beginning, everything had always been in order. So he had trusted Dvorak completely. Of course he had never been to the sand quarry. Franz said, "Let's leave that for the moment. I think that Eva has already prepared something. You, Sivacek, don't be angry with me when I say that we have to first talk with Dvorak alone. Thank you very much for all your efforts. We'll meet up later." Sivacek said, "That's fine. We'll see each other later."

Dvorak came, wearing his suit with his ruffled hair under his hat. Saying that he had not had time to make the payments, he placed a bundle of banknotes on the table and pushed forward a piece of paper which should be signed to confirm payment. Franz convinced him that Emer and Willi would be working with him from now on so that the business would move better forwards. Dvorak hesitated. "But I have to make some repairs before we can take on any contracts," he explained, "In about a week everything will be operational. Then we can start work again." Franz asked, "Since when has the sand quarry not been operational? Just what is broken? Can't we do it ourselves?" Dvorak answered, "Well, there is the lorry and the conveyor belt has a split in it. We can't repair these things ourselves. You have to give me some time." Franz said, "We have also examined the contract. It will have to be changed. You can read it through and tell us if you agree." Dvorak asked, "Do I have to do that now? You know I'm Croatian and my German is not very good. I'll have to look at it back home." Eva said, "I can explain everything to you. It won't take long," Franz said, "We have to go back to work. Do you still need us?" Eva replied, "One of you has to count the money which Mr. Dvorak brought with him, and sign here. Apart from that, we can carry on alone."

Sivacek was not satisfied and left to pick up the lorry. He drove it into the courtyard and then ran off.

Emer was the first to see the smoking lorry drive in.

Willi, Aloisia's husband came into the workshop nervously. "Aloisia said I should come here. She can't wait until I get a decision from the glass factory. I'll get by even without you." Franz greeted his son-in-law and got straight to the point. "Tell me, do you know anything about repairing motor vehicles? There's a lorry standing there. Can you have a look at it? It belongs to the sand quarry. We can't deliver any building sand, before the lorry is fixed." Willi said, "Do you mean the blue rusty crate over there?"

Without waiting for an answer he went out to take a closer look at the lorry. The handle on the driver's door was missing, so he got in on the other side. The ignition key was in the lock, but he could not get it out. Emer brought a pad of paper and a pencil. Willi said, "You can write it down if you want, but it's going to be a long list." Emer wrote and also noted the approximate costs which Willi gave him. He calculated on parts that he could get from the scrap heap. "Have you got money'" he asked, "then we can get the most important parts and I can repair it in the municipal courtyard. That could take a bit longer than in a garage. I've got some tools and I can borrow some more." Willi took a blood stained handkerchief out of his trouser pocket and wiped his hands on it. Emer asked, "Have you cut yourself?" It was then that Will realised that he always had this handkerchief in his pocket. "No, no. That's old."

But Emer saw that it was fresh blood, but he said nothing about it. He simply said, "I'll tell father what we intend to do, then we can go." Franz came towards them with Dvorak at his side. Willi told them what was wrong with the lorry and got into the driver's seat. Dvorak did not fully agree, but Willi insisted on how dangerous the worn out brakes and tyres were, so Dvorak had to agree. However, he insisted on taking all his personal belongings out of the lorry before Emer and Willi drove off and for that he needed a box. Franz gave him a leather shopping bag, which he had every intention of getting back later. Eva immediately got stuck into the bank statements and accounting which Dvorak had had to produce and asked Franz for all papers concerning the sand quarry. Franz said, "That's not so important right now." But Josefine gave her a show box, which had the words 'Sand quarry', written on it and nodded. Willi drove off without Emer, so he went on foot to the courtyard. When he got there he met Aloisia. "Willi's just gone to fetch some tools." She turned to face him, "Please tell Father to speak to Willi so that he doesn't hit me again. Now he doesn't even hold back when the children are there. He hits me without any reason. I only wanted to help him get a job with father. When I told him he could work there he went crazy. I'm afraid of him. Please, tell Father he should talk to him today." Emer said, "What a swine! Good, but go now, before he comes back." He though about the poor children. Two had bow legs. Their legs were so arched that they looked as though they had a barrel between them. He knew that came from malnutrition, but with time it would correct itself. Aloisia was thin and the children were timid and shy. On the other hand, Willi looked strong and well fed and made sure he was always well dressed. When he laughed, you could see that he had a golden tooth. He wore a gold chain and his wedding ring was on his little finger. His black wavy hair was fixed with Brilliantine. Later, when they were together in the lorry, Emer asked innocently how Aloisia and the children were. He was considering visiting them more often in future. "Maybe the children would like to come with me in the gymnastic club," I haven't seen them for a long time," he lied, "it's really time I got to know them better. I'll tell Father he should pay more attention to Aloisia. After all, she is his oldest daughter. I remember her being very pretty and playful."

That is what Emer said and all the time he looked straight at the road. Now he knew why Willi's handkerchief was full of blood. Willi said, "Oh. Don't worry about them. I've got everything under control." Emer said, "Whatever, our family have really neglected Aloisia and the children and that has to change from now on. Obviously in future we're going to work more closely together. Then we'll automatically have closer contact." Changing the subject Willi started to talk about the motor repairs.

In the meantime Eva had looked at all Dvorak's documents and told Emer about what she had already suspected. "He is a complete swindler. I don't understand how your father could let it go on! We have to get Mr. Dvorak here. I'll send Reinhard on his bike to him." But Reinhard soon came back. "Mrs. Dvorak and the three children were alone. After Mr. Dvorak left us he went straight home; took a packed suitcase, which he had packed days before and hidden under the bed and ran off. That is what his wife told me. She was very distressed. She said she did not think he was ever coming back. He had wanted to go to Canada for a long time." And that is exactly how it was. He went off and left his wife and children for good.

Eva was seething with anger. She put all the documents back in the shoe box labelled, 'Sand quarry' and put it away. Josefine had told her that she should have thought of that before, because she had nothing else to do. Then she left the office early and went to the café. She was going to order a strong coffee. In front of the coffee shop she met Christine with the milk can in her hand. "What are you doing with the milk can? Are you going to get some milk?" She nodded. Isabella came up to them. "Let me carry the can," she laughed, "you can have it again when it's full." Eva said, "You know what, Isabella? Today you can go all alone for the milk. I want to talk to Christine about something." Isabella made a dark face. Eva said, "What's the matter? Go on." She turned the girl in the direction of the milk shop and went into the coffee house with Christine. "Mother wouldn't allow this," Christine remarked. "Of course she would. I'm with you."

Eva wanted to do Christine a favour, but Christine did not feel in the least bit comfortable. She did not want to drink anything and kept looking at the door. Isabella went straight as an arrow to the workshop and told them that Christine was sitting in the coffee house with Eva and that she would have had to collect the milk on her own. Franz and Josefine were still annoyed about Mr. Dvorak. Franz said, "Josefine, you go on ahead and get her out of the café. I'll read the riot act to her later."Josefine did not hold back in using the opportunity to say what she thought to Eva and Christine in front of all the people in the café. She stormed into the café and looked at Christine, who stood up immediately and made for the door suspecting that something bad was going to happen. But Josefine grabbed her by the hair and swore at her as she had never done before. "Let Christine go; don't make a scandal; I'm to blame," Eva said and tried to get Josefine's hand out of Christine's hair, but all she got was a fist in her face. Christine was dragged out by her hair over the doorstep, out into the street and shaken. The people stood still and wanted to intervene, but Josefine became even more angry and shouted, "My daughter will not be a whore. I'll kill her first." Christine fainted and hung there with her hair in her mother's hand.

She did not come to until she found herself back home and saw Mrs. Reisin from the Red Cross and also the neighbour's wife leaning over her. "My head hurts. I can feel every single hair." "It'll be all right. You should try to forget everything that has happened," Mrs. Reisin said, "I'll give you a headache pill." Reinhard came from the workshop. He whispered to Christine, "Father is really angry. You have to run away before he also hits you. Mrs. Reisin came with a small case full of tablets and bottles and said, "Here, take this." Reinhard, gathered up a box of pain killers and stuffed them in his pocket. Mrs. Reisin said, "All right. Now I want to measure your pulse and if that's normal, I have to go. She left almost immediately.

Reinhard: "Come on. Quickly. Pack some things in a bag. Benni is in the park. He'll take you to the main station. Now you can finally visit your favourite Aunt Anna in Wienerneustadt. I've got the address and money for the journey." Christine said, "I don't have to run away. Mum only pulled my hair. I shouldn't have gone to the coffee shop. I only fainted because I was so ashamed. Father has never hit me. I don't think he would do that." Reinhard was very angry- "You had a shock. Mother has really worked on Father. He has sacked Eva without notice. Eva doesn't even know about it yet. He told me to tell her. He said, she doesn't need to come any more. I'm supposed to cycle there and tell her." Christine stood up, but she was still shaky on her legs. She cleared out her part of the cupboard; fetched a few hidden things and Reinhard put them all into a bag, which he had ready.. Then they hurried out of the house to the park.

Benni was leaning on his car, totally relaxed. A few of his friends were standing around. "The whole town knows about it," he said, grinning, "Your mother was loud enough for everyone to hear." Then he looked at the large bag and asked, "Reinhard do you want to run away with her?" Reinhard said, "She has to leave. She's going to visit her aunt until everything has quietened down. Let's just say that Christine is finally going on holiday." Benni said, "That's great! So, let's go on holiday!" Everyone there laughed. And Christine was also pleased to go somewhere else and left on the night train.

When she arrived in Wienerneustadt she took out the address which Reinhard had given her. It was not Anna's address. It was Aunt Rosa's address. She went to the information desk and asked for the post office. She could not find the name Anna Pfeifer there, so she asked how she could get to the Aunt Rosa's address.

She was very surprised to see Christine at her door. "Why. Hello! Who else is there? You'll have to excuse us, we weren't expecting visitors." Christine said, "I'm on my own." Aunt Rosa : "And your father allowed that? I suppose my sister wants to get rid of you. I remember well when she once gave you to a Russian woman under some pretext or another. She was unlucky. A pregnant cat bit your hand and so the doctor sent you back home." Christine: "No. Mother just wanted to sort something out and had only left me there for a moment." The aunt said, "But she was at home when they brought you back. Oh, well! Let's forget all that. They're just old stories. No, wait. There was something else. She once tried to sell you to a pottery dealer at the market. He was quite serious when he told me about it. He's an old acquaintance of ours. He once gave you an enamelled coffee cup because he felt so sorry for you. You must remember it. Don't you remember it?" Yes. Christine did remember it, he had also kissed her on the forehead and he smelt magnificently of perfumed pipe tobacco, just like Grandfather.

But why was Aunt Rosa talking like this about her sister Josefine? "You can't stay here long. We haven't got much space as you can see. But we're still very happy to see you." Christine: "Maybe Aunt Anna has more room. I asked for her address at the post office. Doesn't she live in Wienerneustadt any more?" Aunt Rosa said, "Yes, yes, but she has a new name and a new address since she got married." Christine said, "I didn't know she had married." Aunt Rosa: "Well, she really didn't want to get married but her husband was also single and had no family. They have known each other for a long time. Anna is a beautiful, elegant woman and he is well off. She is well situated now, therefore, he doesn't want her to work outside the house. So now she's a bit bored and, it must be said, she's put on weight. She's losing her figure and that's not good, if you ask me. He's also taught her to read and write and he buys her books and magazines, but she›s still finding it hard to learn. I've learnt a bit with the children, but not really enough. And then, after my second husband and then a few months later my eldest son Pauli died as a result of a motorbike accident, I haven't had much time. I have to earn our daily bread for both my daughters and myself. I was lucky enough to be able to buy a fairground shooting stand and I'm making good money. This afternoon I have to set up the stand for the annual fair. If you want, you can help me. Anna will be there as well."

Happy holiday! If only Reinhard knew!

Christine helped to set up the stand. Her two cousins came after school. "Hello! Finally we've got visitors! If you want to serve behind the stand then you'll have to paint your lips and eyebrows, otherwise Mother will not let you behind the stand. Come on. It's fun. Then some of the men look at you in a completely different way." They giggled. "Christine, there is Aunt Anna," Rose shouted. Christine was just having her lipstick put on.

"What? Is Christine really here? I can hardly believe that anyone from the von Dorns would actually visit us. Come here, Christine. Lipstick doesn't suit you. Get that make-up off. What an idea! Who said you should colour your lips. That's so horrible and common." While they were setting up the stand

Aunt Anna chatted with Christine and later she showed her her flat. "In actual fact, nothing here belongs to me, so please don't touch anything which is on display. My husband sees everything, even if it has only been moved a millimetre. Come, sit here and tell me something. Would you like a warm chocolate? I should be practising my writing. I should write a whole side before he comes home. Look! From this paper I have to write down several things, but I still can't read them properly."

Aunt Anne laughed about herself and when she laughed she showed her pearl white sparkling teeth. Christine put her hands behind her back and looked at all the things which were standing around. "I've really got a good life. My husband does the shopping and cooks, because I can't cook very well. I always have to watch how he prepares the food, so that one day I'll be able to put something presentable on the table. But most of the time I just sit around and get fatter. He also doesn't like it if I go to the fair alone, even though he knows I only go there to visit my friends. I'm sorry, I should be happy instead of whining all the time."

Christine asked, "Can I stay here? Aunt Rosa doesn't have much room and I can only stay there for a short while." "Yes, I know, but unfortunately my husband doesn't want anyone else in his flat. How long do you want to stay?" "I don't know," Christine said, embarrassed. "Is something wrong? I have a feeling you didn't come here of your own free will." Christine said, "I just need a break; just to get away from home and the workshop. That's why I'm here. Reinhard and I thought you were still living alone. I would have felt at home with you." Aunt Anna put her arms around her and said, "You know what. Just stay here for a moment. Ferdinand will soon be home."

She had just said this when the door opened and Ferdinand came in. Anna went to him, greeted him warmly and gave him a kiss. "Look, Ferdinand, we've got a lovely visitor. This is my niece, Christine," she said to Ferdinand and then to Christine, "this is Ferdinand." "Hello," he said and nothing more. He disappeared into the kitchen with the shopping. Anna ran after him and shut the door behind her. Christine heard them discussing. When Anna came back, she took her by the shoulders, led her out of the house and said, "I'm sorry, Christine. You're going to have to stay with Rosa. I'll come a little way with you, but then I have to go back." She brushed a tear from her eye and wiped her nose. Sadly Christine said, "That's all right. I can find my way back alone. I'm sure we'll see each other again before I go home." Anna just nodded and waved for a long time. Christine told Aunt Rosa what had happened. "I think he keeps her like a prisoner," Rosa said, "I once wanted to visit her and she couldn't open the door. She told me that he had locked her in by mistake. But I tell you, he did it on purpose. Let's see if she comes here tomorrow." Rosa became fractious. "Girls, make sure we're doing business. Christine, you can replace the plaster pipes which have been shot into the corner and put some new flowers in them." At the first shot Christine flinched, plaster splinters flew everywhere and she pressed herself into a corner. "Come on. Sit here in front and watch the money," her older cousin said to her. It was 4 o'clock in the morning before they finally got to bed. And they were three in one bed.

That went on for two nights. Then the police knocked on the door. Rosa went out and when she came back and started to grumble. "She ran away because Franz wanted to beat her, because she had been in a coffee shop." "Just for that?" one of the cousins asked and laughed out loud, "I don't believe it. If that were so we would have been dead long ago. Now tell us really what happened?" Christine's eyes filled with tears and she told them everything, her voice broken by her sobs. Aunt Rosa said, "Since when has Josefine been so hysterical? She was always the fine lady. What! She pulled you by your hair into the town square? If that's true, then it's not normal! What a scandal! Our mother told us that Josefine never touched you or took you in her arms. Emer and Fredi were her favourite children. I don't know how it was or is with Reinhard. I love my children equally."

The oldest cousin booed., "Yes, yes. let's leave it. You shouldn't be telling such stories now. That is not nice from you. Mother. Grandmother told these stories the way she saw them. When you have so many children you can't take them all on your lap at the same time. And she was always pregnant. Let›s hope that with the birth of her 9th child, Jolanda, it's finished." Aunt Rosa and her children giggled. "You shouldn't take it so hard," Rosa said, "the last time I saw your mother she said you were a very industrious, and responsible girl. You were much younger then. So she was proud of you. Normally she only spoke about Emer. By the way, the police told me that he was coming to collect you."

XXII

Emer arrived. He and Christine had to travel back in an overcrowded train. For much of the journey they had to stand in the corridor in front of a compartment. Then a man left his place and Emer pushed himself in between two men. "Come here, little sister and sit on my lap." Christine did not want to. But a firm grip on her wrist forced her to do as he had asked. The conductor forced two more people into the compartment so that he could get through. It was a horribly tight squeeze. Emer held Christine tightly on her upper thighs. His inquisitive fingers started to wander and found their way into her pants. She wanted to stand up. "Stay here, you can't get through this crowd." He held her tightly and tried again. Christine started to cry. "I don't feel well. I have to get out of here." The man who was standing in front of her moved to one side so that she could go out. She made it to the toilet, which stank terrible, shut the door behind her, stood on the edge of the toilet and forced the window with all her strength so that she could finally get some fresh air. She pressed her face to the upper open gap and breathed deeply with closed eyes. Tears were running down her cheeks. She did not hear someone rattling the door. Only when she heard loud knocks on the door did she leave the window. She washed her face and thighs with cold water and calmed herself down. Emer was standing outside. "Come out. Some people will be even more sick with all this perfume," he said jokingly and stroked her shoulders. She stepped back. She would never forget what had happened and the memory stayed with her always. She could not free herself from it; could not switch off the memory, even though he had not achieved his goal.

Once they got home Franz was very authoritarian. From early to late Christine had to pull the shoe uppers over the last and stud bags together. Her knees swelled up and were bruised. She could hardly straighten her back, from sitting so long.

After several days, in the main square Christine suddenly bent low and had the most awful pains in her stomach. She could go no further. Her mother was called and she asked what the matter was. "Come on, don't behave like this in front of all these people. They'll thing you're losing a child." The old lady Dr. Zernic passed by and said to two young men who were standing around, "Lay her down on the bench over there. "Show me exactly where it hurts."

She touched Christine's stomach and said that it could be a ruptured appendix. "We need an ambulance and a doctor. We have to treat her quickly. Is someone going to telephone?" Dr. Zernic asked the people who were standing around and gave the number which she knew by heart, to someone who offered to make the call. Christine was not taken to the hospital in Vordersberg but 35 kilometres further to the regional hospital. Her mother did not want to go with her. Christine heard her say, "I can't go with her. I've seven other children who need me."

On the way to the hospital her details were noted. The young doctor who was taking care of her asked her if she wanted something for the pain. She nodded, but when she saw the hypodermic she panicked and started to scream. That did not help. The nurse held her down and the injection landed in her upper thigh. The doctor gently pressed her stomach, but was not able to make a diagnosis. "Just try to rest. We'll examine you more fully later." He also asked how long she had had such swollen knees, and he also saw the shoe glue on her hands. "That's from making shoes," she answered and fell asleep.

The injection worked. She was already in the hospital bed when she woke up and saw an angel bending over her. It was Sister Zitta, a nun wearing a blindingly white, winged bonnet and a large, white collar. She smiled at her and said, “Everything’s all right, young lady. The doctor has examined you. Everything is good, good, good. You have been in a deep sleep for a long time.” Her voice had a nice ring. She spoke with a Hungarian accent. Christine said, “My mother is also Hungarian.” “Ah! You heard that right away? My home town is Budapest. I was born in Buda. Where does your mother come from?” “From Friese.” “Oh, sorry, I don’t know it. I’ve been away from my home land for a long time. Doctor will come soon. There’s another girl sleeping in the bed by the window. The poor little thing is very ill.” She went to the small girl’s bed and shook the bed covers back into place. “After visiting you get food. Aren’t you hungry?” “Yes, I’m hungry and thirsty.” “I’ll bring you a glass of water right now. Then, first doctor and then eat.”

After two days just lying in bed Christine could not sleep at night. She crept to the door, which was standing open and looked into the hall. Opposite she saw Sister Zitta in a small room stuffing dolls. All the doors were open. Christine said, “I can’t sleep. What are you doing, Sister Zitta?” I make little dolls for small girls. For presents. They really like them and they comfort them.” “Can I help?” You can stuff the arms and the legs right to the end. Come here and sit on the cushion. Then we sew them on the body. Red wool goes on the head, like hair. Look, just like a pretty, young Hungarian girl. I have given her red cheeks, like it is back home.”

From then on Christine helped every night for a few hours and slept during the day. She told Sister Zitta all about her home and the workshop, where about 30 people worked. She also talked about her father, who would not let her go on with her studies, because all girls get married sooner or later. But she did not want to marry and she did not want to have children. Since she had always had to look after her younger siblings, she knew what it was like. Sister Zitta asked if she would like to go to a convent school, because that could be arranged. “I’ll talk to your parents about it when they come to visit. Maybe we can arrange something. Come, let's ask God about it. Kneel down here on the floor next to me."

Christine had been in the hospital for almost a week. She had no visitors. They treated her knees, where water had gathered, which they drained off. When the doctor came he said that she had suffered from exhaustion and your body reacted with stomach pains. But now you have recovered well. If you want, you can go home on Saturday. Tell the sister if you have the feeling that you feel well."

Then he went to the bed by the window where little Nanni was lying. Every day Christine had gone to Nanni's bed to see if she had finally woken up. The doctor removed the tube and had it taken away. The sister closed the curtains so that the sun would not disturb her. They left the room looking very serious.

Christine felt tired and fell asleep. She was woken by a woman shaking her and calling her 'Nanni'. "Nanni! Nanni! Please don't leave us," she wept loudly and pressed her head on Christine's shoulder. Appalled, Sister Zitta hurried to Christine's bed and said, "Jesus, Maria! Please, not here! Nanni is over there!" She took the woman by the shoulders and led her to the bed by the window, then she said to Christine, "Come. We'll go to another room. Sorry. She made a mistake. Don't upset yourself my love. Here's some raspberry juice to drink. I'm sorry. I have to go. I'll be back soon." She left the door open.

After a while Christine saw them rolling out a bed. It was Nanni lying on the bed and they had covered her face. The woman who had come into the room was being supported by Sister Zitta.

The next day Christine's mother came. "Good morning, Sister!" Christine heard her mother saying in a very friendly voice, "My husband sent me to ask how our daughter is. Well, you know, the one who had stomach pains." Josefine could not bring herself to say her daughter's name. "Ah! You mean Christine? A lovely girl I'm very pleased to meet you."

Then Christine heard both of them chatting in Hungarian. She also heard her mother blow her nose, x-times, which meant that she was performing her weeping act. At the same time she asked herself why she always did that in front of other people. I know my mother well enough to know that this conversation can go on for a long time, Christine thought and slid under the down cover, as she thought, for the last time and tried not to listen. Sister Zitta had given her a doll, which she held on to tightly. She prayed deeply to God that she could go to the convent school. "Come, Christine. You've slept long enough." Sister Zitta put her hand on her forehead. "You're in luck. Your mother has agreed that you can go to the convent school. I'll take you there. We'll be there in an hour. We've already arranged everything." Christine sat up and was suddenly wide awake. "What, as quickly as that? I'll get dressed right away." She jumped out of the bed, put on her clothes and hid the little doll under her blouse. Then she washed her face and combed her hair. When she was ready she stood in front of her mother. Sister Zitta noticed the mother's cold attitude towards her daughter.

All three of them went in the bus to the convent school. They were greeted together and then interviewed separately. The Mother Superior and a couple of other people left them to discuss the matter. Sister Zitta served them tea and cakes, which had already been put there by a younger nun. It took a long time! Finally their discussion was over. Josefine had to sign an agreement and was asked if she wanted to look at the school, but she showed no interest. She simply said that she had other things to do. "Yes. Then you can take your leave from your daughter." Sister Zitta said, "Come, Christine. Give your mother a hug and a kiss on the cheek." Josefine put a hand on Christine's shoulder and pouted her lips in a kiss which she did not give. She put the visiting paper and the agreement in her bag and went down the stairs. Christine watched her mother through the little side window and saw her turn and look back at the convent building.

Christine was given blue clothes which she put on later. There was a large room with many beds, a small cupboard by every bed and curtains to separate them. That was the dormitory for the convent pupils. Everyone was fully occupied from early to late with praying, keeping silent, studying books, class work, handicrafts, house work and gardening. There was little free time, but when the weather was good they could gather in the garden. There were quiet corners there, where they could retreat. Christine enjoyed the regulated order of the days. She learnt easily and she learnt many new things. She started each new day without any problems and went to bed tired, but satisfied every night. Some of her school colleagues found it difficult to adapt, but they got a lot of help from the nuns. Of course, a few of them left the convent after the trial period. Some others were advised to leave the convent.

Only about three weeks later did Franz realise that Christine was not yet home. There were new employees in the workshop, most of them relations. That is why he did not have everything under control. Willi had settled in to working in the sand quarry and seemed to have understood everything. Emer sometimes had to help sieve the sand or shovel it on to the conveyor belt. Since he had a well trained, muscular body which was clear to see from his 'washboard' stomach, everyone expected him to do this work with ease. Unfortunately this was not the case. He suffered all the time from aching muscles and did not want to go on shovelling sand. So Reinhard went to help.

"Now Christine has really got to come back to work in the workshop," Franz said, "it won't be long before Emer has got everything ready for the circus and then we'll have one more person less. Where is she, anyway?" Josefine turned to face the wall and said, "She's been taken care of. Don't count on her. She won't be coming back." "What are you saying? Can't you speak clearly? Where the devil is she?" "What do you mean by the devil? She's in the convent, by the winged nuns. She's been there for three weeks and," she stressed, "she went there of her own free will." "And you tell me that now? Get her back immediately out of this holy….., out of the claws of the convent before she is brainwashed. You did that on purpose, because she was always in your way. Do you think you could make her disappear behind the convent walls?" "That's not true," Josefine said, defensively, "she was happy to go to the convent, without any influence on my part. Ask her yourself. I'm not going to fetch her. You can do that. I have signed that as far as I'm concerned, she can stay there." "We'll see about that. Without my permission nothing can happen here; absolutely nothing. Do you understand?" Josefine put a copy of the agreement on the table and went out with Jolanda, her youngest child. She stayed away for three days and told no one where she had been.

Franz asked Sivacek, if he could drive him to the convent and they went of to the convent school to bring Christine back.

When Christine was sent to the Mother Superior she was totally surprised to see her father.

She greeted her father warmly and also gave her hand to Mr. Sivacek with a smile. She had no idea that it was more than a visit. "I'm going to get you out of here," her father said. Christine looked at the Mother Superior in despair, because she did not want to go with him. She refused and stood behind the desk next to the Mother Superior, cried and her whole body shook. "Please, please, leave me here." Franz threatened to go to the police and to the court and shouted at the Mother Superior, "You want to take my daughter from me. You've already brainwashed her and I'm not going to allow this to go on! She has to come with us now; right now! She is still a minor and that means I decide what is right for her."

The Mother Superior asked him and Mr. Sivacek to wait in the visitor's room. Sister Zitta happened to be in the school and was called to help Christine calm down and to explain that, as soon as she had reached majority, then she could come back to them and that they would always be there for her. She was also told that whenever she had any problems, whatever they should be, she would always be welcome. One of the sisters would always have time for her. She did not need to make an appointment. The door would always be opened for her.

Franz was called into the Mother Superior's office. He had to show his identity card and sign the release papers. She then told him how everything had happened and said that she hoped, with the 'help of God' he and his wife would be able to understand each other better. Was he really convinced that Christine would be better cared for in the outside world? She made it clear to him that the sisters worked in many places outside and did not just sit in the convent and pray. The convent could not exist if that were the case. "Even we have to work hard. We only have well schooled people and the best teachers you can find. Every pupil can decide later if they want to become a nun or would rather leave as a free person. I know of no convent where people are forced to stay. This school has already produced several, worldly women and we are proud of them." The Mother Superior made a short pause and looked at Franz challengingly. "Mr. Remi, we have not asked for any financial support. Because you have other children to support, we decided against any such request."

He wanted to interrupt her, but she held up her hand. "Let me finish." Her voice sounded severe, "Do you still believe that Christine is better protected in your workshop or in a circus and better prepared for life than here, with us? If that's your opinion, then please, in God's name, take her, All I can say is that it is regrettable." Franz stood up angrily, "You've spoken long enough. I'll wait outside for her."

He was obviously aggravated and said to Sivacek, "She almost got me where she wanted me. It wouldn't have taken much more and I would have left Christine there," then he grinned and went on, "She can talk! I could use her to write my speeches for the Communist party then the majority of the people would come over to our side." Sivacek said, "Communism! We've got that in Yugoslavia. Then I could go home right now. No, I don't need that." "That's because you don't understand anything about it.

You should come to one of our meetings. Then you'll learn what is meant by Communism. You've got no idea what you're talking about."

Sivacek just laughed, shook his head and went to the car. Right here, in front of a convent he was confronted, for the first time, with the hard headedness of someone who so firmly believed in Communism. Or, Sivacek thought, does he think he's better than me because of the way he thinks? Oh my God, I'll have to watch out with him, or else we'll get into a real conflict.

Then Christine appeared with Sister Zitta looking like a real angel. "Have courage, Christine. Maybe God is testing you. Every evening, look up to the stars, then we'll pray together and everything will turn out right." She gave her a gentle push and remained standing at the tops of the steps. Christine pressed her lips together, turned round once more, before she got into the car and waved at Sister Zitta. She stood in front of the great entrance door and waved until she could not see the car. Sivacek saw, in his rear-view mirror that Christine was fighting against her tears and looking sadly out of the window. He was very sorry for her. He promised himself that he would try to support her a little and, if possible, help her somehow.

Back home, Christine had to share a bed with Hanni, one of the two remaining housemaids who had not yet been sacked, until a different solution could be found in the next few days.

In the middle of the night Christine realised that Hanni had put a chair out of the window and that someone had climbed into the room. She heard a man's voice ask, "Is she asleep?" and she thought she recognised Emer's voice. "Yes," the girl answered "we can put her in Reinhard's bed." Reihard was sleeping at the other end of the same room.

Christine pretended to sleep, but strained, with half open eyes, to see what was going on. The man took her in his arms. Hanni showed the way over the floor with a hand torch. Reinhard must have heard something, because he was lying in bed close to the wall. It was not long before you could hear both of them grunting quietly. Suddenly Reinhard shook himself. Had he also got an erection? Christine moved further away and was now lying on the edge of the bed. Reinhard coughed on purpose and turned himself against the wall. The man stood up and carried Christine back into the bed, which was now empty. Where was Hanni? Then he left through the window and closed the shutters from outside. Christine spread herself out on the bed and was soon asleep. She did not wake up until midday and was amazed that no one had woken her and called her to go to work. She was alone in the house. Hanni was taking the midday meal into the workshop and already put out a plate for Christine.

Christine had only just got dressed and done her hair when someone started knocking loudly on the door and then the window. She opened the door. Walter, the second son of Willi and Aloisia jumped back and Luise, father's divorced wife stood in front of her. "Please come quickly. Walter heard that something bad had happened to his mother. I don't want to go there alone." Christine said, "Come on. We'll go together. There's no one else here." They ran down the street to Willi and Aloisia's flat.

A car stopped. It was Sivacek. "I didn't see you in the workshop," he said to Christine. "Come with us," she called to him, "We've heard that something has happened to Aloisia; something bad."

Sivacek drove on, parked his car in the courtyard and ran up to the first floor. He did not knock, but opened the door and looked around the kitchen. Franzli, the youngest was crouching in a corner. He heard noises from the bedroom. The door was not fully closed. "Is anyone there?" Sivacek asked and wanted to open the door. At first he saw the shoes and then the legs. It was Aloisia. In the silence behind the door he heard Willi's voice. "I cut her down from the cord." Sivacek saw what had happened. Aloisia's tongue was hanging out, her eyes were contorted, Sivacek tried to loosen the cord and while he was bumping her chest to try to bring her back to life, he shouted "Bring a doctor and the police." But his efforts were in vain. He closed her eyes and covered her tongue with a handkerchief. He took out a pencil and made a few marks around her body on the floor and he said to Willi, who was sitting on the sofa in the kitchen, "Come. We'll lay her on the bed." Willi hesitated at first and then they lifted her onto the bed, which was close to the window. A neighbour reacted quickly and called a doctor and the police who came immediately. Luise took care of the children. She was afraid of looking at her dead daughter. The neighbour took her into her flat until the investigation was over.

Two of the four children were still in school. Through the window Christine saw straight into Aloisia's face and how the doctor examined her and looked into her eyes. The cord had been loosened, but was still round her throat. Her tongue was hanging out of the side of her mouth. A policeman looked at the door knob from which Aloisia had apparently hanged herself. An other policeman made a note of the details, made some sketches and measurements. Two short marks made by Aloisia's rubber soles were critically examined. The knot on the noose did not look exactly as though she had made it herself. Willi sat upright on a chair and answered every question. He had been lying on the sofa in the kitchen and did not notice that something was happening. The children were playing in the courtyard. When he wanted his lunch to be served, he had called his wife. He thought she was holding the door closed from the inside, and he pushed it. When he saw his wife hanging from the doorknob he got a knife right away and cut through the cord. Walter arrived and Willi was sent him straight away to Aloisia's mother. He had to tell her that something bad had happened to his mother. She should come right away. That was Willi's statement. Later the children could not tell the police anything else. But Franzli said, "My dad beat my mother until she was kaputt. She was often kaputt. But then everything was all right again." Walter wanted to know if they were going to lock his father up, so that he could not hit his mother any more. The older children were told what had happened. Out of breath they arrived just as their mother, covered, was being put in the ambulance. Alisa snatched the sheet from her mother's head. Her face was lying to one side, half covered by her hair; her tongue was still hanging out a little between her teeth; her eyes were half open. Alisa had a terrible shock and started to scream. Wilhelm started to hit his father wildly. The he looked up to the sky and collapsed. Both of them were put into the doctor's car and taken to the hospital. They stayed there and were cared for by the doctors until the day of the funeral.

Sivacek drove straight to Franz in the workshop and took him to one side. Franz was totally bewildered, "What's the matter?" Sivacek: "Your daughter, Aloisia has taken her own life or has been murdered. No one knows exactly what has happened. I'll drive you to the police station where Willi is being interviewed.

They've already taken Aloisia away. Come on. Get your jacket." Emer wanted to know what it was all about and ran after them. Sivacek told him, briefly what had happened. Emer said, "The swine! She told me that he would one day beat her to death. I warned him. I told him, I'll beat you to a pulp if you lay a finger on her again. And now he's pulled a cord round her neck." He cried in anger and grief. "Be careful what you say." Sivacek said, Willi is saying that she hanged herself on the door knob." He leapt into the car and drove off. Franz sat next to him and said not a word.

At the police station they interviewed Sivacek and he described what he had seen. "The scuff marks up to the door..., the knots used... that Willi was lying on the bench in the kitchen and had heard nothing; that the two small children were alone in the courtyard. That doesn't sound like a mother committing suicide." He looked at the policeman, "Or does it?" he asked. Franz, who was now trembling listened and was asked repeatedly what he thought. He let out a brief cry and held his well worn hands in front of his face. "You can go now," the policeman said, "if we need you again we'll come to you or send someone for you." Then he gave Franz his hand, "My deepest condolences, Mr. Remi. We understand your incomprehensible shock and pain. We'll do our best to clear up the case." He opened the door and they both went out. Since Franz had not said a word, Sivacek drove him home. Hanni was there and Christine was sitting with a tear streaked face. Sivacek said to Christine, "I think what your father needs now is a strong Cognac, and I could do with one too." Hanni: "We've only got slivovitz." She fetched two spirit glasses and poured the plum brandy into them. Christine's food was standing untouched on the stove. "Father, did you have something for lunch?" He shook his head. "Hanni, is there also something for Mr. Sivacek?" Franz looked at the plate in front of him and said, "I can't eat all that. Half of it is enough. Come on, Sivacek you can at least eat the other half." Hanni looked at Christine. It was her plate which was being divided. Christine said, Come on, Hanni. Here's another plate." While Hanni served the two men, Christine went into the adjoining room. Hanni brought her bread and a glass of cold milk which she took gratefully.

According to the police report and the doctor's assessment nothing could be proved against Willi. Franz went to the police again, but was told that because there was no proof, Willi could not be held. There had already been suicides committed in this way, even if such cases were very rare, "It was him! I'm telling you," Franz insisted, "he had often beaten her, but I've only found out about it now." The policeman: "If you think that every man who beats his wife becomes a murderer, then more than three quarters of our women would be lying in the cemetery, believe me. Mr. Remi, I beg you not to burden your grandchildren and your whole family with such statements. Everyone can think what they want, but marking your son-in-law, without any proof, as the murderer of your daughter, well that's character assassination and that is a punishable offence. I know that it would be easier for the family to have a culprit behind bars, but in this case the conclusion will be suicide, even though the case is not completely clear."

The day of the funeral came. Franz and Luise's oldest child, Franzi, came from Vienna. He was in the process of leaving Vienna when he heard about his sister's death. He wanted to try his luck in Vorarlberg, because he could then cross the border into Germany and earn more money. Franz did not go to the funeral and did not let anyone from his current family go. Later he heard how dramatic it had been, when the children saw their much loved mother's coffin being lowered into the grave. Alisa started to scream in despair and wanted to drag it out. At the last moment Franzi managed to hold her back, otherwise she would have fallen on the coffin. Willi clenched his teeth. What thoughts were going through his head? The mourners looked at him as the muscles in his face twitched.

After the funeral Franzi went to Willi. He wanted to hear what he had to say. The children clung to Franzi and wanted to go with him. They did not want to stay with their father. They were afraid he might kill them as well. He wondered if he should take Wilhelm, Walter and Alisa with him to Vorarlberg. Fransli would stay with his father. Franzi telephoned his wife in Vienna, but he already knew she would not agree. She did not want to leave Vienna and her friends. Her answer was that she would rather be divorced. From the beginning it had been a very open marriage, which Franzi now wanted to end. He was in contact with a former field hospital nursing aid and he sent an express letter to her asking if she could imagine living with him. Soon after he got a telegram:

> FINALLY stop ON MY WAY TO YOU stop
> I LOVE YOU stop WILMA

Franzi told his father what he planned to do. He asked for the money which he had once lent to Josefine before he had gone to Vienna. Franz knew nothing about this and called her. "What money?" she said, "I have never had money from you." Franzi's nerves were at an end after all that had happened in the past few days. "I'm not going to argue. Give me back my money," he demanded. Josefine shouted, "What are you talking about! He comes here and has the cheek to tell me that I owe him money. I don't remember anything." Franzi boiled over with anger and hit her in the face. Her topknot released. Franz wanted to hit him, but Josefine came between them. "Stop it!" she screamed and called for Emer. "Emer, give Franzi his money back." Emer asked how much it was and gave Franzi the amount and a little extra. He took the money and left the workshop without a word.

Christine sat in front of Luise's door. Wilhelm, who was the same age as her and Walter joined her. "We can go with Uncle Franzi to Vorarlberg, We're just waiting until Wilma comes and then we're leaving." They were living in a confined space with their grandmother Luise. Wilhelm was sad, "Tomorrow we're going to go to the cemetery again." Christine: "I'll come with you, then I can also visit Fredi's grave. Nobody else goes there." Franzi came through the park. "Hello, Christine. How are you?" "I'd like to come with you to the cemetery. Father didn't let us go to the funeral. What time are you going?" "Let's say about nine. Erwin is coming as well. We'll meet at the bridge."

Alisa was very tired. She just wanted to sleep. Franzi borrowed Reinhard's bike. He put Alisa on the luggage rack, took Franzli on the cross bar and pushed them to the cemetery. Franzi had prepared Alisa for the visit, "Listen to me! Where ever you go your mother will accompany you behind a cloud in the sky, and wave to you by the stars at night; warm you with the sun and knock on your window with rain drops." Walter added, "I know the last words. They're from a love song which is often played on the radio." Franzi went on. "You know that we must all die sooner or later. Now we're going to visit your mummy's resting place before we leave. Then we're going to go 100, 200, 300, no a thousand kilometres a long way from here and we'll start a new life together. We'll stick together and then for sure we'll finally find happiness." He wiped his face with his hand and looked up at the clouds.

There was a candle burning on Aloisia's grave and the flowers were still fresh. Christine added two candles and let Franzli and Alisa light them. After a while they visited Fredi's grave. The cross was rotten and had fallen down. Christine took the stump which was still in the ground out. Erwin found a shovel and planted the short, upper part again. They all removed the weeds which had grown over the grave and just left the green ivy.

Many years later Christine visited her half brother Franzi and his wife Wilma in Vorarlberg. She also met Wilhelm and Walter. They were both doing well. They were upstanding, good looking and loved their new home town. Alisa was happily married and lived close by in Germany, but she went only rarely to Vordersberg. Franzli stayed with his grandmother.

Shortly after his wife Aloisia's death Willi brought a pretty blonde home. Most of the people in the town did not give him the time of day and whispered behind his back whenever he was seen with his 'new one'. He had one heart attack after another and after the third all help was too late. His blonde did not stay for the funeral, but before she left, she looked for Franzli and gave him, crying, the key to the flat. Willi was not buried in his wife's grave. The priest in charge did not want the surviving dependants, because at the time he had refused to give Aloisia the last blessing. According to his belief, since she had committed suicide she had committed a deadly sin.

Luise, Franzli and Reinhard went to the cemetery. They were able to watch the funeral from Aloisia's grave, but, at first, they did not want to be any closer. There were only a few people there. Luise couldn't leave it like that and she persuaded the other two to take part in the funeral. "We still don't know what really happened. How it got to such a point. The truth is buried in the graves. It started with a deep seated love and for years everything went well. We have to forgive whatever happened. Otherwise I can't go on living."

She took hold of both of them and dragged them to the graveside.

Emer got an engagement with Circus Althof in Germany to work with a really great artiste. They became interested in him because he was the seventh best floor acrobat in Austria. He decided to work with them for one season. His partner had superb new ideas which they were able to work out and it did not take long before photographs of them started to appear in the German and Austrian press. Everything went well until just before the end of the season when his partner died suddenly.

Emer came home and wrote many applications to various circuses. Finally he got an engagement with the Rotondo Circus, which he accepted.

It started in spring. Against her will Christine had to go with them to look after Rosita and Isabella and take care of the household. Christine, Emer, Rosita and Isabella had worked out an acceptable acrobatic routine. The girls started in a new, unknown world in a large caravan, of which the half was for their use.

The compartment had two wide beds on the dividing wall. Next to the door there was a two flame gas cooker on the kitchen cupboard. Under the window there was a folding table and two folding chairs. On the wall overhead there was a row of small cupboards. Everything they had brought with them was put away carefully. Franz had sent them off with a jute sack full of pre-stamped leather parts, studs, hammers and an iron plate. His idea was that while they were away they could assemble bags.

When they stopped in Graz, Christine saw her old school friend Adelheid, who was at a college there, standing staring with wide open eyes. "Hello!" Christine shouted and waved at her out of the window. "I must be going crazy! Is it really you, Christine in the circus with your sisters? What are you doing? Can I come with you, or must you be able to do something special?" she called excitedly. "I didn't want to take part," Christine said and wiped a few tears from her eyes, "but without me my father wouldn't let the others go. I'd much rather be in school." "Christine, you're crazy! You're free. You can travel; see other towns, away from this everyday routine. I'd love to swap places with you. My father could stop working double shifts for this stupid school, which I hate." The caravan jerked and drove on. "The world is so unfair," she shouted, "I'll come to a performance. Bye! Bye!" They waved at each other. Christine lay down on the bed and slept for a while.

Emer came in, "Come on. Put on your costume. We've got a dress rehearsal and our first performance in front of the audience is at seven thirty. Put your second costume on the bed. It'll be a quick change. Here is some powder, an eyebrow pencil and lipstick. Put your hair into a pony tail. Don't' forget the large bows for Rosita and Isabella. It must sit firmly on their heads." Christine had a flashy green and pink swimsuit with foam breasts sewn into it. Rosita and Isabella had sparkling red skirts, short embroidered tops and tight flounced pants. Emer put a lot of make-up on them. Afterwards Christine did not want to look in the mirror. With such flashy make-up she felt like another person and in actual fact, that made it easier for her to go into the ring.

Dress rehearsal. They waited for their entrance behind a large curtain. They went through their routine in their heads. "Don't look at the audience. If you do, then look at the last row, so that you always hold your heads high." The props which Emer had requested were carried into the tent. When he heard his name announced he strode proudly into the arena. Christine with Rosita and Isabella behind him. Emer bowed and went with them to the apparatus. "Stop! Stop!" he heard over the microphone, "whenever possible, don't turn your back to the audience. You only bow after the act. OK, start again." Then Emer somersaulted into the middle of the ring and grinning, held up his hands." "Bravo!" shouted the Ring Master. Emer raised the girls on a special chair with hands and feet into the air and spun them round. The other artistes applauded.

The floor gymnastics were interwoven. After the interval the ring and the rope was let down into the arena. Christine turned herself on the hook which Emer had in his mouth and made her figures while he was making a handstand on the ring. The ring was lowered and he wrapped Christine round his hips and then the ring was pulled up again. In this fashion he completed his act with the ring. That was always very exciting for the audience. Finally Christine slid down a long sheet and Emer made his elegant descent on the rope. The applause from their colleagues was frenetic. The circus directrix was very pleased with their act and shook their hands.

Make something to eat. If there was time, rest for a while. There was little time to rest, because on Wednesdays, Saturdays and Sundays there were also afternoon shows. In the meantime they trained; polishing the act, Emer called it. Every morning she had to bring fresh water in buckets; make sure the cooking gas did not run out; get petrol for the lamps; shop almost every day, because there was no fridge. Every two or three days she had to do the washing by hand and help to erect and dismount the tent; send Rosita and Isabella and the other children to school and finally help them with their homework. Emer knew how to break into the public electricity supply, so they could iron their clothes and, when it was hot, use a fan. They went from one town to another, but saw very little. That was the 'romantic, interesting life in the circus! Which so many envied!

The direction told everyone in the circus to make sure that no strangers came near the caravans or the installations. That was often very difficult. In every place there were always a few girls hanging around the male employees. Emer encouraged them by flexing his muscles and took every opportunity to kiss them on the lips. Christine also had her followers, but if Emer noticed that someone was getting too close, he shouted "Close the door!" He hated it when she did not remove her make-up right after the performance. He said, right away, "Get that stuff off."

Emer could not manage money. Luckily he did not like alcohol or cigarettes. When he went shopping he normally bought too much of the same things. When he wanted to eat he preferred to go alone to a restaurant. He had a healthy appetite and began to put on weight. He started to sweat more and more during the act and his costume was almost ready to burst.

He was always looking for something new together with other artistes and for that he spent a lot of money. All he said was, "Christine will have to make a few shopping bags in her spare time. Then they can be traded for food in the shops and they can sell the bags to their customers. I haven't got any more money and I'm not going to ask for an advance, otherwise people will think I'm a poor so-and-so." Christine decided that the next time they were paid she would ask Emer for housekeeping money for the whole week. Up to now she had kept account of what she had received and spent. So she knew how much money she needed. Emer was not at all pleased, but Christine insisted. She wanted to get together enough for tickets to go home and she had already hidden a few bank notes in the lining of her red rain hat.

She finished three bags, went to the nearest shop and asked if they were interested in the goods and if they would be prepared to pay half in food and half in cash. At first they were suspicious; asked where she came from and where she had got the bags. Very politely she told them about her home and the circus. She kept telling them what she needed and how much the bags would cost. She bargained until both parties were happy and did not forget to give them the address of the workshop in Vordersberg in case they wanted to order some more. She also said that they should visit the circus and they said, "You're very smart. Is that what you learn in the circus?" "Actually, I never wanted to be in the circus. I wanted to continue in school, but my father had other ideas.

He said there was no point in girls being educated because they always get married, so it's a waste of money and time." "Wait, I'll give you a few sweets. God bless you. My husband and I'll bring our grandchildren to the performance on Sunday afternoon. They'll be really pleased."

Christine had to put down her full shopping bags a few times and a young man with his foot in plaster spoke to her. "Hi! Aren't you the girl in the ring? I was sitting in the first row. I liked you a lot – I mean I still like you a lot." He laughed. She looked at him and thought, he›s good looking and from the way he is behaving, I think he knows it too. "Thank you for the compliment," she said "what happened to your foot?" "Broken. Next week I have to go back to boarding school. How long are you here? I'd like to invite you for an ice or something. How about right now? Look, there's an ice cream man over there. Come on. I can carry one of your bags to the bench over there. Then I'll get the ices." Then he grabbed one of the bags and, with the other hand supported himself on his stick. Christine followed him and sat down on the bench. "I'm Rudi, and you?" "Christine." "Christina! Christina! What a romantic name and what a beautiful young woman. What sort of ice do you want? Vanilla would suit you. I'll be right back." Rudi turned on one leg and waved his stick in the air. He was back soon and stood in front of her, smiling and with an ice. "Thank you." Rudi: "Mmm, it tastes good. Do you know the vanilla flower? Small white and pink flowers, which smell wonderful. From now on I'll only eat vanilla ice. Then I can close my eyes and think of you and stay cool." He took her hand and held it tight. "May I?" She felt a cold kiss on her cheek. "Oh! Your lips are cold. You are overwhelming me with your behaviour. Please move a little further away." "A little? Oh, how sweet. So that means not totally rejected?" He looked at her impishly and raised an eyebrow. "Watch out, your ice is dripping." She thought he was very amusing. What a pity that we won't see each other again. They took out their handkerchiefs and wiped their fingers and then their mouths. Rudi: Come on, let's exchange them. Then we'll have some thing to remind us of each other." Slowly he took her handkerchief and gave her his and looked deep into her eyes.. The he kissed the tips of her fingers. Christine felt warmth flowing through her body. "But now I have to go," she said, "I can carry that by myself. Thank you and goodbye." She picked up the shopping bags and ran off. Rudi stayed sitting there. Christine's heart was beating fast and she was happy that no one was in the caravan. She quickly put the money inside the lining of her rain hat and unpacked the food which she had brought back. She had bought quite a lot of preserves which would last for some time. In this way she had made amble provision for their needs.

That same evening she saw Rudi outside the circus tent. He gave her a sign that she should go round the outside of the tent, "Christina, please come later after your performance. Promise me that you'll come. I have to see you. I have something important to tell you. Please!" His eyes begged so much that she could not resist. "I'll be there. I promise." She put her hand on her heart and Rudi did the same. Then she went back.

The evening was muggy. Christine's hands were moist. She could hardly rub them dry. That was dangerous for the performance. The trapeze artistes wanted to have a safety net. The directrix promised to get one tomorrow. "Today, just be careful. Please don't take any risks. Just leave something out rather than let something happen. As far as I'm concerned tomorrow you can fall into the net like dead flies," she joked. When Christine was hanging around Emer's waist, she had problems keeping hold of him with her slippery hands. "Stop," she called. Emer reacted immediately and was able to catch her. The audience held its breath and the applauded loudly.

Applause was the nicest thing about the circus. When the applause was enthusiastic, you forget everything going on in the world; you felt happy as if you were floating on a cloud. It was a really great feeling. Emer collected his props together. Christine ran round the tent to Rudi. She almost tripped over a tent rope. Her foot hurt, but she gave it no thought and ran on. "Christina," she heard Rudi call softly. It was very dark. "Christina," he whispered and took her in his arms. "You wanted to say something important," she whispered back. "Yes. That I like you. That I love you," he said, hoarsely. When my foot is out of plaster I'm going to come and work in the circus so that I'm always close to you." He kissed her again and again on the cheek. Then she interrupted his kisses, "Listen to me. I've also got something important to tell you. It was not my idea to join the circus. I was in a very good convent school. However, my father did not agree and he took me out of there. Back home I have to do heavy work and I'm still doing it. I don't want to tell you about all the things I have to do every day, but one day I'll go back to school. Please, go back to the boarding school. We can stay in contact and write to each other. You can send me letters 'poste restante'. I'll inform you early enough in every letter, where to post yours. You must do that. Do you hear? Because I think I love you as well. You're such a crazy guy; I really like you, really Rudi ...Oh! How I like you. She put her arms around him. He spelt out his name into her ear and she did the same. Then they kissed each warmly. "You're wonderful. Do you sometimes do crazy things?" "No. I have to go otherwise my brother will come looking for me." "We'll meet here again tomorrow. I have to see you tomorrow, otherwise I'll die." He kissed her. "Don't say stupid things. I'll be here tomorrow." She pulled herself out of his embrace and ran to the artistes' entrance. A Moroccan wearing a red uniform pointed to a mirror which was standing in the entrance. She looked in it and was shocked to see that her whole face was smeared with make-up. She put her hands in front of her face and went to the caravan. Emer was not there and Rosita and Isabella were already in bed. The petrol lamp was turned down to a minimum. The make-up removal cream was still standing open. Then she washed her face with cold water and then climbed into bed, as always, at the end of her sisters' bed. Today there was no fan and it was still muggy. It stank of leather. Father had sent a sack full of leather by rail. Emer must have asked for it. Then he came into the caravan, took off all his clothes, washed himself all over, cleaned his teeth well and wiped the droops of water off the floor. He lay down naked on his bed and put out the light. Christine lay as if she was sleeping and prayed that the five weeks would soon be over. She took Rudi's handkerchief from under her pillow and held it in front of her nose and mouth. Then she heard Emer say, "Come on. Rosita, it must be really hot up there for the three of you without a fan. You can sleep next to me." He laid her on the bed. She was only wearing her pants and Emer was still naked. Christine had a really bad feeling about it. She remembered the train journey and she could not sleep at all. She got out of bed to get a drink of water and said, "Rosita, you can sleep in my place." "I'll sleep here," was her answer. Emer did not stir. Christine pulled his underpants from under his clothes and threw them in his face. "Put them on." He did not do it immediately, so she kicked him with her injured foot, "Ow!" "What's wrong?" he asked and pulled on his underpants, "have you hurt yourself?" She did not answer and they both got back in their beds.

Such things happened a few times. Rosita often kissed her on the mouth. Christine told her that one did not do that. "But I do it in the ring." "I'll tell Emer that in future he should only kiss you on the cheek. Don't let him kiss you on the lips again." Rosita looked at her sister as if in a dream, "If you want to say something to me, then say it. Has he …." Christine said, "Listen, if he or anybody else touches you down there, then scream. No one should touch you there. That belongs to you and to you alone. Anyone who touches as minor goes to prison and we don't want this shame to come on our family, so no one touches us. Have you understood? Rosita, you must never again sleep on the lower bed. You cannot sleep next to your half brother. Mother would be really upset about it." Isabella said, cheekily, "We shouldn't call him half brother. Father told us that. Mother explained everything. You don't need to explain it again." Christine said "Well then, don't forget." Isabella asked, "Who says we've forgotten?" Christine would have liked to pack up everything and take both of them home. The responsibility was a heavy burden on her shoulders and she had no one to talk to. So she fell back to her work and both the girls helped her. After the midday meal they lay down under a tree next to the caravan and rested. After the next performance while Emer was bathing in the applause, Christine took both the girls by the hand and led them out of the ring, thus avoiding the kissing scene. Emer did not trust himself to say anything. He knew what was bothering Christine. In the act after the interval when only Emer and Christine were in the ring, she allowed him to kiss her on the cheek and then wiped the kiss off. The audience thought that was amusing, clapped their hands and laughed. Even the other artistes behind the curtain clapped and shouted "Bravo, Christine!" behind her. As soon as she left the tent she went to look for Rudi. This time she had not put on such heavy make-up and she wiped her lipstick off on a cloth. She looked around but could see no one. Someone stuck his head threw a gap in the circus tent. "Rudi?" she asked. It was Rudi. "Why did the people laugh? I didn't see a clown." "The clown is standing in front of you," she joked. He kissed her on the throat. "I've brought you something. Sweets for my sweetie," he said and gave her a pretty box of chocolates. "Thank you, Rudi, that's very nice of you. Hey. I'm sorry you got make-up on your face from me last night. Was it bad?" "You little witch. You did that on purpose, didn't you? For that I'm going to get a thousand kisses. Let's start right now, otherwise we won't be finished today." "Let's save a few for morning," she murmured between their close pressed lips. "Tomorrow! Darling, tomorrow you'll get a letter at the post office which I wrote to you today." "Why didn't you bring it with you?" "I think it's more exciting to send a letter 'poste restante'. I've never done that before. From next week you can write to me at this address, but I've left my name off, just in case." "Rudi, we're leaving tomorrow and tomorrow is already next week." "Yes, Christina." "It's Christine with an 'e' at the end." "For me you will always be Christina!!! Basta!!!!." "And for me you are Rrrrrudi." "I like it when you roll my 'r'," he joked. They stayed together and kissed until they heard the final of the performance. Rudi let some light fall on her face through the gap in the tent. She pulled him closer so that she could see his face. They looked into each other's eyes, deeply and seriously. Rudi said, "Please, please write to me. Have you got a photo for me?" "I'll send you one. Can you give me one of you?" "Do you want two photos of me?" "Why? What? Oh! Is there one in the box of chocolates?" "No." "Ah! It's in the letter, which you have sent to me. I'll collect that tomorrow as soon as the post office opens. Come, give me one more kiss. I love you." He gave her a kiss and then, with heavy hearts they parted.

The next day she went to the post office, "Do you have proof of identity, Miss?" "No, I've nothing with me." Her heart started to race. "That's all right. I've seen you in the circus. Letters to the circus are almost always 'poste restante'. But next time you have to bring an identity card with you, otherwise one could collect post addressed to other people." Christine sat down on the nearest bench and read the loving lines from Rudi several times. The photo was in the envelope. He was sitting on a gilded, high backed chair wearing a dark suit with a blue shirt and diagonally striped tie. He looked older and more decisive than he did face to face. On the back of the photo he had written, "See you soon, darling. Your Rudi" Who are his parents, she asked herself. The writing paper was not exactly cheap. As agreed there was no address on the envelope. They went on writing letters to each other and it worked well. Even when she was only able to write a few lines Rudi was happy.

They installed a safety net in the circus tent. After that Emer and Christine had to change their act, because up to now most of what they did had taken place on the ground. They had to practise. Falling into the net had to be safe, but must look good. It was still hot and humid. The sweat came out of all their pores.

Emer had damp hands and Christine also had to keep wiping the sweat from her arms.

The evening performance started. Emer used a large amount of talcum powder and pulled on his costume which was stretched to the limit, because he had gained weight. So the inevitable happened. Emer made the splits, pushing two chairs away from each other. Christine was posing next to him when she suddenly saw Emer's testicles suddenly emerging between his legs. She jumped forward in her pose and whispered to him what had happened, but he was not about to stop the act. The circus people standing next to the curtains, having seen what took place, sent a clown with a red scarf into the ring, who with a lot of noise and clowning drew attention away from Emer and as quick as lightning wrapped the red scarf around his waist.

Christine remembered that even in Vordersberg people had remarked about his scandalous swimming trunks. When he practised his gymnastics the children standing around giggled and when he saw the pool attendant or adults approaching, he slowly packed up his things and left the pool area.

One time Christine told her parents, because she was ashamed, but they said he had certainly not done it on purpose, and, for them, that was the end of it. The circus directrix called Emer after the performance. Something was in the air. Emer put on a different costume and after the interval went, nervously, with Christine for the second acrobatic number into the ring. For the first time he forgot to take his beloved sweat cloth with him, which, even when it was not muggy, he used to 'span out the time,' as he put it. So he wiped his hands on his costume and, clowning, Christine copied him and the audience laughed. He gripped her hard under the arms and Christine knew that he did not like it. When she was hanging from his mouth piece, Christine could feel his sweat falling on her head and body. Nervously he wrapped her round his waist and let himself be carried up with the ring. Suddenly she felt that his sweaty hands could not hold her ankles. She slipped down and fell, thank God, into the net, but her upper thighs caught the taut edge of the net. The crowd cried,"Oohh!" Then she made an exquisite roll out off the net, pointed to Emer up above and the audience clapped with relief. Nothing bad had happened, but she had a very large bruise. Even though she put raw meat and cold vinegar cloths on it immediately her upper thigh went all the colours of the rainbow.

At one point, the circus was in a place where there was thermal spring water. Christine used the water for cooking the midday meal. She had no idea what was in the spring water. She did not know that, even when boiled the water was unpalatable. A young police cadet had seen her and told her where she could get drinking water. He stayed around the circus all day. It was the weekend and he had nothing else to do. He came to the performance in the afternoon and in the evening; clapped the loudest and longest. In the evening other police cadets came and threw sweets and flowers into the ring. The clown went into the ring, collected everything and later gave it to Christine. On Sunday the police cadet came again and in the morning met her at the fountain. He wanted to know where she would be going at the end of the season and if he could meet her. He had found out her family name and he even knew how old she was. His name was Michael, but people called him Michi. Could he call her Tini? Christine did not care what he called her. She had absolutely no interest in getting to know him, but she was polite. "You're a real detective," she said, "you know so much about me and you still want to know more." He looked at her with his beautiful blue eyes, "I find you very attractive. May I use the familiar form? I'd like to meet you somewhere else." "That's not possible. My brother would never allow it. Circus people have to take care of their reputation."

Michi carried the brimming water bucket to the caravan. Suddenly he was in a rush, "I have to go to church. I'll come back later." She was happy that he left. She was overcome with a strong longing for Rudi. She took his last letter out of her rain hat and pressed it to her heart, looked for his handkerchief and lost a few tears on it. Someone knocked on the door, "Christine," Vera called. She was the person who looked after the children and Christine opened the door. "Isabella, Rosita and the other children have gone off with Emer to hang out placards. They won't be back until after midday, so you only have to cook for yourself. Or, what are you going to do in the meantime? Do you know what, that gives us a chance to take a look at the town and then eat lunch somewhere." Christine was very keen. "Oh, yes!" she said, "I'll just make myself presentable and we'll meet at the exit in ten minutes." She closed the door, kissed Rudi's letter and hid it back in her rain hat; took some money out of it and hid it in her skirt.

The two girls met at the exit. Both of them were overjoyed to get away from the circus and to have a look at the small town and they soon noticed that the people were looking at them as they passed by. The youths made comments. They were very amused. Vera was a little older than Christine and she smoked and drank in secret. They came to a tobacco shop which was open. Vera coloured her lips red and gave the lipstick to Christine. At first she did not want to use it. "Come on. We want to have fun. We'll get a few cigarettes and smoke one. You'll soon see that it's a real pleasure. OK, now let's go into the shop." They went up two steps, greeted the woman politely and asked for an unusual brand of cigarette, which the woman did not have. Then a different brand. But the woman in the shop refused to sell them any cigarettes. "You rascals. Do you really think that just because you've smeared some lipstick on you're going to get cigarettes from me? Get out, right now." She came from behind the counter and went on scolding. Christine turned away and wiped the lipstick off her lips with the back of her skirt. Vera took her time. "Then I'll buy my cigarettes somewhere else," she snapped. "What a stupid cow! In Vienna I could buy cigarettes everywhere," she said to Christine and then, quietly, "and even very special ones."

A young man came towards them. Vera spoke to him, "Hello, young man, may I ask you for a light?" Then she fumbled in her bag and said, "Oh, no! I've forgotten my cigarettes." She took some money out of her bag. "Would you be so good and go and buy some for me. I think the shop over there is open." She pressed the money into his hand and gave him the name of a brand. "Well, all right," the young man said. "We'll wait here," Vera whispered and gave him a provocative look and a little shove. He came back quickly, gave her the cigarettes and the change. "And now what are you ladies going to do?" Vera said, "We want to go somewhere to eat and drink a glass of good wine. You can come with is if you want." "I'll be happy to drink a glass of wine with you, but I'm going to eat with my parents. I'm just here on a visit. On the edge of town there's a very nice garden restaurant. Would that be all right?" "OK." He placed his arms so that they could take them. Vera was not shy and took his arm. Christine thanked him, but said she would walk alongside them.

It was a very pleasant garden. The waitress kept saying "please, thank you". It was very enjoyable. Schandor, that was the young man's name, ordered for each of them an eighth of the red house wine and then another eighth. The wine was sweet. It was called Bull's Blood. They were recommended to order "Wiener Schnitzel" with potato salad dressed with pumpkin oil. Schandor was a very funny man; he told a lot of jokes and pulled Vera towards him. They constantly whispered in each other's ears and laughed. Schandor said, "Excuse us, Christine, but we're only whispering dirty stories to each other." Vera said, "That's not true. How can you say something like that? From now on there'll be no more whispering. Understand?" All three laughed and were happy. They talked about the circus and he told them about his work in Vienna.

"I'll come to the afternoon performance. Where should I sit so that I can chat with you?" "While Christine is doing her act, no body chats." Vera told him where to sit and said, "And don't come without flowers for both of us, even if you have to pick them from your parent's garden. You must bring flowers. You can throw Christine's in the ring and I know how I can get my bouquet." She grinned. "Oh, you are so lovely and think of every one." The "Wiener Schnitzel" were served. They were so big that they hung over the edge of the plate. Christine clapped her hands together, "Oh my God! In my whole life I have never seen such large Schnitzel." Schandor: I'll go inside and pay. Enjoy your meal. I have to go to my parents, they're certainly waiting for me and I'm hungry. Goodbye to both of you. See you later." He kissed both of them on the cheek.

Vera asked, "Can you eat that? Even half of it is too much for me." "For me too." Vera stood up and came back with a newspaper . "Come on. We'll pack one for your sisters or for you later. They divided one of the Schnitzels and ate it eagerly. Christine called the waitress to pay. "Everything has been already paid by the man you were with and you also a coffee and cake, please, thank you. "With the best will in the world I can't drink a coffee and certainly not eat any cake. What do you think, Vera?" "I can't either, but could we get the money back?" "Of course, please, thank you." The waitress brought them the money. Vera divided it and lit another cigarette." "Come on. Smoke one." "Yes, maybe another time. I'm sure to feel sick. Don't forget that I have to perform in front of our admirer. Oh, no. I'll leave him for you. I already have a secret love, but I'm not going to tell you who he is now. He's certainly not someone you know." Vera said, "Hey! I wouldn't have thought that of you. That stays with us. It's good to have secrets with someone. I think we'll be good friends." "I've got the same feeling," Christine said sceptically and wanted to know how Vera had suddenly acquired the expensive cigarette lighter. "I'm not going to tell you right now. Come on. We have to go." They hurried back to the circus.

Christine hid the money in her rain hat, put the cutlet into a pan, got ready for the afternoon performance and laid out the costumes for the others. Then she tried to do some stretching exercises, but her stomach was still too full and she also had wind, probably from the potato salad. This may not be that funny, she feared and laughed to herself a little shamefaced.

In the circus tent Vera showed her where Schandor would be sitting. He came early with two enormous bouquets, which he placed at his feet. The circus people wondered who was going to get them. Vera noticed that Schandor was very neatly dressed, gave him a secret wave and a radiant smile. He touched his fingers to his lips. As the performance started she crept to him. "You must give Christine the flowers after her second act, and when am I going to get mine?" Schandor: "You must know that today I am going to announce my engagement. My fiancée will come into the middle of the ring and she'll get a passionate kiss and, of course, the bouquet." He held out his hand in her direction. Vera was confused, "Oh! So that's how it is. That's why you're wearing such elegant clothes." Schandor took her hand, looked deep into her eyes and said, "Do you agree? Do you want to be my wife? That's not a joke. I'm totally serious. I'll ask you again – Do you want to be my wife?" "You're crazy. How can you give me such a shock?" She put her hands to her head. "We don't even know each other, but yes, I think I could go along with it. I mean, yes, we could give it a try." She hugged him, "I think I'm dreaming. If it's real pinch me." He pinched her on the hip. "Ow!" Schandor said, "It is true. Are you ready? Will you come when I call you?" Vera: "Yes, sure, of course I'll come."

She trusted him completely and went back into her caravan compartment. She took out an evening dress which she had not worn for a long time. The last time she had worn it was at her sister's wedding. She put up her hair and looked at her face in the mirror. She looked happy and radiant. Then the doubts started. What if he's just playing a joke on me? No! No!, she shook her head, he would not do that. He means it, even if he is completely mad.

She heard the music for Christine's entrance coming from the circus tent; took her shoes in her hand and ran barefoot through the entrance. Christine was just making an elegant somersault from the net and landed on the ground. Schandor was already standing on the edge of the ring. Christine saw him, took a couple of steps forward, bowed and held out her hand to Emer. Then Schandor came to her and gave her the flowers. She thanked him with a hug. The clown made fun of it, saw the second bouquet and asked if they were for him.

Schandor stood there and with determination said, "No. This is for my Vera. With these flowers I'm announcing our engagement. Vera, come to me!" He held out his arm towards her. Vera had butterflies in her stomach, stepped over the low barrier and they went towards each other. They embraced and kissed each other. The people stood up, applauded and shouted "Bravo!" Schandor took Vera on his arm turned her round once and carried her out of the ring.

From behind the curtains Emer said, "This bitch has stolen my show, with all the applause and everything. I work my fingers to the bone and this woman comes with her pimp and takes everything from me. That should not happen. That doesn't happen anywhere! I could have had her, but I have my pride."

The directrix was very pleased with the surprise addition. She congratulated the couple with loud applause. "That was a one off and very moving. I had to hold back my tears. It seems that only Christine knew something about it." Christine said nothing. She was as surprised as the others. She went to the engaged couple. "You're very elegant. Tell me; is it real or was it just an act?" Schandor said, "It's crazy, but it's serious. Vera, darling, tell her. I knew it from the first time I saw you. The circus is no place for you, Vera. Pack your things and come with me. Quickly, before the performance is over. Hurry up." Christine said, "I'm really happy for both of you. I wish you all the luck in the world. Schandor: "I'll give you my address so that you can visit us. Write to us wherever you are." "OK. Come on, Vera, I'll help you pack."

Vera changed into more comfortable clothes and stuffed her things into two bags. She said, "I think I'm going crazy. My parents threw me out of the house when I was a child and now a total stranger comes and picks me up lovingly. I must be dreaming! Or maybe not?" She started to cry. "Don't cry, Vera, pull yourself together. I know you can do this. Schandor is not a bad person. I'm sure of that, even though you have only just met. Come on now. He's waiting for you. We'll stay in contact and that's a promise. Write to me if you have problems. I'll try to help you as best I can." The two girls hugged each other. "Thank you. So much happiness all at once doesn't happen to everyone. I still haven't got my wages from last week." "Come, forget it. I'd like to go off with you. Go!" Schandor and Christine hugged each other as though they were old friends. Then the couple disappeared behind the large trees and Christine could no longer hold back her tears.

That was a day; we laughed and cried, she whispered to herself. She buried her face in the bouquet and went to the caravan. Just before she got there, she turned back, went to the artiste's entrance and gave the flowers to the directrix. "I'm sorry I couldn't give you the bouquet in the ring. I would have loved to have done that. Please take it." "Thank you, Christine. You should know that I love flowers. But these were for you." "But I want to give them to you. It's your birthday the day after tomorrow." "That's very nice of you. Many thanks." She gave Christine her hand and with a smile looked at the big, beautiful bouquet.

Christine heard Isabella and Rosita laughing and shouting. The were playing 'blind man's buff' with the other circus children. Emer was washing his hair in the caravan. "Please, can you bring me fresh water from the trough? I've already used what was here." Christine took the bucket and another water jug and went to the trough. When she had almost filled both, Michi crept up from behind and put his arms round her. She had not heard him coming because of the noise from the flowing water. She was so shocked that she wanted to cry out. He turned her round, pressed his mouth on her lips and tried to force his tongue between her tightly clenched teeth. She pinched him where she could and tried with all her energy to push him away with her knee. She could not breath and started to feel his tongue in her mouth. Her stomach rose, but he let go of her at the last minute. She choked and was disgusted "You idiot," she shouted. "But Tini, I love you. I just wanted to show how much I want you. Have I done something wrong? I'm sorry. Please forgive me."

Christine rinsed her mouth and did not listen to his griping. "Disappear! Get out of my way! Do you hear! Just get lost!". But he picked up the bucket and the jug full of water, carried them to the caravan and put them down. "I'm coming to the evening performance. I must see you. Don't be angry. I'll put everything right." Walking sideways, he sent her hand kisses and then disappeared.

Emer, with soapy hair, looked out to see where the water was and grabbed the jug. Christine fetched a hand towel and washed herself behind the caravan. Luckily, she thought, the tent will be taken down tonight and morning we shall be somewhere else.

Michi came to the evening performance and behaved outrageously, so that everyone noticed him. Even before the interval, when Emer, Isabella and Rosita were in the ring and Christine was arranging the props, he came to her and gave her flowers. He wanted to take her in his arms but she turned away and waving at the audience with the flowers, ran out of the ring. The audience laughed and Michi applauded franticly. Christine put the flowers on a small table behind the curtain and only then did she notice that there was a piece of paper attached to one of the roses. She undid the ribbon and withdrew the piece of paper. She had to change and prepare herself for her second act.

Emer came to her. "Now you've been given flowers twice. Watch out! The other broads will get jealous." He grinned and pressed a wet kiss on her cheek. "Yuk! Stop that!" She twisted her face and wiped it away. Emer went on grinning. Isabella and Rosita arrived. Each of them had a piece of cake. "It's the directrix's birthday," they shouted. "I know. I gave her Schandor's bouquet," Christine said. Emer:"Oh. So you gave your flowers to her. I wondered where they were." "If you want you can also give her this beautiful rose." She put the ribbon back on the stem, put the other flowers in a vase and placed the rose in his hand. "Come on. She'll be really pleased. Now we have to go. It's almost our turn."

Michi was still sitting in the gallery, but now he was holding his head in his hands and presented a very sad picture. She felt a bit sorry for him. After the performance Emer put on his work clothes. Like all the others he had to help to take down the tent. Christine had to secure anything which might fly around. The caravan was coupled to a tractor. Isabella and Rosita were already in bed. Christine was pouring dirty water down the drain when she heard Michi's voice. "Tini! Tini!" he called softly. "Hello Michi. Thanks for the flowers," she said and kept her distance. "Did you read my letter?" "Your letter? Oh, yes. It was fastened on the rose. No, not yet. I wanted to read it in peace, but now I have to work." Michi: "I'd like to write more letters to you. I've always wanted to have a pen-friend like you, Tini. It would make me very happy."

He gave her the address of the Police Academy, where he was studying, "Please, Tini, give me your address." "OK. You can fetch water for me and in the meantime I'll write my address." She shook some cleaning powder into the bucket and scrubbed it with a brush, "Please rinse it out thoroughly before you put fresh water into it." Michi went off. Christine wrote the next three addresses in their tour on a picture postcard. He came back and gave her the bucket full of water. Christine gave him the picture postcard, which he read in the dim light from the caravan. "Poste restante?" "Yes. I always go to the post office when we arrive and then again before we move on. That's how it is with us. So, Michi; here's to a good friendship." She held out her hand and he kissed it tenderly and looked up at her, "To our friendship. Thank you Tini." She wanted to give him a hug, but did not, because she did not want to give him any false hopes. "Gooodbye, Michi and all the best!" Michi: "Thank you. And all the best to you, Tini. Take care!" Christine went into the caravan and closed the door. When they were driving off Michi knocked quietly on the door and called "I love you," and repeated it several times until they were far away. Christine looked for the letter which she had put under her bed cover and read the lines by the petrol lamp. She was surprised that he had such lovely handwriting and his words were also wonderful.

For me you are like a budding rose; so beautiful and so sweet scented. My greatest wish is to be there when it slowly unfolds, sprays its perfume over me and envelopes us both in a cloud full of inexpressible happiness.

Up to then she had thought that such things only came from novels and in the cinema. Now she was a little proud to have such an admirer. The season was not yet over. Who knows what would happen. The caravan jerked. Christine put out the lamp. With her head full of sweet thoughts she crept under the cover and let herself be shaken to sleep.

In the next place someone knocked loudly on the door. "Open up! Open the door right now!" Emer pulled on his underpants and opened the door. Two policemen with hand torches forced their way in, pushed him down on a chair, nervously shone their torches around and examined his bed. Emer said, "What's going on?" "Are those the trousers and shirt which you wore last?" "Yes. Why?" Rosita looked down from the upper bed and saw the police putting her underpants into a bag. "Hey! Those are mine. They fell onto the lower bed when I was undressing." Like lightning she grabbed her underpants from the policeman.

"Get dressed," a policeman said to Emer, "we'll sort this out at the station. Closely observed he dressed. "There must be some mistake. I've done nothing wrong." He took his wallet, comb and watch. Without a word the directrix, in her dressing gown, gave the police Emer's papers.

When the fuss was over and the police car had driven off, Christine heard the directrix, outside the door, say, "I've been expecting that. It's a miracle it hasn't happened before. I've warned Emer and the others not to lay a finger on the young girls. Now it's happened. I've always told you to chase these young girls away from the circus area. The stupid things were always around him like moths on a street light. Now he's made a mistake and has probably gone too far. We'll see. Luckily the season is almost over and we've only got a few small towns yet to go to. What a disgrace! Hopefully our name won't appear in a bad column in the newspapers. I demand that all of you keep absolutely silent about this. So! Hold your tongues. I don't want people talking about it. Understood? We've got enough other things to do. People are always looking for a scandal. What a disgrace!" Someone said, "It won't be so bad. Go back to sleep and forget it. It'll come right in the end. We'll know more in a few hours."

Naturally Christine could not go back to sleep. As soon as it got light she removed Emer's bedding, stirred up some lye and soaked the bedding in it. She pulled the underpants, which the police had almost taken, from under Rosita's pillow. Christine could not stop herself from looking at them. There! The cotton lining was stuck together. With shaking hands she compared them with Isabella's underpants which were soiled normally. "So, he has been playing around with Rosita," she said to herself and angrily washed the underwear and hung them on the washing line which she had stretched between two trees.

As if in a trance she packed her personal things and those from Rosita and Isabella, put the three travel bags on Emer's bed and covered them with a blanket. It was time for breakfast. Rosita and Isabella should have gone to school, but Christine wanted to speak to the directrix first. If Emer did not come back then they had to go home, because the programme was so arranged that without Emer it was impossible to perform.

The directrix had already sent her manager and book keeper to the police station. "He'll be back soon," she told Christine, "I think the investigation will take about two to three days. I've been thinking about what we can do with you three in the meantime. Arnold is a skilful man. He used to do a balancing act with his partner. The best thing is to ask him if he would be prepared to work out a routine with you. We'll leave out the number with the ring. The trapeze number will have to be longer, because I don't want to shorten the show."

She told someone to fetch Arnold. When Christine saw him, she thought, Oh! No! He was an insignificant cock of the wall type who worshipped the ground the directrix stood on. He had his own, luxuriously fitted caravan and had money in the bank from his parents. He had not wanted to stay in his parent's business. The circus was his life. "My dear Arnold," the directrix said, "I wanted to ask you if you could work something out with the three girls until Emer gets back. You know their act." Arnold: "Oh-oh. Me and the girls? I used to balance a board on the soles of my feet and move two girls around. I'm sure I can think of something. I'll go and find a good plank of wood. Come into the ring in ten minutes then we can try out a few tricks. We'll make it funny. Then if something goes wrong we can pretend it was just a joke." He laughed and his eyes twitched nervously. His body looked a bit bloated.

Let's see, Christine thought, but in truth she wanted to leave immediately and would be happy when the circus season finally came to an end. Everything was so embarrassing for her. Rosita and Isabella went to the ring to rehearse. Christine said, "Show Arnold the props. Emer won't be happy about other people using them. He's very pedantic." She took the bicycle which Vera had always used, and rode off in secret to the post office. There was a telegram for Emer and Christine and a letter from Rudi, but it was not postmarked from the place where he was in the boarding school. She stopped by a small duck pond; dropped the bicycle on the grass, sat down and read the telegram first.

HAVE YOU STILL GOT MATERIAL? Stop
TELL US WHERE WE SHOULD SEND IT stop
GREETINGS FATHER

If only he knew! Then she pressed Rudi's letter to her heart and against her lips and closed her eyes before she opened it carefully. What she saw was just a barely readable scribble on tissue paper.

Darling, my precious darling!

I'm sorry that I was such a fool! We have to find another way. I'm in hospital because of my leg and very confused. Mama found the letters and does not agree to our friendship. She wanted to write to you. Have you already received a letter? I'm in despair!!!!. I don't even have your handkerchief any more. I always caught my tears in it. Now they're just flowing into emptiness.

Since Friday my letters to the boarding school have been confiscated. I'm being kept here like a prisoner. Everyone checks me. I'm burning up with love and longing for you!

We're leaving soon. A nurse is going to send this letter. Hopefully! Believe me, I'll search for you and find you again. I'm sealing this with my own blood as a sign of my love for you. If you put your blood on it then we are joined forever.

Chirstinaaaaa! I miss you!!!!

For always. Your Rudi

In tears Christine re-read the letter many times. She looked for a thorn with which to prick herself, found a splinter of glass and cut her finger tip. A drop of blood appeared which she pressed on Rudi's blood. She folded up the tissue paper very carefully and put it back in the envelope. She wiped her tears with Rudi's folded handkerchief, which she always carried with her and had never washed.

She cycled back to the caravan; hid the letter with the others in her rain hat and went over to the circus. She arrived just as Rosita flew off the plank and hurt herself. Of course Isabella also flipped off. "Have you hurt yourself?" Christine asked. "No. It's OK. We just have to practice more." Arnold got cramp in his leg and grimaced. "Ow! I get that a lot. It'll soon pass." Christine stayed there and after three turns she grabbed the plank. Rosita did the splits and Rosita made a somersault. They really tried to improvise. Christine stood with one foot on Arnold's bent knee and put the other foot round his neck. They became a flowing pair of figures. Someone stopped the clock and thought that it would be enough for an act.

On that day there was a special performance for school, so they could check if their act was good enough for the evening. The trapeze artiste was still practising so that she could lengthen her act. She had no problems with it.

Christine went to the directrix's caravan and asked about Emer. "Unfortunately I still don't have any news. The investigation will certainly go on all week and he can't have any visitors. Someone will come and collect a few things which he has requested and written down here." She gave her the piece of paper. Toothbrush, pencil, eraser, exercise books, clothes etc. His half sister collected all the items and put them in a medium sized suitcase. Christine watched Rosita as she smuggled all the bonbons into the suitcase, even though she knew that he did not eat a lot of sweet things. Isabella put in the mirror which he had always used to check his hair from behind and Christine put in his Eau de Cologne. That was enough. Then all three of them set about cleaning the caravan until it shone; ate their lunch and then, as always, rested for a while before the performance. Christine let both of them sleep, cycled to the train station and asked when there was a train to Vordersberg. After two changes she could be there by eleven o'clock in the evening.

She reckoned that if it did not work in the afternoon performance (which she secretly hoped) and she went straight to the station then she could catch the train. Now, somehow, she had to manage to get her wages. She went to the directrix and asked if she could have her outstanding wage. Emer had debts with various people which she wanted to pay off she fibbed. There was some truth in it, but he only owed one person a small amount. She needed the rest for housekeeping. The directrix called her book keeper, who advised her to hold back the money for the last three days and pay out the rest. Once more she hid the money in her rain hat. Realising that it no longer fitted her head, she took out all her letters and hid them in the travel bag to make more room. She put the rest of Emer's clothes in a suitcase and wrote his name on it. She looked around for food and put Emer's small water container ready so that she could possibly take any milk which remained with her. She laid out a knife which had belonged to her grandmother, the enamelled coffee pot and a change of clothes ready to take with her. The rest would have to be stuffed into the three travel bags.

The performance for the children started. They had to perform before the interval. Arnold was wearing a costume which had seen better days. He was sweating freely and his make-up had started to run. The three sisters helped to put all the props in the right place and the act began. Arnold lay on the balancing couch. Isabella and Rosita jumped onto the plank at the same time, but after the second round Arnold could not go on. The girls jumped away, somersaulted and did the splits; Christine grabbed the plank and put it on one side. Arnold just lay there, "I can't see a thing! Ow! My leg!" People came to help and a clown was sent into the ring until it was time for the interval. Christine grabbed her sisters right away and they ran together to the caravan. "Hurry up. We have to get the train to Vordersberg. We can't stay here or we'll even loose our return fare. They took of their costumes and packed the remaining things in the bags. Rosita and Isabella got the hidden treasures from under the mattress. Christine hung her red rain hat round her neck. "Forgotten anything? Think quickly!" Christine heard them say, "I've got everything." "Me too." They each carried their own bag. Christine was also carrying the food and they left. Taking a short cut, they fought their way over the banking and managed to get to the station just in time, but gasping for breath. By the time they had bought the tickets the train had already arrived. In the train, still a little out of breath, they let the world rush by. Calming down, they held the bags on their knees. The warm wind through the open window played gently with their hair.

The first connection went well. At the next change their train was late and they had to cross the rails so as not to miss the connecting train. Isabella, Rosita and their bags were just on the train when it started. Christine put her bag on the train but had to run after it to jump on. She had the handle in her hand, but the steps were too high, she slid and had to let go. She fell off and was bleeding from her knee and shin. A railway official came to her.

"My God, that could have been very serious." He helped her over the rails back into the station. Christine was crying. "My younger sisters are alone with all the luggage in the rail car. Hopefully nothing happens. What can I do now?" "No problem. We'll stop the train at the next station and they should send the children and the luggage back here with the mail train." He knocked on the Station window and gave the order.

"There isn't another train to Vordersberg today. Do you know anyone here?" Christine shook her head, "Can we telephone someone? Somebody must be waiting for you," the railway official said. "No. It was supposed to be a surprise." "In the cellar we've got a room with beds run by Caritas. If we're lucky they'll have a free bed. Then you can also have your injuries attended to. I'll go and look what we can do."

He came back with a Caritas sister. "We still have a narrow bed free." Christine said, "Thank you. I'll just wait for my two sisters. I've been told they'll be here soon." "Three people? That's not possible." "They can certainly pay something," the railway officer said and looked at Christine, "that's right, isn't it?" "Yes. Of course." The Caritas sister went back into the cellar. Christine fished out a few notes. "How much do I have to pay?" The man named an amount which seemed to her to be very little."

They're collecting money everyday. Take the money down there. Maybe they'll find one more bed." He grinned to encourage her. Christine went into the cellar. It was a badly lit room with bunk beds. The sister was in the process of showing a man the narrow bed. "I think that if you hunch up that'll be all right for one night." Christine gave her the money and asked for a bandage. The sister invited her into a small corner, unfolded the notes and pushed them into a slit under the registration book. Then she looked at her knee and leg. "We'll wait until your sisters are here. Then I'll disinfect the wounds and bandage them. No point in doing it in haste. Are you in pain? I can give you a tablet." She fetched a glass of cool water and gave Christine a pain killing tablet. Later Isabella and Rosita arrived and they were tired.

The mail train did not come into the station, so they had had to walk. "We already thought we would never see you again. The conductor grumbled because the guard hadn't waited until you were on the train." Isabella said, "We're hungry and thirsty." Christine took some provisions and gave them each a piece of bread, half an apple and some milk. Then she wiped their faces and went to bed. Christine put the bags under the bed and her rain hat under her vest. Then she went to the sister to have her wounds seen to. When the blood was washed off, it did not look so bad. The iodine burned, but then the ointment cooled her wounds. After they were bandaged she lay down to sleep.

The train to Vordersberg was supposed to leave at 7 o'clock in the morning. At six everyone had to get up and leave the cellar. They were given a piece of bread and sweetened black tea on the platform. The train took about an hour to arrive in Vordersberg. They had to walk about one kilometre to get to the central park where their house was.

The bags were heavy and seemed to get heavier. They had to put them down many times. But then they went through the park and they were finally there. Everyone was already in the workshop. There was no housemaid and they did not see any neighbours. "You can stay here and eat what we have brought with us," Christine said, "I'll go and get the house key. Isabella said, "Wait. Reinhard always hid skeleton keys under the cellar steps. Maybe we can open the lock." They found the rusty ring which had various hooks on it. Isabella asked, "Now, which is the right one?" Rosita looked at them all very closely. "Look. The rust has been scraped off the front of this one. I think that will fit." And, indeed, it did not take long before the lock sprang open.

Christine: "Oh, my God. Just look at this. I don't think we still have a housemaid. The pile of washing, the mountain of dishes in the water and the bed covers simply thrown back, even the windows haven't been cleaned for a long time." Isabella said, "But you're not going to start cleaning right now? We'll hide our things under the beds and go to the swimming pool. It's such lovely weather." Rosita whined, "We haven't been swimming for such a long time. We could spend the whole day there without anyone noticing. Come on. We'll do it. The work here isn't going to run away." Christine agreed. "OK. After all this stress we've really earned a bit of free time. Don't touch anything. We'll just take a blanket with us." Isabella and Rosita dug out their swimsuits. Christine took the green circus costume, which was really a swim suit, but was a bit conspicuous. It was all she had. She also took a toothbrush, shampoo, Emer's sun cream and mirror, hand towels and the letter in a linen bag. She made sure that the hidden bags could not be seen and closed the door behind her.

It was rather difficult to close the door, but she succeeded and Isabella put the ring with its hooks back in its place. Christine: "We'll go through the river, but look at the church clock. The pool doesn't open until ten o'clock. We're too early. If we are the first visitors we'll be noticed." Rosita said, "We can hide under the wooden sun bathing area. Nobody goes there right away and we'll be the first to put a towel on the sun beds. They won't be able to see us from the till." They laughed about the trick which they were planning.

There was little water in the river and it was easy to cross. They only had to go up the bank, behind the sun beds and then lie down on the blanket which they had brought with them. Christine opened the bag of food. All that was left was a sip of milk for all of them, half an apple and a little bread. Anyway, she wanted to go to the savings bank before she went to the workshop to pay into her account the money from her rain hat, which she now had under her vest. Isabella and Rosita should not notice this, so she asked them both what they would like to eat and went to the nearest shop to buy something. Isabella said, "There's a path along the wooden fence, then you only have to cross the road and you'll find a large shop. They're certain to be already open."

Up to now Christine had not let go of the rain hat. She had hidden the letters in it again. She took the shopping, found her way down the bank and then continued on her way behind the fence. I hope that after I've done the shopping the savings bank will be open, she thought. And it was. In the savings bank she sat in the corner where she had sat with Reinhard, took the money out of her rain hat, counted it twice and passed it over the counter. "Do you have a savings book with us?" Christine told them her password and signed the new entry, looked at the total and was very pleased. The money would be enough to follow Franzi to Vorarlberg in east Austria. Franzi had a passport, so he was probably working in Germany she mused and decided to go to the council offices and ask about her own passport. She had bought a lot of food, so they could feast the whole day long. The girls were really happy and enjoyed every bite.

While Christine was lying in the sun, her conscience started to prick her. Maybe she should not have simply run away from the circus, but informed her parents about what had happened. But then she saw how much Isabella and Rosita were enjoying playing in the water and banned all doubts from her mind. Because of the bandages on her leg she only went under the shower. She noticed how some of the others round the pool looked at her.

She looked very pretty with her unusual swimsuit and her long hair piled high on her head. She put Isabella's sun glasses on her nose, took the hidden letters out of her rain hat and read them again. Strange. Now, she found them all very childish. Rudi only wanted to have something to keep secret from his parents, she convinced herself. That's normal with young people. Everyone wants to have an exciting secret. You tell your best friend about and usually it does not remain a secret for long before everyone knows about it. Then you'll be in for a ribbing. All right. I think we really love each other, but now it's likely over. She did not read his last letter. She wondered if she should throw the letters away. No. She put them back inside her hat, stretched herself out and fell asleep. Isabella and Rosita were soon blue from the cold water and were shivering from top to toe. They lay down next to Christine in the sun.

The beautiful day was coming to an end. Christine removed the loose bandage. Just once she wanted to dive from the high platform. She climbed up the steps to the five meter high tower, concentrated for a few seconds, tested her spring a couple of times and landed with an elegant head dive in the water. A few people clapped when she came up. She had practised the double dive with Emer. Sitting on his shoulders and diving backwards. They always had fun together, even when they entered the water badly, which was painful. Then she noticed that the rubber breasts sewn into her costume were full of water. She pushed them back into place and pressed the water out of them as best she could before she got out of the pool.

Christine changed, put her hair into a pony tail, left Isabella and Rosita at the pool until it closed and marched through town until she came to the "Shoe and bag Factory". That was what was now written in large letters over the door. She took a deep breath and went in.

When the family saw her she was bombarded with questions, but first she wanted to talk to her parents alone. "Has something happened? The season can't be over yet. Are Emer and the children here as well?" She sat down on a work bench at some distance from them. Her parents were standing in front of her and they were tense. "Isabella and Rosita are at the swimming pool, but they'll be here soon. I just wanted to have a few moments alone with you and tell you about everything which has happened.

The season isn't over. Emer is in custody. He's suspected of having had inappropriate relations with under age girls." Father: "What! They must be wrong. How could they get such an idea? How long has he been there?" Mother interrupted, "I simply don't believe it. Just what are you saying? You come home and don't have anything else to say but this stupid story. I'm not going to listen to such idiotic things. They've certainly mixed things up. They were not under age girls. Just look around. They run around today as though they are already adults. How can anyone know?"

Christine knew that her mother had already suspected that Emer had a few sexual lapses, so she did not understand her anger. She became angry. Now she wanted to tell them everything and started off, "He has already fumbled with Rosita in bed and before that he tried it with me. The circus directrix said he should have gone to a psychiatrist long ago." Josefine raised her hand and wanted to hit Christine, but her fist hit the wall. "Never, ever tell that to anyone. Otherwise you know what you'll get:" Franz did not listen to the rest. He went to the others who were waiting expectantly. "Emer is in custody – under suspicion. He's in prison, but I know him well and he'll soon be free." Josefine's eyes were nervous and incandescent.

Before anyone could ask any more questions Franz called, "Let's go, let's go! The goods must be in the post today. How's the packing going? Come on! You and you, help them quickly." Christine left the workshop and went down the street into town. She saw Isabella and Rosita pressing their noses against a shop window. "Hey! Both of you. Come home with me. They have so much work to do. They haven't got time for us. I think we'll have to wash the dishes and there are a lot of other things to do. For today I think you've had enough free time; now we have to do some work." Reinhard was the first to come to the door. "You're already here? We weren't expecting you so soon. What a surprise! And you've already started washing up and tidying. Who are you doing that for? Everyone is so ungrateful. Just sit down and tell me about it. Look, my small corner is as tidy as always. I don't care what the other's places look like." "Come, brother, throw this water out and bring us fresh water. We're not just cleaning up for the others, but for you as well. Now, go on," Christine ordered and smiled at him, "I'll tell you why we're already here, while we're working."

Reinhard was shocked when he heard about Emer's behaviour. "Do you understand that? With children! I always thought he liked children. If you do, you don't do things like that. I mean, all the women run after him. He can take his pick. He doesn›t need to start with under aged girls. Let's hope it soon turns out to be a big mistake. Otherwise I'm telling you, I'll leave just like Franzi and the others. I don't want to have to be ashamed if it's all true.

By the way, Adelheid's sister Maria is going to Sweden to get married. I heard that she is expecting a child and has arranged with her parents that, when it's born it will be brought up here, with them for the time being. Adelheid herself wants to go to England because of the language and Lilli is looking for a job in Zürich. She's already got her passport. On Friday we're all going to go out together. We're all still in the same clique. You'll see. It'll be fun.

They'll be really happy that you're back. We all missed you. They all envy you; an artiste; the circus life; freedom and getting to see other towns. That's really something." Christine did not spoil his dreams. She had recounted enough for one day. Reinhard helped her to scrub the floors in all the rooms which Isabella had already swept. Rosita was sorting out the clothes which would be washed the next day. "Not long ago father started up a wash and spin-dry rental company. Business is good, because most people don't have their own machines," Reinhard told them. Rosita: "A washing machine? Then tomorrow we can do all the washing."

Reinhard: "But you'll have to get up very early, because most of the machines are already reserved." She calculated the time when she had to start washing and put all the dirty clothes in a pile so she could work out how many machines she would need.

They all made their beds. Christine and Isabella used the vegetables that were there to make a thick soup which they cooked in a large pan. Later, they ate some of it before the rest of the family arrived and then they went to bed.

Most of the time families got together to rent a washing machine. Delivery was difficult on a cycle trailer, especially in winter. You could only carry a small washing machine and a small spin dryer. Christine and Reinhard helped with the deliveries. Christine preferred going to the neighbouring village, Rosenheim, which was five kilometres away, because two kilometres further on there was a small town with two cinemas, and one or other of them always had an afternoon show. She always got the rental money in advance and then cycled to the cinema. She enjoyed watching the films in the warmth of the cinema and while she was there she ate something which she had brought with her. Most of the films were exciting films about the Alps and very emotional folklore films, which always had a happy end. She wasn't too keen on the Italian spaghetti westerns.

Christine's friend Lilli often came to the workshop. She was very welcome, because she spoke very quietly and also helped. Lilli was waiting for her Swiss residence permit. Once she called Christine's father and asked if Christine could also go to Switzerland. "You can learn many different languages there," she told him, "it just depends what region of Switzerland you go to. But she would have to apply for a passport now, because it takes an eternity for the council to issue one." "She'll get her passport when she's seventeen and not a moment before," was his answer. Lilli said, "Oh, Christine. You're exactly sixteen and a half. I don't think your father knows that." She looked at him mischievously. "What? Really? I must have mixed her up with Charlotte. Yes, well, if that's so." He said nothing more and went away.

Lilli said, quietly to Christine, "Today we've arranged to go to the film ball. You, Adelheid, Reinhard, Benni and his friend Harry. You don't know Harry yet, but he's already heard everything about you and he's dying to meet you." She giggled. "Listen," Christine said indignantly, "I won't let any of you start match making for me." "No, of course not. He's just inquisitive about what a circus princess looks like." "What sort of nonsense have you all been spreading about?" Christine did not feel in the least bit comfortable, but asked about the entrance tickets. "They must be very expensive. Are there still some available? Which film stars are coming?" "The ones from the film 'When the church bells ring'. They want to encourage people to go to the cinema. They dance with a few people who are important for them and then they travel on. Just a promotion. I got three free tickets from my uncle, because he's providing the dance music with a couple of others. Oh, and Adelheid bought a ticket because she really wants to go. She did not tell anyone for a long time until she heard that I was also going. I wouldn't have had a ticket for her. She's so boring. Then she begged to go with us; otherwise she would be there all alone. I said yes, without asking Benni, but she gave me money for the petrol." Christine said, I think she's so stuffy and conservative because of the way she was brought up."

Lilli said, "Ah, let's forget about it. I've got something more important in mind. I bought myself a red see through blouse and a black corset for underneath and I'm going to wear them tonight, with high heeled sandals. I'm already excited about it." Christine asked, "The blouse with the corset out of the window? I wanted to buy them, but I didn't know when I would wear them. They weren't very expensive. Yes, tonight would have been a good occasion. You don't want to outshine all the actresses do you?" Lilli said, "You know what? I'm going to buy you the same blouse and corset. We've both got the same taffeta skirts. The 'twin look' is very fashionable right now. Come on, give me the cash and I'll buy them right now. That'll be a big hit."

Christine looked in the pouch which was sewn into her skirt and put all the money she had on the work bench. Lilli counted it and saw that it was not enough, but she put it in her purse. "What are you doing there?" they suddenly heard Josefine shout. Lilli said, "I was supposed to buy something before midday, but I've left my money at home." "How much do you need? I can lend you some until you come again." Lilli mentioned an amount which was the full price for the clothes she wanted to buy and a little bit more. Christine shrank back. Her mother gave Lilli the money and said, "Here, take that. You don't need to pay me back. You've always worked hard helping us and have never had a penny. You have really earned it." "Thank you Mrs. Remi, but I didn't think you were wearing your charitable pants today," Lilli answered, opened her eyes wide and added, cheekily, "Then Christine should also get the same, otherwise I won't take it." "Now look here. You're not shy, I'll say that. Now you want me to give her something." Yes. I think she's earned a lot more than me." "If that's what you think, I can't say no, but I don't have so much in my bag." Lilli said, "Yes you have. There's more than enough in it. You've already shown me the money." "All right then, for the sake of peace and quiet. Hesitantly Josefine put a little more than she would have liked on the work bench because she did not have anything smaller. Christine thanked her and gave it, secretly, to Lilli, who rushed off.

She soon came back. "Christine, I only got the corset. They didn't have any more blouses." "I can't do anything with just the corset," Christine said. Lilli said, "Shall I take it back?" Christine said, "I've just thought of Gries Square in the main town. There's a branch of the same shop there. The shop here will almost certainly call them for you. If they have one they'll definitely reserve it for you. You've got enough money. You've taken all my money with you." "What an idiot I am, but I'll need at least three hours." Christine: "Hurry up. There's a bus in twenty five minutes which goes straight to Gries Square. Then you should take the train back." "Thirty five kilometres for a blouse! I think we're crazy," and she was gone. It was 5 o'clock when she came back and asked an employee who came by, to send Christine out to her. Lilli waited behind the house wall and when Christine arrived she fished out the blouse with a big grin on her face. "There!!! I hope it's not too big. They didn't have any in your size. Try it on, now, with the corset. Christine took the things, but hesitated. She said she still had to work. "Oh, come on. Just leave. Reinhard has already left," Lilli insisted and joked, "I bet he's gone with Frieda dadadada…" Christine said, "Yes. I should stop. My back is already aching, but I have to finish something off and clean up my work space. Same time? Same place?" "Yippie," shouted Lilli and rushed off home.

Christine saw steam coming from the laundry room. She wondered about it and took a quick look. A hot bath would not be bad. A plump blonde with a happy face and curls fastened up on top of her head looked at her. "Hello, Christine. I know you don't know me, but I've seen you in the circus. I was looking for Emer and came here today. Your mother said that I could wait here with you until he comes. In the meantime I can make myself useful here." Christine was amazed; thought that was typical of the Remis. Then, almost croaking said, "Oh! Hello. I just thought I could take a hot bath. My back hurts. I'm meeting a few friends later and I want to be on top form." "I can understand that. I'll put some hot water in that tub over there. If it doesn't bother you, I'll stay here. I won't disturb you; won't talk; won't look," she said in a melodious voice. "Oh, thank you! What's your name?" "You can call me Sindi." "Pleased to meet you." Sindi: "If you want I can wash your back." "Oh, that feels good. I've been working hard all day and I feel it." Sindi washed her back and massaged it. That did her good. Then she washed her hair. Now just lie back, close the eyes for a moment and relax. After a while Christine got dressed, thanked her and left the laundry room as though she were newly born.

Back home she put her hair in rollers and tried on the corset and blouse. The corset was not filled out at the top and the blouse was one size too big, but it was just about OK when she stuffed it under the skirt, which was quite tight round the waist. She looked for her circus costume with the rubber breasts which she now had to sew into the corset. And that was it. The corset looked tighter and shaped a charming décolleté, but the whale bones stuck in her stomach when she bent forward. Then she heard someone at the door. She put on a vest, stuffed everything into a bag, took the rollers out and brushed her hair into place. The door opened and Reinhard stuck his head round it. "Hello! I've already heard where you're going today. That's not for me. I'm going somewhere else I'm just surprised that prudish Adelheid is going with you. You won't have any fun with her. She's always afraid of losing her self control. She is seriously buttoned up." He grinned and then said, "Watch out. The others will soon be home. Let's grab our things and get changed somewhere else." They crept through the park to the town theatre and then into the changing rooms. People were rehearsing on the stage, so they were not disturbed.

As always Benni was leaning, nonchalantly, on his blue Thunderbird and talking to friends. As expected Adelheid arrived with her hair scraped back, a white granny blouse buttoned right up and closed with an oval porcelain broach and a floor length dark skirt. She looked very demure.

Some youth whistled through his teeth as he saw Lilli and Christine in 'twin look' approaching. "Hands off! You uncouth louts. Both of them are in my care." He took them by the shoulders and said quietly, "Listen. My friend Harry will soon be here. You have to get him into the mood. He's got love problems. His hot bride has just left him." Then he saw Harry in the distance wandering towards them and opened the car door. "Ladies, please get in. We'll drive to him.

Adelheid: "Wow! He's good looking. I'd like one like him. What's his job? He's certainly a bit older." They were amused by Adelheid's reaction and Benni said, "You can ask him yourself." Harry opened the door and looked at the young ladies on the back seat. "Hello, my pretties. I'm Harry and who are you?" He gave each one his hand and they introduced themselves. "Adelheid! That's the first time I've heard that name. I might not be able to remember it so easily." Adelheid said, "Then I'll make it easier for you to remember. Adel means noble and Heide is very common and easy to remember, but Adel and Heide together is rather unusual." Lilli and Christine giggled. Harry said, "But noble Adelheid, you can call me Harry. Benni: "There you are. You've got it, but I'll ask you again later, then we'll see if you remember."

They started to enjoy themselves. When they got to the venue, Benni drove straight up to the entrance, leapt out of the car and opened the door for the ladies, ignoring the man in uniform who waved him on. Harry stayed with them on the steps until Benni came back from the car park. He collected the entrance tickets from the three ladies. Harry did not have a ticket, but Benni knew about that and managed to get him through with a trick.

"Ladies first," Benni said, and stood protectively in front of them. He waved to the ticket collector and while he distracted her, Harry slipped by unnoticed and managed to avoid being checked.

Once in the room they looked for a table. Lilli's uncle was on the stage putting the instruments in their place. When he saw his niece he showed her to a table close to the stage. There was a card on the table which said, 'Reserved', but a waiter came and took it away. Benni leant back with relish and looked at Lilli and Christine. "The usual?" he asked, grinning. They both said yes and explained to Harry and Adelheid what that was about. Harry said, "Yes, of course. The usual." Adelheid hesitated. Harry looked at her. She looked confused. They had something more to laugh about. Benni explained it to the waiter and said, jokingly and loud, "of course, honoured guests, the usual." A few people were already looking at them. Harry said, "You're really good company. I think I'm going to have a very enjoyable evening." The waiter came and poured the drinks. Harry paid immediately. "Girls, can I offer you the first round?" Benni grinned. They had already agreed that if Harry got in without a ticket, then he would pay for the first round. Lilli said, "I hope you're not up to no good." "Us? No, of course not. You know me." Benni said with a grin.

Then it started to get exciting. The film stars and starlets were presented. The ladies were wearing low cut evening dresses. One dress was a little too tight so that the starlet could only take very small steps and so everyone was looking at her. After that they danced and sang songs from their films. Then they gave their autographs whilst sipping champagne. Some of their photographs looked a little 'antique' when compared to the person in the flesh. They laughed, talked a lot but said very little. After about an hour they all came back on stage and sang, "Goodbye, goodbye, I'll sing you just a last goodbye…" The ladies were all presented with a bouquet of flowers and thanked the 'charming audience.' Every one applauded as they left the stage. At the table there was a lot of discussion about the stars and a lot of criticism. "He's a lot smaller and fatter than in the film." – "The one with the bleached hair has a crooked nose. You don't see that on the screen." – "The lips were painted a lot larger than her actual lips and her eyebrows were too thick and higher than her own." – "She had wrinkles on her breasts. Her whole décolleté was covered in brown patches." – "Well, for me there was only one who I fancied, if his shoes had not such a high heel. Is that the fashion nowadays?" This last remark was from Lilli. Benni: "You haven't a good word to say for anyone. The one with the tight dress got my interest. I'll bet she gets to be a big star! Although she is a bit skinny. She'll have to be nourished first." He turned to Harry, "Before our beautiful gossipy women go on criticizing, you say something!" Harry stood up and bowed to Adelheid, "Lovely lady, may I invite you to dance with me?" Christine and Lilli were astonished. Benni grinned. "So! What's the matter? Are you envious?" A young man came to ask Lilli to dance. "Me? Why?" she asked in amazement and went on to the dance floor with him. Christine was also invited to dance by someone she knew by sight.

The band played another hour for the public. Benni danced with all three girls, but soon others came to claim them. Harry held Christine very tightly around her waist. She felt dizzy when he did this. She said nothing, went with the music and floated over the dance floor. They danced cheek to cheek; to wistful songs and then more lively music. He would not let her go. Suddenly Christine felt that her false breasts had begun to slip. At every turn she tried to hold them back, but they would not stay in the right place. So she danced very close to Harry and of course he misunderstood. When they danced by their table, she snatched up her hand bag and ran towards the toilets, shouting a quick, "Excuse me, please."

Adelheid and Lilli were already in the toilets. Christine said, "My God, my breasts keep slipping out of my corset and look, my waist is red from the sewn in stays." She showed them the red patches. But the pair of them just giggled.

Lilli had an invitation for the following Friday. "I don't know if I should go or not." Adelheid asked, "Who is it. You must show us the guy. We'll give him the quick once over." She was tipsy and laughing all the time. "Come on. We have to go back. The music is almost over." Lilli: "Maybe Christine has also got an invitation?! From Harry?! You were dancing very close together…!" "No! I don't. I just wanted to get him over his love sickness. That's all." They laughed loudly. Laughed and laughed. Adelheid: "That was really funny! I haven't laughed so much in a long time. My stomach is aching."

Harry tried to force Christie to come home with him. Benni got annoyed. "Come on. Leave her in peace. Anyway, your mother wouldn't allow it. She would notice it right away. I don't want to be your driver. How's she going to get home? Didn't you hear? She doesn't want to." "Yes, yes. Bloody women! My woman has run off with someone else. The cow really insulted me. Just wait. I'll get even with her." Benni: "It's better to say nothing more, right now. We don't want to spoil a nice evening, do we?" Harry: "Stop over there. I'll get out and have a drink."

Benni: "Come on. I'll drive you home, otherwise you'll do something stupid." Harry: "It's OK. I've calmed down. I just need a coffee." "Then we'll go and drink a coffee together. First of all I'll take our lovely companions home." Christine said, "Thank you Benni." Adelheid, Lilli and Christine put something in Benni's money bag which Lilli had hung discreetly in the car. Harry thought that was great. "Girls, please excuse me. If I've said anything wrong, then I'm sorry. It was really good to get to know you. Next Sunday there is a fair in Heiligenberg. Who'd like to come? Let's say we'll meet at eleven at the lower church." Christine said, "I'll come." The others said nothing, as if they already had something planned. Harry: "Please, Christine, come, even without your friends. I promise to behave very correctly." She thought: It would be all right. In daylight with lots of people about, and I've never been to Heiligenberg. So she accepted.

Christine did not have any suitable clothes for the fair in Heiligenberg. So she asked one of the employees, who had already done some sewing for her, to make a traditional Austrian dress – a dirndl – from three different coloured, but traditionally patterned remnants. The backless upper part was red, the skirt was blue and the apron was white and under it was a puffed sleeved blouse made of transparent organza. As she wandered through the town she saw a pair of strap sandals made of black patent leather with a seven centimetre high heel. They just had one pair left and it was a half size smaller than her shoe size, but the sandals were open toed, so that should not be a problem. She could not resist them and she bought them.

The Sunday festival started. It was a hot, sunny day. Harry was waiting at the lower church with his sister Lorry, who, she was soon to discover, was a former classmate. Lorry did not now want to go up to the Heiligenberg and took her leave. So Christine knew now who Harry's family were. She had already delivered wash machines there. The father was an alcoholic and the mother was not particularly faithful. There were four children. In the cramped flat, she remembered that two of them slept together in a bunk bed in the kitchen. Harry and Christine started out on the path. They had only covered about a quarter of the mountainous route when Christine's feet started to hurt. The straps cut into her feet and in the heat her dress was too tight under her breasts, the organza blouse scratched her throat and blew up like a balloon on her back. It was torture. About a hundred metres from the pilgrim place she sat down on a rock, took off her sandals and opened the front of her dress so that she could breathe more easily. Harry: "Come on. We'll go further. I can already hear the music." A few people laughed about her shoes. "They're not exactly hiking boots!" Harry: "You can go barefoot. Do you think you can do that? I'll help you stand up." Before she stood up she pulled her blouse down into her underpants. The material scratched her everywhere. She tried to walk on the hot asphalt, tried to walk from stone to stone on the edge of the road. Harry watched for a while and then swept her into his arms and carried her over the last few metres to the meadow where she could sit on a wooden bench. He then brought her some cool cider.

Christine tried to clean her feet from the sticky tar in a water trough. The straps had already caused some little blisters. She slipped her feet half way into the sandals and went into the guest house, which was close by, to ask for some plasters. She was in luck and they gave her some.

Harry and Christine wandered around, listened to the music and took a look at the tiny chapel which had been lovingly painted with holy figures. Outside on a hill there was a life size, dramatic figure of Jesus on the Cross with the two sinners on either side.

Christine had drunk the fermented apple juice too quickly and began to feel the alcohol. Her cheeks were burning. She felt hungry and bought bread and sausages for her and Harry. The church service was held in the open air and then there was more music and magnificent folk dancing. After about two hours Harry wanted to go down from the mountain, but suggested another route which went directly to the house where he lived. Christine did not know that. She put on her sandals and then took them off again and they made their way down the mountain. When they got to the house he beckoned her that she should come in, but she did not want to. He claimed that a friend would be coming soon with a car and he could give her a lift back to Vordersberg. In the meantime she should come in and have something to drink. She was not convinced about this, but Harry took her by the hand. The door was scarcely closed behind them when he kissed her passionately and Christine felt butterflies in her stomach. They were soon lying on the lower bunk and she noticed that he had an erection.

Suddenly the door opened and his mother was standing there. "I'm just getting something to drink," she said, but Harry shouted at her. Christine pushed him aside, grabbed her sandals and, pulse racing, ran out of the house. She crossed a bridge which led to the main road and signalled passing cars. It was not long before a car stopped. "That's my little Christine. I hardly recognised you." "Viktoria! Thank God!" Christine breathed a sigh of relief.

"Come on, Hansche, drive on. Look over there. I think Christine is being chased. By the way, let me introduce you. This is my husband." Harry ran after the car. Viktoria and Christine looked through the window and saw him getting smaller and smaller. They had a lot to tell each other on the short journey and Christine mentioned that she wanted to go to Switzerland. Viktoria : "I'd like to go to Switzerland some time. I've read that the people there are very friendly and everything is very clean." After a while she called, "Hansche. Stop. Is this OK for you?" "Yes. Thank you so much! Best wishes and hopefully we'll meet again soon." Viktoria stroked her cheek. "Take care of yourself, little miss." Hansche said a few words in his mother tongue, gave her his hand and smiled.

Christine searched through all the newspapers she could get her hands on for advertisements offering jobs abroad. Wanted: "Au pair girl, near Biel, west Switzerland" she read. West Switzerland? That is where they speak French! She applied immediately and soon got a reply, even if there were a few mistakes in it, but they could also speak German so she was pleased.

She had already filled out the forms for her passport at the council office. She just had to get some photographs. So she made an appointment with the photographer for passport photos.

First she went to the hairdresser. She wanted to have her hair cut and curled. The hairdresser said, “For that you’ll have to have a perm. Otherwise it won’t last long. After a lot of discussion, not least because of the expense, Christine finally let herself be persuaded.

The catastrophe was perfect! Christine’s hair stood up from her scalp; frizzy curls. The manager of the salon got involved and tried everything to give some shape to her hair. Christine just sat there without moving and could not look in the mirror. “We’ll have to cut the hair even shorter. Then it will look better. I’m really sorry. This has never happened before, but you have very fine hair.”

She started to cut the hair shorter and shorter. Christine was desperately unhappy. She stood up and ran off without paying.

In the meantime Josefine asked the post office to call the small town where Emer was being held on remand, to find out if there was any post for him. They told her there was also a letter for Christine. She had everything sent to Vordersberg. Since the woman in the post office knew all the people concerned she trusted herself later to hand the post to their mother.

Josefine took it on herself to open all the letters and read them. There was a letter to Emer from a Miss Elke who worked with her parents in the butcher's. The letter to Christine was from Michi, who had written several pages of wonderful poetry. When Josefine read it, she was deeply moved, but she could not keep it to herself and read it out, dramatically, to some of the employees, while Christine was at the hair dressing salon for the first time. Michi also wrote that his brother managed a food shop in Vordersberg. Eventually, Christine was given the letter with the remark that it had been opened 'in error'. She took it and as she later read it burst into tears . She was already very upset about her disastrous perm and now she had a letter which had already been opened!

The next day, with swollen eyes she went to the photographer. "I'm sorry, but I don't want to be photographed today. I'll come another time." "No, just come in. I can correct that with light and shadow. Believe me, it's my speciality." She let herself be persuaded. Luckily she was wearing her new black jacket with the stand up collar. The photographer's wife came to help. She put some powder on Christine's face, a delicate lipstick, mascara and re-arranged her hair. "You'll see. My husband takes very good photographs. Now, just smile a little; a little more, and look straight into the camera. Yes. That's good. The photos will be ready next week. Thank you and goodbye." Christine said, "I'll have to remove the make-up before I can go home."

Sindi was packing her things. "So, Christine, I'll make a fine breakfast for us. The others have already left. Here is some money. Go and buy two large croissants and two chocolate drinks. There's still some butter and jam here." Christine went to do the shopping and then they enjoyed their breakfast together. Sindi: "You know, Christine, you really should get away from here. Look, I also had to leave my family, but without being angry with them. You know, you can't buy your mother's love. You'll see, you will make it since you are as hard working and reliable as me, also very responsible, that will still keep the bond to your family. I've let myself be used here, to a certain extent, because I thought I would meet Emer again, but he's certainly already found someone else. I think to myself, go further, other mother's also have handsome sons. 'Don't cry for your lover, on the earth there is certain another... Do you know the song? Well, the world is beautiful and now I'll get going". Christine hugged her. "You are always so cheerful. I'm going to miss you. Thank you, Sindi, for everything you've done for us and especially for me". "Oh, do you really mean that then I will come back and visit you again." Then she laughed. "Now, bye, bye, baby". She picked up her rucksack and set off waving her hand.

One evening, Christine's father brought a new typewriter into the office. He wanted Christine to try it out. "What shall I write". "Just write anything". But her mother who stood behind her, started to dictate. "O.K, write. Dear Miss Elke.." Christine wanted to know who that was. "Oh, it's just a name, now go on". "Just for your information, my brother, Emer, has six children and is no longer available". She leant forward and pulled the page out. "Let's see if the machine writes well. Yes that's easily readable." Christine had no idea that Josefine would send this page to Elke and that with Father's agreement, who even signed it with Christine's name.

Josefine tried the trick with postal deliveries once more, but was told that Emer had collected his post personally. Now she knew that he had been released and was obviously relieved.

Emer heard about the scheming letter from Elke and that she had sent a reply to Christine. On the telephone he told Charlotte about it. Charlotte said to Christine, "Of course he's angry with you. He claimed that Elke and he got on well together. He was ready to stay with her and maybe even work in the butcher's. Now he's making your letter responsible for the separation." Christine was very angry and told Charlotte about the lines which she had typed. Charlotte laughed. "It's very funny, because Emer could not look at blood", opinionated Christine. "If a hen was slaughtered, he ran away." Charlotte knew about the letters and other things which Josefine had hidden in a cardboard box and among them were two letters to Christine. One from Elke and the other from Emer. Elke's letter contained the following:

To Christine!

It's a shame that Emer has such a lying, vicious sister like you. He did not deserve that! Luckily I'm not expecting to get a sister in law like this. From my side, there was never anything serious between me and Emer. Life in a circus is not for me and I can't imagine Emer without the circus. This is just for your 'information'. Elke.

Christine's heart stood still. "Please, please, dear God," she prayed, "the passport and residence permit in Switzerland! Help me. I can't stand it any longer." But why had mother and father done that to me and Emer? Then, with tears in her eyes, she read Emer's accusations. "You are the last person I would expect to do something like this. How easy it is to be deceived, etc." Emer stuck to his accusations for ever. He never wanted to believe the truth of the matter, even though Christine gave him Elke's letter to read, in which it was written, black on white, that it was never a serious relationship. With time she realised that with those words he was hiding from disappointment.

Christine showed Reinhard the letters. "Why did you write that? Couldn't you have typed something else?" Christine said, "Had? Should have? They tricked me. They used me to write this filthy letter."

Reinhard changed the subject, "How much money do you have in your savings account now? Is it enough to get to the west of Switzerland?" "No. I need a bit more. I've asked how much the journey costs and you can only buy a ticket at the main stations, because you have to cross the border.

I'll also need a few clothes and shoes, but I could get them in the clothes shop where I have bought remnants. I've already told them there what I want to do. When the time comes I can go to them and pay off my debts later from Switzerland. She really trusts me."

Reinhard, "You have to scrape a bit more money together. You can't expect anything from the parents. I've got an idea. On Friday and Saturday they are showing a super film and they've only started selling tickets today. We'll buy several tickets. You know how people are. They always want to be the first to see the film. Then they are really keen to get tickets. Then we can make out that we are ready to sell our tickets. Obviously always two together and we can ask for twice the price." Christine said, "I'm not going to do that. That's not fair." "Doesn't matter. I'll persuade Frieda to help me. You can watch from a distance."

So Chrsitine and Reinhard invested money in cinema tickets. Frieda sad she could not put her few pennies in the pot. Reinhard bought twelve and Christine bought eight. Then Frieda bought another ten for Reinhard. Frieda was very clever. She said to the people at the end of the queue for tickets, "I've got some tickets" and left. A couple followed her. When she asked for twice the price, they were amazed. "Well, I have to add my costs, if I can only go to the cinema tomorrow." She got exactly what she had asked. When the couple left, Christine spoke to two others and sent them to Frieda.

That also worked. Reinhard did not even let the people get to the queue. "There are no more tickets," he said, "but if you really want to see the film, I'll sell you ours." Christine sent the people either to Frieda or to Reinhard. Finally all the tickets were sold. "That was exciting," Frieda said. Reinhard went round the corner and they both followed him. He had a piece of paper on which he had written down how much money he should have after all the tickets had been sold. They all counted and he said, "Three tickets are missing and gave them a serious look, but then he felt in his breast pocket and took out three tickets. "The three best seats, my ladies! May I invite you to the cinema and afterwards to the coffee house? The girls laughed and punched Reinhard from right and left. "We have to wait until the lights are dimmed, so that the people who bought our tickets don't recognise us. I'll take off my jacket." In the interval he bought both of them ice creams. It was an exciting and gripping film and a lovely, amusing evening for all three.

The next day Christine collected her photos. Her eyes only looked a little swollen and her perm did not look too bad. The next step was to get her father's signature.

Through a Christian organisation, Adelheid had got a job in a hospital in London and was the first to leave. Two weeks later Lilli went to Zürich, but first she went with Christine to her father to get the signature for her passport. He hesitated at first, but Lilli did not leave her side until he signed. Then she checked all the documents and noticed that the doctor's report was missing. "The doctor's report for entry is missing. Have you already asked for it somewhere?" she asked Christine, "I went to Dr. Zernic." Christine: "Tomorrow I'll make an appointment with him. What does he actually check?" Lilli: "Well, you know, the things they check normally; blood, urine, lungs, heart and throat. Then he tested my eyes and my hearing and then he did something with drawings. You have to tell him what you can make of them. It's like when you see figures in the clouds or something. That and something else annoyed me." She wanted to change the subject, but Christine wanted to know exactly what that 'something else' was. "You will feel it. Oh, why do I have to tell you? It's about sexually transmitted diseases and, well, you know where that examination is." Christine: "If you can't speak clearly, then I know what you mean. Ugh! That's horrible. I can imagine it." Lilli: "It takes at least a week until you get the report."

Lilli and Adelheid soon sent her densely scribbled postcards. One was of Lake Zürich and one was of 'Big Ben' in London. Christine met Adelheid's mother on the street and asked if she had an address for Adelheid, because she had not written it on the card. "If she wants to give you her address, then she'll send it to you herself, maybe at Christmas. The English send Christmas cards to everyone they know. I've read about this. It's a custom there. I think it's stupid. Buying so many cards and stamps! Imagine what that costs! Sorry, but I have to get on."

Christine got a letter from Switzerland. She could start as an au-pair at the end of April 1956. She would get the residence permit and the permission to enter the country one month in advance if she sent the necessary documents. Then it said:

"We shall be happy to get to know you. Until then, we send you friendly greetings from our beautiful Switzerland".

When she read the card from Lilli she noticed that she had written "Grüezi" – Greetings. In Switzerland they seem to speak a different German.

It was time to collect her doctor's report. The assistant let Christine wait. The doctor had not yet signed it, but it was ready on his desk. Christine said that she had to get it in the post, but that did not help. The post office was closed when she finally left the doctor's surgery. She put the report in the envelope without reading it, went back to the workshop and put the envelope on the workbench next to her. Reinhard arrived with Grossmeier, the taxi driver. "Hello Christine," Mr. Grossmeier said, "I've heard you want to leave us." Reinhard: "She still has to get some more money together. Otherwise, when she gets to Switzerland she'll have to walk the last few kilometres." Christine: "I still have some time". Reinhard left them. Grossmeier: "I've got a book in the car which I would like to give you. Come outside, quickly. I don't have much time. I've got to collect a client." Christine got up and followed him into the courtyard which was already dark. He stood behind the taxi door, put some rolled up money into her hand and gave her a small travel guide about Switzerland. She thanked him and wanted to go, but he took hold of her arm and held her back. "Not so fast. I've earned a little kiss." He held his cheek to her. When she tried to kiss his cheek he turned his head so quickly that the kiss landed on his moist, open lips. She pulled herself away and wiped her mouth. He just laughed loudly and drove off. Christine did not find it in the least bit funny.

Josefine used Christine's absence to look into the envelope. She was so nosey about what was in the report. She took out the doctor's report and read it secretly in the office. When Christine came back from the courtyard she heard her mother sobbing and reading something to a few of the employees. As soon as Christine appeared the group split up. "None of my children will ever bring a child home out of wedlock. I swear it," Josefine said loudly. Christine had no idea why she seemed so proud to say this. The youngest, Jolanda was only four years old.

Franz came into the office, "What's going on?" "Here! Read this," Josefine said, with the paper in her hand, "it's written here. 'Still a virgin.' I've just read it." "Show me," Franz said and took the paper from her, "What is that? Oh, it's a doctor's report." Then he saw Christine's name and was disgusted. "You don't read something like that to the workers." He gave the paper to his daughter and said, "There. Take it back."

That was when Christine realised that her mother had read her doctor's report to the workers! She quickly read the report and, with trembling hands, put it back in the envelope which was still lying on the workbench. She felt her throat close, "So mean!" she managed to say and left the workshop. Reinhard and Rosita ran after her. "You can be proud of it," Reinhard said, "right now with all this flower power, free love is everywhere. In your age there are hardly any virgins left. You have to go out into the country to find one. That's the way it is."

Rosita: "Come on. I'll go home with you. Reinhard are you coming too?" "Yes, of course! Today we're taking Aunt Grete with us to Datschka City. Uncle Alfred is working on the night shift. He was very mean to her, to-day. She needs a change of scenery for a few hours. I've already arranged it with her. Now we only have to find a way of getting her out of the flat without anyone seeing her." Rosita: "Datschka City? That's the first time I've heard of it. Where is it?" Reinhard laughed, "It's not very far. We've changed the name. Datschka means frog – toad. Now do you understand me?" Rosita: "Froschdorf – Frog village – there is a dance there every Friday evening. Christine, are you going?" "No. I'm not really in the mood." Reinhard: "What do you mean? No! I can't take Aunt Grete to the dance hall alone. The people there know me. What would they think? You have to come with us."

In the end Christine went with them. And, of course, reliable Benni. He liked it, as soon as he heard what they had planned for that evening.

Rosita had the idea that they should knock so loudly on Aunt Grete's door that her mother would also look out of the flat. She always did that. "Then I'll give Aunt Grete a bag with a note in it," Rosita said, "we'll write on it that she should climb out of the back window. When Peter was still living there he often jumped out of this window. Reinhard, you must go to the back of the house, take the chair which our aunt will pass through and put it under the window. Then you can both run along the back alley. We'll wait for you there. You'll see. That will work." Benni: "This girl is smart. Right. Let's go. Take your positions." Benni reversed into the narrow alley with Christine and turned off the engine and lights. They did not have to wait long before Reinhard and Grete came running to them. Aunt Grete had to duck down on the rear seat next to Reinhard. A little further on they picked up Rosita and took her home. Grete gave her some money to keep her mouth shut.

Then she told them why Alfred was so angry. "It's a long story. First of all, I have to tell you that I'm a great fan of Errol Flynn and I got to see all of his films. Up to now I've always managed to go to the cinema without anyone knowing. Then I got the idea of writing to the film star: Eroll Flynn, Hollywood, California, America. Of course I put my photo with the letter which was, of course a mixture of German and English and raved about him." Everyone started to laugh out loud. Giggling she went on. "Can you imagine? Eroll, my darling, wrote back immediately and sent me a large photo on which he had written: 'For Grete, all the best, Eroll Flynn'. I had the photo set in a gilded frame and hung it in the bedroom, so that I could see it before I fell asleep. It was also the first thing I saw when I opened my eyes in the morning." Benni had to stop the car. He got out and doubled up with laughter. Reinhard asked, "And Alfred could see the photo as well?" Grete: "Yes. I hung it at the end of the bed." Christine asked, "Is the photo no longer there?" Grete wiped her face; she cried and shook her head. "No! Alfred tore it down and jumped on it. He got glass splinters in his foot which I was expected to pull out, but I ran to mother and sent her to him. She took the photo and the gilded frame and now it's in a drawer in the kitchen, all stained with blood. Oooh, oooh, oooh," she sobbed into her handkerchief. "Oooh," Christine tried to soothe her, "I think the photographer can put that right. If you want I can take it to him." Aunt Grete opened a bottle of red wine which she had in her bag and took a few good sips from it. Christine took the bottle from her. "Sorry. No alcohol in the car," Benni thanked Christine and Aunt Grete said that she was sorry.

From that time on Christine often went to the cinema secretly with Aunt Grete. With Aunt Grete she did not have to worry about being dragged out of the cinema by the ears, because the film was only allowed for people over 18. That once happened with Lilli. The shame of it! Of course the other people in the cinema found it very amusing. Only Adelheid, the tall beanstalk, was allowed to stay there.

Aunt Grete was a very romantic and amusing person and because she was so cheerful could start up a conversation with total strangers. One day her brother Herbert arrived and brought with him, Hans, a Swiss man who had been in the Foreign Legion. Hans was staying in an inn for just one night and wanted to invite a few people for a lively evening. Grete's husband, Alfred was not at home, but Christine was there, because she was collecting shoe uppers which her aunt had sewn. Grete and Christine were happy to be invited. So Grete went to the inn with her brother and after delivering the uppers Christine joined them. The next day Hans set off for his parents who lived in central Switzerland. He gave Christine his address and invited her to spend a few days with him before she went further west to her job. He said he would be happy to show her something of his country. Herbert and Hans talked about an expired criminal action. It became clear that, after breaking the law, Hans had gone to Marseilles and joined the Foreign Legion and from there he had gone to Algeria. Now he was hoping that what his parents had told him was true and that his crime in Switzerland had really expired and that he would not fall into a trap.

Then Christine's parents had another idea for Christine. They wanted to keep her with them and apprentice her to Mrs. Hoppe as a tailor. But the idea of working nine hours a day in a dark room, sewing seams on pre-drawn lines was not exactly what she wanted from life. She had kept it up for fourteen days. In fact she would have liked to have learnt tailoring, but not like that. It was just too boring.

XXVIII

It was Christmas eve. Christine, Rosita and Isabella tried to find a present for everyone to put under the Christmas tree. For the first time they should have a real Christmas. Sweets wrapped in fringed silk paper, Christmas cookies, nuts, apples, mandarins and oranges had been prepared to hang on the tree. Reinhard made a tree stand and laid a pretty sheet around it on the floor.

Now they only needed the fir tree, which Christine said she would buy. She had money for it. In the market square which was now almost empty, she saw a beautiful large fir. The remaining trees were about to be loaded up. She went to the dealer and asked him how much the fir cost. She bartered until almost all the trees had been loaded and finally they agreed on a price. Christine, beaming with joy, dragged the tree through the snow, across the street towards the house. Reinhard came to meet her. "Isn't the tree too big? We'll have to cut it down. It's really getting late, the others will soon be home." They had only just set up the tree when the children came to decorate it.

The twigs which they had cut off in the glowing stove, together with the freshly baked Christmas cookies and cakes created a festive scent throughout the house. Aunt Berta and Aunt Senta had seen Christine dragging the Christmas tree through the streets and followed her, nosily. Now they knocked on the window and wished them a happy Christmas. Charlotte invited them in and quickly found a present for both of them. Aunt Berta went back to her flat and brought the old crib which grandfather had carved by hand, with all the figures. She put it in the middle of the table so that everyone could see it.

Water was put on for tea and it was not long before Rosita shouted, "Light the candles! They're coming!" Reinhard put a bucket of water ready, in case a fire started. They switched off the electric light and Charlotte started to sing "Silent night, holy night…" loudly. The others joined in. The door opened and father said, in a trembling voice, "Just look here!" He cleared his throat and mother blinked her eyes dry. It was the first time that the family had sat round the Christmas tree together. They switched the lights back on and handed out the presents. There was joy, and surprise in their shining eyes. After that there was tea, for the adults with schnapps. Aunt Berta turned out to be really good at creating a happy atmosphere. She had lots of jokes and humour. Mother looked at all the good things to eat on the table and addressing Christine asked, "Where did you buy all this and where did you get the money?". Charlotte heard the question. "From the last delivery. We've all done this together," she lied, "otherwise we would not have been able to have a real Christmas. Now enjoy it and don't begrudge it." Mother knew very well that Christine had organised everything. "It's high time, before all the children leave the nest. Who knows when we will all be together again." Reinhard kept standing up, making sure that all the candles were standing straight and that nothing went up in flames.

There was a knock at the door. It opened and there stood Emer. Rosita jumped up and hugged him, "Thank God you're back home." Everyone greeted him warmly, and he even took Christine in his arms and kissed her on the head. "I can see you're having a really good Christmas. I've come at the right moment. I'm dying of hunger. Some farmer brought me close by, but I had to walk the last three kilometres. There's no one out on the roads. I've come straight from the last stage performance in Germany, but the journey took a long time. I had to make it in stages. Now I'm here, and the scent of fir tree branches, cakes and tea is wonderful. Finally a really fantastic Christmas celebration." Isabella: "Come here. Sit down and eat something." Suddenly

Rosita found a present wrapped in paper and gave it to Emer. She had watched carefully that everyone had opened their presents very carefully, so that the paper could be used again. "Is that for me? My God. You even thought of me! You have no idea how happy that makes me. I just hope that in the future our family will have many wonderful Christmases like this." He was really moved. Reinhard said, jokingly, "Christine discussed everything with us and we had to do as she told us." The two youngest, Hermine and Jolanda, fell asleep side by side on a cushion under the Christmas tree. Jolanda still had a piece of cake in her hand.

The church bells rang, inviting the people to the midnight mass. Mockingly, Reinhard said, "Christine, now you have to go to the church, otherwise it's not a real Christmas." Christine: "You better come with me." "No. I'm much too tired. I'd only fall asleep, but you can pray for all of us." Christine did not let herself be dissuaded and went to the midnight mass. She heard her father say, "The saint is now going to church!" "It won't harm the family, when at least one of us goes to pray," she heard her mother say.

On the way to the church Christine remembered when, shortly after Jolanda's birth, she had seen her mother running away with the baby in her arms and a travelling bag in her hand. She had convinced her to stay and had asked her where she wanted to go. But her mother had shaken her off. "I have to get away! I can't stand it here a moment longer! It's too much for me!" Christine had cried and gone into the workshop to tell her father. "Oh! Don't worry about it. She'll be back soon. We'll just have to get along without her for a few days. She travelled around a lot in the old days and sometimes she misses it." About a week later, on her way to the workshop, she heard a "Psst! Psst!" coming from a cellar window. She bent down and saw her mother with Jolanda in her arms, standing at the window. "Is father angry because I left?" "No. No, you can come out. He said you would come back soon, but I was shocked when you left."

Now she remembered the scene which was firmly seated in her memory. Her mother's frightened face, with the baby in her arms, through the cellar window. And now the picture of Jolanda sleeping under the Christmas tree and her mother, happily sitting there and wanting to hear Emer recounting everything about circus life in Germany.

The day for her departure for Switzerland came closer. She had all the necessary documents. The date had already been fixed: two days after her 17th birthday. She had four pieces of clothing and a pair of shoes which she had bought on credit. She had the money for a second class ticket and enough for the journey. Reinhard thought that she should at least take a couchette, but she did not want to use all her money for the journey. She saved where she could, "Who knows what will happen to me."

It was not difficult for her to take her leave. Everyone seemed to be pleased for her and that she had the courage to go to a foreign country. Everyone hugged her. She only had to pull her father and mother to her so that she could give them a kiss on the cheek. She heard someone say, "Write to us when you arrive."

No one accompanied her. She went to the station with her grey, cardboard suitcase, her black handbag and her jacket over her arm. When she was sitting alone at the window in the night train, tears trickled down her cheeks. Tears of sorrow or tears of joy? She was not sure.

Very early in the misty morning in Feldkirch the customs officers and border controllers came on to the train. "Do you have anything to declare?" They opened bags and suitcases and checked everything. "All passports and visas!" Christine showed him her passport and the other documents. "Leave the train at Buchs." The border officer kept her passport and put the residence permit between the pages. Christine went into the stinking toilet to arrange herself in the almost blind mirror. Men came with buckets and cleaning materials. She had to leave the toilet and go back to her seat. Of course, she was now in the neat and tidy Switzerland where everything was cleaned.

Many people from southern countries left the train at Buchs. Holding up the passports the border controller shouted, “Follow me!” She went into a building. “Women in this room!” Then they had to stand in line. They all had their doctor’s reports in their hand. Some of them had to go to the doctor, open their mouths and say “Aah!” Then they had to take off their upper clothing and go into an X-ray machine. They then got a stamp on their doctor’s report and another in their passports. Almost all of them were allowed to continue their journey in a Swiss train.

The train went to Sargans, where Hans, the one time foreign legionary was supposed, as arranged, to get on the train. In Sargans she leant out of the window and looked up and down the platform. The train went on and there was no trace of Hans. Disappointed she sat down again and leant against the window, but then, a few minutes later, he was standing in front of her.

The train travelled along the Walensee where the rising sun was reflected in the water. Then it continued to Näfels, Hans’ home town. His family was waiting there for him. The food was already on the table and the taller people had to stoop in the room because the ceiling was low. Soon all were sitting at the table. The bread was passed round. Christine took a slice, broke it in half and put it in her mouth. She had not noticed that everyone else had put the bread on a small plate and waited for the grace to be said. She put her hand in front of her mouth and pretended to take the bread out of her mouth. After breakfast Hans showed her the small town and then Christine said that she had to continue her journey because she wanted to start her au-pair job that evening.

“You can come and visit me, if you want,” she laughed as the train moved off.

Now Christine felt that she was finally free!